Starting to pray, he felt ready to drive away all his foolish ideas, but they fell on him like flies. As he prayed, he sighed. He wanted to be a man of standing, but his head was full of distractions. A man should love his wife, but to think of her night and day was not right. He couldn't get her off his mind. He remembered her playful words when he had come to her in bed on those nights when she was ritually pure, and the outlandish nicknames she had called him as she curled his earlocks, tickled him, bit him, kissed him. The truth was, he should never have tolerated such loose behavior. . . .

—from "The Riddle"

Fawcett Crest Books
by Isaac Bashevis Singer:

Isaac Bashevis Singer

A Friend
of Kafka
and
other stories

Of the stories in this collection, the following appeared originally in *The New Yorker:* "A Friend of Kafka," "Guests on a Winter Night," "The Key," "Dr. Beeber," "The Cafeteria," "The Mentor," and "The Joke." "Pigeons" appeared originally in *Esquire;* "The Riddle" and "The Blasphemer" in *Playboy;* and "Altele" in *TriQuarterly.* Other stories have appeared in *The Saturday Evening Post, Israel Magazine, Works in Progress, Commentary, Menorah Journal, The Critic,* and *Harper's Magazine.*

Of the stories in this collection, the following appeared originally in *The New Yorker:* "A Friend of Kafka," "Guests on a Winter Night," "The Key," "Dr. Beeber," "The Cafeteria," "The Mentor," and "The Joke." "Pigeons" appeared originally in *Esquire;* "The Riddle" and "The Blasphemer" in *Playboy;* and "Altele" in *TriQuarterly.* Other stories have appeared in *The Saturday Evening Post, Israel Magazine, Works in Progress, Commentary, Menorah Journal, The Critic,* and *Harper's Magazine.*

A Fawcett Crest Book

Published by Ballantine Books

Copyright © 1962, 1966, 1967, 1968, 1969, 1970 by Isaac Bashevis Singer

ISBN: 0-449-20695-5

This edition published by arrangement with Farrar, Straus & Giroux

Printed in Canada

First Fawcett Crest Edition: December 1980
First Ballantine Books Edition: June 1984

Contents

AUTHOR'S NOTE

The stories in this collection were all written in my later years, some of them quite recently. About one third are about immigrants in the United States, where I have now lived a longer time than in the country of my birth, Poland. I have translated these stories with the assistance of collaborators, and I find that I do much revision in the process of translation. It is not an exaggeration to say that over the years English has become my "second" language. It is also a fact that the foreign-language editions of my novels and stories have been translated from the English.

My translators, whose names appear at the end of each story in this book, are not only my first readers but also my first constructive (I hope) critics. I have been a translator all my adult life and I consider translation the greatest problem and challenge of literature. The "other" language in which the author's work must be rendered does not tolerate obscurity, puns, and linguistic tinsel. It teaches the author to deal with events rather than with their interpretation and to let the events speak for themselves. The "other" language is often the mirror in which we have a chance to see ourselves with all our imperfections and, if possible, to correct some of our mistakes.

A good half of these stories were edited by Rachel MacKenzie, senior editor of *The New Yorker,* and the whole collection was edited by Robert Giroux. I dedicate this book to my translators and editors.

New York, June 2, 1970   I.S.

A Friend of Kafka

I had heard about Franz Kafka years before I read any of his books from his friend Jacques Kohn, a former actor in the Yiddish theater. I say "former" because by the time I knew him he was no longer on the stage. It was the early thirties, and the Yiddish theater in Warsaw had already begun to lose its audience. Jacques Kohn himself was a sick and broken man. Although he still dressed in the style of a dandy, his clothes were shabby. He wore a monocle in his left eye, a high old-fashioned collar (known as "father-murderer"), patent-leather shoes, and a derby. He had been nicknamed "the lord" by the cynics in the Warsaw Yiddish writers' club that we both frequented. Although he stooped more and more, he worked stubbornly at keeping his shoulders back. What was left of his once yellow hair he combed to form a bridge over his bare skull. In the tradition of the old-time theater, every now and then he would lapse into Germanized Yiddish—particularly when he spoke of his relationship with Kafka. Of late, he had begun writing newspaper articles, but the editors were unanimous in rejecting his manuscripts. He lived in an attic room somewhere on Leszno Street and was constantly ailing. A joke about him made the rounds of the club members: "All day long he lies in an oxygen tent, and at night he emerges a Don Juan."

We always met at the club in the evening. The door would open slowly to admit Jacques Kohn. He had the air of an important European celebrity who was deigning to visit the ghetto. He would look around and grimace, as if to indicate that the smells

7

of herring, garlic, and cheap tobacco were not to his taste. He would glance disdainfully over the tables covered with tattered newspapers, broken chess pieces, and ashtrays filled with cigarette stubs, around which the club members sat endlessly discussing literature in their shrill voices. He would shake his head as if to say, "What can you expect from such schlemiels?" The moment I saw him entering, I would put my hand in my pocket and prepare the zloty that he would inevitably borrow from me.

This particular evening, Jacques seemed to be in a better mood than usual. He smiled, displaying his porcelain teeth, which did not fit and moved slightly when he spoke, and swaggered over to me as if he were on-stage. He offered me his bony, long-fingered hand and said, "How's the rising star doing tonight?"

"At it already?"

"I'm serious. Serious. I know talent when I see it, even though I lack it myself. When we played Prague in 1911, no one had ever heard of Kafka. He came backstage, and the moment I saw him I knew that I was in the presence of genius. I could smell it the way a cat smells a mouse. That was how our great friendship began."

I had heard this story many times and in as many variations, but I knew that I would have to listen to it again. He sat down at my table, and Manya, the waitress, brought us glasses of tea and cookies. Jacques Kohn raised his eyebrows over his yellowish eyes, the whites of which were threaded with bloody little veins. His expression seemed to say, "This is what the barbarians call tea?" He put five lumps of sugar into his glass and stirred, rotating the tin spoon outward. With his thumb and index finger, the nail of which was unusually long, he broke off a small piece of cookie, put it into his mouth, and said, *"Nu ja,"* which meant, One cannot fill one's stomach on the past.

It was all play-acting. He himself came from a

Hasidic family in one of the small Polish towns. His name was not Jacques but Jankel. However, he had lived for many years in Prague, Vienna, Berlin, Paris. He had not always been an actor in the Yiddish theater but had played on the stage in both France and Germany. He had been friends with many celebrities. He had helped Chagall find a studio in Belleville. He had been a frequent guest at Israel Zangwill's. He had appeared in a Reinhardt production, and had eaten cold cuts with Piscator. He had shown me letters he had received not only from Kafka but from Jakob Wassermann, Stefan Zweig, Romain Rolland, Ilya Ehrenburg, and Martin Buber. They all addressed him by his first name. As we got to know each other better, he had even let me see photographs and letters from famous actresses with whom he had had affairs.

For me, "lending" Jacques Kohn a zloty meant coming into contact with Western Europe. The very way he carried his silver-handled cane seemed exotic to me. He even smoked his cigarettes differently from the way we did in Warsaw. His manners were courtly. On the rare occasion when he reproached me, he always managed to save my feelings with some elegant compliment. More than anything else, I admired Jacques Kohn's way with women. I was shy with girls—blushed, became embarrassed in their presence—but Jacques Kohn had the assurance of a count. He had something nice to say to the most unattractive woman. He flattered them all, but always in a tone of good-natured irony, affecting the blasé attitude of a hedonist who has already tasted everything.

He spoke frankly to me. "My young friend, I'm as good as impotent. It always starts with the development of an overrefined taste—when one is hungry, one does not need marzipan and caviar. I've reached the point where I consider no woman really attractive. No defect can be hidden from me. That is impotence. Dresses, corsets are transparent for me. I can no longer be fooled by paint and perfume. I have lost my own teeth, but a woman has only to open her mouth and I spot her fillings. That, by the way, was Kafka's problem when it came to writing: he saw all the defects—his own and everyone else's. Most of literature is produced by such plebeians and bunglers as Zola and D'Annunzio. In the theater, I saw the same defects that Kafka found in literature, and that brought us together. But, oddly enough, when it came to judging the theater Kafka was completely blind. He praised our cheap Yiddish plays to heaven. He fell madly in love with a ham actress—Madam Tschissik. When I think that Kafka loved this creature, dreamed about her, I am ashamed for man and his illusions. Well, immortality is not choosy. Anyone who happens to come in contact with a great man marches with him into immortality, often in clumsy boots.

"Didn't you once ask what makes me go on, or do I imagine that you did? What gives me the strength to bear poverty, sickness, and, worst of all, hopelessness? That's a good question, my young friend. I asked the same question when I first read the Book of Job. Why did Job continue to live and suffer? So that in the end he would have more daughters, more donkeys, more camels? No. The answer is that it was for the game itself. We all play chess with Fate as a partner. He makes a move; we make a move. He tries to checkmate us in three moves; we try to prevent it. We know we can't win, but we're driven to give him a good fight. My opponent is a tough angel. He fights Jacques Kohn with every trick in his bag. It's winter now; it's cold even with the stove on, but my stove hasn't worked for months and the landlord refuses to fix it. Besides, I wouldn't have the money to buy coal. It's as cold inside my room as it is outdoors. If you haven't lived in an attic, you don't know the strength of the wind. My windowpanes rattle even in the summertime. Sometimes a tomcat climbs up on the roof near my window and wails all night like a woman in labor. I lie there freezing under my blankets and he yowls for a cat, though it may be he's merely hungry. I might give him a morsel of food to quiet him, or chase him away, but in order not to freeze to death I wrap myself in all the rags I possess, even old newspapers— the slightest move and the whole works comes apart.

"Still, if you play chess, my dear friend, it's better to play with a worthy adversary than with a botcher. I admire my opponent. Sometimes I'm enchanted with his ingenuity. He sits up there in an office in the third or seventh heaven, in that department of Providence that rules our little planet, and has just one job—to trap Jacques Kohn. His orders are 'Break the keg, but don't let the wine run out.' He's done exactly that. How he manages to keep me alive is a miracle. I'm ashamed to tell you how much medicine I take, how many pills I swallow. I have a friend who is a druggist, or I could never afford it. Before I go to bed, I gulp down one after another—dry. If I drink, I have to urinate. I have prostate trouble, and as it is I must get up several times during the night. In the dark, Kant's categories no longer apply. Time ceases to be time and space is no space. You hold something in your hand and suddenly it isn't there. To light my gas lamp is not a simple matter. My matches are always vanishing. My attic teems with demons. Occasionally, I address one of them: 'Hey, you Vinegar, son of Wine, how about stopping your nasty tricks!'

"Some time ago, in the middle of the night, I heard a pounding on my door and the sound of a woman's voice. I couldn't tell whether she was laughing or crying. 'Who can it be?' I said to myself. 'Lilith? Namah? Machlath, the daughter of Ketev M'riri?' Out loud, I called, 'Madam, you are making a mistake.' But she continued to bang on the door. Then I

heard a groan and someone falling. I did not dare to
open the door. I began to look for my matches, only
to discover that I was holding them in my hand.
Finally, I got out of bed, lit the gas lamp, and put on
my dressing gown and slippers. I caught a glimpse of
myself in the mirror, and my reflection scared me.
My face was green and unshaven. I finally opened
the door, and there stood a young woman in bare
feet, wearing a sable coat over her nightgown. She
was pale and her long blond hair was disheveled.
'Madam, what's the matter?' I said.

" 'Someone just tried to kill me. I beg you, please
let me in. I only want to stay in your room until
daylight.'

"I wanted to ask who had tried to kill her, but I
saw that she was half frozen. Most probably drunk,
too. I let her in and noticed a bracelet with huge
diamonds on her wrist. 'My room is not heated,' I
told her.

" 'It's better than to die in the street.'

"So there we were both of us. But what was I to do
with her? I only have one bed. I don't drink—I'm not
allowed to—but a friend had given me a bottle of
cognac as a gift, and I had some stale cookies. I gave
her a drink and one of the cookies. The liquor seemed
to revive her. 'Madam, do you live in this building?' I
asked.

" 'No,' she said. 'I live on Ujazdowskie Boulevard.'

"I could tell that she was an aristocrat. One word
led to another, and I discovered that she was a
countess and a widow, and that her lover lived in the
building—a wild man, who kept a lion cub as a pet.
He, too, was a member of the nobility, but an out-
cast. He had already served a year in the Citadel, for
attempted murder. He could not visit her, because
she lived in her mother-in-law's house, so she came
to see him. That night, in a jealous fit, he had beaten
her and placed his revolver at her temple. To make a
long story short, she had managed to grab her coat

and run out of his apartment. She had knocked on the doors of the neighbors, but none of them would let her in, and so she had made her way to the attic.

" 'Madam,' I said to her, 'your lover is probably still looking for you. Supposing he finds you? I am no longer what one might call a knight.'

" 'He won't dare make a disturbance,' she said. 'He's on parole. I'm through with him for good. Have pity—please don't put me out in the middle of the night.'

" 'How will you get home tomorrow?' I asked.

" 'I don't know,' she said. 'I'm tired of life anyhow, but I don't want to be killed by him.'

" 'Well, I won't be able to sleep in any case,' I said. 'Take my bed and I will rest here in this chair.'

" 'No. I wouldn't do that. You are not young and you don't look very well. Please, go back to bed and I will sit here.'

"We haggled so long we finally decided to lie down together. 'You have nothing to fear from me,' I assured her. 'I am old and helpless with women.' She seemed completely convinced.

"What was I saying? Yes, suddenly I find myself in bed with a countess whose lover might break down the door at any moment. I covered us both with the two blankets I have and didn't bother to build the usual cocoon of odds and ends. I was so wrought up I forgot about the cold. Besides, I felt her closeness. A strange warmth emanated from her body, different from any I had known—or perhaps I had forgotten it. Was my opponent trying a new gambit? In the past few years he had stopped playing with me in earnest. You know, there is such a thing as humorous chess. I have been told that Nimzowitsch often played jokes on his partners. In the old days, Morphy was known as a chess prankster. 'A fine move,' I said to my adversary. 'A masterpiece.' With that I realized that I knew who her lover was. I had met him on the stairs—a giant of a man, with the face of a murderer. What a funny end for Jacques Kohn—to be finished off by a Polish Othello.

"I began to laugh and she joined in. I embraced her and held her close. She did not resist. Suddenly a miracle happened. I was a man again! Once, on a Thursday evening, I stood near a slaughterhouse in a small village and saw a bull and a cow copulate before they were going to be slaughtered for the Sabbath. Why she consented I will never know. Perhaps it was a way of taking revenge on her lover. She kissed me and whispered endearments. Then we heard heavy footsteps. Someone pounded on the door with his fist. My girl rolled off the bed and lay on the floor. I wanted to recite the prayer for the dying, but I was ashamed before God—and not so much before God as before my mocking opponent. Why grant him this additional pleasure? Even melodrama has its limits.

"The brute behind the door continued beating it, and I was astounded that it did not give way. He kicked it with his foot. The door creaked but held. I was terrified, yet something in me could not help laughing. Then the racket stopped. Othello had left.

"Next morning, I took the countess's bracelet to a pawnshop. With the money I received, I bought my heroine a dress, underwear, and shoes. The dress didn't fit, neither did the shoes, but all she needed to do was get to a taxi—provided, of course, that her lover did not waylay her on the steps. Curious, but the man vanished that night and never reappeared.

"Before she left, she kissed me and urged me to call her, but I'm not that much of a fool. As the Talmud says, 'A miracle doesn't happen every day.'

"And you know, Kafka, young as he was, was possessed by the same inhibitions that plague me in my old age. They impeded him in everything he did—in sex as well as in his writing. He craved love and fled from it. He wrote a sentence and immediately crossed it out. Otto Weininger was like that, too—mad and a genius. I met him in Vienna—he spouted aphorisms and paradoxes. One of his sayings I will never forget: 'God did not create the bedbug.' You have to know Vienna to really understand these words. Yet who did create the bedbug?

"Ah, there's Bamberg! Look at the way he waddles along on his short legs, a corpse refusing to rest in its grave. It might be a good idea to start a club for insomniac corpses. Why does he prowl around all night? What good are the cabarets to him? The doctors gave him up years ago when we were still in Berlin. Not that it prevented him from sitting in the Romanisches Café until four o'clock in the morning, chatting with the prostitutes. Once, Granat, the actor, announced that he was giving a party—a real orgy—at his house, and among others he invited Bamberg. Granat instructed each man to bring a lady—either his wife or a friend. But Bamberg had neither wife nor mistress, and so he paid a harlot to accompany him. He had to buy her an evening dress for the occasion. The company consisted exclusively of writers, professors, philosophers, and the usual intellectual hangers-on. They all had the same idea as Bamberg—they hired prostitutes. I was there, too. I escorted an actress from Prague, whom I had known a long time. Do you know Granat? A savage. He drinks cognac like soda water, and can eat an omelette of ten eggs. As soon as the guests arrived, he stripped and began dancing madly around with the whores, just to impress his highbrow visitors. At first, the intellectuals sat on chairs and stared. After a while, they began to discuss sex. Schopenhauer said this. . . . Nietzsche said that. Anyone who hadn't witnessed it would find it difficult to imagine how ridiculous such geniuses can be. In the midst of it all, Bamberg was taken ill. He turned as green as grass and broke out in a sweat. 'Jacques,' he said, 'I'm finished. A good place to die.' He was having a kidney or a gall-bladder attack. I half carried him out and got him to a hospital. By the way, can you lend me a zloty?"

"Two."

"What! Have you robbed Bank Polski?"

"I sold a story."

"Congratulations. Let's have supper together. You will be my guest."

2.

While we were eating, Bamberg came over to our table. He was a little man, emaciated as a consumptive, bent over and bowlegged. He was wearing patent-leather shoes, and spats. On his pointed skull lay a few gray hairs. One eye was larger than the other—red, bulging, frightened by its own vision. He leaned against our table on his bony little hands and said in his cackling voice, "Jacques, yesterday I read your Kafka's *Castle*. Interesting, very interesting, but what is he driving at? It's too long for a dream. Allegories should be short."

Jacques Kohn quickly swallowed the food he was chewing. "Sit down," he said. "A master does not have to follow the rules."

"There are some rules even a master must follow. No novel should be longer than *War and Peace*. Even *War and Peace* is too long. If the Bible consisted of eighteen volumes, it would long since have been forgotten."

"The Talmud has thirty-six volumes, and the Jews have not forgotten it."

"Jews remember too much. That is our misfortune. It is two thousand years since we were driven out of the Holy Land, and now we are trying to get back in. Insane, isn't it? If our literature would only reflect this insanity, it would be great. But our literature is uncannily sane. Well, enough of that."

Bamberg straightened himself, scowling with the effort. With his tiny steps, he shuffled away from the table. He went over to the gramophone and put on a dance record. It was known in the writers' club that he had not written a word for years. In his old age, he was learning to dance, influenced by the philosophy of his friend Dr. Mitzkin, the author of *The Entropy of Reason*. In this book Dr. Mitzkin attempted to prove that the human intellect is bankrupt and that true wisdom can only be reached through passion.

Jacques Kohn shook his head. "Half-pint Hamlet. Kafka was afraid of becoming a Bamberg—that is why he destroyed himself."

"Did the countess ever call you?" I asked.

Jacques Kohn took his monocle out of his pocket and put it in place. "And what if she did? In my life, everything turns into words. All talk, talk. This is actually Dr. Mitzkin's philosophy—man will end up as a word machine. He will eat words, drink words, marry words, poison himself with words. Come to think of it, Dr. Mitzkin was also present at Granat's orgy. He came to practice what he preached, but he could just as well have written *The Entropy of Passion*. Yes, the countess does call me from time to time. She, too, is an intellectual, but without intellect. As a matter of fact, although women do their best to reveal the charms of their bodies, they know just as little about the meaning of sex as they do about the intellect.

"Take Madam Tschissik. What did she ever have, except a body? But just try asking her what a body really is. Now she's ugly. When she was an actress in the Prague days, she still had something. I was her leading man. She was a tiny little talent. We came to Prague to make some money and found a genius waiting for us—*Homo sapiens* in his highest degree of self-torture. Kafka wanted to be a Jew, but he didn't know how. He wanted to live, but he didn't know this, either. 'Franz,' I said to him once, 'you are a young man. Do what we all do.' There was a brothel I knew in Prague, and I persuaded him to go there with me. He was still a virgin. I'd rather not speak about the girl he was engaged to. He was sunk to the neck in the bourgeois swamp. The Jews of his circle had one ideal—to become Gentiles, and not Czech Gentiles but German Gentiles. To make it short, I talked him into the adventure. I took him to a dark alley in the former ghetto and there was the brothel. We went up the crooked steps. I opened the door and it looked like a stage set: the whores, the pimps, the guests, the madam. I will never forget that moment. Kafka began to shake, and pulled at my sleeve. Then he turned and ran down the steps so quickly I was afraid he would break a leg. Once on the street, he stopped and vomited like a schoolboy. On the way back, we passed an old synagogue, and Kafka began to speak about the golem. Kafka believed in the golem, and even that the future might well bring another one. There must be magic words that can turn a piece of clay into a living being. Did not God, according to the cabala, create the world by uttering holy words? In the beginning was the Logos.

"Yes, it's all one big chess game. All my life I have been afraid of death, but now that I'm on the threshold of the grave I've stopped being afraid. It's clear, my partner wants to play a slow game. He'll go on taking my pieces one by one. First he removed my appeal as an actor and turned me into a so-called writer. He'd no sooner done that than he provided me with writer's cramp. His next move was to deprive me of my potency. Yet I know he's far from checkmate, and this gives me strength. It's cold in my room—let it be cold. I have no supper—I won't die without it. He sabotages me and I sabotage him. Some time ago, I was returning home late at night. The frost burned outside, and suddenly I realized that I had lost my key. I woke up the janitor, but he had no spare key. He stank of vodka, and his dog bit my foot. In former years I would have been desperate, but this time I said to my opponent, 'If you want me to catch pneumonia, it's all right with me.' I left the house and decided to go to the Vienna station. The wind almost carried me away. I would have had to wait at least three-quarters of an hour for the streetcar at that time of night. I passed by the actors' union and saw a light in a window. I decided to go in. Perhaps I could spend the night there. On the steps I hit something with my shoe and heard a ringing sound. I bent down and picked up a key. It was mine! The chance of finding a key on the dark stairs of this building is one in a billion, but it seems that my opponent was afraid I might give up the ghost before he was ready. Fatalism? Call it fatalism if you like."

Jacques Kohn rose and excused himself to make a phone call. I sat there and watched Bamberg dancing on his shaky legs with a literary lady. His eyes were closed, and he leaned his head on her bosom as if it were a pillow. He seemed to be dancing and sleeping simultaneously. Jacques Kohn took a long time—much longer than it normally takes to make a phone call. When he returned, the monocle in his eye shone. "Guess who is in the other room?" he said. "Madam Tschissik! Kafka's great love."

"Really."

"I told her about you. Come, I'd like to introduce you to her."

"No."

"Why not? A woman that was loved by Kafka is worth meeting."

"I'm not interested."

"You are shy, that's the truth. Kafka, too, was shy—as shy as a yeshiva student. I was never shy, and that may be the reason I have never amounted to anything. My dear friend, I need another twenty groschen for the janitors—ten for the one in this building, and ten for the one in mine. Without the money I can't go home."

I took some change out of my pocket and gave it to him.

"So much? You certainly must have robbed a bank today. Forty-six groschen! Piff-paff! Well, if there is a God, He will reward you. And if there isn't, who is playing all these games with Jacques Kohn?"

Translated by the author and Elizabeth Shub

Guests on a Winter Night

The stove was heated. The hanging kerosene lamp cast a bright glow over the room. Outside, it had been snowing for three days. Our balcony was cushioned in snow. At the head of the table, my father sat in a black velvet robe beneath which a yellowish fringed garment showed. He wore a skull-cap. His high forehead gleamed like a mirror. I looked at him with love, and also with astonishment. Why was he my father? What would have happened if someone else had been my father? Would I have been the same Isaac? I observed him as though I were seeing him for the first time. The reason for these reveries was something my mother had told me the day before—that the matchmaker had tried to marry her off to a young man from Lublin. Would she still have been my mother if she had married that young man? The whole thing was a puzzle.

My father was fair, his sidelocks dark, his beard red like tobacco. He had a short nose and blue eyes. A strange thought occurred to me—that he resembled the czar whose picture hung in our cheder. I knew well enough that a comparison like that was a sacrilege. The czar was a vicious man, and my father was pious and a rabbi. But my brain was full of crazy thoughts. If people knew what I was thinking, they would put me in prison. My parents would disown me. I would be excommunicated like the philosopher Spinoza, of whom my father spoke at the Purim dinner. That heretic had denied God. He said the world was not created but had existed for eternity.

An open book lay on the table in front of my

father, and he put his sash in it as a sign that he was interrupting the study only for a short while. On his right stood a glass of tea, half full. On his left lay his long pipe. Opposite him sat my mother. My father's face was almost round, and my mother's face, her nose, her chin were angular. Even the gaze of her large gray eyes was sharp. She wore a blond wig, but I knew that under it her hair was fiery red, like mine. Her cheeks were sunken, her lips thin. I was always afraid that she was reading my mind.

To my father's right sat Abraham, the ritual slaughterer, a corpulent man, black as a gypsy, with a round beard like a brush. There was gossip that he trimmed it. Abraham had a big belly, a straight neck, a broad nose, and thick lips. He pronounced his r's hard, and he spoke unusually fast. He felt wronged by everybody, but most of all by his third wife, Zevtel. Though he was supposed to be speaking to my father, he constantly glanced at my mother. His dark eyes embedded in bluish puffs flashed with anger. I had heard that all slaughterers were born under the sign of Mars and if they had not studied to become slaughterers they would have been murderers. I imagined Abraham lurking in a thick forest with an ax in his hand, attacking merchants who were going to Leipzig, Danzig, or Lentshno. He took their bags of gold and chopped off their heads. When they implored him to let them live, he answered, "A murrrderer knows no merrrcy."

But here was Abraham sitting and complaining like a schlemiel about his wife. He said, "All day long I stand and slaughter; at night I want to have rest, but then the fire begins. She wages war against me. Her mother was like that, too. I only learned about her when I visited Zelochow. She buried three husbands—you know it's forbidden to marry a three-time widow, but she has a fourth husband now. Zevtel also had two husbands before me. I am the third. Both divorced her. The first was a gentle

young man, fine as silk, a nephew of the rabbi of
Zychlin. What could she have had against him? She
simply fell in love with the other one, they told
me—that boor of a coachman. She behaved so
shamefully the whole town was scandalized."

"God save us—phooey," my father said. He reached
with his right hand for the glass of tea. With his
other hand he held his beard.

Even though I was still a boy, I knew that my
father understood little about such matters. He judged
everything according to law. A deed was either
permitted or forbidden. For him there was no difference between touching a candlestick on the Sabbath
and behaving in a loose way. My father was brought
up on the Torah, prayer, the sayings of wonder
rabbis. His real passion was visiting rabbinical courts,
conversing with Hasidim about miracles, but each
time he suggested going away my mother reminded
him that we had rent to pay, and tuition for the
children, and that we also had to eat. One does not
make a living by wandering among rabbis.

I heard my mother ask Abraham, "If this is the
case, why did you marry her?"

Abraham bit his thick lower lip. "The truth doesn't
show itself immediately. She made everything look
smooth. When she wants to, she can be as sweet as
honey. After my Luba died, I was all at sea. What
can a man do alone? I upset my stomach by eating in
restaurants. They told me her father was a scholar.
With Luba—peace be with her—I had no children.
She suffered from a female ailment and they removed her womb. I wanted to leave a son to say
Kaddish for me. The matchmaker brought Zevtel
and me together, and she spoke pleasing words.
According to her, the Zychliner rabbi's nephew was
half mad and an unworldly dreamer. When she
brought him food to the study house, he didn't recognize her and thought that she was the maid. He
didn't know which side of the coin was up. He

remained a schoolboy—there are such men. Anyway, he was no match for Zevtel. I understood this later. Excuse me for saying so, she was a woman who needed a real male. I don't want to slander, and also there is a holy scroll here in the Ark, but I could tell you things that would make your hair stand up. About her second husband, she told me he was a grain merchant and an important elder but she couldn't get along with her stepdaughters. I didn't have time to look into all this. It happens that people divorce. Even rabbis sometimes divorce. But right after we were married she began to show her true colors. She wanted me to become a community slaughterer. It didn't please her that I was just an unofficial slaughterer in Warsaw. I said, 'What's the difference so long as I make a living?' The city slaughterers have a sinecure—it passes from father to son. They were all born in Warsaw, and anyone from the provinces is an outsider. They're stuffed with money and live in high style. The rabbi of Gur, who supports them, may be a holy man, but he's also powerful. If you're one of his followers, all doors are open to you. If not, it's persecution. He's supposed to be in touch with heaven, but he knows too well what goes on below."

My father put down his glass of tea. "What are you saying, Reb Abraham? The rabbi of Gur is a saint. He loves all Jews."

"Yes. But even Moses cut corners. Anyhow, she began to go from one elder to another, looking for pull. She ordered a wig that only half covered her head. She didn't cut her hair but combed it into her wig. I came into the room and there she stood in front of the mirror making curls with a crimping iron. I said to her, 'What does this mean?' And she said, 'Don't rack your brains about it.' In short, she was getting ready to go to see the elder for my sake and she wanted to charm him. It made me burn. I said, 'I don't want to be a community slaughterer, and don't make yourself pretty for them.' The way she went at me I could have been her worst enemy."

My father reached for his pipe. "The Talmud says, 'A man does not live with a snake in a basket.' "

"Don't I know! I haven't told a thousandth part of it. In Zelochow I learned the truth—that the grain merchant she had fallen in love with was no grain merchant but a common drayman who carried merchandise. Once in a while, he took passengers. She went on a wagon with him to Sochaczew. He had a nasty tongue, said things that would make a Cossack blush. She developed a taste for him. She left her husband, refused to be his wife. You know what I mean."

My mother shook her head. My father said, "Such a woman may be divorced without a settlement."

"She already had plenty of money from the first one. But then she got jealous. He went on the road and always had a wagon full of women—a crude fellow, a scoundrel. Never without a bottle of vodka in his breast pocket, they said, and he could eat a bowl of buckwheat with chicken fat as big as a washtub. He left her in town, miserable and alone, and came home just for the Sabbath—sometimes not even then. Now she was the one who wanted a divorce and he demanded payment—he threatened to go to America and leave her a deserted wife unless she paid. What she extorted from the first she had to give to the second, and she even had to sell her jewelry in addition."

"A wanton," my mother said. "Why do you stay with her?"

"She refuses to give me a divorce. All I can do is get permission from a hundred rabbis."

My father glanced into the book. "Rabbi Zadock from Lublin, blessed be his memory, had a damned woman like this. She shook hands with an officer. When Rabbi Zadock found out, he immediately wanted to divorce her, but she refused to be divorced. And Rabbi Zadock had to go to a hundred cities to get a hundred signatures."

"All for shaking hands with an officer?" Abraham asked.

"It's light behavior. Once you take one step from Jewishness, you are already sinking into the Forty-nine Gates of Defilement," my father replied.

"Perhaps the Russian held out his hand and she was afraid not to take it?" my mother asked.

"One should only be afraid of the Almighty," my father said judiciously.

2.

It was quiet. I heard the wick sucking the kerosene. Outside, the dry snow was falling and the wind was blowing. My father reached for his pouch of tobacco to fill his pipe but found it empty. He looked at me half questioningly and half imploringly. "Itchele, I am without tobacco."

My mother became tense. "You are not going to send the child out in the cold. Besides, all the stores are closed now."

"If I don't have tobacco in the morning, I cannot study. Neither can I prepare myself for the morning prayer."

"Eli's store may still be open," Abraham said.

I guessed that Abraham wanted to get rid of me, as he was about to tell secrets not meant for a boy's ears. But I wanted to go down the street anyhow. If only it weren't so dark on the steps. I said, "I will go."

"Give him twenty groschen," my father said.

My mother frowned, but she gave in. My father was an ardent smoker. Every morning, he smoked his pipe, drank many glasses of watery tea, and wrote commentaries on narrow pads. Saturday at dusk, he could hardly wait for the appearance of three stars in the sky. My mother dressed me in a

warm vest and put a muffler around my neck. She
left the kitchen door open as I went down the steps,
because she knew that I was afraid. How could I not
be afraid, knowing that the world was full of demons, devils, hobgoblins? I remembered the neighbors' little daughter, Jochebed, who had died the
year before. And a ghost who haunted a house in
Bilgoray, broke windowpanes, threw the dishes
around. And the boy who had been carried away by
an evil spirit to the castle of Asmodeus and forced to
marry one of the Evil Host. It was good that we lived
no higher than the second floor. But the gate was
dark, too. A man often stood there with a face that
looked as though it had been skinned. He had a piece
of black plaster for a nose. I could never learn who it
was he waited for there alone for hours in the cold
and dark. Most probably he also was connected with
the unclean spirits.

But the moment I passed the gate everything
became cheerful. Though there were neither moon
nor stars in the sky, it shone with a yellowish light,
as if illuminated behind the clouds by heavenly
lamps created for this particular night. The gas
lamps wore caps of snow, the glass was white from
frost, and the light coming through had the colors of
the rainbow. Each lamp dragged a trail of fog behind
it. The snow covered the poverty of Krochmalna
Street, and it looked rich now. I imagined that
Warsaw had in some strange way moved deep into
Russia—perhaps Siberia, where according to my
brother Joshua the winter is one long night and
white bears travel on ice floes. The gutter became a
skating rink for boys. Some of the stores were closed,
their windowpanes framed in ice and covered with
frosty palm branches, like the ones used in the Feast
of Tabernacles. In others, customers were let in
through the back doors. The delicatessen was brightly
lit. Long sausages hung from the ceiling. Behind the
counter stood Chayele, slicing sausage, liver, breast

of veal, roast beef, or a mixture of everything—cold cuts. Salt pretzels could be had here, as well as hot frankfurters with mustard. At a small table a couple were sitting, eating a late supper. I knew that they were engaged. Who else ate supper in a delicatessen? He was dressed half old-fashioned, half new-fashioned, in a short gaberdine, a small cap, a stiff cardboard collar, and a paper dickey. The hair beneath his cap was sleek and pomaded. I knew him. He was Pesach, who specialized in sewing uppers for boots. On the Sabbath morning, he used to come to the prayerhouse, but after the Sabbath meal he took his fiancée to the moving pictures or to the Yiddish theater, where they played *Shulamith, Chasia the Orphan, Prince Chardas*. I learned all this from what the boys in the courtyard told me. I knew the girl, Feigele, well. Only a year ago she used to play with girls in the courtyard, throwing nuts at a target. She was also deft with a Diabolo. But suddenly she became engaged, was a grownup. She rolled her black hair into a bun. My father officiated at her engagement party and brought home a piece of cake for me. Tonight, she was wearing a green dress trimmed with fur. She held the frankfurter elegantly, crooking her little finger and taking tiny bites. For a while, I stared at this pair. I had a great desire to call "Pesach! Feigele!," but I restrained myself. Other boys could afford to act freely, but not the son of a rabbi. If I did not behave, there was gossip and I was denounced to my parents.

It was even more interesting to look into Chaim's coffee shop. Many couples sat there, all of them emancipated, not Hasidic. The place was frequented by thieves and "strikers"—the young men and girls who only a few years before were throwing bombs and demanding a constitution from the czar. What a constitution was I had not yet learned, but I knew that on Bloody Wednesday scores of these young people fell before bullets. Still, many remained alive, and some of those who were put into prison had later been released. They sat in Chaim's coffee shop, ate rolls with herring, drank coffee with chicory, sometimes took a piece of cheesecake, and read the Yiddish papers. They tried to learn about other strikes deep in Russia or abroad. The strikers were dressed differently from the thieves. They wore collarless shirts closed with tin studs. The visors on their caps were not pulled down so far over their eyes. The girls were poorly clothed, their hair caught up in combs. The thieves sat at one large round table, and their girls wore summer dresses in the middle of winter— red, yellow, some with flowers. Their faces looked to me as though they had been smeared with borsch; their eyes, rimmed in black, shone uncannily. My mother said that these sinful creatures had lost both this world and the world to come.

Occasionally, my father sent me to that coffee shop to summon a boy or a girl to his court. My father had no beadle, and I served as one. When I entered, all the guests began to chide me. The workers pointed to me and made fun of my red sidelocks. One time one of them asked me, "You are studying the Torah, aren't you? What will you become—a Talmud tutor, a middleman, a peddler?" He added, "Tell your father that his time is over." The thieves would call me "schlemiel," "yeshiva boy," "bench hugger." The girls would defend me. "Don't bother the child." Once, one of them kissed me. I spat and ran away. Everybody in the coffee shop laughed.

Eli's store was still open. I got a package of tobacco. Composition books, crayons, erasers, steel pens, pencils could be bought there, but these were for rich boys, not for me, who got a penny a day and sometimes not even that.

I did not go home immediately. I lifted a handful of snow and licked it with the tip of my tongue. Even though it was winter, I thought I heard behind the snow the chirping of crickets. Or perhaps it was the

bells on the necks of horses pulling sleighs around
Iron Street, where the gas lamps appeared small and
where I could see a trolley car as tiny as a toy. I
never dared to go there by myself. On the way back
near our gate, I saw my sister, Hindele, and my
brother Joshua. I was overjoyed that I would not
have to walk up the dark steps alone. To see my
brother and sister together on the street was something out of the ordinary. First, because it did not
behoove a Hasidic young man to walk in the street
with a girl—even his sister—and, second, because
they were not on good terms. They seemed to have
met by accident—he returning home from Krel's study
house on Gnoyna Street, and she coming home from
her friend Leah. Hindele, too, was afraid to walk up
the dark steps. I ran toward them, screaming,
"Hindele! Joshua!"

"Why do you shout like a wild man?" Joshua
scolded me. "We are not deaf."

"What are you doing in the street so late?" Hindele
asked. She was dressed like a lady, in a hat fastened
with rhinestone pins, a fur collar trimmed with the
little head of an animal, and a muff. She was already
engaged and her trousseau was being prepared.
Joshua wore a long gaberdine and a small cap. He
had sidelocks, too, but they were trimmed. Joshua
had become enlightened—"spoiled," my father called
it. He refused to study the Talmud, he read secular
books, he was opposed to the use of a matchmaker.
Almost every day my father had a discussion with
him. Joshua insisted that the Jews in Poland lived
like Asiatics. He mocked their sidelocks, their gaberdines down to their shoe tops. How much longer
were they going to study the law concerning the egg
that was hatched on a holiday? Europe, my brother
said, had awakened, but the Jews in Poland were
still in the Middle Ages. He used modern words I did
not understand. I listened to him dispute with my
father, and I was always on his side. I wanted to cut

off *my* sidelocks, put on a short jacket, study Polish, Russian, German, and learn what makes a train go, how to build a telephone, a telegraph, a balloon, a ship. I never dared to take part in these arguments, but I knew very well that men in long gaberdines and women in wigs and bonnets were not allowed inside the Saxony Gardens. My father kept promising me that when the Messiah came those who studied the Torah would be saved and the unbelievers would perish. But when would the Messiah come? Perhaps he would not come at all.

My sister, Hindele, was no longer pious, either. She and Joshua were both grownups, but I was still a boy. Between Joshua and me there had been two other children, both girls, who had died of scarlet fever.

Hindele and Joshua each took one of my hands and led me to the dark gate and up the dark steps. Now I wasn't afraid even of Satan himself. My brother said to my sister, "See how dark it is here. In houses on other streets, there are gas lamps along the stairways. Here it is dark physically and spiritually."

"The landlord tries to save the penny for kerosene," my sister said.

We all entered the kitchen. Abraham the slaughterer was leaving. His belly blocked the door for a moment.

3.

This night there was no dispute. My father was writing his commentaries. My mother, Hindele, Joshua, and I stayed in the kitchen. The stove was heated and tea was boiling. My mother was rendering goose fat for Hanukkah. Joshua told stories about America. There were robbers there who called themselves the Black Hand. They didn't steal linen from attics, like the thieves on Krochmalna Street, but attacked millionaires. They used blackmail to extort money. The police were afraid of them. Joshua spoke to my mother, but from time to time he glanced at me. He knew that I devoured his words. My sister also listened as she turned the pages of a Yiddish newspaper. She was reading a serialized novel. My brother and my mother used to take a look at it, too. My sister said, "My! The Countess Louisa has escaped."

"How did she escape?" my mother asked.

"Through the window."

"But she was on the fifth floor."

"Wild Max helped her get out with a ladder."

"Oh, what a writer can invent!"

"That stuff in the newspaper is trash," my brother explained. "But Tolstoy was a great writer. Publishers are offering a quarter of a million rubles for his manuscripts."

"Well, one painting in Paris was appraised for twenty million francs," my mother said. "And when it was stolen all of France went into mourning, as though it were Tisha b'ov. When it was found, people kissed in the streets. There is no lack of lunatics," she added.

"The *Mona Lisa*," my brother said, nodding. "Why do you call them lunatics? This is art. Leonardo da Vinci took many years to paint it. No artist before or after has brought out such a smile."

"Who cares how some female is smiling?" my mother asked. "It's all idolatry. In olden times, the wicked served idols. Now they call it Art. One can smile very beautifully and be a hussy just the same."

"What do you want, Mother? Should the French make a pilgrimage to the rabbi of Gur and pick up crumbs from his table? In Europe, they want beauty, not the Torah of an old man who recites the Psalms and has a rupture."

"Phooey—what a way to speak! It is possible to have a rupture and be more acceptable to God than a

thousand good-looking *shiksas*. The Almighty loves
a broken heart, not a chiseled nose."

"How do you know what the Almighty loves?"

"Mother, in Paris the women are now wearing
pants!" my sister exclaimed.

"A time will come when they walk with their
heads down and their feet up," my mother said as
she covered the pot with a lid. "The gluttony, the
drunkenness, and the wantonness get boring, and
they have to invent something new."

I listened to each word: Countess Louisa, Mona
Lisa, Paris, Art, Tolstoy, Leonardo da Vinci. I didn't
know what all these words stood for, but I grasped
that they were essential to the debate. No matter
what was talked about at our house, the conversation always led to the topic of the Torah and the
world, and Jews and other peoples.

After a while, my brother took out a Russian
grammar and began to study—*imia sushchestvitelnoye,
imia prilegatelnoye, glagol* (noun, adjective, verb).
He resembled my mother, but he was tall and manly.
I knew that the matchmakers had offered him a
bride with a thousand-ruble dowry and six years'
board at her father's house. But he refused. He said
that one should marry only for love.

Hindele took some samples from her pocketbook:
silk, velvet, satin. She was engaged to a young man
from Antwerp. She had been chosen by his father,
the preacher Reb Gedalya, who, though his sons
went abroad, found them their brides. Hindele had
large bright eyes and her face was rosy. Her hair
was brown. The women in our courtyard used to say
that she was blooming—save her from the Evil Eye.
But we in the family knew the truth—she had sick
nerves. One moment she laughed, the next she cried.
One day she covered mother with kisses, another
day she accused her of being her enemy and of trying
to send her into exile. One day she was overly pious,
the next she was blasphemous. She often fainted.

She had even tried to throw herself out of the window.

To me and to my younger brother, Moshe (who was asleep in the bedroom), she was always good. She brought us candy. She told us stories about a wild man with one eye in his forehead, about an island of fools, and about a young man who found a single golden hair and went to Madagascar to seek its owner.

While Hindele sorted through her samples, I made use of the pause to say, "Hindele, tell me a story."

The moment I said this, I heard unusually heavy steps on the stairs, deep breathing, and sighing. Then someone knocked on the door. My mother said, "Who can this be?"

"Mother, don't open," my sister warned. She was always afraid. She believed Warsaw was full of murderers and men who ride about in carriages, seduce girls, take them to Buenos Aires, and sell them as slaves. She even suspected that her father-in-law-to-be, Reb Gedalya, was one of these, that he let his white beard and sidelocks grow just to fool people.

My mother opened the door and we saw an old woman dressed in clothes from the time of King Sobieski—a bonnet with a high crown hung with many colored ribbons, a beaded velvet cape, and an unusually long wide skirt, pleated and flounced, with a train. She wore long earrings. Her wrinkled face looked like a patchwork. In one hand she grasped a satchel with copper locks and outside pockets, in the other a bundle tied up in a flowered kerchief. It's my grandmother Tamerl, I thought.

The old woman looked around with beaming eyes. "Is this the residence of Pinchos Mendel?" she asked.

I had never heard anyone call my father by his first names. My mother looked at her in astonishment. "Yes, it is. Come in."

"Woe is me! Why do you live so high up?" the old

woman asked in a voice that was both soft and strong.

Snow fell from her shoes, of which only the tips were visible. "Alas, this Warsaw is not just a city but a whole country," she complained. "The people run as though—God forbid—there were a fire. The train arrived even before the time of the pre-evening prayer, but no matter how many times I asked the way I could not find your street. You are most probably Bathsheba," she said to my mother. "And these are your children." She pretended to spit to ward off the Evil Eye. "They all take after their grandmother Tamerl. Where is Pinchos Mendel?"

"Please sit down. Put down your satchel. Warm yourself." My mother pointed out a chair.

"I am not cold, but I want to wash my hands for the evening prayer."

This was not like a woman speaking but more like a man and a scholar. My brother raised his eyes from the Russian grammar and looked at her, half in wonder and half in mockery. My sister gaped. The old woman put down her satchel and cried, "Children, I have brought you cookies! I baked them myself."

She opened the bundle and it was full of cookies. They smelled of cinnamon, almonds, clove, and spices whose names I didn't know but my nose recognized. It became Purim in our kitchen in the middle of winter. The chair that my mother offered was too narrow for the guest's billowing skirt. My mother helped her to remove her cape, but under it was another cape. She was all wrapped up in silk, velvet, bows, beads. Even though it was no holiday, she wore around her neck a thick golden chain and a string of pearls.

"Great Matriarch Sarah!" my brother muttered.

My father entered the kitchen.

The old woman exclaimed, "Pinchos Mendel, it's you!"

My father did not look at her, since it was not correct to look at women, but he stopped. "Who are you?" he asked.

"Who am I? Your aunt, Itte Fruma."

My father's face lit up. "Itte Fruma!"

If it had been a man, he would have known what to say: "Peace be with you," or "Blessed be your arrival." But how does one greet a female? After a pause, he said in his simple manner, "Why did you come to Warsaw?"

"It's a long story. I was left without a house."

"Did it—God forbid—burn down?"

"No. Someone gave it as dowry for his daughter."

"What do you mean?"

"There is in our town one Shachno Beiles. He has been my neighbor for many years. The poor man has ugly daughters—the youngest already over thirty and still not married. From where shall a pauper like this get a dowry? In short, he promised the young man my house. I learned about it only after their wedding. The bridegroom came to me and showed me in the engagement contract that my house was his house. I didn't want to shame Shachno Beiles. He is some kind of a scholar—and he did it because he was in distress. If I told his son-in-law that he had been deceived, he might have run away from his wife. I am already old, I thought, and they are just beginning to live. How long will I stay in this house? I have no one to leave it to but you, Pinchos Mendel. But since you live in Warsaw, why do you need a house in Tomashov? Besides, you are not a worldly man. To get some income from a house you have to be shrewd. The roof needs fixing and there are other repairs. The expense of traveling there and back would be more then you could make from it. Well—so I left them the house. One must leave everything anyhow. One takes nothing to heaven except good deeds. So I packed my bundle and came here."

My mother looked at her with both sympathy and derision. I saw that Hindele was choking with suppressed laughter. My brother's face expressed ridicule. His lips moved, and I knew what they were saying: "Asia—Asiatics." The only one who did not seem surprised was my father. He said, "Well, I understand. Where will you live?"

Aunt Itte Fruma answered, "With you."

4.

My mother spoke plainly to my father: if his Aunt Itte Fruma was going to stay in our house, my mother would take me and my brother Moshe to her father's in Bilgoray. My brother Joshua let it be known that he would move out the next day. My sister Hindele cried, laughed, and warned that she would return the engagement contract and go to America. All this talk went on when Aunt Itte Fruma was absent. She had another relative in Warsaw, and she went to visit him. At night, my father gave his bed to his aunt. He made himself a bed on a bench in the study.

Aunt Itte Fruma slept little; she conducted herself like an ancient Hasidic scholar. She prayed three times a day. She got up in the middle of the night and lamented the destruction of the Temple. She did not eat meat on weekdays, only on the Sabbath; Monday and Thursday she fasted. We had never heard of an old woman going to the ritual bath—it was for young women who cleansed themselves for their husbands—but Aunt Itte Fruma went to the ritual bath. Joshua, who liked to make fun of people, assured us that Aunt Itte Fruma wore a fringed undergarment like a man. It could have been true. I had a great-grandmother, Hinde Esther, the one my sister was named for, and she really wore a fringed garment and went on pilgrimages to the rabbi of Belz. Her husband, Isaac, whose namesake I was,

went to the rabbi of Tshernoble. In our family,
everything was possible. Aunt Itte Fruma's skirt
and train took up half a room. She could hardly pass
through the door. She blew her nose with a kind of
kerchief only rabbis use. She snuffed tobacco from a
carved bone box. With every step she took, she
caused damage. She broke dishes, knocked over an
inkwell, upset a kerosene lamp. Our apartment was
turned topsy-turvy. We noticed that she was wearing all the clothes she owned. In her satchel, which
she left open, there was only a huge prayer book and
some jewelry.

"Where is her linen?" my mother asked herself
and the rest of us. "Has she lost her mind?"

My brother Joshua said, "She's senile." He now
slept at the house of a friend. He had wanted to move
out for a long time. He planned to wear modern
clothes and study painting.

The third day after her arrival, Aunt Itte Fruma
had a conversation with my sister. When Hindele
told her she was engaged, Aunt Itte Fruma took the
heavy gold chain from her neck and gave it to her.
My sister refused to take it, but Aunt Itte Fruma
insisted. "What do I need a chain for?" she said. "I
can't take it to the grave."

My sister showed the chain to all of us. It had the
kind of clasp that goldsmiths no longer made. The
chain itself must have weighed a pound. Hindele
went with it to a jeweler, and he told her that it was
fourteen-carat gold.

All our neighbors and everyone on the street heard
about the unusual visitor. Pious women, charity
workers came to meet her and converse with her.
Aunt Itte Fruma told them of numerous miracles
performed by the wonder rabbis. She spiced her
Yiddish with Hebrew expressions. She recommended
magic cures for headaches, pressure around the heart,
ringing in the ears, catarrh. She sat in our kitchen
and held court like a lady of the manor. She didn't

have a single tooth in her mouth. And when she ate, it was only oatmeal and borsch in which she dipped crusts of bread. My mother spoke quietly, but Aunt Itte Fruma had a loud voice. She could be heard in all the rooms.

I was pleased with this aunt's visit. I ate all her cookies. I had heard my mother say that she would take me and my brother to Bilgoray, which meant that we would go on a train, see fields, forests, and not go to cheder. Aunt Itte Fruma's stories fascinated me. She told about the thirty-six concealed saints, of demons disguised as yeshiva boys, of hobgoblins, mocking spirits, werewolves, imps. She had seen for herself the famous virgin of Krashnik who was possessed by a dibbuk. Aunt Itte Fruma had spoken to the dibbuk, and she told us about it. When she asked the dibbuk why he had taken possession of this girl, he answered, "A new meddler has arrived on the scene! Pick up and go back to where you came from." He called her a hypocrite, a holier-than-thou, an oil anointer. He told her that she had a birthmark on her left breast, and it was true.

The women of Krochmalna Street listened to the stories and sighed, blew their noses, shook their heads. They brought the old woman little offerings—a slice of honey cake, a roasted apple, a dish of stewed prunes. Aunt Itte Fruma gave them all to us children. I kissed her hand and she pinched my cheek.

She said to me, "Your great-grandfather, whose namesake you are, could have become a rabbi, but he refused. He studied all day long, and your great-grandmother, Hinde Esther, provided for the family. I knew them both well. She had a dry-goods store, but between one customer and the next she read *The Heritage of the Deer*. Once, a merchant from Lublin entered her store and saw a Turkish shawl there that he liked and bought for his wife. He gave her a a five-ruble banknote, and she returned the change. A few hours later, your great-grandmother figured

out that the merchant overpaid her six pennies. She
immediately closed the store and went to the inn to
look for this merchant. But he had already left. She
didn't know his address, not even his name—only
that he was from Lublin. And Hinde Esther knew
the law that if one takes so much as one penny that
doesn't belong to one, repentance will not help. One
had to find the person and give him back his property even if he had gone overseas. Your pious
great-grandmother—may she intercede in heaven
for us all—left her business and went to Lublin to
find the merchant. For a week and a half, she sought
him in all the synagogues, all the study houses,
hostelries, and stores, until she finally found him
and gave him back his six pennies. It cost her a lot of
money, in addition to the fact that her store was
closed. This was your great-grandmother."

One day, Aunt Itte Fruma went to spend the night
with her other relative. My father moved back to his
bed again and I slept with him. In the middle of the
night I awoke. I heard my father speak, but he
wasn't in bed with me. His voice seemed to come
from my mother's bed, which was placed head to foot
with his bed. How was this possible, I asked myself.
Could my father have gone to my mother's bed?
Could my father, the rabbi, defile himself in this
way? I held my breath. I heard my father say, "She
is a saint. It is a privilege to have her in our house."

"She is too much of a saint," my mother replied. "If
this man gave her house as dowry, he is a swindler.
It is not written in any book that one must allow the
daughter of a swindler to take over one's house—and
then become a burden to others. Forgive me, but this
is sheer folly."

"It is written that it is better to be burned in a kiln
than to shame another," my father said. "Everyone
in town would have found out what this man had
done and he would have been degraded. His son-in-law
might have run away."

I wanted to cry out "Daddy!" but some instinct told me to be silent. I closed my eyes and went right to sleep.

The next day, my Aunt Itte Fruma returned and let us know that she was moving out. She was going to live with this other relative, who wasn't kindred of ours. He was a connection of her late husband's. He was a watchmaker, and all his children were married. He had a large apartment on Prosta Street.

For a year and a half, Aunt Itte Fruma lived there. She used to visit us, and she always brought a kerchief with Sabbath cookies, walnuts, raisins. She spoke to my father about the Torah. She told us many stories about grandfathers, great-grandfathers, great-uncles, great-aunts. On my father's side, I had family in Hungary and Galicia. My brother Joshua grew fond of her, and without her knowledge he drew her portrait. When my sister, Hindele got married, the wedding took place in Berlin. Aunt Itte Fruma gave her a wedding present. My mother regretted that she had spoken against her. She now admitted that Itte Fruma was a holy woman, like one of the ancients.

One day, I was told that Aunt Itte Fruma had died. She was in her late eighties. Even though she had resided in Warsaw only eighteen months, she had quite a large funeral. The community elders gave her a plot among the distinguished citizens. She left my mother her earrings and her thick prayer book, which was bound in wooden covers and had a brass clasp. I often browsed in this prayer book. It had prayers and lamentations not to be found in other prayer books—recitals for fast days in memory of martyrs of Chmielnitzki's time, Gonta's time, ordeals in Prague, in Frankfurt, even in France. The pages were yellow from age, spotted with droppings of tallow from candles and with traces of tears. God knows how many grandmothers and great-aunts had used it. It had an aroma of the Days of

Awe, of smelling salts used on Yom Kippur; it reminded one of Gentile edicts and God's miracles for His tried people. Some of the supplications and liturgies were translated into Yiddish-German with a script that looked half written and half printed.

One morning, I heard my father say, "She gave up a house in Tomashov and has built herself a mansion in Paradise."

"Will we visit her there?" I asked.

"Who knows? If we deserve it."

"Look at this boy!" My mother suddenly became angry. "Wash your face. Go to cheder. Don't ask such silly questions!"

Translated by the author and Dorothea Straus

The Key

At about three o'clock in the afternoon, Bessie Popkin began to prepare to go down to the street. Going out was connected with many difficulties, especially on a hot summer day: first, forcing her fat body into a corset, squeezing her swollen feet into shoes, and combing her hair, which Bessie dyed at home and which grew wild and was streaked in all colors—yellow, black, gray, red; then making sure that while she was out her neighbors would not break into her apartment and steal linen, clothes, documents, or just disarrange things and make them disappear.

Besides human tormentors, Bessie suffered from demons, imps, Evil Powers. She hid her eyeglasses in the night table and found them in a slipper. She placed her bottle of hair dye in the medicine chest; days later she discovered it under the pillow. Once, she left a pot of borsch in the refrigerator, but the Unseen took it from there and after long searching Bessie came upon it in her clothes closet. On its surface was a thick layer of fat that gave off a smell of rancid tallow.

What she went through, how many tricks were played on her and how much she had to wrangle in order not to perish or fall into insanity, only God knew. She had given up the telephone because racketeers and degenerates called her day and night, trying to get secrets out of her. The Puerto Rican milkman once tried to rape her. The errand boy from the grocery store attempted to burn her belongings with a cigarette. To evict her from the rent-controlled apartment where she had lived for thirty-five years,

the company and the superintendent infested her
rooms with rats, mice, cockroaches.

Bessie had long ago realized that no means were
adequate against those determined to be spiteful—not
the metal door, the special lock, her letters to the
police, the mayor, the F.B.I., and even the President
in Washington. But while one breathed one had to
eat. It all took time: checking the windows, the gas
vents, securing the drawers. Her paper money she
kept in volumes of the encyclopedia, in back copies
of the *National Geographic,* and in Sam Popkin's old
ledgers. Her stocks and bonds Bessie had hidden
among the logs in the fireplace, which was never
used, as well as under the seats of the easy chairs.
Her jewels she had sewn into the mattress. There
was a time when Bessie had safe-deposit boxes at
the bank, but she long ago convinced herself that the
guards there had passkeys.

At about five o'clock, Bessie was ready to go out.
She gave a last look at herself in the mirror—small,
broad, with a narrow forehead, a flat nose, and eyes
slanting and half closed, like a Chinaman's. Her
chin sprouted a little white beard. She wore a faded
dress in a flowered print, a misshapen straw hat
trimmed with wooden cherries and grapes, and shabby
shoes. Before she left, she made a final inspection of
the three rooms and the kitchen. Everywhere there
were clothes, shoes, and piles of letters that Bessie
had not opened. Her husband, Sam Popkin, who had
died almost twenty years ago, had liquidated his
real-estate business before his death, because he
was about to retire to Florida. He left her stocks,
bonds, and a number of passbooks from savings
banks, as well as some mortgages. To this day, firms
wrote to Bessie, sent her reports, checks. The Inter-
nal Revenue Service claimed taxes from her. Every
few weeks she received announcements from a funeral company that sold plots in an "airy cemetery."
In former years, Bessie used to answer letters, de-

posit her checks, keep track of her income and expenses. Lately she had neglected it all. She even stopped buying the newspaper and reading the financial section.

In the corridor, Bessie tucked cards with signs on them that only she could recognize between the door and the door frame. The keyhole she stuffed with putty. What else could she do—a widow without children, relatives, or friends? There was a time when the neighbors used to open their doors, look out, and laugh at her exaggerated care; others teased her. That had long passed. Bessie spoke to no one. She didn't see well, either. The glasses she had worn for years were of no use. To go to an eye doctor and be fitted for new ones was too much of an effort. Everything was difficult—even entering and leaving the elevator, whose door always closed with a slam.

Bessie seldom went farther than two blocks from her building. The street between Broadway and Riverside Drive became noisier and filthier from day to day. Hordes of urchins ran around half naked. Dark men with curly hair and wild eyes quarreled in Spanish with little women whose bellies were always swollen in pregnancy. They talked back in rattling voices. Dogs barked, cats meowed. Fires broke out and fire engines, ambulances, and police cars drove up. On Broadway, the old groceries had been replaced by supermarkets, where food must be picked out and put in a wagon and one had to stand in line before the cashier.

God in heaven, since Sam died, New York, America—perhaps the whole world—was falling apart. All the decent people had left the neighborhood and it was overrun by a mob of thieves, robbers, whores. Three times Bessie's pocketbook had been stolen. When she reported it to the police, they just laughed. Every time one crossed the street, one risked one's life. Bessie took a step and stopped.

Someone had advised her to use a cane, but she was
far from considering herself an old woman or a
cripple. Every few weeks she painted her nails red.
At times, when the rheumatism left her in peace,
she took clothes she used to wear from the closets,
tried them on, and studied herself in the mirror.

Opening the door of the supermarket was impossible. She had to wait till someone held it for her.
The supermarket itself was a place that only the
Devil could have invented. The lamps burned with a
glaring light. People pushing wagons were likely to
knock down anyone in their path. The shelves were
either too high or too low. The noise was deafening,
and the contrast between the heat outside and the
freezing temperature inside! It was a miracle that
she didn't get pneumonia. More than anything else,
Bessie was tortured by indecision. She picked up
each item with a trembling hand and read the label.
This was not the greed of youth but the uncertainty
of age. According to Bessie's figuring, today's shop-
ping should not have taken longer than three-
quarters of an hour, but two hours passed and Bessie
was still not finished. When she finally brought the
wagon to the cashier, it occurred to her that she had
forgotten the box of oatmeal. She went back and a
woman took her place in line. Later, when she paid,
there was new trouble. Bessie had put the bill in the
right side of her bag, but it was not there. After long
rummaging, she found it in a small change purse on
the opposite side. Yes, who could believe that such
things were possible? If she told someone, he would
think she was ready for the madhouse.

When Bessie went into the supermarket, the day
was still bright; now it was drawing to a close. The
sun, yellow and golden, was sinking toward the
Hudson, to the hazy hills of New Jersey. The buildings on Broadway radiated the heat they had absorbed. From under gratings where the subway trains
rumbled, evil-smelling fumes arose. Bessie held the

heavy bag of food in one hand, and in the other she
grasped her pocketbook tightly. Never had Broadway
seemed to her so wild, so dirty. It stank of softened
asphalt, gasoline, rotten fruit, the excrement of dogs.
On the sidewalk, among torn newspapers and the
butts of cigarettes, pigeons hopped about. It was
difficult to understand how these creatures avoided
being stepped on in the crush of passersby. From the
blazing sky a golden dust was falling. Before a
storefront hung with artificial grass, men in sweated
shirts poured papaya juice and pineapple juice into
themselves with haste, as if trying to extinguish a
fire that consumed their insides. Above their heads
hung coconuts carved in the shapes of Indians. On a
side street, black and white children had opened a
hydrant and were spashing naked in the gutter. In
the midst of that heat wave, a truck with micro-
phones drove around blaring out shrill songs and
deafening blasts about a candidate for political office.
From the rear of the truck, a girl with hair that
stood up like wires threw out leaflets.

It was all beyond Bessie's strength—crossing the
street, waiting for the elevator, and then getting out
on the fifth floor before the door slammed. Bessie
put the groceries down at the threshold and searched
for her keys. She used her nail file to dig the putty
out of the keyhole. She put in the key and turned it.
But woe, the key broke. Only the handle remained
in her hand. Bessie fully grasped the catastrophe.
The other people in the building had copies of their
keys hanging in the superintendent's apartment,
but she trusted no one—some time ago, she had
ordered a new combination lock, which she was sure
no master key could open. She had a duplicate key
somewhere in a drawer, but with her she carried
only this one. "Well, this is the end," Bessie said
aloud.

There was nobody to turn to for help. The neighbors were her blood enemies. The super only waited

for her downfall. Bessie's throat was so constricted
that she could not even cry. She looked around,
expecting to see the fiend who had delivered this
latest blow. Bessie had long since made peace with
death, but to die on the steps or in the streets was too
harsh. And who knows how long such agony could
last? She began to ponder. Was there still open
somewhere a store where they fitted keys? Even if
there were, what could the locksmith copy from? He
would have to come up here with his tools. For that,
one needed a mechanic associated with the firm
which produced these special locks. If at least she
had money with her. But she never carried more
than she needed to spend. The cashier in the supermarket had given her back only some twenty-odd
cents. "O dear Momma, I don't want to live any
more!" Bessie spoke Yiddish, amazed that she suddenly reverted to that half-forgotten tongue.

After many hesitations, Bessie decided to go back
down to the street. Perhaps a hardware store or one
of those tiny shops that specialize in keys was still
open. She remembered that there used to be such a
key stand in the neighborhood. After all, other people's keys must get broken. But what should she do
with the food? It was too heavy to carry with her.
There was no choice. She would have to leave the
bag at the door. "They steal anyhow," Bessie said to
herself. Who knows, perhaps the neighbors inten-
tionally manipulated her lock so that she would not
be able to enter the apartment while they robbed her
or vandalized her belongings.

Before Bessie went down to the street, she put her
ear to the door. She heard nothing except a murmur
that never stopped, the cause and origin of which
Bessie could not figure out. Sometimes it ticked like
a clock; other times it buzzed, or groaned—an entity
imprisoned in the walls or the water pipes. In her
mind Bessie said goodbye to the food, which should
have been in the refrigerator, not standing here in

the heat. The butter would melt, the milk would turn sour. "It's a punishment! I am cursed, cursed," Bessie muttered. A neighbor was about to go down in the elevator and Bessie signaled to him to hold the door for her. Perhaps he was one of the thieves. He might try to hold her up, assault her. The elevator went down and the man opened the door for her. She wanted to thank him, but remained silent. Why thank her enemies? They were all sly tricks.

When Bessie stepped out into the street, night had fallen. The gutter was flooded with water. The street lamps were reflected in the black pool as in a lake. Again there was a fire in the neighborhood. She heard the wailing of a siren, the clang of fire engines. Her shoes were wet. She came out on Broadway, and the heat slapped her like a sheet of tin. She had difficulty seeing in daytime; at night she was almost blind. There was light in the stores, but what they displayed Bessie could not make out. Passersby bumped into her, and Bessie regretted that she didn't have a cane. Nevertheless, she began to walk along, close to the windows. She passed a drugstore, a bakery, a shop of rugs, a funeral parlor, but nowhere was there a sign of a hardware store. Bessie continued on her way. Her strength was ebbing, but she was determined not to give up. What should a person do when her key has broken off—die? Perhaps apply to the police. There might be some institution that took care of such cases. But where?

There must have been an accident. The sidewalk was crowded with spectators. Police cars and an ambulance blocked the street. Someone sprayed the asphalt with a hose, probably cleaning away the blood. It occurred to Bessie that the eyes of the onlookers gleamed with an uncanny satisfaction. They enjoy other people's misfortunes, she thought. It is their only comfort in this miserable city. No, she wouldn't find anybody to help her.

She had come to a church. A few steps led to the

closed door, which was protected by an overhang and
darkened by shadows. Bessie was barely able to sit
down. Her knees wobbled. Her shoes had begun to
pinch the toes and above the heels. A bone in her
corset broke and cut into her flesh. "Well, all the
Powers of Evil are upon me tonight." Hunger mixed
with nausea gnawed at her. An acid fluid came up to
her mouth. "Father in heaven, it's my end." She
remembered the Yiddish proverb "If one lives without a reckoning, one dies without confession." She
had even neglected to write her will.

2.

Bessie must have dozed off, because when she opened
her eyes there was a late-night stillness, the street
half empty and darkened. Store windows were no
longer lit. The heat had evaporated and she felt
chilly under her dress. For a moment she thought
that her pocketbook had been stolen, but it lay on a
step below her, where it had probably slipped. Bessie
tried to stretch out her hand for it; her arm was
numb. Her head, which rested against the wall, felt
as heavy as a stone. Her legs had become wooden.
Her ears seemed to be filled with water. She lifted
one of her eyelids and saw the moon. It hovered low
in the sky over a flat roof, and near it twinkled a
greenish star. Bessie gaped. She had almost forgotten that there was a sky, a moon, stars. Years had
passed and she never looked up—always down. Her
windows were hung with draperies so that the spies
across the street could not see her. Well, if there was
a sky, perhaps there was also a God, angels, Paradise. Where else did the souls of her parents rest?
And where was Sam now?

She, Bessie, had abandoned all her duties. She
never visited Sam's grave in the cemetery. She didn't
even light a candle on the anniversary of his death.
She was so steeped in wrangling with the lower

powers that she did not remember the higher ones.
For the first time in years, Bessie felt the need to
recite a prayer. The Almighty would have mercy on
her even though she did not deserve it. Father and
Mother might intercede for her on high. Some Hebrew words hung on the tip of her tongue, but she
could not recall them. Then she remembered. "Hear,
O Israel." But what followed? "God forgive me,"
Bessie said. "I deserve everything that falls on me."

It became even quieter and cooler. Traffic lights
changed from red to green, but a car rarely passed.
From somewhere a Negro appeared. He staggered.
He stopped not far from Bessie and turned his eyes
to her. Then he walked on. Bessie knew that her bag
was full of important documents, but for the first
time she did not care about her property. Sam had
left a fortune; it all had gone for naught. She continued to save for her old age as if she was still young.
"How old am I?" Bessie asked herself. "What have I
accomplished in all these years? Why didn't I go
somewhere, enjoy my money, help somebody?" Something in her laughed. "I was possessed, completely
not myself. How else can it be explained?" Bessie
was astounded. She felt as if she had awakened from
a long sleep. The broken key had opened a door in
her brain that had shut when Sam died.

The moon had shifted to the other side of the
roof—unusually large, red, its face obliterated. It
was almost cold now. Bessie shivered. She realized
that she could easily get pneumonia, but the fear of
death was gone, along with her fear of being homeless. Fresh breezes drifted from the Hudson River.
New stars appeared in the sky. A black cat approached
from the other side of the street. For a while, it stood
on the edge of the sidewalk and its green eyes looked
straight at Bessie. Then slowly and cautiously it
drew near. For years Bessie had hated all animals—
dogs, cats, pigeons, even sparrows. They carried
sicknesses. They made everything filthy. Bessie

believed that there was a demon in every cat. She
especially dreaded an encounter with a black cat,
which was always an omen of evil. But now Bessie
felt love for this creature that had no home, no
possessions, no doors or keys, and lived on God's
bounty. Before the cat neared Bessie, it smelled her
bag. Then it began to rub its back on her leg, lifting
up its tail and meowing. The poor thing is hungry. I
wish I could give her something. How can one hate a
creature like this, Bessie wondered. O Mother of
mine, I was bewitched, bewitched. I'll begin a new
life. A treacherous thought ran through her mind:
perhaps remarry?

The night did not pass without adventure. Once,
Bessie saw a white butterfly in the air. It hovered for
a while over a parked car and then took off. Bessie
knew it was a soul of a newborn baby, since real
butterflies do not fly after dark. Another time, she
wakened to see a ball of fire, a kind of lit-up soap
bubble, soar from one room to another and sink
behind it. She was aware that what she saw was the
spirit of someone who had just died.

Bessie had fallen asleep. She woke up with a start.
It was daybreak. From the side of Central Park the
sun rose. Bessie could not see it from here, but on
Broadway the sky became pink and reddish. On the
building to the left, flames kindled in the windows;
the panes ran and blinked like the portholes of a
ship. A pigeon landed nearby. It hopped on its little
red feet and pecked into something that might have
been a dirty piece of stale bread or dried mud. Bessie
was baffled. How do these birds live? Where do they
sleep at night? And how can they survive the rains,
the cold, the snow? I will go home, Bessie decided.
People will not leave me in the streets.

Getting up was a torment. Her body seemed glued
to the step on which she sat. Her back ached and her
legs tingled. Nevertheless, she began to walk slowly

toward home. She inhaled the moist morning air. It smelled of grass and coffee. She was no longer alone. From the side streets men and women emerged. They were going to work. They bought newspapers at the stand and went down into the subway. They were silent and strangely peaceful, as if they, too, had gone through a night of soul-searching and come out of it cleansed. When do they get up if they are already on their way to work now, Bessie marveled. No, not all in this neighborhood were gangsters and murderers. One young man even nodded good morning to Bessie. She tried to smile at him, realizing she had forgotten that feminine gesture she knew so well in her youth; it was almost the first lesson her mother had taught her.

She reached her building, and outside stood the Irish super, her deadly enemy. He was talking to the garbage collectors. He was a giant of a man, with a short nose, a long upper lip, sunken cheeks, and a pointed chin. His yellow hair covered a bald spot. He gave Bessie a startled look. "What's the matter, Grandma?"

Stuttering, Bessie told him what had happened to her. She showed him the handle of the key she had clutched in her hand all night.

"Mother of God!" he called out.

"What shall I do?" Bessie asked.

"I will open your door."

"But you don't have a passkey."

"We have to be able to open all doors in case of fire."

The super disappeared into his own apartment for a few minutes, then he came out with some tools and a bunch of keys on a large ring. He went up in the elevator with Bessie. The bag of food still on the threshold, but it looked depleted. The super busied himself at the lock. He asked, "What are these cards?"

Bessie did not answer.

"Why didn't you come to me and tell me what happened? To be roaming around all night at your age—my God!" As he poked with his tools, a door opened and a little woman in a housecoat and slippers, her hair bleached and done up in curlers, came out. She said, "What happened to you? Every time I opened the door, I saw this bag. I took out your butter and milk and put them in my refrigerator."

Bessie could barely restrain her tears. "Oh, my good people," she said. "I didn't know that . . ."

The super pulled out the other half of Bessie's key. He worked a little longer. He turned a key and the door opened. The cards fell down. He entered the hallway with Bessie and she sensed the musty odor of an apartment that has not been lived in for a long time. The super said, "Next time, if something like this happens call me. That's what I'm here for."

Bessie wanted to give him a tip, but her hands were too weak to open her bag. The neighbor woman brought in the milk and butter. Bessie went into her bedroom and lay down on the bed. There was a pressure on her breast and she felt like vomiting. Something heavy vibrated up from her feet to her chest. Bessie listened to it without alarm, only curious about the whims of the body; the super and the neighbor talked, and Bessie could not make out what they were saying. The same thing had happened to her over thirty years ago when she had been given anesthesia in the hospital before an operation—the doctor and the nurse were talking but their voices seemed to come from far away and in a strange language.

Soon there was silence, and Sam appeared. It was neither day nor night—a strange twilight. In her dream, Bessie knew that Sam was dead but that in some clandestine way he had managed to get away from the grave and visit her. He was feeble and embarrassed. He could not speak. They wandered through a space without a sky, without earth, a tunnel full of debris—the wreckage of a nameless structure—a corridor dark and winding, yet somehow familiar. They came to a region where two mountains met, and the passage between shone like sunset or sunrise. They stood there hesitating and even a little ashamed. It was like that night of their honeymoon when they went to Ellenville in the Catskills and were let by the hotel owner into their bridal suite. She heard the same words he had said to them then, in the same voice and intonation: "You don't need no key here. Just enter—and *mazel tov*."

Translated by the author and Evelyn Torton Beck

Dr. Beeber

In the Writers' Club in Warsaw, everyone knew Dr. Mark Beeber, a tall, broad-shouldered man with a mass of dark hair graying at the temples. His brown eyes, shining beneath bushy brows, always reminded me of the shrunken cherries in cocktail glasses. In professorial style, he wore a large-brimmed plush hat. He was known as a Bohemian, even though he came from a rich Hasidic family. Before the First World War, he studied philosophy in Switzerland. For years, he had been jobless. He lived somewhere in one of the Gentile neighborhoods, in a rented room.

The members of the Writers' Club were amazed that Dr. Beeber managed to get along without earning anything. Some believed that he derived a small income from his father's dissipated estate. (Mendel Beeber, his father, in his old age had married a nineteen-year-old girl, who had then born him eleven children.) Others said he was a gigolo, supported by old women. Certain members of the Writers' Club knew that he ate at a different house every night, like a yeshiva student; old friends and relatives invited him for dinner, supper, and sometimes to their villas between Warsaw and Otwock. Occasionally, the Writers' Union gave him the opportunity to substitute for some journalist or proofreader who had gone on vacation.

However he existed, Mark Beeber remained good-natured and full of a lust for life. Poor as he was, he smoked fine cigars. Though his suits were shabby, they were English tweeds. For hours, he would tell stories about Switzerland. He had known everyone personally: Lenin, Kropotkin, Bergson, Kuno Fischer,

Wundt, Georg Kaiser—even a number of princes and pretenders to thrones. In Monte Carlo, he had played roulette. During his student years, he drank numerous steins of beer with Prussian Junkers, and he once served as a second for one of them in a duel. He was a hedonist in theory and practice. Writers' Club members doubted that his doctor's title was valid. He had never written a dissertation. But he was familiar with all the German philosophical movements. Although he considered himself an epicurean, he had a high opinion of David Hume, Kant, and Schopenhauer. He gave me two books written by personal friends of his, Professor Messer and Professor Bauch, both Kantians. I noticed that the books were stamped with the name of the university library at Berne.

In spite of his being twenty-odd years older than I, we were friends. I addressed him as "you"; he employed "thou." He called me Tsutsik (Puppy). He would say, "Keep on writing, Tsutsik. I tried it but don't have the patience to sit still. The moment I lift the pen, the telephone rings. I don't like to waste time scribbling. Who needs so many books? If I have to eat, I eat; when I have schnapps, I drink. Females are always available. That commodity isn't scarce."

I knew he was telling the truth. He had a talent for meeting divorcées, widows, spinsters, and just women who were looking for affairs. In the Writers' Club, he was constantly wanted on the telephone. Romantic, talkative women made him impatient. He sought out those who didn't require what he called "a prologue and an epilogue."

My earnings began to increase around that time. I translated Thomas Mann's *The Magic Mountain* into Yiddish, and several other German novels for the Yiddish press. Occasionally, I invited Dr. Beeber to lunch. He would order a drink and a dinner of seven courses and eat all the rolls from the basket on the table. Between courses, puffing his cigar, he told innumerable anecdotes. He had traveled extensively, lived in almost all the capitals of Europe. Besides Yiddish, he knew German, Russian, French, and Italian. Hebrew, too. As a boy, he had studied at the yeshiva. He had been a mountain climber for a while, and told me of excursions in the Alps. His stories always came to the same conclusion: everything is vanity, all philosophers are mistaken, all ideals silly and hypocritical. Man is nothing but a sly ape. However, when one can't pay the rent, there's trouble.

As time went on, I found him often in a bad mood. Then he would pour out his problems. He was getting old and had missed everything. He was sick and tired. A doctor had told him there was fat around his heart, had forbidden him to smoke, drink, or eat fatty foods. He had also warned him against too much sex. Dr. Beeber said that what he needed was spiritual rest. But how can a person rest if every dawn repeats the question of how one is to get through the day? More than anything else, he feared old age. What would he do when his hair turned white altogether? Who would take care of him then? And if he became ill, what would happen? He would lie forgotten in a hospital. He had rejected his family, and they had renounced him; he would not recognize his sisters and brothers on the street.

His hair became grayer, his clothes shabbier. Several times I noticed the ties of his long underwear dangling over his shoe tops. He had begun to smoke cheap, stinking cigars. Food spotted his clothing as he ate. His stories and jokes grew repetitious. If he didn't settle down soon, he would fall to pieces. One day, I told him there were matchmakers in Warsaw.

He looked at me mischievously, blowing smoke rings. "Be quiet, Tsutsik. I haven't sunk that low."

For a few weeks I had vacationed in a village near the Baltic Sea. On my return, I was informed that

Dr. Beeber had married. The next day Dr. Beeber telephoned me. Never having spoken to him on the telephone before, I scarcely recognized his voice.

"Tsutsik," he said, "I've been looking for you. I took your advice. You're speaking to a respectable Warsaw citizen."

"*Mazel tov!* I heard the good news. You couldn't have done anything wiser."

"It happened overnight. Someone brought us together and things got going. You know, I hate long-drawn-out productions. The Talmud forbids one to talk too much to a woman; this means she's limited to yes or no. My wife is bourgeois but charming, has more formal education than I—finished *Gymnasium*. And she's far from ugly. Deeply in love with me, too. What more can one ask at my age, in my situation? Now I have a home—everything. I can't believe I've been footloose so long. Really, I must have an iron constitution. Wait—Saltsche wants to talk to you. She knows about you. I gave her one of your little stories to read. She adores it. One moment."

I heard a typical Polish-Yiddish accent. "Tsutsik, may I call you Tsutsik? It's a marvelous name. You can call me Saltsche. Mark told me everything. His friends are my friends. We wanted you to attend the wedding, but you were out of town. We're so sorry. I read your sketch. Beautiful! Are you busy this evening?"

"Not especially."

"In that case you must come for supper. Please don't refuse. He's always talking about you. I've heard all your jokes. He believes in your talent. When will you come? Make it early. We have a large apartment, all the conveniences. If you stay late, there's a guest room; you can sleep here. Mark jokes about adopting you. . . ."

At six o'clock in the evening, having got a shave and a haircut, I put on my best suit and tie. I bought a bouquet of roses in a flower shop and hired a droshky. The Beebers lived in a neighborhood of Christians and wealthy Jews. I went up to their apartment in an elevator. On a broad mahogany door I found a brass plate with the name "Dr. Mark Beeber." A Gentile maid opened the door. Beeber and his wife came to greet me. Saltsche was a woman in her forties, small, round, dark, with a high bosom and large black eyes—sad and cheerful Jewish eyes, as old as the Jewish exile. She extended her arms as if to embrace me, and told the maid to place the flowers in a vase. A string of pearls enclosed her plump neck, and a diamond glittered on her left hand.

Dr. Beeber wore a fancy smoking jacket and slippers. He looked young; his wrinkles were gone, and so were the bags under his eyes and the gray hair. His cigar was set in an amber holder. His eyes beneath the bushy brows were full of a jovial mockery. "Saltsche, this is Tsutsik," he said.

"May I kiss him?"

"By all means."

I entered a conventionally furnished living room, with rugs, chairs, a chaise longue, candelabra, and pictures. After a while, we went into the dining room. There a huge glass closet was filled with china and silver. Dr. Beeber had found himself a rich wife. Raising one brow, he smiled. "See what's happened to me? I've betrayed poverty."

"Why is it so good to be poor and suffer?" Saltsche said. "A man like Mark should be working on his books, not deteriorating in an attic. When I saw where he lived, I nearly collapsed. I didn't let him bring along anything from that place except his manuscripts. How can such a brilliant man neglect himself so? Oh, men have no compassion on themselves! He would surely have gone to pieces by now. You, Tsutsik, are still young. But let this be a lesson to you—get married and settle down. Don't follow his example. One can't create on an empty stomach. His life is disciplined at last. He stays in his room until noon. No one may disturb him. I don't even call him to the telephone. Up to this point, his relatives didn't want to hear about him; suddenly all his sisters, brothers, and cousins come around. But they can wait. A real friend is a friend in need, not those who wait until your luck changes. Therefore, Tsutsik—"

"Well, Saltsche, enough. Tell the cook to bring in the tasty dishes she's prepared."

"What? Don't worry. He won't starve."

Saltsche tinkled a glass bell, and a cook in white apron and cap appeared. To have a cook in addition to a maid, one must be rich. What didn't they serve that evening! Lox, fish in sweet-and-sour sauce, sardines, cold cuts, caviar. Dr. Beever devoured his food with gusto. Indicating an assortment of cheeses, he told me their names and where they were from, then washed down his food with wine.

"She keeps me incarcerated every day between nine and two," he said. "I've been going through some old manuscripts. Really, I'm amazed. What I wrote so long ago seems incredible to me now. One forgets. The trouble is that I can't remember enough German. And Hebrew is no use to me—it has no modern philosophic terminology."

"Why don't you write in Yiddish?"

"For whom? For the yeshiva boys? But I'll manage somehow. Actually, I can't believe in anything any more. I even lack the spark of faith one needs to become a skeptic."

"Don't go looking for excuses," Saltsche intervened. "Keep on writing and everything will turn out all right. Nobodies and ignoramuses become gr~at and famous, but a man of his intellect neglects h I read German; I understand. Every sen writes is profound. He's a genius, absolu' nius."

"I think you prepared *kreplach?*" Dr. Beeber said.

"Wait. The *kreplach* are on their way. Eat, Tsutsik. Please forgive me for calling you Tsutsik. What flavor that name has! My father, may he rest in peace, used to call my brother by the same name. They're both in another world now." Saltsche wiped away a tear with a lace handkerchief.

2.

From the way we spoke that evening, I assumed that I would visit the Beebers frequently. I would eat, sleep, and work there. But weeks, months passed before we met again. Several times Dr. Beeber or Saltsche called me by telephone to ask me to supper, but I happened to be busy or had no desire to eat a heavy meal and stay up late. Dr. Beeber stopped appearing at the Writers' Club. There they began to say that he had turned into a snob.

One day Dr. Beeber phoned me, saying, "Tsutsik, have you forgotten me?"

"No, Dr. Beeber, I'll never forget you. How are you?"

He stammered and sighed. "People envy me," he said. "They think I've come into a great fortune. I hear there's a lot of gossip about me at the Writers' Club. But I'm not happy. Really, I begin to regret the whole business."

"What happened? Aren't you and your wife getting along?"

"We get along too well. But what good does it do me? She's trying to make me into an immortal. Tsutsik, those illusions are too remote from me. What if I do publish another book? Who's waiting for it? Only today I found an essay I wrote about Schleiermacher. Who cares about Schleiermacher? Until dinnertime she keeps me imprisoned. After dinner, I have to lie down for an hour to digest the ¹. The cook is an Eighth Wonder. She prepares delicacies that I can't resist. I stuff myself until I'm unable to budge. There's another feast in the evening. After supper, Saltsche wants to go somewhere—the movies, the theater, the opera. She has innumerable relatives who keep coming here and inviting us to return the visit. My family also rose from the dead. They sit and babble banalities all night. I told you, didn't I, Saltsche was an old maid—a kosher virgin. Now she wants to make up for lost time. None of this is for me. I long for some kind of adventure. She won't let me answer the phone; she's afraid I'll be robbed of my time for contemplation."

Dr. Beeber laughed and grunted at the same time.

"Things will straighten out," I said.

"How? Every day I have to report my progress. She reads every word I write. Already, she's got in touch with a publisher, and God knows what. When a woman begins to run a man's life, he's lost. I'm so enslaved I began a little affair with the maid."

"Be careful."

"Tsutsik, let's get together."

The winter passed and summer arrived. I went away on vacation once more, this time to Zakopane, in the mountains. I returned in August. When I entered the Writers' Club, somebody said, "Did you hear the latest about Dr. Beeber?"

"What happened?"

"He lost forty thousand zlotys in the casino at Zoppot."

"Forty thousand?"

"All his wife's cash. They had a joint account at the bank. He went to Zoppot and lost everything."

"Where was she?"

"I don't know the details."

I telephoned Dr. Beeber, but nobody answered. As I was walking up Przejazd Street a day or two later, Dr. Beeber approached me: bent, pale, disheveled, with bags under his eyes. Previously he had not carried a cane; now he had one, and it seemed to me he was limping. Raising his bushy brows, he looked at me balefully, with silent reproach, as if we had had an appointment and I was late.

I said, "Can this be you?"

"Tsutsik, I've been looking for you. Where did you disappear? I'm in a real jam. Did you hear what happened to me?"

"Yes, I heard."

"Well, I must have lost my mind, or the devil knows what. I'm beginning to think I'm *meshugga* altogether. It all happened out of boredom. She dragged me to Zoppot with all my manuscripts, rented a villa, and whatnot. Suddenly she had to leave for Warsaw—her brother-in-law had become mortally ill. As a matter of fact, he died. While she was away, I went to the casino just to observe, but it's a quagmire. You put a foot in and begin to sink. She had given me a checkbook, and the bank has a branch in Zoppot. Why go on? I lost everything, to the last zloty."

"Where is Saltsche?"

"She simply threw me out. Her family wanted to put me in the insane asylum."

"They were right."

"Tsutsik, I'm penniless. I don't even have a bed to sleep in. According to the law, she wasn't allowed to throw me out. But who wants to start in with the police? She has a cousin, a lawyer, and he threatened me with jail. Maybe I can sleep at your place?"

"I only have one bed."

"Could you possibly spare a few zlotys?"

"What's the sense of losing forty thousand zlotys?"

"Forty-three. I don't know. I don't know. I used to think I knew myself, but now I'm convinced that I don't. All of modern psychology is worth no more than a pinch of tobacco. A dibbuk or a demon must have taken possession of me. Now I understand why you write about demons. It's not just folklore; it's true. At least give me ten zlotys."

"I don't have ten zlotys. But you can sleep overnight in my room."

"How? You're probably going somewhere. Well, fine. I haven't slept in two nights, or eaten either. Give me at least three zlotys for cigars. I can't go to your room by myself—you'll have to introduce me to your landlady; she might take me for a thief. When things begin to turn badly, anything can happen."

"Let's go in and have some coffee."

"What? My legs won't carry me any farther. All right. Let's go. I always knew this would be the outcome. It was too good. The whole thing was like a prank of Asmodeus's—or who else rules the world? What can I do now? I used to be skilled at getting along without money, but I've lost that. I don't know how to start in again. If I had the courage, I'd kill myself."

"Perhaps there's a possibility of making peace between you."

"Try. She has a high opinion of you. Actually, the life I was leading almost destroyed me. Who can be with a woman twenty-four hours a day? I was used to being alone. A bachelor can have a dozen mistresses and still remain his own man. Tsutsik, never get married. Run from it as from a fire. Unless you want to procreate."

"I don't."

"Schopenhauer was right. It's all that blind will to prolong the human tragedy. Fortunately, she was too old to conceive. I don't want my loins to produce generations of storekeepers, janitors, coachmen, and harlots. I'd like to enjoy a few more years and then finish. But what can I do now? Perhaps they'll take me into an old people's home? Or I could commit a crime that would put me in prison. But what kind of crime? Unless I set the Belvedere Castle on fire?"

We drank coffee. Dr. Beeber muttered and groaned

as he drank. He wiped his forehead with a dirty handkerchief. His suit was filthy. Unwashed, unshaven, he sat there, one eye half closed, the other open wide. His nails were grimy. From his pocket he drew a cigar stub, lit it, and blew out a cloud of stinking smoke.

"What's so great about gambling?" I asked.

"What? One is completely in the hands of the powers that rule the universe. Whether you believe in it or not, you try to hypnotize the little ball and send it where you please. You wage war with the laws of physics, but they make a mockery of your commands. I had won fifteen hundred zlotys. Suddenly everything began to go wrong. You believe in luck, don't you?"

"I believe in all superstitions."

"You're right. Rationalism is the worst disease of the human species. Reason will reverse evolution. *Homo sapiens* will become so clever that he won't know how to breed, eat, or go to the toilet. He'll even have to learn how to die."

Dr. Beeber laughed and snorted, exposing a mouthful of blackish teeth. "What I'm afraid of really," he said, "is that Saltsche may decide to forgive me."

Translated by the author and Elaine Gottlieb

Stories from Behind the Stove

Outside, a heavy snow was falling. Toward evening, frost set in. An icy wind blew from the Vistula, but in the study house the clay oven was burning hot. Beggars roasted potatoes on the coals. Boys who studied at night marked their places by laying their sashes on their open books, and listened to stories. There was talk about people and things vanishing, and Zalman the glazier lifted up his tobacco-stained index finger as a sign that he had something to tell. He had a thick beard that looked like dirty cotton, and bushy eyebrows over eyes that were small and dark like those of a hedgehog. Before he began to talk, he murmured and grunted like a clock getting ready to strike.

"People do vanish," he said. "Not everyone is like the Prophet Elijah, who was taken to heaven in a fiery chariot. In the village of Palkes, not far from Radoshitz, a peasant was plowing with an ox. Behind him walked his son, sowing barley from a bag. The boy looked up and the ox was there but his father had gone. He began to call, to scream, but there was no answer. His father had disappeared in the middle of the field. He was never heard from again."

"Perhaps there was a hole in the earth and he fell in?" Levi Yitzchock suggested.

"There was no hole to be seen—and if there had been a hole, why didn't the ox fall in first? He was in the lead."

"Do you mean that the demons carried him away?"

"I don't know."

"Perhaps he ran away with some woman," Meir the eunuch suggested.

"Nonsense, an old man of seventy—maybe more. A peasant does not run away from his earth, his hut. If he wants a woman, he goes with her into the granary."

"In that case, the Evil Ones took him," Levi Yitzchock said judiciously.

"Why just him?" Zalman the glazier asked. "A quiet man, Wojciech Kucek—that was his name. Before the Feast of the Tabernacle, he used to bring branches for covering the Sukkoth. My own father bought from him. These things do happen. Near Blonia there lived a man, Reb Zelig the bailiff. He had a store and a shed where he kept kindling wood, flax, potatoes, old ropes. He had a sleigh there too. He got up one morning and the shed was gone. He could not believe his eyes. If during the night there had been a wind, a storm, a flood! But it happened after Pentecost—calm days, quiet nights. At first he thought he had lost his mind. He called his wife, his children. They ran out. 'Where is the shed?' There was no shed. Where it had been, everything was smooth—high grass, no beams, shingles, no sign of a foundation. Nothing. Well, if the night creatures seize a man, they may have some claim, but what would they want with a shed? And how can grass grow up overnight? When they heard about this in Blonia, they ran as though to a fire. Even cheder children came running. Everybody knew Zelig the bailiff. Saturday, after the pudding, when the tailor boys and shoemaker apprentices went for a walk they always passed the shed. If it happened to rain, they used to wait there, inside, to keep dry. Zelig did not have a lock on the door. He just bolted it from outside. There were no thieves in Blonia. At that time I was boarding with my father-in-law. Since the whole town was running, I ran too. Squire Jablowski came, and even the Russian officials. They stood and stared at each other like graven images. People pinched their cheeks to make sure they were not dreaming. Jablowski hollered, 'Either I am crazy or the Jews trick me!' In a small place, everybody knows each house, each alley, each store. 'Witchcraft in the middle of the day!' he yelled. He waved his whip. He had a huge dog that barked ferociously. 'If the shed does not stand where it has always stood, and at once, I will whip you all to death.' He had forgotten that the serfs had been freed. Zelig defended himself. 'Your Excellency, is this my fault?' The chief of police stood near the squire, gaping. He had long mustaches almost to his shoulders. A Dr. Chalczynski had his practice in Blonia. He was there with the others. A strange man. Even though he was a Gentile, he could speak Yiddish. He never went to church. He was a friend of the enlightened Jews—Falik the druggist, Baruch the petition writer, Bentze Kaminer. Each night they used to sit until one o'clock around the samovar, mocking everybody and playing cards. Their wives did not cover their hair. That morning Falik stood behind the counter, weighing some herbs. A young man came in and told him what had happened, and Falik ridiculed him: 'If you have lost your mind, go to a madhouse.' But soon others came—all witnesses. They swore holy oaths that it was true. Falik said to them, 'What other tall tales will you invent? Perhaps the rabbi became pregnant and gave birth to a calf?' Nevertheless, he locked the drugstore and went to have a look for himself. The other skeptics were already there. Falik said to the Gentiles, 'My good people, a shed has no legs and cannot walk. There must be some reason. Let's go and find it.' So they all went off to look for the shed. They walked around for half a day, but there was no sign of anything. A heavy shed built of logs had burst like a bubble.

"How long can one stand around and wonder? Merchants have to do their business. Mothers must feed their children. The squire went to the tavern

and got drunk; he only needed an excuse to begin.
He ranted against the Jews. 'It's all a Jewish trick,'
he said. But Dr. Chalczynski would not leave Zelig's
place. He kept on investigating, measuring, sniffing.
He stayed around Zelig's house until night. At first
he joked, then he became sad. He said to Falik, 'If a
thing like this is possible, what sort of a doctor am I?
And what kind of druggist are you?' 'There is some
swindle here,' the druggist replied. He stretched out
on the grass and examined the earth. He asked for a
spade. He wanted to dig. But Zelig said, 'I kept the
spade in the shed. It's gone.' The next day the whole
lot of enlightened ones arrived with spades. They
dug a ditch six feet deep. The earth was full of roots
and stones. The shed could not have sunk in.

"Two weeks passed. The simple people had other
things to worry about. We young men in the study
house did discuss the matter, but for all our pondering
we came to the same conclusion: it was done by
mocking demons. Doesn't the Bible tell us that even
a house can become leprous? The Evil Ones are
capable of anything. But Dr. Chalczynski, Falik the
druggist, and the other doubters kept on searching
and inquiring. Dr. Chalczynski had a phaeton with
two horses. Falik had a britska. They drove for
miles, trying to locate the lost shed. They asked the
peasants, but no one had heard or seen anything. At
night the enlightened ones no longer played cards;
they brooded. If a shed can dissolve like snow, perhaps there is a God. Dr. Chalczynski went to the
rabbi. He wouldn't go to the priest, because he had
maligned the Church and evil tongues informed the
priest. They had become enemies. The doctor stayed
in the rabbi's study for hours. 'Is anything like this
mentioned in the Torah?' he asked. 'Is it a punishment for some sin?' The rabbi did not know what to
answer. 'With God everything is possible,' he said.

"Well, two weeks passed. Then early one morning
Zelig came out of his house and saw the shed. He

went wild—screamed and knocked his head. The
whole household came out, barefoot, half naked.
There stood the shed as if nothing had happened.
Someone carried the news to Blonia town. Again
there was a commotion. They came running from all
sides—some laughed, others cried. Squire Jablowski
galloped up on a horse. The shed stood where it
always had. They went inside; everything was as
before. The only change was that the potatoes had
started to sprout as they always do late in the
summer.

" 'What new prank is this?' Jablowski shouted. 'I
will knock your heads in. I will hound you out of
here to the ends of the earth!' He had already had
one too many. He pounded the shed and kicked it.
Dr. Chalczynski was as white as chalk. Falik the
druggist scratched his head. His wife was moaning
as if at a funeral. 'Why do you lament? It's not Yom
Kippur,' he scolded her. 'For me today is Yom Kippur,'
she answered.

"Why should I go on? The druggist's wife turned
pious—she began to bless the candles on the Sabbath eve; she cut off her hair, put on a wig; she came
to the rabbi with questions. As for Falik, he remained
stubborn. He said, 'Just because a shed plays
hide-and-seek, I am not going to become a Hasid.' He
looked up at the sky and blasphemed. 'If there is a
God, let him punish me right here on the spot. Let
him send lightning to strike me.' He and his wife
started to quarrel. She baked a Sabbath pudding,
and he wanted her to fry pork chops for him. Dr.
Chalczynski lost his head completely. They called
him to a sick man and he barely examined him. He
prescribed a medicine, but the sick man grew worse.
The chief of police ordered that the floor of the shed
be torn up. Underneath, there was no sign of grass
or that any ditch had been dug. The earth was bare,
dusty, full of worms. The whole thing must have
been an illusion. But how can a whole town be

deluded? The news of the event spread over half of
Poland. They came from Gombin and Lowicz to look
at the freak shed. The peasants said that Zelig was a
sorcerer and his wife a witch. I happened to be back
in Radoshitz at the time. Later I was told that Falik
and his wife were divorced. She married an elder
from Sochaczew. Falik moved to Warsaw and converted to Christianity. One night Dr. Chalczynski
left town. He didn't say goodbye to anybody—left
behind all his books and instruments.

"I forgot the main thing. The shed burned down.
On the night of the Feast of Rejoicing of the Law,
when Zelig and his family were sleeping, the maid
saw that it was as light outside as day. The shed was
flaming like a torch. Zelig and his sons tried to put it
out, but you cannot put out a fire from Gehenna. In a
half hour, only coals and ashes remained. There was
no lightning that night and there was nothing in the
shed that could have ignited by itself."

"Does this mean that it was all done by the Powers
of Darkness?" Levi Yitzchock asked.

"What did they have against the shed?" Zalman
asked back.

2.

Levi Yitzchock took off the blue glasses that he wore
even at night. Although he was an old man, his
beard was streaked with yellow. There was a deep
scar on the bridge of his nose. Under his inflamed
eyes with their swollen, lashless lids, hung double
bags of withered flesh. He wiped his glasses with a
dirty handkerchief and groaned. "Nowadays God
conceals His face," he said. "If a miracle does happen, it is explained as natural. In my time we could
find miracles everywhere. My father—peace be with
him—was a Hasid of the rabbi of Kapelnitza. In
olden days, Rabbi Dan had quite a large following.
Even so, each Hasid was a chosen man, a person

known for worthy deeds. But Rabbi Dan's children
died during his lifetime and there was nobody to
take his place. His wife choked to death at the
Sabbath meal; a daughter drowned in a well; his
son, Levi Yitzchock, after whom I was named, collapsed while he was making the benediction of the
palm branch and lemon fruit. His whole life, Rabbi
Dan waged war with the demons. They did not have
the power to destroy him, so they took revenge on
his family. The old Hasidim slowly died off. The
young men defected to Kotzk or to Gur. The study
house turned into a ruin. The oven of the ritual bath
broke and there was nobody to mend it. The rabbi's
courtyard crawled with polecats, rats, hedgehogs.
Moles made their little hills, weeds and thorns grew
everywhere. Once, the rabbi had four beadles. In my
time, only one was left—Izie, an old man in his
eighties, blind in one eye and a drunk to boot. Rabbi
Dan used to fast even in his youth, but in his old age
he almost stopped eating. He ate just enough bread
to be able to bless the food. His hangers-on were all
tottering old men. On the Days of Awe a few score
Hasidim made their pilgrimage to the rabbi, but at
other times of the year it was difficult to get even a
quorum for prayer. The rabbi stopped reciting Torah.
My father was one of the inner circle, and he took me
to Kapelnitza when I was a boy. When I saw the
rabbi for the first time, I was terrified. He was small,
bent, shrunken, with a beard that reached to his
loins. You couldn't see his eyes. When the rabbi
wanted to look at someone, he had to lift an eyebrow
out of the way with his index finger and thumb. My
father introduced me. The rabbi stretched out a
hand that was as dry as parchment and as hot as
fire. All he said was 'Nu,' and this nu I will never
forget. It was a voice from the very depths—not of
this world.

"They expected the rabbi's demise every day. But
years passed and still he lived on. The walls of the

study house grew black as a chimney. The books were nibbled away by mice. An owl settled on the roof and hooted in the night. For a time there were a good many deaths in Kapelnitza, then the Angel of Death seemed to forget the place. The hangers-on crept around like shadows. An old woman cooked soup for them in a caldron and patched their linen. When I went with my father to Kapelnitza for the last Rosh Hashana, there was not even a small crowd present. The old men were sitting in torn prayer shawls, their robes riddled with holes. One was praying, another was dozing. The rabbi stood in a corner and did not utter a sound. The man who blew the ram's horn was short of breath. Instead of a blast, there was a groan that might have come from a slaughtered animal. I said to my father, 'Don't bring me to this place again.'

"As a rule, my father stayed for the Ten Days of Repentance and Yom Kippur. But this time we left the day after Rosh Hashana. On the wagon my father said to me, 'I doubt if the Saint will last past the Feast of the Tabernacle. Already he is more there than here.' Nevertheless, he lived until Hanukkah. At Hanukkah we got a telegram announcing his death. I did not want to travel to the funeral, but my father argued that the passing away of saints should not be ignored—there wouldn't be another Rabbi Dan until the Resurrection of the Dead. We expected a large gathering, because it is the nature of people to forget a saint while he is alive and give him all honors at his death. But a deep snow had fallen, and Kapelnitza could not be reached by cart or sleigh. We got there with the greatest difficulty. I was present when the rabbi was buried. The earth was frozen. A moribund man recited Kaddish. Heavy snow was still falling, and the mourners all turned white. The burial took place Friday, and so it was impossible to go back home. We had to remain in Kapelnitza over the Sabbath.

"I thought that there would be no Sabbath meal in the study house, but someone prepared food. For the first time in sixty years, the rabbi's chair stood empty. The old men tried to sing; what came out was a gasp. One of them recited some of the rabbi's sayings, but they hardly heard him; most of them were deaf. So it went during Friday's supper and Saturday's midday meal. In Kapelnitza the most revered repast was the third one, which began at dusk. The people of the town had long since lighted their candles, said the Valedictory prayer and the chapter that is read Saturday evening, but in the study house it was still dark and the 'Sons of the Mansion' was being sung. The rabbi used to reveal mysteries of mysteries at this hour.

"What can a boy do on the Sabbath after dark, especially in winter? I remained in the study house. Night fell quickly. The hangers-on munched their dry bread with herring and chanted in mournful voices, all eyes fastened on the rabbi's chair at the head of the table. I sat in the darkness and a strange yearning seized me. I kept on thinking of the rabbi. His holy body is already in the grave, but where is his soul? Most probably in Paradise at the Throne of Glory, in the Mansion of the Messiah. For the first time, it occurred to me that I too would not be young forever. Outside, the sky cleared and I saw the new moon of the month of Taveth. The stars glittered. It was dark in the study house; only a faint glow entered. The singing of the hangers-on cannot be conveyed by words. With hoarse voices they intoned the variations of one theme. Each sigh, each accent carried you up to the highest spheres. Bodies cannot sing that way. It was the humming of souls pleading with the Lord of the Universe: How long, God, will the darkness of Egypt last? How long will the sacred sparks remain imprisoned in the morass of darkness? Let there be an end to the suffering, to pettiness, to material vanities. I was still a youngster, but I was transfixed. I looked toward the door and the rabbi entered. I was so astonished that I forgot to be afraid. I recognized him—the same image, beard, shape. He seemed to float over to the empty chair and sit down. For a long time there was an awesome silence—such a silence I have never experienced before or since. Then the singing resumed, quietly at first and then louder. It was as it is written, 'All my bones shall speak.' In the song there was joy to make the soul expire. Those who haven't heard this singing will never know what Jews are and what spirit is. I feared that I might faint from exaltation and I called out, 'Father!' If I hadn't done this, I wouldn't be sitting here today."

"You got frightened, huh?" Zalman the glazier said.

"The rabbi vanished immediately. The old men seemed to wake up. Izie lit a candle. My father took me outside and rubbed my temples with snow. He was as white as a corpse. When I could talk, I asked, 'Daddy, did you see?' And he answered, 'Keep quiet.' I was afraid to go back into the study house and my father took me to the inn. He half carried me. He recited the Havdalah, bathed my eyelids with wine, and made me sniff spices. I think that I missed the night prayer. I soon fell asleep.

"That night three of the hangers-on died. By Passover, the whole group had gone. My father was never willing to talk to me about that Sabbath evening. Not until the day of my marriage, before I was led to the ceremony, did he admit to me that he, too, had seen the rabbi."

Meir the eunuch clutched his naked chin where a beard should have grown. "What's so unusual about it?" he asked. "The same thing happened with Rabbi Jehudah. After his demise he came home every Friday night to recite the benediction over the wine. You'll find it in the Talmud."

"Still, in our times—"

"What are our times? The Lord is the same. No change occurs in Him. If fewer miracles happen, the fault is ours—not His."

"What happened to the rabbi's court?" Zalman asked.

"It fell to dust," Levi Yitzchock answered. "It seems that the rabbi kept it together with his spirit. The moment he was summoned to the Yeshiva on High, the walls began to crumble, the roof disintegrated. The whole court became one ruin."

"What keeps all the world together?" Meir the eunuch asked. "It's all by a word of the Almighty. If He takes His word back, the whole creation returns to primeval chaos."

3.

Meir the eunuch rose and began to pace back and forth. Even though he had a hunchback, he was tall, and although his cheeks were smooth he looked masculine, with a high forehead, an aquiline nose, and the sharp eyes of a scholar. He touched the stove and he must have burned himself because he blew on the palm of his hand. Meir the eunuch belonged to those the Talmud describes as "sometimes sane, sometimes insane." When the moon was full, he acted like a madman. He talked to himself, rubbed his hands together, laughed and grimaced. When the moon diminished, his thoughts became more ordered again. Now he sat down and began to talk:

"There is nothing strange about seeing a ghost. My mother died when I was five years old, but whenever I am in danger I hear her voice. She warns me. She calls, 'Meir!' and I know that I must be on guard. There is no death. How can there be death if everything is part of the Godhead? The soul never dies and the body is never really alive. Well, but there is something between—not completely matter, not completely form. Perhaps I should not talk about it,

but while we are on the subject I want you to know
the truth. As I said, I lost my mother when I was
five. My father never remarried. He was a forester
and was more in the woods than at home. We had a
servant, Shifrah, and she had a sister with children
in town. When my father traveled, she spent almost
all her time with her sister. Nobody took care of me.
When I wanted to study I studied, and when I
wanted to be idle there was no one to reproach me.
We had a library. Its four walls had shelves up to the
ceiling filled with books. I always had a pocketful of
money and I used to order books from Lublin and
even from Warsaw. I bought from the book peddlers,
too. By the time I was sixteen, I had gone through
the thirty-six tracts of the Talmud. I became attracted
to the cabala. I knew very well the law that one
should not delve into these mysteries before reaching
the age of thirty. But I found extenuating circum-
stances. I began to look into the Zohar, the *Vine-
yard,* the *Tree of Life,* the *Tracts of the Hasidim.*
From the intellectual cabala there is only one step to
the magic cabala. And from the latter, one can
easily fall into sorcery. However, I learned somewhere that the Sanhedrin were required to study
witchcraft. I had the desire to become an unseen one,
to make seven-mile steps, to tap wine from the wall.
An old man came to our town. He was born in
Babylon and journeyed all over the world working
miracles. If someone placed his finger between the
pages of a book, he could tell what was written
there. He said the letters appeared before his vision.
He also cured the sick. In our town he healed an
epileptic. He asked for a live rooster to be brought to
him. He uttered an incantation and the rooster was
seized by epilepsy. Those who have not seen this
rooster shaking and having a fit will never know the
power of spells. However, there are holy spells and
unholy ones. The power of darkness is like a monkey; it mimics the power of light. The rabbis in

Poland brought an injunction against anyone having anything to do with the black magician. But if you have an only son who every few days is taken with a seizure in the middle of the street, foaming at the mouth and knocking his head against the curbstone, you forget all about injunctions. That Jew from Babylon cured only the rich. He asked to be paid with golden coins. What did he need so much money for? He ate less than a fly. His wife had divorced him. Such people don't have children. He possessed a house somewhere in Lublin and the demons danced in it even in the middle of the day. He stands before my eyes—tall, emaciated, wearing a fez like a Turk, a long coat striped in red and white and sandals on his bare feet. His face was peeling like a leper's, his cheeks were sunken. He had a sparse white beard and it was always awry as though a wind blew through it. His eyes were set unevenly and Samaél looked out from them. He spoke half Aramaic, half Yiddish.

"When the Jew of Babylon came to our town I immediately went to the inn where he was staying. I spoke simple words to him: 'I want to be your pupil.' He said to me, 'Young man, why go into the sickroom when you are in good health? Look at me. I am one of those who have gazed into the abyss and been damaged. The Evil Ones never give me any rest, either waking or sleeping.' As the Jew of Babylon was talking, I heard a strange knocking. It came neither from outside nor from inside. It was as if a woodpecker had entered the chair where he sat—or perhaps the creature with a copper beak who pecked the brain of Titus the Wicked. 'What is that noise?' I asked. And the Jew of Babylon answered, 'Space is full of naked souls and they all have their illusions and claims. At the same time I am conversing with you, I can see Alexander of Macedonia and his legions. The dead don't know that they are dead,' he said, 'just as the living don't know that they are alive. Napoleon is still waving his sword.'

"I sat with him for three hours. I have never met a greater sage. He admitted to me that he was the reincarnation of King Solomon. When he had convinced himself that he couldn't get rid of me, he said, 'Meir, I have warned you, but if you insist, here is a pamphlet written on parchment and from it you will be able to create your own teacher.' He quoted to me from the Mishnah, 'Make your master.' The next day he left. He got lost somewhere in the Forty-nine Gates of Defilement. He had most probably married a Lilith.

"I began to study the pamphlet and it was filled with holy names—or so it seemed to me. It would take a year to tell you all that pamphlet contained. First I had to fast seven days and seven nights. Then there was a long list of charms, incantations, meditations, and all kinds of magic doings. The combination of letters is not something to fool around with. An error in one letter or one vowel accent could destroy the earth. You light a wax candle, you burn incense, you utter a sacred name, and a creature begins to grow before your very eyes like an embryo in its mother's womb. The uttering of the name is not enough. In the cabala, thoughts are objects. The slightest imperfection can turn everything upside down. The Evil Powers try to get hold of sacred things all the time. What happened in Egypt? Everything that Moses did, the magicians imitated. But Moses was Moses, and Meir was a boy not yet eighteen years old. Every day some mishap occurred. It was midnight, the world was asleep. I stood at the window of my attic room ready to read the Shema and to go to sleep. Suddenly there was a commotion, a whistling, a wind, a confusion. The table began to dance, there was a howling as of a thousand female voices, the walls trembled, the whole building shook like a ship at sea. I said a word to quiet the storm. Just as suddenly there emerged freaks, monsters, grimacing, laughing, crying, struggling—to make it short, I had omitted the stem of the letter 'jud,' and instead of an angel as was created by the holy Joseph Karu, I had conjured up a misbegotten creature, a goblin. One moment I saw a head without a body and then a body without a head. Legs walked by themselves and entered the wall. A muzzle with the beard of a he-goat was delivering a sermon. It spoke like a cabalist but suddenly it started to babble in rhymes like a wedding jester, peppering its talk with obscenities and blasphemy. I myself spoke in a strange language. Later on when I wrote, my handwriting could only be read in a mirror. My father happened to be at a fair in Leipzig and the maid lay sick at her sister's. I was alone. But how long would I be able to hide all these goings on? It is true that the pamphlet gave directions for destroying unwanted entities, but in the magical cabala it is more difficult to erase than to create. My goblin began long debates with me—a lot of nonsense, all for spite. I wanted to sleep and he woke me. He twisted my sidelocks. He tickled the soles of my feet; he licked me with his tongue and begged me to find a spouse for him.

"One night when I was half asleep he came to my bed and tried to persuade me to have sexual relations with him. I was on the verge of falling into the trap but my God-fearing ancestors must have interceded for me. I jumped out of bed and drove him away. I got dressed, packed my phylacteries, the *Book of Creation,* and ran out of town. My father was a follower of the rabbi of Partzev and I found a wagon to take me there. It wasn't the rabbi who is residing there today, but his grandfather, Rabbi Kathriel. All along the way the fiend I had created tried to pull me into his net with good and bad words. But besides the *Book of Creation,* I had with me a bag full of charms that hung around my neck. I managed to reach the rabbi's yeshiva and there I remained for twenty years, until the evil spirit perished."

Meir the eunuch was silent.

Zalman the glazier shook his head. "Didn't he bother you in Partzev?"

"In Partzev the Evil Host did not hold sway."

"What do they want?"

"The small ones just make fools of themselves. The big ones attempt to take over the rule of heaven."

"And God will let them?"

"It's a war."

"Why did He create them?"

"In order that there be free choice."

It became quiet and the clock struck twelve. Through the half-frozen window a three-quarter moon shone in. Meir the eunuch began to pinch his naked chin with the tips of two fingers, as if to pull out a hair. He said, "The Jew of Babylon told me something that day which I won't forget to my last hour."

Levi Yitzchock took off his glasses. "What did he say?"

"The moment the Infinite Light shrank and grew dim, and Creation began, insanity was born. The demons are all crazy. Even the angels are not completely sane. The world of matter and deeds is an insane aslyum."

"How about a stone?" Zalman the glazier asked.

Meir the eunuch uttered a laugh that began in a masculine voice and ended in a feminine falsetto. "Really, a good question. With the exception of God and a stone, everything is mad."

Translated by the author and Dorothea Straus

The Cafeteria

Even though I have reached the point where a great part of my earnings is given away in taxes, I still have the habit of eating in cafeterias when I am by myself. I like to take a tray with a tin knife, fork, spoon, and paper napkin and to choose at the counter the food I enjoy. Besides, I meet there the *landsleit* from Poland, as well as all kinds of literary beginners and readers who know Yiddish. The moment I sit down at a table, they come over. "Hello, Aaron!" they greet me, and we talk about Yiddish literature, the Holocaust, the state of Israel, and often about acquaintances who were eating rice pudding or stewed prunes the last time I was here and are already in their graves. Since I seldom read a paper, I learn this news only later. Each time, I am startled, but at my age one has to be ready for such tidings. The food sticks in the throat; we look at one another in confusion, and our eyes ask mutely, Whose turn is next? Soon we begin to chew again. I am often reminded of a scene in a film about Africa. A lion attacks a herd of zebras and kills one. The frightened zebras run for a while and then they stop and start to graze again. Do they have a choice?

I cannot spend too long with these Yiddishists, because I am always too busy. I am writing a novel, a story, an article. I have to lecture today or tomorrow; my datebook is crowded with all kinds of appointments for weeks and months in advance. It can happen that an hour after I leave the cafeteria I am on a train to Chicago or flying to California. But meanwhile we converse in the mother language and I hear of intrigues and pettiness about which, from a moral point of view, it would be better not to be informed. Everyone tries in his own way with all his means to grab as many honors and as much money and prestige as he can. None of us learns from all these deaths. Old age does not cleanse us. We don't repent at the gate of hell.

I have been moving around in this neighborhood for over thirty years—as long as I lived in Poland. I know each block, each house. There has been little building here on uptown Broadway in the last decades, and I have the illusion of having put down roots here. I have spoken in most of the synagogues. They knew me in some of the stores and in the vegetarian restaurants. Women with whom I have had affairs live on the side streets. Even the pigeons know me; the moment I come out with a bag of feed, they begin to fly toward me from blocks away. It is an area that stretches from Ninety-sixth Street to Seventy-second Street and from Central Park to Riverside Drive. Almost every day on my walk after lunch, I pass the funeral parlor that waits for us and all our ambitions and illusions. Sometimes I imagine that the funeral parlor is also a kind of cafeteria where one gets a quick eulogy or Kaddish on the way to eternity.

The cafeteria people I meet are mostly men: old bachelors like myself, would-be writers, retired teachers, some with dubious doctorate titles, a rabbi without a congregation, a painter of Jewish themes, a few translators—all immigrants from Poland or Russia. I seldom know their names. One of them disappears and I think he is already in the next world; suddenly he reappears and he tells me that he has tried to settle in Tel Aviv or Los Angeles. Again he eats his rice pudding, sweetens his coffee with saccharin. He has a few more wrinkles, but he tells the same stories and makes the same gestures. It may happen that he takes a paper from his pocket and reads me a poem he has written.

*   *   *

It was in the fifties that a woman appeared in the group who looked younger than the rest of us. She must have been in her early thirties; she was short, slim, with a girlish face, brown hair that she wore in a bun, a short nose, and dimples in her cheeks. Her eyes were hazel—actually, of an indefinite color. She dressed in a modest European way. She spoke Polish, Russian, and an idiomatic Yiddish. She always carried Yiddish newspapers and magazines. She had been in a prison camp in Russia and had spent some time in the camps in Germany before she obtained a visa for the United States. The men all hovered around her. They didn't let her pay the check. They gallantly brought her coffee and cheese cake. They listened to her talk and jokes. She had returned from the devastation still gay. She was introduced to me. Her name was Esther. I didn't know if she was unmarried, a widow, a divorcée. She told me she was working in a factory, where she sorted buttons. This fresh young woman did not fit into the group of elderly has-beens. It was also hard to understand why she couldn't find a better job than sorting buttons in New Jersey. But I didn't ask too many questions. She told me that she had read my writing while still in Poland, and later in the camps in Germany after the war. She said to me, "You are my writer."

The moment she uttered those words I imagined I was in love with her. We were sitting alone (the other man at our table had gone to make a telephone call), and I said, "For such words I must kiss you."

"Well, what are you waiting for?"

She gave me both a kiss and a bite.

I said, "You are a ball of fire."

"Yes, fire from Gehenna."

A few days later, she invited me to her home. She lived on a street between Broadway and Riverside Drive with her father, who had no legs and sat in a

wheelchair. His legs had been frozen in Siberia. He
had tried to run away from one of Stalin's slave
camps in the winter of 1944. He looked like a strong
man, had a head of thick white hair, a ruddy face,
and eyes full of energy. He spoke in a swaggering
fashion, with boyish boastfulness and a cheerful
laugh. In an hour, he told me his story. He was born
in White Russia but he had lived long years in
Warsaw, Lodz, and Vilna. In the beginning of the
thirties, he became a Communist and soon afterward a functionary in the Party. In 1939 he escaped
to Russia with his daughter. His wife and the other
children remained in Nazi-occupied Warsaw. In
Russia, somebody denounced him as a Trotskyite
and he was sent to mine gold in the north. The
G.P.U. sent people there to die. Even the strongest
could not survive the cold and hunger for more than
a year. They were exiled without a sentence. They
died together: Zionists, Bundists, members of the
Polish Socialist Party, Ukrainian Nationalists, and
just refugees, all caught because of the labor short-
age. They often died of scurvy or beriberi. Boris
Merkin, Esther's father, spoke about this as if it
were a big joke. He called the Stalinists outcasts,
bandits, sycophants. He assured me that had it not
been for the United States Hitler would have overrun all of Russia. He told how prisoners tricked the
guards to get an extra piece of bread or a double
portion of watery soup, and what methods were used
in picking lice.

Esther called out, "Father, enough!"

"What's the matter—am I lying?"

"One can have enough even of *kreplach*."

"Daughter, you did it yourself."

When Esther went to the kitchen to make tea, I
learned from her father that she had had a husband
in Russia—a Polish Jew who had volunteered in the
Red Army and perished in the war. Here in New
York she was courted by a refugee, a former smuggler

in Germany who had opened a bookbinding factory
and become rich. "Persuade her to marry him,"
Boris Merkin said to me. "It would be good for me,
too."

"Maybe she doesn't love him."

"There is no such thing as love. Give me a cigarette. In the camp, people climbed on one another
like worms."

2.

I had invited Esther to supper, but she called to say
she had the grippe and must remain in bed. Then in
a few days' time a situation arose that made me
leave for Israel. On the way back, I stopped over in
London and Paris. I wanted to write to Esther, but I
lost her address. When I returned to New York, I
tried to call her, but there was no telephone listing
for Boris Merkin or Esther Merkin—father and
daughter must have been boarders in somebody
else's apartment. Weeks passed and she did not
show up in the cafeteria. I asked the group about
her; nobody knew where she was. "She has most
probably married that bookbinder," I said to myself.
One evening, I went to the cafeteria with the premonition that I would find Esther there. I saw a
black wall and boarded windows—the cafeteria had
burned. The old bachelors were no doubt meeting in
another cafeteria, or an Automat. But where? To
search is not in my nature. I had plenty of complications without Esther.

The summer passed; it was winter. Late one day, I
walked by the cafeteria and again saw lights, a
counter, guests. The owners had rebuilt. I entered,
took a check, and saw Esther sitting alone at a table
reading a Yiddish newspaper. She did not notice me
and I observed her for a while. She wore a man's fur
fez and a jacket trimmed with a faded fur collar. She
looked pale, as though recuperating from a sickness.

Could that grippe have been the start of a serious illness? I went over to her table and asked, "What's new in buttons?"

She started and smiled. Then she called out, "Miracles do happen!"

"Where have you been?"

"Where did you disappear to?" she replied. "I thought you were still abroad."

"Where are our *cafeterianiks?*"

"They now go to the cafeteria on Fifty-seventh Street and Eighth Avenue. They only reopened this place yesterday."

"May I bring you a cup of coffee?"

"I drink too much coffee. All right."

I went to get her coffee and a large egg cookie. While I stood at the counter, I turned my head and looked at her. Esther had taken off her mannish fur hat and smoothed her hair. She folded the newspaper, which meant that she was ready to talk. She got up and tilted the other chair against the table as a sign that the seat was taken. When I sat down, Esther said, "You left without saying goodbye, and there I was about to knock at the pearly gates of heaven."

"What happened?"

"Oh, the grippe became pneumonia. They gave me penicillin, and I am one of those who cannot take it. I got a rash all over my body. My father, too, is not well."

"What's the matter with your father?"

"High blood pressure. He had a kind of stroke and his mouth became all crooked."

"Oh, I'm sorry. Do you still work with buttons?"

"Yes, with buttons. At least I don't have to use my head, only my hands. I can think my own thoughts."

"What do you think about?"

"What not. The other workers are all Puerto Ricans. They rattle away in Spanish from morning to night."

"Who takes care of your father?"

"Who? Nobody. I come home in the evening to make supper. He has one deisre—to marry me off for my own good and, perhaps, for his comfort, but I can't marry a man I don't love."

"What is love?"

"You ask me! You write novels about it. But you're a man—I assume you really don't know what it is. A woman is a piece of merchandise to you. To me a man who talks nonsense or smiles like an idiot is repulsive. I would rather die than live with him. And a man who goes from one woman to another is not for me. I don't want to share with anybody."

"I'm afraid a time is coming when everybody will."

"That is not for me."

"What kind of person was your husband?"

"How did you know I had a husband? My father, I suppose. The minute I leave the room, he prattles. My husband believed in things and was ready to die for them. He was not exactly my type but I respected him and loved him, too. He wanted to die and he died like a hero. What else can I say?"

"And the others?"

"There were no others. Men were after me. The way people behaved in the war—you will never know. They lost all shame. On the bunks near me one time, a mother lay with one man and her daughter with another. People were like beasts—worse than beasts. In the middle of it all, I dreamed about love. Now I have even stopped dreaming. The men who come here are terrible bores. Most of them are half mad, too. One of them tried to read me a forty-page poem. I almost fainted."

"I wouldn't read you anything I'd written."

"I've been told how you behave—no!"

"No is no. Drink your coffee."

"You don't even try to persuade me. Most men around here plague you and you can't get rid of them. In Russia people suffered, but I have never met as many maniacs there as in New York City. The building where I live is a madhouse. My neighbors are lunatics. They accuse each other of all kinds of things. They sing, cry, break dishes. One of them jumped out of the window and killed herself. She was having an affair with a boy twenty years younger. In Russia the problem was to escape the lice; here you're surrounded by insanity."

We drank coffee and shared the egg cookie. Esther put down her cup. "I can't believe that I'm sitting with you at this table. I read all your articles under all your pen names. You tell so much about yourself I have the feeling I've known you for years. Still, you are a riddle to me."

"Men and women can never understand one another."

"No—I cannot understand my own father. Sometimes he is a complete stranger to me. He won't live long."

"Is he so sick?"

"It's everything together. He's lost the will to live. Why live without legs, without friends, without a family? They have all perished. He sits and reads the newspapers all day long. He acts as though he were interested in what's going on in the world. His ideals are gone, but he still hopes for a just revolution. How can a revolution help him? I myself never put my hopes in any movement or party. How can we hope when everything ends in death?"

"Hope in itself is a proof that there is no death."

"Yes, I know you often write about this. For me, death is the only comfort. What do the dead do? They continue to drink coffee and eat egg cookies? They still read newspapers? A life after death would be nothing but a joke."

3.

Some of the *cafeterianiks* came back to the rebuilt cafeteria. New people appeared—all of them Europeans. They launched into long discussions in Yiddish, Polish, Russian, even Hebrew. Some of those who came from Hungary mixed German, Hungarian, Yiddish-German—then all of a sudden they began to speak plain Galician Yiddish. They asked to have their coffee in glasses, and held lumps of sugar between their teeth when they drank. Many of them were my readers. They introduced themselves and reproached me for all kinds of literary errors: I contradicted myself, went too far in descriptions of sex, described Jews in such a way that anti-Semites could use it for propaganda. They told me their experiences in the ghettos, in the Nazi concentration camps, in Russia. They pointed out one another. "Do you see that fellow—in Russia he immediately became a Stalinist. He denounced his own friends. Here in America he has switched to anti-Bolshevism." The one who was spoken about seemed to sense that he was being maligned, because the moment my informant left he took his cup of coffee and his rice pudding, sat down at my table, and said, "Don't believe a word of what you are told. They invent all kinds of lies. What could you do in a country where the rope was always around your neck? You had to adjust yourself if you wanted to live and not die somewhere in Kazakhstan. To get a bowl of soup or a place to stay you had to sell your soul."

There was a table with a group of refugees who ignored me. They were not interested in literature and journalism but strictly in business. In Germany they had been smugglers. They seemed to be doing shady business here, too; they whispered to one another and winked, counted their money, wrote long lists of numbers. Somebody pointed out one of them. "He had a store in Auschwitz."

"What do you mean, a store?"

"God help us. He kept his merchandise in the straw where he slept—a rotten potato, sometimes a piece of soap, a tin spoon, a little fat. Still, he did

business. Later, in Germany, he became such a big
smuggler they once took forty thousand dollars away
from him."

Sometimes months passed between my visits to
the cafeteria. A year or two had gone by (perhaps
three or four; I lost count), and Esther did not show
up. I asked about her a few times. Someone said that
she was going to the cafeteria on Forty-second Street;
another had heard that she had married. I learned
that some of the *cafeterianiks* had died. They were
beginning to settle down in the United States, had
remarried, opened businesses, workshops, even had
children again. Then came cancer or a heart attack.
The result of the Hitler and Stalin years, it was said.

One day, I entered the cafeteria and saw Esther.
She was sitting alone at a table. It was the same
Esther. She was even wearing the same fur hat, but
a strand of gray hair fell over her forehead. How
strange—the fur hat, too, seemed to have grayed.
The other *cafeterianiks* did not appear to be interested in her any more, or they did not know her. Her
face told of the time that had passed. There were
shadows under her eyes. Her gaze was no longer
clear. Around her mouth was an expression that
could be called bitterness, disenchantment. I greeted
her. She smiled, but her smile immediately faded
away. I asked, "What happened to you?"

"Oh, I'm still alive."

"May I sit down?"

"Please—certainly."

"May I bring you a cup of coffee?"

"No. Well, if you insist."

I noticed that she was smoking, and also that she
was reading not the newspaper to which I contribute
but a competition paper. She had gone over to the
enemy. I brought her coffee and for myself stewed
prunes—a remedy for constipation. I sat down. "Where
were you all this time? I have asked for you."

"Really? Thank you."

"What happened?"

"Nothing good." She looked at me. I knew that she saw in me what I saw in her; the slow wilting of the flesh. She said, "You have no hair but you are white."

For a while we were silent. Then I said, "Your father—" and as I said it I knew that her father was not alive.

Esther said, "He has been dead for almost a year."

"Do you still sort buttons?"

"No, I became an operator in a dress shop."

"What happened to you personally, may I ask?"

"Oh nothing—absolutely nothing. You will not believe it, but I was sitting here thinking about you. I have fallen into some kind of trap. I don't know what to call it. I thought perhaps you could adivse me. Do you still have the patience to listen to the troubles of little people like me? No, I didn't mean to insult you. I even doubted you would remember me. To make it short, I work but work is growing more difficult for me. I suffer from arthritis. I feel as if my bones would crack. I wake up in the morning and can't sit up. One doctor tells me that it's a disc in my back, others try to cure my nerves. One took X-rays and says that I have a tumor. He wanted me to go to the hospital for a few weeks, but I'm in no hurry for an operation. Suddenly a little lawyer showed up. He is a refugee himself and is connected with the German government. You know they're now giving reparation money. It's true that I escaped to Russia, but I'm a victim of the Nazis just the same. Besides, they don't know my biography so exactly. I could get a pension plus a few thousand dollars, but my dislocated disc is no good for the purpose because I got it later—after the camps. This lawyer says my only chance is to convince them that I am ruined psychically. It's the bitter truth, but how can you prove it? The German doctors, the neurologists, the psychiatrists require proof. Everything has to be according to the textbooks—just so and no different. The lawyer wants me to play insane. Naturally, he gets twenty per cent of the reparation money— maybe more. Why he needs so much money I don't understand. He's already in his seventies, an old bachelor. He tried to make love to me and whatnot. He's half *meshugga* himself. But how can I play insane when actually I *am* insane? The whole thing revolts me and I'm afraid it will really drive me crazy. I hate swindle. But this shyster pursues me. I don't sleep. When the alarm rings in the morning, I wake up as shattered as I used to be in Russia when I had to walk to the forest and saw logs at four in the morning. Naturally, I take sleeping pills—if I didn't, I couldn't sleep at all. That is more or less the situation."

"Why don't you get married? You are still a good-looking woman."

"Well, the old question—there is nobody. It's too late. If you knew how I felt, you wouldn't ask such a question."

4.

A few weeks passed. Snow had been falling. After the snow came rain, then frost. I stood at my window and looked out at Broadway. The passersby half walked, half slipped. Cars moved slowly. The sky above the roofs shone violet, without a moon, without stars, and even though it was eight o'clock in the evening the light and the emptiness reminded me of dawn. The stores were deserted. For a moment, I had the feeling I was in Warsaw. The telephone rang and I rushed to answer it as I did ten, twenty, thirty years ago—still expecting the good tidings that a telephone call was about to bring me. I said hello, but there was no answer and I was seized by the fear that some evil power was trying to keep back the good news at the last minute. Then I heard a stammering. A woman's voice muttered my name.

"Yes, it is I."

"Excuse me for disturbing you. My name is Esther. We met a few weeks ago in the cafeteria—"

"Esther!" I exclaimed.

"I don't know how I got the courage to phone you. I need to talk to you about something. Naturally, if you have the time and—please forgive my presumption."

"No presumption. Would you like to come to my apartment?"

"If I will not be interrupting. It's difficult to talk in the cafeteria. It's noisy and there are eavesdroppers. What I want to tell you is a secret I wouldn't trust to anyone else."

"Please, come up."

I gave Esther directions. Then I tried to make order in my apartment, but I soon realized this was impossible. Letters, manuscripts lay around on tables and chairs. In the corners books and magazines were piled high. I opened the closets and threw inside whatever was under my hand: jackets, pants, shirts, shoes, slippers. I picked up an envelope and to my amazement saw that it had never been opened. I tore it open and found a check. "What's the matter with me—have I lost my mind?" I said out loud. I tried to read the letter that came with the check, but I had misplaced my glasses; my fountain pen was gone, too. Well—and where are my keys? I heard a bell ring and I didn't know whether it was the door or the telephone. I opened the door and saw Esther. It must have been snowing again, because her hat and shoulders of her coat were trimmed with white. I asked her in, and my neighbor, the divorcée, who spied on me openly with no shame—and, God knows, with no sense of purpose—opened her door and stared at my guest.

Esther removed her boots and I took her coat and put it on the case of the Encyclopedia Britannica. I shoved a few manuscripts off the sofa so she could sit down. I said, "In my house there is sheer chaos."

"It doesn't matter."

I sat in an armchair strewn with socks and handkerchiefs. For a while we spoke about the weather, about the danger of being out in New York at night—even early in the evening. Then Esther said, "Do you remember the time I spoke to you about my lawyer—that I had to go to a psychiatrist because of the reparation money?"

"Yes, I remember."

"I didn't tell you everything. It was too wild. It still seems unbelievable, even to me. Don't interrupt me, I implore you. I'm not completely healthy—I may even say that I'm sick—but I know the difference between fact and illusion. I haven't slept for nights, and I kept wondering whether I should call you or not. I decided not to—but this evening it occurred to me that if I couldn't trust you with a thing like this, then there is no one I could talk to. I read you and I know that you have a sense of the great mysteries—" Esther said all this stammering and with pauses. For a moment her eyes smiled, and then they became sad and wavering.

I said, "You can tell me everything."

"I am afraid that you'll think me insane."

"I swear I will not."

Esther bit her lower lip. "I want you to know that I saw Hitler," she said.

Even though I was prepared for something unusual, my throat constricted. "When—where?"

"You see, you are frightened already. It happened three years ago—almost four. I saw him here on Broadway."

"On the street?"

"In the cafeteria."

I tried to swallow the lump in my throat. "Most probably someone resembling him," I said finally.

"I knew you would say that. But remember, you've

promised to listen. You recall the fire in the cafeteria?"

"Yes, certainly."

"The fire has to do with it. Since you don't believe me anyhow, why draw it out? It happened this way. That night I didn't sleep. Usually when I can't sleep, I get up and make tea, or I try to read a book, but this time some power commanded me to get dressed and go out. I can't explain to you how I dared walk on Broadway at that late hour. It must have been two or three o'clock. I reached the cafeteria, thinking perhaps it stays open all night. I tried to look in, but the large window was covered by a curtain. There was a pale glow inside. I tried the revolving door and it turned. I went in and saw a scene I will not forget to the last day of my life. The tables were shoved together and around them sat men in white robes, like doctors or orderlies, all with swastikas on their sleeves. At the head sat Hitler. I beg you to hear me out—even a deranged person sometimes deserves to be listened to. They all spoke German. They didn't see me. They were busy with the Führer. It grew quiet and he started to talk. That abominable voice—I heard it many times on the radio. I didn't make out exactly what he said. I was too terrified to take it in. Suddenly one of his henchmen looked back at me and jumped up from his chair. How I came out alive I will never know. I ran with all my strength, and I was trembling all over. When I got home, I said to myself, 'Esther, you are not right in the head.' I still don't know how I lived through that night. The next morning, I didn't go straight to work but walked to the cafeteria to see if it was really there. Such an experience makes a person doubt his own senses. When I arrived, I found the place had burned down. When I saw this, I knew it had to do with what I had seen. Those who were there wanted all traces erased. These are the plain facts. I have no reason to fabricate such queer things."

We were both silent. Then I said, "You had a vision."

"What do you mean, a vision?"

"The past is not lost. An image from years ago remained present somewhere in the fourth dimension and it reached you just at that moment."

"As far as I know, Hitler never wore a long white robe."

"Perhaps he did."

"Why did the cafeteria burn down just that night?" Esther asked.

"It could be that the fire evoked the vision."

"There was no fire then. Somehow I foresaw that you would give me this kind of explanation. If this was a vision, my sitting here with you is also a vision."

"It couldn't have been anything else. Even if Hitler is living and is hiding out in the United States, he is not likely to meet his cronies at a cafeteria on Broadway. Besides, the cafeteria belongs to a Jew."

"I saw him as I am seeing you now."

"You had a glimpse back in time."

"Well, let it be so. But since then I have had no rest. I keep thinking about it. If I am destined to lose my mind, this will drive me to it."

The telephone rang and I jumped up with a start. It was a wrong number. I sat down again. "What about the psychiatrist your lawyer sent you to? Tell it to him and you'll get full compensation."

Esther looked at me sidewise and unfriendly. "I know what you mean. I haven't fallen that low yet."

5.

I was afraid that Esther would continue to call me. I even planned to change my telephone number. But weeks and months passed and I never heard from her or saw her. I didn't go to the cafeteria. But I often thought about her. How can the brain produce

such nightmares? What goes on in that little mar-
row behind the skull? And what guarantee do I have
that the same sort of thing will not happen to me?
And how do we know that the human species will
not end like this? I have played with the idea that all
of humanity suffers from schizophrenia. Along with
the atom, the personality of *Homo sapiens* has been
splitting. When it comes to technology, the brain
still functions, but in everything else degeneration
has begun. They are all insane: the Communists, the
Fascists, the preachers of democracy, the writers,
the painters, the clergy, the atheists. Soon technology, too, will disintegrate. Buildings will collapse,
power plants will stop generating electricity. Gen-
erals will drop atomic bombs on their own popula-
tions. Mad revolutionaries will run in the streets,
crying fantastic slogans. I have often thought that it
would begin in New York. This metropolis has all
the symptoms of a mind gone berserk.

But since insanity has not yet taken over altogether, one has to act as though there were still order—
according to Vaihinger's principle of "as if." I
continued with my scribbling. I delivered manuscripts
to the publisher. I lectured. Four times a year, I sent
checks to the federal government, the state. What
was left after my expenses I put in the savings bank.
A teller entered some numbers in my bankbook and
this meant that I was provided for. Somebody printed
a few lines in a magazine or newspaper, and this
signified that my value as a writer had gone up. I
saw with amazement that all my efforts turned into
paper. My apartment was one big wastepaper basket. From day to day, all this paper was getting drier
and more parched. I woke up at night fearful that it
would ignite. There was not an hour when I did not
hear the sirens of fire engines.

A year after I had last seen Esther, I was going to
Toronto to read a paper about Yiddish in the second
half of the nineteenth century. I put a few shirts in

my valise as well as papers of all kinds, among them
one that made me a citizen of the United States. I
had enough paper money in my pocket to pay for a
taxi to Grand Central. But the taxis seemed to be
taken. Those that were not refused to stop. Didn't the
drivers see me? Had I suddenly become one of those
who see and are not seen? I decided to take the
subway. On my way, I saw Esther. She was not
alone but with someone I had known years ago, soon
after I arrived in the United States. He was a
frequenter of a cafeteria on East Broadway. He used
to sit at a table, express opinions, criticize, grumble.
He was a small man, with sunken cheeks the color of
brick, and bulging eyes. He was angry at the new
writers. He belittled the old ones. He rolled his own
cigarettes and dropped ashes into the plates from
which we ate. Almost two decades had passed since I
had last seen him. Suddenly he appears with Esther.
He was even holding her arm. I had never seen
Esther look so well. She was wearing a new coat, a
new hat. She smiled at me and nodded. I wanted to
stop her, but my watch showed that it was late. I
barely managed to catch the train. In my bedroom,
the bed was already made. I undressed and went to
sleep.

In the middle of the night, I awoke. My car was
being switched, and I almost fell out of bed. I could
not sleep any more and I tried to remember the
name of the little man I had seen with Esther. But I
was unable to. The thing I did remember was that
even thirty years ago he had been far from young.
He had come to the United States in 1905 after the
revolution in Russia. In Europe, he had a reputation
as a speaker and public figure. How old must he be
now? According to my calculations, he had to be in
the late eighties—perhaps even ninety. Is it possible
that Esther could be intimate with such an old man?
But this evening he had not looked old. The longer I
brooded about it in the darkness, the stranger the

encounter seemed to me. I even imagined that somewhere in a newspaper I had read that he had died.
Do corpses walk around on Broadway? This would
mean that Esther, too, was not living. I raised the
window shade and sat up and looked out into the
night—black, impenetrable, without a moon. A few
stars ran along with the train for a while and then
they disappeared. A lighted factory emerged; I saw
machines but no operators. Then it was swallowed
in the darkness and another group of stars began to
follow the train. I was turning with the earth on its
axis. I was circling with it around the sun and
moving in the direction of a constellation whose
name I had forgotten. Is there no death? Or is there
no life?

I thought about what Esther had told me of seeing
Hitler in the cafeteria. It had seemed utter nonsense, but now I began to reappraise the idea. If time
and space are nothing more than forms of percep-
tion, as Kant argues, and quality, quantity, causality
are only categories of thinking, why shouldn't Hitler
confer with his Nazis in a cafeteria on Broadway?
Esther didn't sound insane. She had seen a piece of
reality that the heavenly censorship prohibits as a
rule. She had caught a glimpse behind the curtain of
the phenomena. I regretted that I had not asked for
more details.

In Toronto, I had little time to ponder these matters, but when I returned to New York I went to the
cafeteria for some private investigation. I met only
one man I knew: a rabbi who had become an agnos-
tic and given up his job. I asked him about Esther.
He said, "The pretty little woman who used to come
here?"

"Yes."

"I heard that she committed suicide."

"When—how?"

"I don't know. Perhaps we are not speaking about
the same person."

No matter how many questions I asked and how much I described Esther, everything remained vague. Some young woman who used to come here had turned on the gas and made an end of herself—that was all the ex-rabbi could tell me.

I decided not to rest until I knew for certain what had happened to Esther and also to that half writer, half politician I remembered from East Broadway. But I grew busier from day to day. The cafeteria closed. The neighborhood changed. Years have passed and I have never seen Esther again. Yes, corpses do walk on Broadway. But why did Esther choose that particular corpse? She could have got a better bargain even in this world.

Translated by the author and Dorothea Straus

The Mentor

When I arrived in Israel in 1955, I met two kinds of acquaintants: those I hadn't seen since 1935, when I left Warsaw for the United States, and those I hadn't seen since 1922, when I left Jadow for Warsaw. Those from Warsaw had known me as a young author, a member of the writers' association and of the Yiddish section of the PEN club; those from Jadow remembered me as an adolescent who tutored Hebrew, sent poems to magazines that were immediately rejected, believed himself deeply in love with a sixteen-year-old girl, and indulged in all sorts of Bohemian activities. The Warsaw people called me by my literary pen name; the Jadower called me Itche, or Itche the rabbi's, because I was the rabbi's grandson.

In Tel Aviv, the Yiddish writers held a reception for me and made speeches. They swore that I had changed little. The Jadower all asked the same question—"What happened to your red hair?" They gathered in the house of a *landsman* who had become rich from his business in leather. There I had a strange experience: former servant girls and coachmen spoke to me in fluent Hebrew. Some of those who spoke Yiddish spoke with a Russian or Lithuanian accent because they had fled from Poland during the Second World War and spent years in Vilna, Bialystok, Jambul, or Tashkent. Girls I had kissed on the sly and who used to call me *Moreh*—teacher— told me about their married children and even of their grandchildren. Faces and figures had changed beyond recognition.

Slowly I began to orient myself. Several of the

Jadow women confided that they had never forgotten me. My boyhood companions reminded me of the wild pranks I played, the fantastic stories I told, and even of my jokes about the old townspeople. Many of the Jadower were missing. They had perished in the ghettos and concentration camps or had died in Russia of hunger, typhoid fever, and scurvy. Some of the Jadower had lost children in the war against the Arabs in 1948. My *landsleit* both laughed and sighed. They prepared a banquet for me, and a memorial evening for those who had not survived.

Since they called me Itche and spoke familiarly, I felt young in this crowd. I began to babble again, telling all kinds of jokes about Berl, the village idiot, and Reb Mordecai Meyer, the Jadower preacher of morality. I spoke to these middle-aged men and women as if they were still boys and girls. I even tried to renew my old romances. Good-naturedly, the Jadower made fun of me and said, "Really, Itche, you are still the same!"

Among the Jadower who came to meet me was Freidl, a former pupil of mine who was now a doctor. She was about ten years younger than I. When I was seventeen, she was eight. Her father, Avigdor Rosenbach, was one of the enlightened, a rich lumber dealer. In Israel, Freidl had Hebraized her name and was called Ditza. Before I left Jadow, Freidl was already known for her sharp mind. She spoke Yiddish and Polish, studied French with one teacher and piano with another. She quickly mastered the Hebrew I taught her. She was a pretty little girl, with black hair, a white skin, and green eyes. She plagued me with all sorts of questions that I could not answer. In her childish way she flirted with me, and after every lesson I had to kiss her. She promised to marry me when she grew up. Later, in Warsaw, I learned that Freidl had finished *Gymnasium* with honors and studied medicine at the Sorbonne. Somebody told me that she knew eight languages. One day, I heard the strange news that she had married a Jadower boy, Tobias Stein. Tobias was a youth of my age; his ideal was to be a chalutz in Palestine. Although his father was a wealthy merchant, he learned carpentry in order to become a builder in the settlements. He was dark, with laughing black eyes and a head of curly black hair. He wore a blouse with a sash, and a white-and-blue cap embroidered with the Star of David to express his Zionistic fervor. Besides carpentry, he learned to shoot a rifle so he could become a guard in Palestine and protect the colonies from Arab attack. He knew the geography of Palestine better than any of us, sang all the Zionist songs, and declaimed Bialik's poems. Sometime after I left Warsaw, Tobias received a certificate to enter Palestine, but it seems that he returned to Europe long enough to marry Freidl. I didn't know the details; neither did I care to know them.

Years after the Second World War, I learned that Freidl had a daughter with Tobias and that the two had separated. Freidl had made a career in Israel; she was a neurologist and had written a book, which was translated into other languages. She was said to have had all kinds of affairs—among others, with a high officer of the English Army. Tobias lived in a remote kibbutz. He was still in love with Freidl. Their daughter had remained with him.

Freidl's entrance that evening into the home of the rich leather dealer created a sensation among the Jadower. She had avoided all their gatherings, and they considered her a snob. The woman who came into the room would have been over forty but looked much younger: a little taller than medium height, slender, with closely cropped black hair, her skin still white, her eyes green. I recognized the Freidl of long ago—only her nose had become that of a grown-up, serious person. Although she did not wear glasses, there were marks on the skin, as if she just removed her pince-nez. She wore a suit of English tweed, with a woman's tie; her purse resembled an attaché case. On her finger sat a large emerald ring. She looked at me in perplexity. Then she called out, *"Moreh!"* and we kissed. I imagined that the smell of all the men with whom she had had affairs still clung to her. After the first sentences, she spoke to me in Yiddish instead of Hebrew. I was embarrassed—I, who had taught her the Hebrew alphabet, could not keep up with her Hebrew, which she spoke rapidly, in a strong voice, and with the modern Sephardic accent. She told me that she was connected with the university in Jerusalem. She also had contacts with universities abroad—even in the United States. The Jadower became silent. They listened to our talk with awe.

I asked, "May I still call you Freidl?"

And she answered, "For you, I will always be Freidl."

2.

After the reception, a number of the Jadower wanted to accompany me to the hotel, but Freidl announced that she had her car and would drive me, and no one dared to contradict her. In the car, Freidl said to me, "Are you in a hurry? It's a beautiful night. Let's go for a ride."

"Yes, with pleasure."

We drove through the city. How strange it was to be in a Jewish country, to read shop signs in the latest created Hebrew, to pass streets with the names of rabbis, Zionist leaders, writers. The day had been a hot one—actually, a chamsin, though not the worst kind. I saw women covering their faces with kerchiefs to keep from breathing in the fine desert sand that the wind carried. The sun had set—large, red, not round as usual but pointed toward the bottom, like a fruit with a stem. Usually in Tel Aviv it cools off after dark, but on this night the hot breeze continued. Gasoline fumes mixed with the freshness that drifted in from the fields, the hills, the valleys. From the sea came the stench of dead fish and the city's refuse. The moon stood low, dark red, half erased, and I had a feeling that it might be falling to earth in a cosmic catastrophe. The stars shook like little lamps suspended from unseen wires. We took the road toward Jaffa. On my right the sea sparkled silvery. Green shadows passed across its surface. Freidl said, "On nights like this I cannot sleep anyhow. I walk around and smoke cigarettes."

I wanted to ask her why she had left Tobias, but I knew that the question should be put in other terms: Why had she married him? However, I waited till she would begin to talk. We passed Arabic houses with many cupolas, like the breasts of mythical beasts. Some of the houses had beaded curtains instead of doors. Freidl pointed out a mosque and a minaret from which the muezzins call the faithful five times a day. After a while, she began.

"It was crazy, the whole business. I remembered him from the time I was still a child, and I was left with a romantic illusion. I belong to the type of woman who is attracted to older men—you know how they call it in Freudian jargon. The truth is I also had a crush on you, but I heard that you were married. I realized early that we Jews had no future in the Diaspora. Not only Hitler—the whole world was ready to tear us to pieces. You were right when you wrote that modern Jews are suicidal. The modern Jew can't live without anti-Semitism. If it's not there, he's driven to create it. He has to bleed for humanity—battle the reactionaries, worry about the Chinese, the Manchurians, the Russians, the untouchables in India, the Negroes in America. He preaches revolution and at the same time he wants all the privileges of capitalism for himself. He tries to destroy nationalism in others but prides himself

on belonging to the Chosen People. How can a tribe
like this exist among strangers? I wanted to settle
here, with my so-called brothers and sisters, and
there was Tobias—an idealist, a pioneer. I had visited
here, and I imagined that I loved him. Even as I
stood with him under the canopy, I knew I'd made a
mistake. I'd convinced myself that he was a hero,
but I soon saw that he was a schlemiel, softheaded,
as sentimental as an old maid. In the beginning, his
Hebrew dazzled me, but when I listened closely I
realized that banalities poured from his mouth. He
parroted all the brochures, all the editorials in the
newspapers. He sang cheap songs with gusto. He fell
in love with me in a sick way, and that love completely
crushed me. There isn't a greater pain than to be
loved by a fool. He makes you frigid and ashamed of
your sex. Near him I became cruel and bitchy. I
immediately wanted to end it, but then our Rina
came. A child is a child. She took after our family,
not his. But he keeps her as a pawn. He has set her
against me until she has become my adversary in
every way. I am disappointed in the kibbutz, too. It
has the faults of Communism along with those of
capitalism. What kind of person can she become
there? A half-educated peasant. Do you smoke?"

"No."

"I hear you don't eat meat, either."

"No."

"What's the sense of it? Nature knows no compassion. As far as nature is concerned, we are like
worms. You taught me the Bible, and my father
stuffed me with the miracles that God performed for
the Jews. But after what happened to them one must
be absolutely stupid and insensitive to believe in
God and all that drivel. What's more, to believe in a
compassionate God is the worst betrayal of the victims. A rabbi from America visited here, and he
preached that all the six million Jews sit in Paradise, gorge themselves on the meat of the Leviathan,

and study the Torah with angels. You don't need to be a psychologist to figure out what that kind of belief compensates for. In Jerusalem there's a group that dabbles in psychic research. I became involved a little—I even attended their séances. It's all fake. If they don't swindle others, they deceive themselves. Without a functioning brain, there is no thought. If a hereafter really existed, it would be the greatest cruelty. Why should a soul remember all the pettiness of its existence? What would be so wonderful if my father's soul continued to live and recall how his partner stole from him, how his house burned down, how my sister Mirele died in childbirth, and then the ghettos, the camps, and the Nazi ovens. If there is one iota of justice in nature, it is the obliteration of the spirit when the body decays. I don't understand how one can think differently."

"If one thinks that way, there is no reason one should not be a Nazi."

"It's not a question of should or should not. Nazis are enemies of the human race, and people must be allowed to exterminate them like bedbugs."

"How about the weak ones? What rights do they have?"

"They have the right to unite and become strong."

"Why not enjoy all the privileges and injustices meanwhile?" I asked.

"We do enjoy them. The fact that at this moment we find ourselves riding in a car, instead of pulling somebody in a rickshaw or standing in a rice field up to our knees in water and working for six piastres a day is already a privilege and even an injustice. Let's end this talk. It leads nowhere. You yourself believe in nothing."

"Someone takes charge of this world."

"Who? Nonsense. Sheer nonsense!"

"What about the stars?"

Freidl lifted her head for a second. "The stars are stars."

We became silent. The road ran through fields and orchards—or perhaps they were orange groves; it was too dark to see. From time to time a light flickered in the distance. I did not ask where we were going. I had already crossed the land in its length and breadth and my curiosity was quenched. We had traveled for half an hour without encountering a single car. A midnight silence hovered over the earth. The wind had stopped. The noise of the motor was overlaid by the chirping of crickets, the croaking of frogs, and the rustle of myriads of insects that lived in this Holy Land, searched for food, protection, mates.

Freidl said, "If you are sleepy, I will turn back. For me, there is no greater pleasure than such a trip in the night."

I wanted to ask Freidl about her affairs, but I restrained myself. I knew that most people like to confess but can't stand having someone force the truth from them with open curiosity. I don't remember how it came about, but Freidl began to talk again.

"What was there to to stop me?" she said. "I didn't love him, and even if I did I would have wanted to taste others. I had men before him, with him, and after him. I had somebody on our what you call honeymoon. There are monogamous women and even men, but I don't belong to them. I feel like de Maupassant: two lovers are better than one, and three are better than two. Naturally, I had to turn away some, but never out of moral motives. I share Mme Kollontai's opinion that my body is my private property. Exactly what love is I don't know and probably never will know. Everyone understands it in his own way. I've heard countless stories from my patients. But there isn't any explanation for human behavior— there are only patterns. Lately, I became a disciple of Gestalt psychology because it doesn't try to find motivations. A cat catches mice. A bee makes honey. Stalin craved power. Modern Jews also crave power— not directly but only through working behind the scenes. In that sense they are like women. The Jew is a born critic. He has to tear things down. Here he cannot belittle everything, and this makes him mad. I am, as you see, a complete hedonist. But there are inhibitions that don't allow one to enjoy things. You won't believe it, but my daughter is the main disturbance in my life. A hundred times a day I tell myself that a child is nothing more than an accidentally fertilized egg and that all the love and loyalty one feels toward it are only blind instinct—or call it what you will. But it bothers me just the same. Her hatred, her complaints make me miserable. It grows worse from day to day. I literally hear how she talks back to me, scolds me, and tries to revenge the wrongs I am supposed to have done her father. I wanted to send her abroad to study, but she refuses to take anything from me. She doesn't answer my letters. When I telephone her—and in a kibbutz it's not an easy thing to get a connection— she hangs up on me. There would be one remedy—to go back to live with Tobias—but the very thought of it makes me vomit. How he managed to implant such hatred is a riddle to me. This has actually become the essence of his life. He appears to be saccharin sweet, but inside he is bitter and malicious. The things he says are baffling in their stupidity, and yet they frighten me, too. There is some mysterious strength in fools. They are deeply rooted in the primeval chaos. You are the only man in the world I have confided this to. I have lost my brothers, and to me you are like an older brother. Thirty-three years is a long time, but somehow I remembered you. Many times I wanted to write to you. However, for me writing a letter is an impossible task. Aren't you sleepy?"

"No."

"Why not? It's late."

"The history in this land doesn't let me sleep."

"Who? Father Abraham?"

"The prophets."

"The first time, I was afraid I wouldn't be able to go to the toilet in Jerusalem, it was so holy, but you get accustomed to it. Are you ready to ride with me the whole night?"

"Yes, but where?"

"Don't laugh at me. I want to take you to my daughter's kibbutz. I stopped visiting her. I've taken an oath—a secular oath; by what can we swear?—that I will never visit her. Every time I go there, she shows her hostility. She is simply possessed by her hatred for me. She refuses to sit with me in the dining hall. She has spit in my face. The reason I want to take you is this. Tobias will be happy to see you. You and he were supposed to be bosom friends. He reads you faithfully. Rina also knows of you. She boasts that you are her father's friend. Here a writer still commands some respect. In that sense, Israel is like Jadow. I can't rest in bed anyhow, and I don't take tranquillizers any more. I'd like to go and have a look at her. Then we will drive back and you will be in the hotel by ten o'clock. I have to be at the clinic, but since you have no work here, you can close the shutters and sleep as long as you wish."

"All right, I agree."

"I am exploiting you, eh? I know I am being weak, but there is some weakness even in the strong. We will be in the kibbutz at daybreak. They have a high school there, and Rina is in the senior class. She works there, too. She has chosen the stable, just to spite me. She milks the cows and cleans away the dung. There is one sphere in which everyone is a genius, and that is in being spiteful."

"What kind of a kibbutz is it?"

Freidl mentioned a name.

"Isn't that a leftist kibbutz?"

"Yes, they are leftists. He, as well as his daughter. Their god is Borokhov. They went there to spread the Torah of revolution directly from Zion. The others have cooled off somewhat, but for the two of them Lenin is still Moses. It's all personal. Just because I make fun of it. She is good-looking, an absolute beauty—clever also. In America, Hollywood would have snapped her up, but here she became a stablemaid."

"Does she go out with boys?"

"Yes, but not seriously. She'll marry some boor, and that will be it."

"She will give you grandchildren."

"For this I have no feeling at all."

"Who is your present lover?"

Freidl was silent for a while. "Oh, there is one. A lawyer, an *orech-din*. He has a wife and children. When I want him he's here, and when I don't want him he's off. Tobias wouldn't divorce me anyhow. I am past forty, and the great desire is over. Once, I had a passion for my work; now even this isn't what it used to be. I would like to write a novel, but no one is waiting for my fiction. Besides, I am actually left without a language. Hebrew is not my mother tongue. To write in Yiddish here makes no sense. I know French fluently, but I haven't used it in years. My English is quite good, but not good enough for writing. Anyhow, I'm not going to become your competitor. Lean back and try to sleep."

"I assure you, I'm not sleepy."

"If you had come a few years sooner, I might have started something with you, but for some time now I've had the feeling that it's late for everything. Perhaps this is the beginning of my menopause, or a presage of death. This daughter has robbed me of all my joy."

"Really, you should be psychoanalyzed."

"What? I don't believe in it. It wouldn't help. All my life I've had one main neurosis and a lot of little ones I called the 'candidates.' When one stepped out, another rose to take its place. They kept on changing, like a clique of politicians. One became the leader for a few years, and then he handed over power to the next. In a few cases, something like a court revolution occurred. This with my daughter is relatively new, but not so new. It grew like a cancer, and I felt it growing."

"What is it that you want of her?"

"That she should love me."

"And what will this bring you?"

"I'm asking you."

I leaned back and began to doze.

3.

I was neither awake nor asleep. I dreamed, and in the middle of my dreams I opened one eye and saw the moon had vanished. The black night lay heavily over the earth, and it reminded me of the darkness in the beginning of creation before God said, "Let there be light!" The insects had become silent. Freidl drove quickly, and I had the uncanny feeling that we were sliding downhill into an abyss. The glowing tip of her cigarette shook upward, downward, sidewise. She seemed to be signaling to someone in a fiery code. You never know who is going to be your angel of death, I thought. It's Freidl from Jadow. I slept again and saw craggy mountains and shadowy giants. They tried to lay a bridge from summit to summit. They spoke an ancient tongue in booming voices and reached out long arms to the edge of the horizon. Below, waters were raging, foaming, throwing up boulders. "Can this be the river Sambation?" I asked myself. "In that case, it's not just a legend. . . ." I opened my eyes, and from behind a hill the sun emerged, bathed and Biblical, casting a light that was neither night nor day. In my half sleep, this scene was somehow connected with the priests' blessing of the Jews, which one is not permitted to look upon lest one become blind. I dozed again.

Freidl woke me. We had arrived at the kibbutz. In the twilight of dawn I saw cactus trees gleaming with dew, beds of flowers, and huts with open doors from which half-dressed men and women came out. They were all sunburned, almost black. Some carried towels, cakes of soap, toothbrushes. Freidl said to me, "You slept like a god."

She took my arm and led me on a narrow path overgrown with wet grass. She knocked at a door, and when no one responded she knocked louder. I heard a hoarse voice, and Freidl answered. The door opened and out came a man with disheveled black hair streaked with white, barefoot, in an unbuttoned shirt that exposed a hairy chest. One side of his face was more wrinkled that the other—raw and red as from a rash. He held up his pants with one hand. "Can this be Tobias?" I asked myself. He had broad shoulders, a thick nose, and a heavily veined neck.

Freidl said to him, "Forgive me for waking you. I brought you a guest."

I was beginning to find some resemblance between this elderly person and Tobias from Jadow. But he blinked sleepily and did not recognize me.

Freidl smiled. "It's Itche the rabbi's, from Jadow."

"Itche," Tobias repeated and stood there bewildered, with his hand on his unbuttoned pants. After a while, he embraced me with his free hand. We kissed, and his beard pricked me like nails.

Freidl said, "I want to see Rina. I will just take a look at her. We have to go straight back."

"Rina isn't home," Tobias answered hesitantly, in a flat voice.

Freidl became tense. "Where is she?"

"Not home."

"Where?"

"With a girlfriend."

"Who? You're lying."

Husband and wife began to bicker in Hebrew. I heard Tobias say, "She is with her mentor."

"With her mentor? In the middle of the night?"

"With her mentor," Tobias repeated.

"Are you crazy, or do you think that I am?"

"She sleeps there." Tobias spoke as if to himself.

Although the sun threw purple flecks on Freidl's face, I saw that she paled. Her lips trembled. Her expression became angry, aggrieved. She said, "A girl of sixteen goes to sleep at a boy's? You shame me before Itche."

"She learned it from her mother." Tobias's eyes beneath his bushy brows were piercing and cold. I saw in them even an expression of mockery. I stepped back. Tobias made a sign with his hand that I should wait. He smiled, and for the first time I really recognized the Tobias from Jadow. He went inside.

Freidl called a name after him. She turned to me. "He's mad. A mad degenerate."

We stood still, apart from one another. Tobias was not in a hurry to come out. Freidl's face seemed set and older. "It's all malice. To spite me, he's making a whore of his daughter. Well, I have no more daughter."

"Perhaps it isn't true."

"Come, let's see."

Freidl walked in front of me, and I followed. My pants and socks became wet with dew. We passed a truck into which men with bare chests were loading crates of live chickens. They clucked in their sleep. We approached a building that looked halfway between a hayloft and a watchtower. There was a weathercock on its cone roof. This was where the mentor lived. A ladder led up to the entrance. Freidl called, "Rina!" Her voice sounded shrill, with a tremor of crying. She called many times, but no one looked out from the open window. Freidl gave me a sidewise glance, as if to ask, "Should I climb up?"

I felt cold; my knees were shaky. It all seemed

without substance—one of those nightmares that
vanish as soon as one wakens. I wanted to tell Freidl
there was no purpose in standing here; it would be
best to go back, but at that moment the face of a girl
appeared. It passed like a shadow. Freidl must have
seen it also. She stood openmouthed. This was no
longer the doctor who had spoken those clever words
this night but a shocked Jewish mother. It seemed
that she wanted to cry out, but she was silent. It was
not full day, and a mist drifted from somewhere. I
said, "Come, Freidl, it makes no sense."

"Yes, you are right."

I was apprehensive that Freidl would take me
back to Tobias's house and begin to quarrel with
him, but she led me in another direction. She walked
so quickly I could barely follow her. We passed the
empty dining hall. Naked bulbs lighted the room. A
girl was spreading paper on narrow tables. A boy
washed the stone floor with a rag mop. The air was
pungent with disinfectant. Soon we reached Freidl's
car.

She drove fast. I leaned back and stared ahead. It
was cold and I shivered. I turned up the collar of my
jacket. Thank God I have no daughters, I thought. In
the east, a cloud spread out like a huge bed of fiery
coals. A long row of birds flew by screeching. We
passed a flock of sheep that seemed to be feeding on
the sandy soil of a barren field. Although I had
doubts about God, His mercy, and Providence, passages from the Bible came to my mind—Isaiah's
admonitions of doom: "A sinful nation, a people
laden with iniquity, a seed of evildoers. . . . They
have forsaken the Lord. They have provoked the
Holy One of Israel. . . ." I had an urge to prove to
Freidl that she was using a double standard—one
for herself and a different one for others—but I knew
that her contradictions were also my contradictions.
The powers that rule history had brought us back to
the land of our ancestors, but we had already defiled

it with abominations. The sun became hot and sul-
phurous yellow. Sparks and little flames fell from it,
as from a torch. It threw a light shadowy and gloomy,
as at a time of eclipse. A dry wind blew from the
desert, sweeping in fine sand. Freidl's face became
ashen gray and sunken. At this moment I saw in her
a resemblance to her mother, Deborah Ita.

We pulled up to a gas station with a sign in
Hebrew, and Freidl said to me, "Where shall we go
from here? If this is a mentor, everything is lost. I
am cured, cured forever!"

Translated by the author and Evelyn Torton Beck

Pigeons

When his wife died, Professor Vladislav Eibeschutz had only his books and his birds left. He had resigned as Professor of History at Warsaw University because he could no longer bear the hooliganism of the students, who belonged to the Orzel Polski fraternity. They would come to class wearing their gold-embroidered fraternity caps, flaunting heavy canes, always ready to provoke a fight. For some reason that Professor Eibeschutz had never been able to fathom, most of them had red faces, pimply necks, snub noses, and square jaws, as if their common hatred of the Jew had turned them into members of the same family. Even their voices demanding that Jewish students sit on ghetto benches sounded alike.

Vladislav Eibeschutz had retired on a small pension. It was barely enough for rent and food, but what else does one need in one's old age? His half-blind maid, Tekla, was a Polish peasant woman. The professor had long since stopped paying her wages. She cooked for both of them the soups and stews they could eat without teeth. Neither one of them needed to buy new clothes, not even a pair of shoes. Suits, coats, shabby furs, as well as Mrs. Eibeschutz's dresses were left from the old days. Everything had been carefully packed away in mothballs.

Over the years the professor's library had grown so large that all the walls from floor to ceiling were covered with bookshelves. There were books and manuscripts in the clothes closets, in trunks, in the cellar and the attic. As long as Mrs. Eibeschutz had been alive, she had occasionally tried to make some order. The books had been dusted and aired. Those

with broken covers or backs had been repaired.
Manuscripts no longer of any use had been burned
in the stove. But after her death the household was
neglected. The professor had by now also collected
about a dozen cages of birds—parrots, parakeets,
canaries. He had always loved birds and the doors of
their cages stood open so that the birds could fly
around freely. Tekla complained that she couldn't
clean after them, but the professor would say: "Little
fool, everything that belongs to God's creatures is
clean."

And as if this were not enough, the professor daily
fed the pigeons of the street. Each morning and
afternoon the neighbors would see him come out
with a bag of feed. He was a small man with a bent
back, a sparse beard, which from white had turned
back to yellowish again, a crooked nose, and a sunken
mouth. His thick-lensed spectacles made his brown
eyes under their bushy brows appear larger and
somewhat crossed. He always wore the same greenish surtout and shoes with elastic inserts and rounded
toes, of a style that was no longer made. Unruly
strands of white hair escaped from his small, round
cap. The moment the professor came through his
front gate, even before he began to call "dush-dush-
dush" (the signal for summoning pigeons, as "zip-zip-
zip" is for chickens), flocks of pigeons converged
from all sides. They had been waiting on the old tile
roofs and in the trees around the Hospital for Skin
Diseases. The street where the professor lived started
at Nowy Swiat Boulevard and slanted its way down
toward the Vistula. In the summertime grass sprouted
between the cobblestones. There was little traffic
here. Once in a while a hearse would come to pick up
the corpse of some patient who had died of syphilis
or lupus, or a police wagon would bring a group of
prostitutes picked up for venereal diseases. In some
of the courtyards hand water pumps were still in
use. The tenants were mostly old people who seldom

went out. The pigeons could escape the noise of the city here.

The professor would tell Tekla that the feeding of pigeons meant the same to him as going to church or synagogue. God is not hungry for praise, but the pigeons wait each day from sunrise to be fed. There is no better way to serve the Creator than to be kind to His creatures.

The professor did not only derive pleasure from feeding the hungry pigeons. He learned from them. He had once read an excerpt from the Talmud in which the Jews were likened to pigeons, and only lately had he grasped the meaning of the comparison. Pigeons have no weapons in the fight for survival. They sustain themselves almost entirely on the scraps that people throw them. They fear noise, flee the smallest dog. They don't even chase away the sparrows that steal their food. The pigeon, like the Jew, thrives on peace, quietude, and good will. But every rule has its exceptions. Among the pigeons, as among the Jews, one finds belligerent specimens, who deny their heritage. There were pigeons who drove the others away, pecked at them and grabbed the seed before they could get to it. Professor Eibeschutz had left the university not only because of the anti-Semitic students but also because of the Jewish Communist students who used the Jew-baiting of the others for their own propaganda purposes.

In the many years that Professor Eibeschutz had studied, taught, rummaged around in archives, and written for scientific journals, he had continued to search for a meaning, a philosophy of history, a law that would explain where mankind was heading and the drive behind man's constant wars. There had been a time when the professor had leaned toward a materialistic interpretation of events. He had admired Lucretius, Diderot, Vogt, Feuerbach. He had briefly even believed in Karl Marx. But that youth-

ful period had passed quickly. Now the professor had
gone to the opposite extreme. One did not need to be
a believer to see the purpose in nature, the truth of
so-called teleology, so taboo in science. Yes, there
was a plan in nature even though it often appeared
to us as total chaos. All of us were needed: Jews,
Christians, Moslems, an Alexander the Great, a
Charlemagne, a Napoleon, even a Hitler. But why
and for what? What can the Godhead achieve by
letting cat eat mouse, hawks kill rabbits, and Polish fraternity students attack Jews?

Of late the professor had as good as given up the
study of history. In his old age he had come to the
conclusion that his real interests lay in biology and
zoology. He had acquired a number of books on
animals and birds. Despite the fact that he suffered
from glaucoma and had almost no sight in his right
eye, he had bought himself an old microscope. His
studies had no professional purpose. He read for his
own edification, in the same way as pious boys read
the Talmud, even nodding and chanting as they do.
Or, he would pull a hair from his beard, place it on a
slide and inspect it through the microscope. Each
hair had its complicated mechanism. A leaf, an
onion peel, a bit of moist earth from one of Tekla's
flowerpots revealed beauties and harmonies that
revived his spirit. Professor Eibeschutz sat at this
microscope, the canaries sang, the parakeets twittered,
talked, kissed, the parrots chattered, calling each
other monkey, sonny boy, glutton, in Tekla's village
dialect. It was not easy to have faith in God's benev-
olence, but God's wisdom shone in each blade of
grass, each fly, each blossom and mite.

Tekla entered. She was small, pockmarked, with
thinning hair, a mixture of straw and gray. She had
on a faded dress and wornout slippers. From above
her high cheekbones there peered a pair of slanting
eyes, green as those of a cat. She dragged one foot.
She suffered from aches in her joints and treated her

ailment with salves and ointments obtained from
quacks. She went to church to light candles for her
saints.

"I've boiled the milk," she said.

"I don't want any."

"Shall I add a pinch of coffee?"

"No, Tekla, thank you. I want nothing."

"Your throat will get dry."

"Where is it written that the throat has to be
moist?"

Tekla made no reply, but she didn't leave. When
Mrs. Eibeshutz had been on her deathbed, Tekla had
sworn that she would take care of the professor.
After a while the professor lifted himself out of the
chair. He sat on a special pillow so that his hemorrhoids would not become irritated.

"You're still here, Tekla? You're as stubborn as
my late wife, may she rest in peace."

"It's time for the professor's medicine."

"What medicine? Silly woman. No heart can pump
forever."

The professor placed his magnifying glass on the
opened page of *The Birds of Poland* and went to take
a look at his own birds.

The feeding of the street pigeons was sheer pleasure, but the caring of scores of birds who lived in
open cages and were free to fly around the apartment at will was fraught with effort and responsibility. It was not only a matter of cleaning up for Tekla.
Not a day passed without some calamity. A parakeet
would get stuck behind a bookcase and would have
to be rescued. The males fought. A female's newly
laid eggs were damaged. The professor had segre-
gated the various species in separate rooms, but
Tekla would forget and leave a door ajar. It was
springtime and the windows could not be opened.
The air smelled stale and sweetish from the bird
droppings. As a rule birds sleep at night, but it

would happen that a parrot, awakened by some birdish nightmare, would fly blindly around in the dark. The lights had to be turned on so that it would not kill itself. Nevertheless, what joy these creatures gave Professor Eibeschutz in return for the few grains they ate! One of the parakeets had learned scores of words and even whole sentences. It would make its perch on the professor's bald spot, peck at the lobe of his ear, climb onto a stem of his spectacles, and even stand like an acrobat on the professor's index finger as he wrote. In his years of experience with birds, Professor Eibeschutz had convinced himself of how complicated these beings were, how rich in character and individuality. After observing a bird for years, he could still be surprised by its antics.

The professor was especially pleased by the fact that these creatures had no sense of history. What was past was past. All adventures were immediately forgotten. Each day was a new beginning. Even so there were exceptions. The professor had seen a male parakeet pine away after it's mate's death. He had noted among his birds instances of infatuation, jealousy, inhibition, even murder and suicide. He would watch them for hours. There was purpose in their God-given senses, their instincts, in the construction of their wings, in the way they hatched their eggs, molted, changed colors. How did all this work? Heritage? What were the chromosomes, the genes?

Since his wife's death the professor had gotten into the habit of talking to himself or to those who had long since died. He would say to Darwin: "No, Charles, your theories don't solve the riddle. Nor do yours, Monsieur Lamarck."

That afternoon, having taken his medicine, the professor filled a bag with linseed, millet, and dried peas, and went out to feed the pigeons. Although it was May, it had rained and a cold wind blew from the Vistula. Now the rain had stopped and sunlight cut through the clouds like a heavenly ax. The moment Professor Eibeschutz appeared, pigeons swooped down from all sides. Some, in their haste, flapped against the professor's hat, almost pushing it off his head. He realized that he had not brought enough food for such a throng. He took care to spread out the grain so that the pigeons would not fight each other, but soon they formed a jostling mass. Some were landing on the backs of others to force their way to an opening. The street was too narrow for this great flock of birds. "The poor things are hungry," Professor Eibeschutz muttered to himself. He knew full well that his feedings could not solve their problem. The more you fed them, the more they multiplied. He had read that somewhere in Australia the pigeons had grown so numerous that roofs had collapsed under their weight. In the long run, no one can outsmart the laws of nature. But neither could the professor let these creatures starve.

Professor Eibeschutz returned to his front hall, where he kept a sack of feed, and refilled his bag. "I hope they wait," he muttered. When he came out, the birds were still there. "Thank God," he said, somewhat embarrassed by the religious implication of his words. He began to throw out the feed, but his hand trembled and the kernels scattered too close to him. Pigeons perched on his shoulders, on his arms, fluttering their wings and pecking at him with their beaks. One bold pigeon tried to land on the edge of the feed bag itself.

Suddenly a stone hit Professor Eibeschutz on the forehead. For a moment he didn't realize what had happened. Then he was hit by two more; one struck his elbow and the other his neck. The pigeons rose all together. Somehow the professor managed to get back to his house. He had read frequently in the newspapers about attacks on Jews by hoodlums in the Saxony Gardens and in the suburbs. But it had never happened to him before. At that moment he did not know which was the greater hurt, the ache in his forehead or his shame. "Have we reached so low," he murmured. Tekla must have seen what had happened through the window. She ran to him with outspread arms and green with anger. She cursed, hissed, and rushed to the kitchen to wet a towel in cold water. The professor had removed his hat and was fingering the bump on his head. Tekla led him to his bedroom, removed his coat, and made him lie down. As she ministered to him, she cursed continuously. "Punish them, God. Punish them, Father in heaven. May they burn in hell. May their guts rot, a black plague on them!"

"Enough, Tekla, enough."

"If this is our Poland, it should go up in flames."

"There are many good people in Poland."

"Dregs, whores, leprous dogs!"

Tekla went out, probably to call the police. The professor heard her screaming and complaining to the neighbors. After a while all was quiet. She seemed not to have gotten to the police, because he heard her return alone. She puttered around the kitchen, mumbling and cursing. The professor closed his eyes. "Sooner or later you have to feel everything on your own skin," he thought. "In what way am I better than the other victims? Such is history, and that is what I've occupied myself with all my years."

A Hebrew word he had long since forgotten came suddenly to the professor's mind: *reshayim,* the wicked. It is the wicked who make history.

The professor lay for a moment amazed. In one second he had found an answer for which he had been searching for years. Like the apple that Newton had seen falling from the tree, the stone thrown by a hoodlum had revealed to him, Eibeschutz, a truth valid for all times. It was exactly as written in the Old Testament. Each generation has its men of falsehood and bloodshed. Villains cannot rest. Whether it be war or revolution, whether they fight under one flag or another, no matter what their slogan, their aim remains the same—to perpetrate evil, cause pain, shed blood. One common aim united Alexander of Macedonia and Hamilcar, Genghis Khan and Charlemagne, Chmielnitzki and Napoleon, Robespierre and Lenin. Too simple? The principle of gravitation was also simple and that is why it took so long to discover it.

Dusk fell. Vladislav Eibeschutz began to doze off. Just before he fell asleep, he said to himself, "Still, it can't be that simple."

In the evening, Tekla got some ice and made the professor a fresh compress. She wanted to call a doctor, but he wouldn't permit her to. He would be ashamed before the doctor and the neighbors. Tekla cooked some oatmeal for him. Usually, before he retired for the night, the professor would examine all the cages, put in fresh water, add grain and vegetables, and change the sand. This evening he relied on Tekla to take over. She had turned off the lights. Some of the parakeets in his bedroom remained in their cages. Others slept perched on the curtain rod. Though the professor was tired, he could not fall asleep immediately. The area over his good eye was swollen and he could barely move the lid. I hope I don't go completely blind, he implored the powers that rule the world. If I must be blind, I would rather be dead.

He fell asleep and dreamed of strange lands, places he had never seen, mountains, valleys, gardens with huge trees, and exotic flower beds. "Where am I?" he asked himself in his dream. "In Italy? In Persia? Afghanistan?" The earth below him moved as if he were traveling in an airplane. He was, however, not in a plane. He seemed to be hanging in space. "Am I out of reach of the earth's gravitation? How did it happen? There is no atmosphere here. I hope I don't choke."

He awoke and for a moment didn't remember where he was. He felt the compress. "Why is my head bandaged?" he wondered. Suddenly everything came back to him. "Yes, history is made by the wicked. I have found the Newtonian formula of history. I will have to rewrite my work." He suddenly felt an ache in his left side. He lay listening to the pulse of pain in his chest. There were special pills for his attacks of angina pectoris, but he had them in a drawer in his study. Stephanie, his late wife, had given him a little bell to call Tekla if he should feel ill during the night. But Professor Eibeschutz was reluctant to use it. He was even hesitant about putting on his night lamp. The birds were frightened by light and noise. Tekla must be tired after her day's work and the unpleasant experience. The attack of the hoodlums had upset her even more than it had him. What else did she have, excepting those few hours of sleep? No husband, no children, no relatives, no friends. He had willed her his possessions. But what were they worth? Of what value were his unpublished manuscripts? The new formula. . . .

For a while it seemed to Professor Eibeschutz that the stabbing in his chest was becoming less painful. Then he felt a violent cutting in his heart, his shoulder, his arm, his ribs. He stretched his hand out toward the bell, but his fingers went limp before he could reach it. He had never imagined that such pain could be possible. It was as if his heart were being squeezed in a fist. He choked and gasped. A last thought ran through his mind. What will happen to the pigeons?

Early the next morning when Tekla went to the professor's room, she could hardly recognize him. The figure she saw was no longer the professor, but a kind of grotesque doll: yellow as clay, stiff as bone, with a gaping mouth, a disfigured nose, his beard pointing upward, the lids of one eye stuck together, the other eye half open in an otherworld smile. A hand with waxen fingers lay on the pillow.

Tekla began to scream. Neighbors came running in. Someone called an ambulance. The sound of its siren was soon heard, but the intern who entered the room glanced toward the bed and shook his head. "We can't help him any more."

"They killed him, killed him," Tekla wailed. "They threw stones at him. They should drop dead, the murderers, a black curse, a cholera on them, the wicked devils!"

"Who are *they?*" the doctor asked.

"They're our own Polish cutthroats, hooligans, beasts, killers," Tekla answered.

"A Jew, huh?"

"Yes, a Jew."

"Well. . . ."

All but forgotten when he had been alive, the professor found fame in death. Delegations arrived from the Warsaw University, the Free University, the Historic Society, and various other organizations, groups, brotherhoods, and societies. The Department of History of the Universities of Kracow, Lemberg, Vilna wired that they were sending their representatives to the funeral. The professor's apartment was filled with flowers. Professors, writers, students kept an honor watch over the body. Since the professor was a Jew, the Jewish burial society sent two men to recite psalms over the dead man. The frightened birds flew from wall to wall, from bookcase to bookcase, tried to rest on lamps, cornices, draperies. Tekla wanted to shoo them back into their cages but they flew away from her. Some disappeared through the doors and windows carelessly left open. One of the parrots screeched the same word over and over in a tone of alarm and admonishment. The telephone rang continuously. The officers of the Jewish community were demanding payment in advance for the burial plot and a Polish major, a former student of the professor's, was threatening them with dire consequences.

The next morning, a Jewish hearse came up the street, the horses draped and hooded in black, with openings only for their eyes. When the coffin was carried out of the house and the funeral cortege began to move downhill toward Tamki Avenue and the Old City, flocks of pigeons began to fly in over the roofs. Their numbers increased so rapidly that they covered the sky between the buildings on either side of the narrow street and darkened the day as if during an eclipse. They paused, suspended in the air for a moment, then, in a body, kept pace with the procession by circling around it.

The delegations, which walked slowly behind the hearse carrying beribboned wreaths, looked up in wonderment. The inhabitants of the street, the old and the sick who had come out to pay the professor their last respects, crossed themselves. A miracle was taking place before their eyes as in Biblical times. Tekla, lifting up her arms from under the black shawl, cried out, "Jesus!"

The throngs of pigeons escorted the hearse until it emerged on Browarna Street. As they circled, their wings, alternating between sun and shadow, became red as blood and then dark as lead. It was obvious that the birds were maneuvering to fly neither ahead nor behind the procession. It was not until they reached the intersection of Furmanska and Marienstadt that the pigeons made one last circle and in a mass turned back—a winged host that had accompanied their benefactor to his eternal rest.

The following morning broke autumn-like and drab. The skies hung low and rusty. The smoke of the chimneys dropped back, gathering on the tile

roofs. A thin rain fell, prickly as needles. During the
night someone had painted a swastika on the professor's door. Tekla came out with a bag of feed, but
only a few pigeons flew down. They pecked at the
food hesitantly, glancing around as if afraid to be
caught defying some avian ban. The small of char
and rot come up from the gutter, the acrid stench of
imminent destruction.

Translated by the author and Elizabeth Shub

The Chimney Sweep

There are knocks and knocks. A knock on the head is no joke. The brain is a delicate thing, or why would the soul be lodged in the brain? Why not in the liver or, if you pardon me, the gut? You can see the soul in the eyes. The eyes are little windows for the soul to look out of.

We had a chimney sweep in town, nicknamed Black Yash. All chimney sweeps are black—what else can they be?—but Yash looked as though he had been born black. His hair was spiky and black as pitch. His eyes were black, and his skin could never be washed free of soot. Only his teeth were white. His father had been the town's chimney sweep, and Yash inherited the job. He was already a full-grown man, but he wasn't married and lived with his old mother, Maciechowa.

He came to us once a month, barefoot, and every step would leave a black mark on the floor. My mother, may she rest in peace, would run to meet him and let him come no further. He was paid by the town, but the women would hand him a groschen or a slice of bread after he had done his work. That was the custom. Children were terrified of him, although he never harmed anyone. And while he was the chimney sweep, the chimneys never caught fire. On Sundays, like all Gentiles, he would wash up and go to church with his mother. But, washed, he seemed even blacker than before; maybe that's why he had never found a wife.

One Monday—I remember it as yesterday—Feitel the water carrier came in and told us that Yash had fallen off Tevye Boruch's roof. Tevye Boruch owned a two-story house in the market square. Everybody felt sorry for the chimney sweep. Yash had always clambered over the roofs as nimbly as a cat, but if a man is fated to suffer a misfortune, it cannot be avoided. And it had to be the tallest building in town, too. Feitel said that Yash had struck his head, but had not broken any limbs. Someone had taken him home. He lived on the outskirts of town, near the woods, in a ramshackle hut.

For a while nobody heard of Yash. But what did a chimney sweep matter? If he could no longer work, the town would hire someone else. Then one day Feitel came again, with two pails of water on his yoke, and said to my mother, "Feige Braine, did you hear the news? Yash the chimney sweep has turned into a mind reader." My mother laughed and spat. "What sort of a joke is that?" she asked. "It's no joke, Feige Braine," he said. "It's no joke at all. He is lying on his cot with a bandaged head and guessing everybody's secrets." "Have you gone crazy?" my mother scolded. Soon the whole town was talking about it. The knock on Yash's head had loosened some screw in his brain, and he became a seer.

We had a teacher in town, Nochem Mecheles, and he called Yash a diviner. Who had ever heard of such a thing? If a knock on the head could make a man a seer, there would have been hundreds of them in every town. But people had gone there and witnessed it with their own eyes. A man would take a fistful of coins from his pocket and ask, "Yash, what have I got in my hand?" And Yash would say, "So many three-groschen coins, so many fours, sixes, kopecks." The coins would be counted, and everything was right to the last groschen. Another man would ask, "What did I do last week at this time in Lublin?" And Yash would say that he had gone to a tavern with two other men. He described them as if they were standing before him.

When the doctor and the town authorities heard

the story, they came running. Maciechowa's hovel
was tiny and so low that the visitors' hats touched
the ceiling. They started questioning him, and he
had all the answers. The priest became alarmed; the
peasants had begun to say that Yash was a saint. A
little more, and they would have started taking him
around on pilgrimages, like an icon. But the doctor
said he was not to be moved. Besides, no one had
ever seen Yash in church except on Sundays.

Well, there he was lying on his pallet, talking like
an ordinary fellow—eating, drinking, playing with
the dog his mother kept. But he knew everything:
what people had in their breast pockets and in their
trouser pockets; where this one had hidden his money;
how much that one had squandered on drink the day
before yesterday.

When his mother saw the rush of visitors, she
began to charge an admission price of a kopeck per
head. She got it, too. The doctor wrote a letter to
Lublin. The mayor of the town sent in a—what do
you call it, now?—a report, and highly placed per-
sonages came down from Zamosc and Lublin. The
governor himself was said to have sent a deputy.
The mayor became frightened and ordered all the
streets cleaned up. The marketplace was swept so
clean that not a stick or a straw remained on the
ground. The town hall was hastily whitewashed.
And all because of whom? Yash the chimney sweep.
The house of Gitel the innkeeper was in an uproar—
who had ever dreamed of such important guests?

The entire company set off to see Yash in his hut.
They questioned him, and the things he said struck
fear into the hearts of the officials. Who knows what
such people can be guilty of? They all took bribes,
and he told them so. What does a chimney sweep
understand? The most important visitor—I forget
his name—insisted that Yash was crazy and should
be sent to an asylum. But our doctor argued that the
patient could not travel, it would kill him.

It was rumored that the doctor and the governor's deputy had strong words, and it had almost come to blows. But our doctor was an official himself; he was the county doctor, and he sat on the draft board. He was a hard man—nobody could ever buy him off, so he had no fear of Yash's second sight. Anyway, the doctor won out. But afterward the deputy reported that Yash was insane, and he must have complained against the doctor, because he was soon transferred to another district.

In the meantime, Yash's head healed and he went back to sweeping chimneys. But he kept his strange powers. He would come into a house for his groschen, and the women would ask him, "Yash, what's there, in the left-hand drawer?" or, "What do I have in my fist?" or, "What did I eat yesterday at supper?" And he would tell everything. They asked him, "Yash, how do you know such things?" He'd shrug his shoulders: "I just know. It comes from the knock on the head." And he would point to his temple. He could have been taken to the big cities and people would have bought tickets to see him, but who thought of bothering with such things?

There were several thieves in town. They stole laundry from attics, and whatever else they could lay their hands on. Now they could no longer steal. The victim would come to Yash, and he would tell him the name of the thief and the place where the goods were hidden. The peasants in nearby villages learned about Yash, and whenever a horse was stolen, the owner came to him to find out where it was. Several thieves were already in jail. The thieves had an eye on him and warned openly that he was a marked man. But Yash knew all their plans beforehand. They came to beat him up one night, but he had hidden himself in a neighbor's barn. They would throw stones at him, but he would jump aside or duck even before the stone came flying.

People mislaid things—money, jewelry—and Yash

always told them where they were. He didn't even
stop to think. If a child got lost, the mother ran to
Yash, and he would lead her to her child. The
thieves began to say that he had stolen the child
himself, but nobody believed them. He was not even
paid for his advice. His mother demanded money,
but he himself was a halfwit. He never rightly knew
the value of a coin.

We had a rabbi in town, Reb Arele. He had come
from a big city. On the Great Sabbath before Passover he preached in the synagogue. And what did he
talk about? Yash the chimney sweep. The unbelievers, he said, deny that Moses was a prophet. They
say that everything must be according to reason.
Yet how does Yash the chimney sweep know that
Itte Chaye the bagel baker has dropped her wedding
ring into the well? And if Yash the chimney sweep
can know hidden things, how can anyone doubt the
powers of the saints? There were some heretics in
our town, but even they had no answer.

In the meantime, news about Yash had reached
Warsaw and other places. The newspapers wrote
about him. And a commission was sent down from
Warsaw. The mayor again sent out the town crier to
order the yards and houses cleaned up. The marketplace was swept again till it was spick-and-span.
After Sukkoth, the rains began. We had only one
paved street—the church street. Boards and logs
were laid out everywhere so that the gentry from
Warsaw would not have to wade through mud. Gitel
the innkeeper prepared pallets and bedding. The
whole town was agog. Yash was the only one who
made nothing of it. He went his rounds and swept
the chimneys as usual. He did not even have sense
enough to be afraid of the Warsaw officials.

Now listen to this: A day before the commission
arrived, there was a snowfall and a sudden frost. On
the previous night, sparks and even tongues of flame
had been seen flying from Chaim the baker's chim-

ney. A baker's oven burns for many hours, and a lot of soot settles in the chimney. As Yash was climbing down, he slipped and fell again. Again he struck his head, but not as hard as the first time. There wasn't even any blood. He picked himself up and went home.

My dear friends, the next day, when the commission arrived and began to question Yash, he did not know anything. The first knock had opened something up, and the second knock closed it. The gentry asked how much money they had, what they had done yesterday, what they had eaten a week ago at the same time, but Yash only grinned like a fool and answered, "I don't know."

The officials were furious. They scolded the police chief and the new doctor. They demanded to know why they had been brought all that way to see this nitwit, this bumpkin who was nothing but an ordinary chimney sweep.

The police chief and the others swore that Yash had known everything only a day or two before, but the visitors would not listen. Somebody told them that Yash had fallen off a roof and banged his head again, but you know how people are: They believe only what they see. The police chief came over to Yash and started banging him on the head with his fist. Maybe the screw would fly loose again. But once the little door in the brain is shut, it stays shut.

The commission returned to Warsaw and denied the story from beginning to end. Yash went on sweeping chimneys for another year or two. Then an epidemic broke out in town, and he died.

The brain is full of all sorts of little doors and chambers. Sometimes a knock on the head upsets the whole business. Still, all of it has to do with the soul. Without the soul, the head would be no wiser than the foot.

Translated by Mirra Ginsburg

The Riddle

The day before Yom Kippur, Oyzer-Dovidl opened his eyes even before the morning star had appeared. On its perch the white rooster, soon to be slaughtered in atonement for his owner's sins, started crowing fiercely. Nechele's white hen clucked softly. Nechele got out of bed and lit a candle. Barefoot and in her nightgown, she opened squeaky bureau drawers, flung open closets, burrowed around in trunks. Oyzer-Dovidl watched with astonishment as she puttered around laying out petticoats, linen, odds and ends. No one airs out clothing on the day before Yom Kippur. But when Nechele wanted something, she didn't ask permission. It was months now since she had stopped shaving her head. Strands of black hair stuck out from under her kerchief. One strap of her nightgown had slipped down, revealing a breast white as milk with a rosy nipple. True, she was his wife, but such behavior ends in evil thoughts.

Lately, Oyzer-Dovidl had no idea how he stood with his wife. She had not gone to the ritual bath as she ought. She had baffled him with constant evasions, with different counts of the days of her period. "Well, today's the day before Yom Kippur!" he warned himself. There was a time when he would have lectured her, tried to win her over with tender words and parables, as the holy books advise. But he had given up. She remained stubborn. Sometimes it seemed as if she simply wanted to make him angry. But why? He loved her, he was faithful to her. When they had married, instead of his boarding with her parents as was customary, she had lived at his parents' expense. And now that they were no longer alive, he supported her from his inheritance. What made her defy him? Why did she bicker with him constantly about meaningless trifles? May the Lord in heaven grant her pardon, he thought. May her heart this Yom Kippur be changed for the better.

"Nechele!"

She turned to face him. She had a thin nose, lips that parted over pearly teeth, brows that grew together. In her black eyes an angry light burned constantly.

"What do you want?"

"It's the day before Yom Kippur!"

"Well? What do you want? Leave me alone!"

"Hurry and finish what you're doing. A day is soon gone. You'll profane the holy day. God forbid."

"Don't worry. You won't roast for my sins."

"Nechele, one must repent."

"If someone has to—you do it."

"Oy, oy, Nichele. We don't live forever."

She laughed insolently. "The little life we have . . . it's still too much!"

Oyzer-Dovidl threw up his hands. It was impossible to talk to her. She answered everything with mockery. He was determined, for his part, to keep his mouth shut. He thought of excuses for her. She must be angry because she did not become pregnant, because after their first child died—might he intercede for them in heaven—her womb had closed. "Well, repentance and prayer and charity are a help in everything!" he told himself.

Oyzer-Dovidl was a puny man. Though he would be twenty-four next Hoshana Rabbah, he still did not have a proper beard; only here and there a few hairs had sprouted. His earlocks were scant, thin, and blond as strands of flax. He was still slight as a schoolboy, with a scrawny neck, pointed chin, sunken cheeks. The clothes his parents had ordered for his wedding, expecting him to grow to fit them, were still too long and baggy. His caftan reached to his

ankles; his fringed undervest was loose; even his
prayer shawl with its braided silver collarband was
too large.

And his thoughts were still childish, too. He imagined all kinds of things. He wondered, for example,
what would happen if he should sprout wings and
begin to fly like a bird. What would Nechele say?
Would she want to be his wife just the same, or
would she marry someone else? Or suppose he found
a cap that would make him invisible! He was
constantly remembering adventures from stories his
aunts had read or told him, though now Nechele was
involved in all of them. At night he dreamed of
gypsy women, of robbers in caves, of sacks full of
gold coins. Once it seemed to him that Nechele was
male, that he saw under her lace drawers the fringed
garment of a boy; but when he had tried to kiss her,
she had clambered to the roof, nimble as a chimney
sweep, and yelled down at him:

> *Kitchen cleaver,*
> *Pudding eater,*
> *Tumble down,*
> *Crack your crown.*

Oyzer-Dovidl did not have a free minute once he
got up. He had first to wash his hands and recite the
early-morning prayers. Next he had to perform the
sacrificial rite. Seizing the white rooster, he gripped
it by its trembling feet and whirled it about his
head. Then he sent it to the slaughterer to be killed
in atonement for his sins. He found this ceremonial
an ordeal: What fault was it of the rooster's?

After that he went to the Trisker prayerhouse.
Starting to pray, he felt ready to drive away all his
foolish ideas, but they fell on him like flies. As he
prayed, he sighed. He wanted to be a man of standing, but his head was full of distractions. A man
should love his wife, but to think of her night and

day was not right. He couldn't get her out of his
mind. He remembered her playful words when he
had come to her in bed on those days she was
ritually pure, and the outlandish nicknames she had
called him as she curled his earlocks, tickled him,
bit him, kissed him. The truth was he should never
have tolerated such loose behavior. If he had stopped
it at the start, he would not have slid into evil
thought.

Should a Jewish wife babble to her husband of
garters and laces and crinolines? Did she have to tell
him of the long stockings she had bought that reached
all the way up to her hips? Of what benefit were her
descriptions of the naked women she saw at the
ritual bath? She aped them all, describing their
hairy legs, flabby breasts, swollen bellies, mocking
the older ones, slandering the younger. She simply
wanted to prove that she was the prettiest. But that
had been months ago. Of late, she wouldn't let him
near her. She claimed she had cramps, or heartburn,
or back pains, or that she had discovered stains on
her linen. She used all kinds of pretexts and fine
points of law to keep him away. But he could not blot
out the images of the past.

Oyzer-Dovidl prayed hard, swaying back and forth,
waving his hands, stamping his feet. Occasionally
he bit his lips or his tongue in his excitement. When
the prayers had ended, the Hasidim refreshed themselves with honeycake and brandy. Oyzer-Dovidl did
not usually touch hard liquor but today he took
some, for it is considered a good deed to eat and
drink on the day before Yom Kippur. The brandy
burned his throat and made his nostrils tingle. His
mood brightened. He thought of what the Tchernobler
rabbi had said: Turn up your nose at the evil one.
Don't be like the *misnagdim,* those dour scholars
who tremble before hell. Samael does what is required of him. You do what is required of you.

Oyzer-Dovidl grew resolute. "I won't deny myself a drink of brandy ever again," he decided. "In heaven, the lowest joy is preferred to the most sublime melancholy."

Oyzer-Dovidl started home for his holiday dinner. At noon on the day before Yom Kippur, Nechele always prepared a feast: white rolls with honey, stewed prunes, soup and dumplings, meat with horseradish. But today when he got there, there was actually nothing to eat. Nechele even did not offer him a plate of gruel. Oyzer-Dovidl was not one to complain about his comfort, but such a meal on the day before Yom Kippur was a slap in the face. "What does she want? To destroy everything?" he thought. The house smelled of dust and moth flakes, unpleasant odors that made him want to sneeze. Nechele, in a red petticoat, was piling clothes on the sofa, the way she did before Passover when the walls were whitewashed. "Is she out of her mind?" Oyzer-Dovidl asked himself. He couldn't control his tongue any longer.

"What's going on, eh?"

"Nothing's going on. Don't meddle in household affairs."

"Who does such things on the day before Yom Kippur?"

"Whoever does, does."

"Do you want to ruin everything?"

"Maybe—"

Oyzer-Dovidl tried not to look at his wife, but his eyes were constantly drawn to her. Her calves shone under the short petticoat, and it irritated him to see her wearing a red one. Red stands for judgment, says the cabala; but Yom Kippur is the time of mercy. It was clear she was acting this way out of spite. But how had he sinned against her?

Although he was still hungry, Oyzer-Dovidl rinsed his hands and said the concluding grace. As he was reciting the blessing, he looked out the window.

Peasant wagons were driving by. A Gentile boy was flying a kite. He had always felt sorrow for those peoples of the world who had not accepted the Torah when the Lord approached them on Mount Seir and Mount Paran. During the Days of Awe, he was more than ever aware that the Gentiles were damned.

Across the street was a pig butcher's house. The hogs were slaughtered in the yard right behind the fence and scalded with boiling water. Dogs were always hanging around there barking. Bolek, one of the butcher's sons, who had become a petty clerk in the town hall, always used to pull the earlocks of the schoolboys, shouting obscenities after them. Today, the day before Yom Kippur, the men over there were carrying out hunks of pork through a gate in the fence and loading them onto a wagon. Oyzer-Dovidl shut his eyes. "Until when, O Lord, until when?" he murmured. "Let there finally be an end to this dark Exile. Let the Messiah have come. Let it grow light at last!"

Oyzer-Dovidl bowed his head. Ever since childhood he had absorbed himself in Jewish matters and yearned to be a saintly man. He had studied the Hasidic books, the morality books, and had even tried to find his way in the cabala. But Satan had blocked his path. Nechele and her wrath were an unmistakable sign that heaven was not pleased with him. A desire took hold of him to talk things out with her, to ask what she had against him, to remind her that the world endures through peace alone. But he knew what would happen: she would shriek and call him names. Nechele was still dragging out bundles of clothing, muttering angrily to herself. When the cat tried to rub against her ankles, she kicked it so that it scrambled away meowing. No, it was better to keep still.

Suddenly Oyzer-Dovidl clapped his hands to his forehead: the day was almost gone!

2.

Oyzer-Dovidl went to the synagogue. To have one-
self flogged on the day before Yom Kippur, though
typical of the *misnagdim,* was not customary among
the Hasidim. But Oyzer-Dovidl, after the afternoon
prayers, asked Getzl the sexton to flog him. He
stretched himself out in the vestibule like a boy.
Getzl stood over him with a leather strap and began
to strike him the thirty-nine times that the rule
prescribes. It didn't hurt. Whom was he fooling,
thought Oyzer-Dovidl. The Lord of the universe? He
wanted to ask Getzl to beat him harder, but was
ashamed to. "Oh, I deserve to be scourged with iron
rods," he moaned to himself.

While he was being flogged, Oyzer-Dovidl counted
up his sins. He had lusted after Nechele on her
unclean days, had unwittingly touched her with
pleasure. He had listened to her tales of events at
the pork butcher's; to her stories about the naked
women at the ritual bath and at the river, where the
younger ones bathed in the summertime. Nechele
had boasted to him constantly of how firm her breasts
were, how white her skin was, of how the other
women envied her. She had even remarked that
other men made eyes at her. "Well, 'Women are
frivolous,' " thought Oyzer-Dovidl, and he recalled
the saying in the Gemara: "A woman is jealous only
of the thigh of another."

After the flogging, he paid the sexton eighteen
groschen for the redemption of his soul, then started
home for the last meal before the fast. The sun was
flaming in the west. Beggars lined the streets behind their alms plates. Sitting on boxes, logs, foot-
stools were deformed persons of all kinds: blind ones,
dumb ones, cripples without hands, without feet, one
with his nose rotted away and a gaping hole instead
of a mouth. Though Oyzer-Dovidl had filled his

pockets with coins, he was soon without a penny. Still the beggars asked, demanded, called out after him, showing their wounds and holding up their plates. He was sorry he had not changed a bank note. "Why should I have money when some people live in such poverty?" he reproached himself. He made his excuses to the beggars, promising to return shortly.

He hurried toward home. Before his eyes he saw the scale in which his good deeds and his bad deeds were being weighed. On one side stood Satan piling up his sins; on the other the Good Angel. But all his prayers, the pages of the Gemara, the money he had given for charity, all this wasn't enough to outweigh the other side. The pointer did not budge. Well, it was still not too late to repent. For that very reason Yom Kippur was provided. A strident wailing rang out through the town: in the court of the synagogue the women were praying for their helpless babes. Oyzer-Dovidl's eyes filled with tears. He had no children. Surely it was a punishment. That was why Nechele was so unstrung. Who knew? Maybe it was his fault; maybe he was the barren one, not she.

Entering the house, he called out: "Nechele, have you got some money?"

"I have nothing."

He looked at her, astounded. She was standing ironing a dress, dampening it by spraying water through her teeth. "God forbid, is she out of her mind?" he thought. "It's almost time to light the candles!" Clothing covered the chairs and bench. Her whole wardrobe was spread about. Skirts, blouses, stockings were piled in disarray. On a small table, her jewelry glittered. "It's all spite, spite," he told himself. "Before Kol Nidre on Yom Kippur she wants to start a fight. This is the Devil's handiwork. But I'm not going to quarrel."

"What is there to eat?" he asked. "This is the last meal before the fast."

"There's challah on the table."

A jar of honey, an apple, and half a challah lay on the table. He glanced at Nechele: her face was wet and drawn. She, who rarely shed a tear, was crying. "I'll never figure her out," Oyzer-Dovidl muttered. She was a riddle; she always had been a riddle to him. Ever since their wedding day he had wanted her to open her heart to him, but it was sealed with seven seals.

Today wasn't the time to think about it, though. He sat down at the table, swaying back and forth in his place. Oyzer-Dovidl was often depressed, but this year on the eve of Yom Kippur he was much more depressed than usual. Some kind of trouble was brewing, some punishment decreed in heaven. A deep melancholy was overtaking him. He could not control himself, but blurted out: "What's the matter with you?"

Nechele did not answer.

"What wrong did I ever do you?"

"Make believe I'm dead."

"What? What are you saying? I love you more than anything else in the world!"

"You'd be better off with a wife who could bear you children."

Sunset was only three-quarters of an hour away, yet the candles were still not fastened in their holders, nor did he see the box of sand in which the large memorial candle would be set. In other years, by now Nechele would have put on her silk cape and holiday kerchief. And the house would be redolent with the odors of fish and meat, rich cakes, apples stewed with ginger. "May I only have the strength to endure this fast!" Oyzer-Dovidl implored. He bit into the apple, but it was too tart and acrid to eat. He finished chewing the stale challah. His stomach felt bloated; nevertheless, he swallowed eleven mouthfuls of water as a precaution against thirst.

He completed the blessings and looked out. A Yom

Kippur sky was spreading over the world. A mass of clouds, sulphur-yellow at the center, purple-red at the edges, was changing shape constantly. At one moment it looked like a fiery river, at the next like a golden serpent. The sky was radiant with an otherworldly splendor. Suddenly Oyzer-Dovidl was seized by impatience: let her do what she wanted. He must hurry to the prayerhouse. Removing his shoes, he put on slippers, his white holiday robe and fur hat, and wound a sash round his waist.

Prayer shawl and prayer book in hand, he went up to Nechele: "Hurry, now! And pray that you have a good year!"

Nechele muttered something that he didn't hear. She lifted the iron abruptly with her slender hand. Oyzer-Dovidl went out, shutting the door behind him. "A riddle, a riddle," he murmured.

In front of the pig butcher's house a wagon was standing, the horse munching oats from a sack, a sparrow pecking at its dung. "The Gentiles don't even know that it's Yom Kippur," thought Oyzer-Dovidl. He felt a wave of pity for these people who had surrendered themselves wholly to the flesh. They were as blind as their horses.

The streets swarmed with men in fur hats, women in shawls, kerchiefs, bonnets. Lights gleamed at every window. Though Oyzer-Dovidl, to ward off temptation, avoided the sight of females, nevertheless he noticed their beaded capes, trailing dresses, ribbons, chains, brooches, earrings. On all sides mournful cries arose. Faces laughed and cried, exchanged greetings, kissed each other. Young women who had lost a child or a husband in the past year ran by with outstretched arms, shrieking. Enemies who had been avoiding each other fell on each other's neck and were reconciled.

The small prayerhouse was already full when Oyzer-Dovidl entered. Lamps and candles shimmered in the glow of the setting sun. The congregation,

sobbing, recited the Prayer of Purity. The room
smelled of candle grease and wax; of hay spread over
the floor so that the congregants could prostate
themselves without soiling their garments; and of a
still nameless odor, something sharp, sweetish,
and peculiar to Yom Kippur. Each man lamented in
his own manner, one with a hoarse sob, another with
a womanly whimper. A young man sighed continu-
ally, waving his fists in the air. A white-bearded old
man, bent in half as if by a heavy burden, recited
from the prayer book, "Woe is me, I have copulated
with beasts, with cattle and fowl. . . ."

Oyzer-Dovidl went to his regular place in the
southeast corner. Putting the prayer shawl on his
head, he pulled it across his face, retreating into its
folds as if into a tent. He implored God once more
that Nechele should not, heaven forbid, light the
candles past the proper time. "I should have talked
to her, persuaded her, won her over with friendly
words," he reproached himself. What could she have
against him? Oyzer-Dovidl laid a hand on his forehead, swayed back and forth. He took stock of his
life, tried to think how he had angered Nechele. Had
he, God forbid, allowed one bad word to fall from his
lips? Had he neglected to praise something she had
cooked? Had he let slip some reproach against her
family? He wasn't aware of having done her the
slightest injustice. But such contrary behavior did
not come from nothing. There must be some solution
to the riddle.

Oyzer-Dovidl began to recite the Prayer of Purity.
But one of the elders had already called out the
introductory words, "With the permission of the
Almighty . . ." and the cantor started to intone Kol
Nidre. "My God," thought Oyzer-Dovidl, "I'm sure
she lit the candles too late!" He braced his head
against the wall. "Somehow she has lost control of
herself. I should have warned her, curbed her." He

remembered the words of the Gemara: "Whoever has it in his power to prevent a sin and does not is punished even before the sinner."

The congregation was in the middle of the prayer, reciting "Thou knowest the secrets of the heart," when a clamor arose in the back. Behind him Oyzer-Dovidl heard sighing, chattering, hands slapping prayer books, even suppressed laughter. "What could it be?" he wondered. "Why are they talking aloud in the middle of the prayer?" He restrained himself from turning his head; it could have nothing to do with him. Someone jabbed him in the shoulder. Oyzer-Dovidl turned round. Mendel the Loafer stood behind him. The boy wore a peasant's cap, fitted boots, and was one of a band of louts who never entered the prayerhouse but stood in the vestibule stamping and talking noisily while prayers were going on inside. Oyzer-Dovidl raised his prayer shawl.

"Well?"

"Your wife ran off . . . with Bolek, son of the pig butcher."

"What?"

"She drove through the marketplace in his wagon . . . right after candle-lighting time . . . taking the road to Lublin."

The prayerhouse was suddenly still. Only the candle flames sputtered and hissed. The cantor had stopped intoning and was peering back over his shoulder. The men stood gaping, the boys' mouths hung open. From the women's section rose a strange hum, a combination of wails and choked laughter.

Oyzer-Dovidl stood facing the congregation, his face pale as his linen robe. Comprehension dawned: "Aha, so that's it! Now everything is clear!" One of his eyes seemed to weep, the other to laugh. After these evil tidings the way to saintliness lay open before him. All temptations were gone. Nothing was left but to love God and to serve him until the last breath. Oyzer-Dovidl covered himself again with his prayer shawl, turned slowly to the wall, and stood that way, wrapped in its folds, until after the closing prayer the following night.

Translated by Chana Faerstein and Elizabeth Pollet

Altele

By the age of ten Altele was already an orphan. First her father died, then her mother. Altele was brought up by her grandmother, the widow Hodele. The widow Hodele made a living at the cemetery. Whenever a woman died on the first day of a holiday, the burial was arranged for the second day. And since sewing is forbidden on holidays, Hodele lent the corpse her own shroud, which she kept ready in a trunk. For this she received a small fee from the burial society. In addition, she earned some money by going into the graveyard to pray for the sick. For those who wished it, Hodele measured the grave of a holy man with a wick; later she dipped the wick in wax, cut it into candles, and had them lit at the synagogue. Hodele also kept the oil replenished in the eternal light in the chapel over the grave of the martyred Reb Zalmon, who had been flogged to death by a landowner for refusing to convert.

How much did Hodele need? On Mondays and Thursdays she fasted. She kept fast days which Jews had long forgotten and which were mentioned only in parchment chronicles and ancient folios. Hodele owned a prayer book that had been printed in old Prague. It had wooden covers, and contained penitential prayers and laments for all possible misfortunes, student riots, and massacres, dating back to the days of the black plague and even earlier.

Hodele was as tiny as a girl of six, and the older she became, the smaller she grew. She was always shivering as if from a draft, even in the heat of summer, and she wore several dresses, one over the other, and wrapped herself in a shawl besides. By

the time she was forty, her face was shrunken and
wrinkled like a fig. On weekdays when there were
no fasts, Hodele ate only once a day; her meal
consisted of bread crusts soaked in beet soup.

Hodele had long lost all her teeth. Her back was
bent; her eyebrows had fallen out; her chin sprouted
an old woman's growth of beard. Her pale lips kept
muttering prayers and good wishes, both for individuals and for all Israel: may they have health,
money, joy from children and grandchildren; may
they bring up their sons in devotion to the Torah,
and lead their daughters to the wedding canopy;
may the Messiah come, and the dead arise.

Hodele wailed and wept at every funeral. Penniless herself, she brought cereals and soups to the sick
in the poorhouse. On Fridays, Hodele made the
rounds of the Jewish homes with a basket, and the
housewives put in whatever they could spare for the
poor: a slice of bread or challah, chicken heads and
feet, the tail of a fish, the head of a herring.

Altele took after her grandmother in piety, but
she inherited her mother's beauty. Altele had a skin
white as cream, blue eyes, and golden hair, which
her grandmother would plait into a braid. She carried her grandmother's *Book of Supplications* and
Book of Prayers Over Graves for her to the cemetery.
Besides, Hodele's shawl often slipped off her shoulders, and Altele would put it back in place. Her
grandmother had implanted a devout fear of God in
Altele, and Altele prayed three times daily, avoided
looking at men, and even kept her eyes away from
dogs and pigs. On the eve of the first and last day of
every month, Altele prostrated herself on the graves
of her mother and father.

When Altele became fourteen, her grandmother
affianced her to a teacher's helper from Shebreshin.
With her beauty, Altele could easily have made a
rich match, but the teacher's helper, Grunam Motl,
was known as a devout man. In addition, he was also

an orphan, and not very strong. He had a big head, a bloated belly, and short legs. He taught the cheder boys the alphabet, spelling, and cantillation; he intoned prayers with them, and whittled pointers for them.

The few kopecks which the teacher paid him every Friday were not enough for Grunam Motl to live on, and he took his meals with various householders on different days of the week. Once, when a fire broke out in Shebreshin in the middle of the night, Grunam Motl went out to rescue the small children who were his pupils. He entered flaming houses and saved many souls from death. His earlocks caught fire and one of his ears was singed. Hodele had heard about his good deeds and chose him to be Altele's husband.

The articles of betrothal were drawn up on the eve of Purim. The wedding day was set for the Sabbath of Comfort, following the Fast of the ninth of Ab. Altele had no dowry. Her grandmother had two dresses made for her; also a pair of shoes and a matron's cap. On the eve of the wedding, the bath attendant shaved off Altele's hair. It was a poor wedding, but everything was done according to the law. On Friday evening, the wedding canopy was set up before the synagogue. On Sabbath evening, the musicians played at Hodele's house, which had an earthen floor and walls as black as the inside of a stable. Hodele had baked a few pans of biscuits and made some candied carrots. The guests had brought wine, brandy, peas, and beans. The couple received wedding presents: a couple of pots, a pail, a pan, a noodle board and a salt cellar. Since Hodele had only one room in her house, a bridal couch was prepared for the newlyweds in the attic.

The bridegroom, Grunam Motl, had yellow hair and many freckles. Although the wedding was in summer, Grunam Motl came to the wedding canopy in a quilted vest, a plush hat with ear flaps over his ears, and a pair of heavy leather boots. He was as shy as a schoolboy. The girls made fun of him and giggled.

Soon after the wedding, Grunam Motl became the helper of the teacher Itchele Krasnostover. The young couple lived with Hodele in her single room. At night, they put a screen before Hodele's bench bed.

Hodele immediately began to wait for Altele to become pregnant, but the winter went by and Altele still had her monthly periods. Hodele went to the holy graves to pray. She ordered a prayer to be written, and left it in the chapel of the martyred Reb Zalmon.

Hodele tried every remedy to make Altele conceive. On Fridays she roasted garlic for Grunan Motl, so that his seed might increase. She fed Altele udders, had her bite off the tip of a citron that had been blessed by Jews on Sukkoth, and recited all sorts of incantations over Altele to open her womb. Altele herself made supplications on Fridays after blessing the candles, praying for children. In the ritual bath, the attendant taught Altele various tricks for arousing her husband's desire for her body, and exorcised the powers that prevent conception and birth. But a year passed and Altele's womb remained locked.

Hodele saw that her prayers and Altele's supplications were not enough. In Zokelkov there lived a miracle worker, Reb Hershele, and Hodele put a loaf of bread, a few onions, and several heads of garlic into a kerchief and went with Altele to Zokelkov.

Since there was no money to pay their fare, the two women set out on foot. Hodele crept so slowly that the journey to Zokelkov took several weeks. At night grandmother and granddaughter slept in the fields, or sometimes at an inn or in a peasant's barn. Kind people, Jews and Christians, would give the two women a slice of bread, a turnip, a radish, or an apple. In the woods there were plenty of berries and mushrooms. Altele knew how to make a fire by rubbing two pieces of wood. During the month of Ab the days were hot and even the nights were warm. And so Hodele and Altele made their way to Zokelkov.

Reb Hershele, the miracle worker, received only six women a day, but the town overflowed with barren and sick women, bewitched brides, girls possessed of dibbuks or suffering from constant hiccuping, abandoned wives looking for their husbands.

The women sat on logs before Reb Hershele's house all day, each with a bundle, waiting to be admitted. A beadle with a black beard and fiery eyes admitted the women one at a time. Those who had bribed him with a few groschen were the first to go in. He bantered with the younger women and scolded the older ones.

Neither Hodele nor Altele knew anything of flattery or bribery. Two weeks went by, and they had still not been allowed into the presence of the holy man. In the end, somebody took pity on them and arranged with the beadle to admit them. Reb Hershele, a tiny man no larger than Hodele, had a white beard down to his loins, white shaggy eyebrows, and white side locks down to his shoulders. His white caftan, belted with a rope, dragged on the ground. His skullcap was also white. Reb Hershele requested a fee, and Hodele gave him the eighteen groschen she had tied up in the corner of her shawl.

Reb Hershele laid his hands on Altele's head and blessed her. He gave her a tiny linen sachet containing an amulet. He told her that, on the night of the ritual bath, when her husband came to her, she was to wet the tip of her finger with the semen he had left within her and smear it on the edge of the wineglass he used in the ceremony of ushering out the Sabbath.

Reb Hershele said: "Go home now. Next year at this time you shall have a son."

It was, however, too late to travel home, for the Days of Awe were upon them. Hodele and Altele

remained in the Zokelkov poorhouse till after
Sukkoth.

2.

A year went by, five years, and ten, and Altele was
still without child. Hodele had died and her remains
were buried near the chapel of the holy Reb Zalmon.
The women who prepared her for the burial swore
that she was as light as a chick and that her lips
were smiling in death. Grunam Motl said Kaddish
for her.

After Hodele's death, the town transferred her
duties to Altele. She was sent to pray for the sick, to
measure graves. But Altele seldom remained in her
home town. She was forever making journeys to holy
men, miracle workers, and even witches, fortune
tellers, and sorcerers. She was constantly trying
new expedients to bring about pregnancy. Her throat
was hung with amulets, wolves' teeth, moon gems,
charmed coins, and pieces of amber. In her bag she
carried a variety of herbs, bottles with magical po-
tions, and salves. Altele ignored no advice, whether
offered by a holy man or by another barren woman.
Who could tell, it might be of help.

Grunam Motl had risen from an assistant to a
teacher of beginners, but he still took his meals with
different householders, because, first, he did not
earn enough, and, second, Altele was seldom home.
She would return on holidays, go to the ritual bath,
and lie with her husband. Soon after the holidays
were over, she would set out again on her journeys
over the width and length of the land, with a stick in
her hand and a sack over her shoulders.

She spent most of her days wandering not only
because this gave her hope but because she had
grown accustomed to the road. Good people did not
let her starve. Almost everywhere there was a poorhouse or a bundle of straw to rest her head on. In

every place she heard new wonders about holy men, about woman who exorcised the evil eye or told fortunes by pouring molten wax; about those who could read the future in cards, who practiced palmistry and phrenology, who looked into black mirrors, or divined by the bones of the dead.

Rabbis in all the towns warned that Jewish daughters must not heed the practitioners of magic and those who invoked the unholy host or conjured by the names of devils and of Lilith, but the barren women persisted in their search. They were ready to do anything to bring a child into the world, even if they had to roll on beds of nails in Gehenna in after-life. Often the rabbis and gypsies offered the same advice. Altele resorted to all kinds of foul remedies: the foreskin of a newly circumcised boy, the virgin blood of a bride, devil's dung and dried frogs, the placenta of a newborn, a stag's testicles. When one seeks help, one cannot be squeamish.

One sorceress told Altele to climb into a shallow pit, and the hag covered her with moss, dry leaves, and rotted straw. Altele remained in that living grave for an hour, in order to deceive the devils into thinking she was dead and so divert their attention from her. One old man who divined the future by drops of oil commanded Altele to recite the names of imps and demons, and to utter words that filled her with terror and disgust.

Years passed, and Altele could not rightly tell how and where they had gone. In wintertime the life of wandering was not easy, but in summer it was a pleasure to walk along paths and highways, through woods and fields, to sleep in cornfields and in haystacks, in shacks and barns, orchards and gardens.

Altele seldom went alone. Everywhere she found kindred souls beset by troubles. Her monthly periods had ceased, but women reassured her that there was still hope. Had not Sarah given birth to Isaac at the age of ninety? If God wills, the womb and the

ovaries can be renewed. In Izhbitza an old woman of
fifty had given birth to twins. In Crasnistow a grandmother and granddaughter lay in labor together. In
Piask a man of ninety married a girl of seventeen,
and she bore him eight children, all boys.

Once, after Sukkoth, when Altele came home with
a sack full of herbs and a heart full of faith that this
time a miracle would finally take place, she found
the house empty. Grunam Motl had gone away somewhere months ago. He never told anyone where he
was going. He left his pupils in mid-term and did not
even collect his tuition fees. Some neighbors said
they had seen him on the road to Lublin. Others
insisted he had gone in the direction of the river
San. Thieves had stolen the few pots and plates from
the kitchen, and Altele's holiday dress, the only
thing remaining from her trousseau. At first Altele
thought that Grunam Motl had gone out in search of
a teaching post, or to see some relatives, and that he
would probably return before long, or write a letter.
But weeks and months went by and nothing was
hear of Grunam Motl. Altele had become an abandoned wife. Now she could no longer hope to bear a
child.

That winter Altele stayed at home. She resumed
her daily visits to the cemetery. The town, as it
happened, was swept by epidemics. Children were
dying of measles, smallpox, the croup, and scarlet
fever. Adults suffered from dysentery. By the time
Purim came around, the epidemics had petered out,
and Altele went to work for a baker as a kneader of
dough for matzos.

Until that winter Altele had still looked young.
Her cheeks had remained as smooth and rosy as a
young girl's. But now her face grew pale, her nose
sharpened, and networks of wrinkles appeared around
her eyes. Since she had no one to celebrate the Seder
for her, she went to the poorhouse Seder, arranged
by the community for beggars and cripples.

The town had thought that Altele would now remain at home. But only a few days after Passover, Altele notified the brokers that she wanted to sell her house.

The winter was over. The sky was clear, the sun was shining and puddles had begun to dry out. Mild breezes blew in from the woods, and Altele decided that she would set out in search of Grunam Motl. This time Altele teamed up with groups of abandoned wives like herself who were looking for their husbands. They wandered from city to city, entered synagogues and prayerhouses among the men, scoured about inns, poorhouses, and fairs, and even scanned the tombstones in the graveyards. Some of them carried writs from rabbis, certifying that they were indeed forsaken wives and asking the community elders to help them.

The abandoned wives spoke of different things, told other stories from her previous companions'. Altele learned about all kinds of strange men: ascetics who refused to lie with their wives as a penance for outlandish sins; Hasidim who journeyed to visit one rabbi's court after another and forgot to return home; men who had set out for Jerusalem on foot or who had gone to look for the lost tribes of Israel on the other side of the river Sambation. Altele learned also about shiftless adventurers, drunkards, and debauchees who found themselves other wives, or even converted and married Gentile women. There were also men who had simply vanished no one knew where.

One abandoned wife told Altele that her husband had gone out to close the shutters on Passover eve; he had risen from the reclining couch in his white Seder robe and house slippers, and was never seen again. It was clear that demons had carried him off somewhere behind the Mountains of Darkness, or to the castle of Asmodeus.

Summer went by and Altele returned home in the

month of Elul. But nothing had been heard of Grunam
Motl. Altele stayed for the holidays; the day after
Sukkoth she set out again. This time she was gone a
whole year. When Altele came back after a year, she
found that her hut had burned down. Altele celebrated
the holidays at the poorhouse.

3.

Almost five years elapsed. One summer day, when
Altele entered a poorhouse in a town in Great Poland
she suddenly saw Grunam Motl. He was sitting on a
bundle of straw, eating a radish. It was the same
Grunam Motl, though he had white hairs in his
beard. Altele recognized the large head, the bloated
stomach, the flat nose. She looked at him and asked:

"Do my eyes deceive me?"

"No, I am Grunam Motl."

"Do you recognize me?"

"Yes, Altele."

"Woe is me, why did you leave me to this misery?"
Altele asked him.

Grunam Motl put down the radish on the straw. "I
don't know myself."

"How could you do such a thing?"

For a while Grunam Motl gaped sheepishly and
raised his shoulders. Then he grew serious. "I was
tired of teaching."

"So if a man is tired of teaching, he has to leave
his wife?" Altele pressed him.

"Eh."

"Answer me. Now that I found you, you won't get
off so easily."

"I went out into the world."

"But why? Why?"

"You were never home anyway."

"Do you have another wife?"

"Heaven forbid."

"What then?"

"Nothing."

"Don't you know it's a great sin to abandon a wife?"

"Yes, you are right."

The other people in the poorhouse heard them and raised an outcry. Men scolded Grunam Motl. Women abused him. He bowed his head in silence.

After a while, he said: "This radish is the only thing I own."

"Come to Rabbi, right now."

"For my part . . ."

The rabbi heard the story and wrinkled his forehead. True, according to the law, when man and wife recognize each other and nobody denies that they are a married pair, they must be believed. Yet all sorts of things happened in the town. Once an abandoned wife had supposedly recognized her husband and he agreed to give her a divorce, but later it turned out that it was not her husband at all: meanwhile, having remarried, she had given birth to a bastard. The rabbi now gathered his beard into his hand and asked Altele: "Do you have any signs?"

"What signs?"

"Something on his body. Something that only a wife could know."

"I remember no signs."

"Does he have a wart anywhere, a mole, a birthmark?"

"I never looked."

"Are there any marks on her?"

Grunam Motl raised his yellow eyebrows. "I don't know of anything."

The rabbi took Grunam Motl to another room to consult with him in private. Soon he returned.

"What tribe is he, a Kohen, a Levite?" he asked Altele.

"I do not know, Rabbi."

"What was his mother's name?"

"My mother-in-law? He was an orphan when we were married."

"He never mentioned his mother?"

"I don't remember."

"And his father?"

"I don't know either."

"Are you certain that he is your husband?"

"Yes, Rabbi, he is Grunam Motl."

"Grunam Motl, do you recognize your wife?"

Grunam Motl blinked. "I think so."

"Do you recognize her, or are you in doubt?"

"I think I do."

"What do you want now? To live together, or to get divorced?" the rabbi asked.

For a long while, both were silent. Then Grunam Motl said: "Whatever she wants."

"What do you want, woman? Do you want to live with him? Or do you want a divorce?"

"Why should we get divorced? He did me no harm," Altele answered.

The rabbi went on questioning them for a long time. Gradually, he elicited from them some proofs of identity. Grunam Motl remembered Altele's grandmother, Hodele. Altele recalled that the big toenail on Grunam Motl's left foot was black. The rabbi ordered Grunam Motl to remove his shoe and unwrap the rag around his foot, and found that the nail was indeed black.

The rabbi said: "You may go and live together."

But where were they to live? Grunam Motl no longer earned any money. He subsisted on alms.

They went back to the poorhouse. The poorhouse attendant added a bundle of straw for Altele. The jolly beggars raised catcalls for man and wife. Altele had a pot in her sack, a handful of groats and an onion, and she put them on the stove to cook for supper for herself and her husband. Grunam Motl went out to gather some sticks of firewood. On Thursday, both set out to beg. The townsfolk had learned that Grunam Motl had deserted his wife and would not give him a groschen. As for Altele, they told her that she had a husband—let him provide for her. In the evening, both returned with empty bags.

The poorhouse was overcrowded and full of smoke and stench. Children cried. Mothers cursed and searched for lice. The poorhouse wags played every sort of nasty trick upon the newly united pair.

A couple of weeks went by, and Grunam Motl made no move to approach Altele. He evidently did not need a wife any longer. He lay awake till late at night, mumbling. Every half hour he crept off to the slop pail to urinate. Before the morning star was out, he went to the study house and remained there until after the evening prayer. Altele suggested that they go to sleep at the community baths, but Grunam Motl replied: "I am afraid of the demons."

"Let's go into the field."

"It isn't right."

"So what's the good?"

"I can give you a divorce."

Altele thought it over. What would come of a divorce? If she was no longer an abandoned wife, she would have to settle in some town and become a servant, or hire out to knead dough or wash clothes. Marry again? But who would take her? And even if anyone would, she no longer had any desire to start all over again. Altele longed for the road, the wayside inns, the abandoned wives with their weird stories, doleful talk, and words of comfort.

One night, when Grunam Motl was snoring, Altele rose, picked up her sack and her cane, and set out wherever God would lead her. Soon she reached a path leading out into the fields. A late moon cast nets of light upon the yellow wheat. Crickets were chirping; frogs croaked. The dew was falling. Shadows of unseen spirits wandering between heaven and earth ran over the cornfields.

Altele knew very well the dangers of being out

alone before daybreak, but she recalled a spell to
ward off the unholy ones who were about at night.
Altele never returned either to the town of her birth
or to the place where she had found Grunam Motl.
Once again she became an abandoned wife. Once
again she went to synagogues and study houses and
fairs to look for her lost husband. With other deserted wives, she read inscriptions on tombstones
and leafed through the records of burial societies. In
time, she even forgot the name of the town where
she had met Grunam Motl.

Altele knew that it was a sin to deceive the community. But perhaps it was not deceit—perhaps the
Grunam Motl she had met was a demon. It often
happened that imps assumed the shapes of men. It
also happened that the dead came out of their graves
and mingled with the living. Altele consoled herself
with the knowledge that she was guilty of no other
sins. Even a saint was permitted a single transgression.

No, the Grunam Motl who had lain on the straw
near Altele and muttered to himself was not the
husband she longed for. A rabbi's wife had revealed
to Altele that true marriage was found only in the
next world, when the sack of bones had been cast off
and only the soul remained. True love between man
and wife begins only in Paradise, where the man sits
on a golden chair and his wife serves as his footstool,
and both are initiated into the mysteries of the
Torah. Here on earth, in the vale of tears, a woman
is an abandoned wife even when she rests her head
next to her husband's on the same pillow . . .

Translated by Mirra Ginsburg

The Joke

Why should a Polish Jew in New York publish a literary magazine in German? The magazine, *Das Wort,* was supposed to come out every three months but barely made it three times a year and sometimes only twice—a little volume of ninety-six pages. None of the German writers who appeared there were known to me. Hitler was already in power and these writers were all refugees. Manuscripts came from Paris, Switzerland, London, and even Australia. The stories were ponderous, with sentences whole pages long. No matter how I tried, I could not finish one of them. The poems had neither rhyme nor rhythm, and as far as I could judge they had no content.

The publisher, Liebkind Bendel, came from Galicia, had lived for years in Vienna, and had become rich here in New York on the stock market and in real estate. He had liquidated all his stocks about six months before the 1929 crash, and at a time when money was a rarity he possessed a lot of cash, with which he bought buildings.

We became acquainted because Liebkind Bendel was planning to publish a magazine like *Das Wort* in Yiddish; he wanted me to be his editor. We met many times in restaurants, cafés, and also in Liebkind Bendel's apartment on Riverside Drive. He was a tiny man with a narrow skull without a single hair, a long face, a pointed nose, a longish chin, and small, almost feminine hands and feet. His eyes were yellow, like amber. He seemed to me like a ten-year-old boy on whom someone had put the head of an adult. He wore gaudy clothes—gold brocade ties. Liebkind Bendel had many interests. He collected autographs

and manuscripts, bought antiques, belonged to chess
clubs, and considered himself a gourmet and a Don
Juan. He liked gadgets—watches that were also
calendars, fountain pens with flashlights. He bet on
the horses, drank cognac, had a huge collection of
erotic literature. He was always working on a
plan—to save humanity, to give Palestine back to
the Jews, to reform family life, to turn matchmaking
into a science and an art. One pet idea was a lottery
for which the prize would be a beautiful girl—a Miss
America or a Miss Universe.

Liebkind Bendel had a German wife, Friedel, no
taller than he but broad, with black curly hair. She
was the daughter of a laundress and a railroad
worker in Hamburg; both her parents were Aryan,
but Friedel looked Jewish. For years she had been
writing a dissertation on Schlegel's translation of
Shakespeare. She did all the work at home and in
addition was her husband's secretary. He also had a
mistress, Sarah, a widow and the mother of an
insane daughter. Sarah lived in Brownsville. Liebkind
Bendel once introduced me to her.

Liebkind Bendel's only language was Yiddish. To
those who didn't know Yiddish he spoke a lingo that
combined Yiddish, German, and English. He had a
talent for mangling words. It didn't take me long to
realize that he had no connection with literature.
The real editor of *Das Wort* was Friedel. The Yiddish
version never came to be, but something attracted
me to that playful little man. Perhaps it was that I
could not fathom him. Every time I thought I knew
him, some new whim popped up.

Liebkind Bendel often spoke about his correspondence with an old and famous Hebrew writer, Dr.
Alexander Walden, a philosopher who had lived for
years in Berlin. There he edited a Hebrew encyclopedia, whose early volumes appeared before the
First World War. The publication of this encyclopedia dragged on for so many years that it became a

joke. It was said that the last volume would appear
after the coming of the Messiah and the resurrection
of the dead, when the names included in it would
have three dates: the day of birth, the day of death,
and the day of arising from the grave.

From the beginning, the encyclopedia had been
supported by a Berlin Maecenas, Dan Kniaster, now
an old man in his eighties. Although Alexander
Walden was supported by Dan Kniaster, he acted
like a rich man. He had a large apartment around
the Kurfürstendamm, owned many paintings, kept
a butler. When he was young, a miracle had happened
to Alexander Walden: the daughter of a Jewish
multimillionaire, a relative of the Tietzs and the
Warburgs, Mathilda Oppenheimer, had fallen in
love with him. She lived with him only a few months
and then divorced him. But the knowledge that Dr.
Alexander Walden had for a time been the husband
of a German heiress and wrote in German made the
Hebraists stand in awe of him. Since he ignored
them, they accused him of being a snob. He avoided
even speaking Yiddish, though he was the son of a
rabbi from a small village in Poland. He was said to
be on intimate terms with Einstein, Freud, and
Bergson.

Why Liebkind Bendel was eager to correspond
with Dr. Alexander Walden is not clear to me to this
day. Dr. Walden had the reputation of not answering
letters, and Liebkind Bendel liked to show that no
one could defy him. He wrote, asking Alexander
Walden to contribute to *Das Wort.* His letters were
ignored. He sent long cables, but still Dr. Walden
kept silent. At this, Liebkind Bendel resolved to get
a letter from Dr. Walden at any price.

In New York, Liebkind Bendel met a Hebrew
bibliographer, Dov Ben Zev, who had become half
blind from too much reading. Dov Ben Zev knew by
heart almost every word Dr. Walden had written.
Liebkind Bendel invited Dov Ben Zeb to his apart-

ment, had Friedel prepare a supper of blintzes and
sour cream, and with the two of them worked out an
elaborate scheme. A letter was sent to Dr. Walden,
supposedly written by a wealthy girl in New York, a
connection of the Lehmans' and the Schiffs', an
heiress to many millions—Miss Eleanor Seligman-
Braude. It was a letter full of love and admiration
for Dr. Walden's works and personality. The knowledge
of Dr. Walden's writings was Dov Ben Zev's, the
classic German was Friedel's, and the flattery was
Liebkind Bendel's.

Liebkind Bendel grasped correctly that in spite of
his age Dr. Walden still dreamed of a new rich
match. What could be better bait than an American
millionairess, unmarried and deeply immersed in
Dr. Walden's work? Almost immediately came an
airmail handwritten letter eight pages long. Dr.
Walden answered love with love. He wanted to come
to New York.

Friedel never wrote more than the one letter; she
protested that the whole business was an ugly trick
and would have nothing more to do with it. But
Liebkind Bendel got hold of an old refugee from
Germany, a Frau Inge Schuldiener, who was willing
to collaborate with him. A correspondence began
that lasted from 1933 to 1938. During these years,
only one thing kept Dr. Walden from arriving in
New York—the fact that he suffered severly from
seasickness. In 1937, Dan Kniaster, his property in
Berlin about to be confiscated, his business taken
over by his sons, had moved to London. He took Dr.
Walden with him. On the short trip across the
Channel, Dr. Walden became so sick that he had to
be carried off the boat at Dover on a stretcher.

One morning in the summer of 1938, I was called
to the pay telephone downstairs in my rooming
house at seven o'clock. I had gone to sleep late, and it
took me some time to get into my bathrobe and
slippers and to go down the three flights of stairs.

Liebkind Bendel was calling. "Did I wake you, huh?"
he screamed. "I'm in a jam. I haven't slept a wink all
night. If you won't help me, I'm ruined. Liebkind
Bendel is a goner. You can say Kaddish for me."

"What happened?"

"Dr. Walden is arriving by plane. Frau Schuldiener
got a telegram for Eleanor from London. He sent her
a thousand kisses!"

It took a few seconds for me to realize what was
happening. "What do you want me to do?" I asked.
"Disguise myself as an heiress?"

"Oy! Have I made a mess of things! If I weren't
afraid that war would break out any day, I would
run away to Europe. What shall I do? I am crazy. I
should be shut up in a madhouse. Somebody has to
meet him."

"Eleanor could be in California."

"But she has just assured him she was staying in
the city this summer. Anyway, her address is a
furnished room in the West Eighties. He will know
immediately that this is not the apartment of a
millionairess. He has her telephone number, and
Frau Schuldiener will answer and all hell will break
loose. She is a *Jaecki* and has no sense of humor."

"I doubt if even God could help you."

"What shall I do—kill myself with suicide? Until
now he has been afraid to fly. Suddenly the old idiot
got courage. I am ready to donate a million dollars to
Rabbi Meir, the miracle worker, that his plane should
fall into the ocean. But God and I are not pals. The
two of us have until eight this evening."

"Please don't make me a partner in your adventures."

"You are the only one of my friends who knows
about it. Last night Friedel was so angry she
threatened me with divorce. That schlemiel Dov Ben
Zev is in the hospital. I telephoned the Hebraists,
but Dr. Walden slighted them so long they have
become his bloody enemies. He didn't even make

hotel reservations. He most probably expects Eleanor
to lead him to the wedding canopy straight from the
airport."

"Really, I cannot help you."

"At least let's have breakfast together—if I can't
talk to someone, I'll lose my mind. What time do you
want to eat?"

"I want to sleep, not to eat."

"Me, too. I took three pills last night. I hear that
Dan Kniaster left Germany without a pfennig. He's
an old has-been of eighty-five. His sons are real
Prussians, assimilationists, half converted. If war
breaks out, this Dr. Walden will become a burden on
my neck. And how can I explain things to him? He
may get a stroke."

We left it that we would meet at eleven o'clock in a
restaurant on Broadway. I returned to bed but not to
sleep. I half dozed, half laughed to myself, playing
with a solution—not because of any loyalty to
Liebkind Bendel but in the same way that I sometimes tried to solve a puzzle in a newspaper.

2.

At the restaurant, I hardly recognized Liebkind
Bendel. Even though he wore a yellow jacket, a red
shirt, and a tie with golden dots, his face looked as
pale as after an illness. He was twisting a long cigar
between his lips and he had already ordered cognac.
He sat on the edge of his chair. Before I managed to
sit down, he called to me. "I've found a way out, but
you must help me. Eleanor has just perished in an
airplane crash. I spoke to Frau Schuldiener and she
will back me up. All you have to do is wait for that
old skirt chaser at the airport and get him into a hotel.
Tell him you are Eleanor's friend or nephew. I will
take a room for him and pay the bill for a month in
advance. After that I am not responsible. Let him go
back to London to find himself a daughter of a lord."

"You could pose as Eleanor's friend as well as I."

"I can't do it. He'd cling to me like a leech. What can he get from you—your manuscripts? You will spend a few hours with him and he won't bother you any more. If worst come to worse, I'll pay his fare back to England. You will be saving my life and I will never forget it. Don't give him your address. Tell him you live in Chicago or Miami. There was a time when I would have given a fortune to be in his company half an hour, but I have lost the appetite. I am afraid of him. I'm sure that the minute I see him and he utters the name Eleanor I'll burst out laughing. As a matter of fact, I have been sitting here laughing to myself. The waiter thought I had gone out of my mind."

"Bendel, I cannot do it."

"Is this your last word?"

"I cannot play such a farce."

"Well, no is no. I will have to do it, then—I'll tell him that I am a distant cousin, a poor relation. She even supported me. What name should I take? Lipman Geiger. I had a partner in Vienna by that name. Wait, I must make a telephone call."

Liebkind Bendel jumped up and ran to a telephone booth. He stayed there about ten minutes. I could see him through the glass door. He was turning the pages of a notebook. He made strange grimaces. When he returned, he said, "I have gotten a hotel and all the rest of it. What did I need the whole *meshuggas* for? I'm going to close down the magazine. I will go to Palestine and become a Jew. All these writers—empty heads, they have nothing to say. At fifty my grandfather woke up every night for the midnight prayers; Dr. Walden wants to seduce an heiress at sixty-five. His last letter was simply a song—the Song of Songs. And who needs his encyclopedia? That Frau Schuldiener is a fool, and in addition she plays the fool."

"Perhaps he would marry Frau Schuldiener."

"She's over seventy. Already a great-grandmother. She was once a teacher in Frankfurt . . . in Hamburg— I have forgotten where. She copied her phrases from a book of standard love letters. Perhaps what I should do is get hold of a female who could play the role of Eleanor. How about the Yiddish actresses?"

"All they can do is weep."

"Somewhere in New York there may be a true admirer of his—an old spinster who would be eager for such a match. But where do you find her? As for me, I'm tired of everything. That Friedel is educated enough but without any imagination. All she thinks about is Schlegel. Sarah is completely absorbed by her crazy daughter. They have a new custom—they send the patients home from the institutions and then they take them back again. One month she is there and the other with her mother. I sit with them and I begin to feel that I am not all there myself. Why am I telling you all this? Do me a favor and come with me to the airport. I will always remember it. Do you agree? Give me your hand. Together we'll manage somehow. Let's drink to it."

3.

I stood behind the glass partition and watched the passengers arriving. Liebkind Bendel was jittery, and the smoke from his cigar almost asphyxiated me. For some reason I was sure that Dr. Walden was a tall man. But he was short, broad, and fat, with a big belly and a huge head. On that hot summer day he wore a long coat, a flowing tie, and a plush hat with a broad brim. He had a thick gray mustache and was smoking a pipe. He carried two leather valises with old-fashioned locks and side pockets. His eyes under his heavy brows were searching for someone.

Liebkind Bendel's nervousness was contagious. He smelled of liquor, he purred like a tomcat. He waved his hands and cried, "Certainly that's he. I recognize him. See how fat he has gotten—broader than he is long. An old billy goat."

When Dr. Walden came up on the escalator, Liebkind Bendel pushed me toward him. I wanted to run away but I couldn't. Instead, I stepped forward. "Dr. Walden?"

Dr. Walden put down his suitcases, removed his pipe from between his blackish teeth and set it, still lighted, in his pocket. *"Ja."*

"Dr. Walden," I said, in English, "I am a friend of Miss Eleanor Seligman-Braude. There was an accident. Her plane crashed." I spoke hurriedly. I felt a dryness in my throat and palate.

I expected a scene, but he just looked at me from under his bushy brows. He cupped his ear and answered me in German. "Would you mind repeating that? I cannot understand your American English."

"A misfortune has happened—a great misfortune." Liebkind Bendel began to speak in Yiddish. "Your friend was flying from California and her plane fell down. It fell right into the sea. All passengers were killed—sixty persons."

"When? How?"

"Yesterday—seventy innocent people—mostly mothers of children." Liebkind Bendel spoke with a Galician accent and singsong. "I was her near friend and so was this young man. We had heard that you were arriving. We wanted to telegraph you, but it was already too late, so we came to greet you. It's a great honor for us, but it's heartbreaking to have to bring such terrible tidings." Liebkind Bendel waved his arms; he shook and screamed into Dr. Walden's ear as though he were deaf.

Dr. Walden took off his hat and placed it on top of his luggage. He was bald in the front but at the back of his head he had a shock of graying blond hair. He took out a soiled handkerchief and wiped the sweat from his forehead. I had the feeling that he still did not understand. He seemed to be considering. His face sagged; he looked dusty, crumpled, unshaved. Clumps of hair protruded from his ears and nostrils. He smelled of medicine. After a while he said in German, "I expected her here in New York. Why did she go to California?"

"For business. Fraulein Seligman-Braude was a business lady. It concerned a big sum—millions—and here in America they say, 'Business before and later pleasure.' She was hurrying back to meet you. But it wasn't destined to be." Liebkind Bendel delivered this in one breath and his voice became shrill. "She told me everything. She worshipped you, Dr. Walden, but man proposes and God imposes, as they say. Eighty healthy people—young women and tiny babies—in the primes of their lives—"

"May I ask who you are?" Dr. Walden said.

"A friend, a friend. This young man is a Yiddish writer." Liebkind Bendel pointed at me. "He writes in Yiddish papers and all the rest of it—*feuilletons* and what have you. Everything in the mother language so that plain people should enjoy. We have many *landsleit* here in New York, and English is a dried-up tongue for them. They want the juiciness from the old country."

"Ja."

"Dr. Walden, we have rented a hotel room for you," Liebkind Bendel said. "My sympathy to you! Really, this is tragic. What was her name?—Fraulein Braude-Seligson was a wonderful woman. Gentle, with nice manners. Beautiful also. She knew Hebrew and ten other languages. Suddenly something breaks in a motor, a screw gets loose, and all this culture is finished. That is what a man is—a straw, a speck of dust, a soap bubble."

I was grateful to Dr. Walden for his dignified behavior. He did not weep, he did not cry out. He raised his brows and his watery eyes, full of red veins, stared at us with astonishment and suspicion.

He asked, "Where can I find the men's room? The trip has made me sick."

"Right there, right there!" Liebkind Bendel shouted. "There is no lack of toilets in America. Come with us, Dr. Walden—we just passed the washroom."

Liebkind Bendel lifted one valise, I the other, and we led Dr. Walden to the men's room. He looked questioningly at us and at his luggage. Then he entered the washroom and remained there for quite a long time.

I said, "He behaved like a fine man."

"The worst is over. I was afraid that he might faint. I am not going to forsake him. Let him stay in New York as long as he wants. Perhaps he will write for *Das Wort* after all. I would make him the main editor and all of that. Friedel is tired of it. The writers ask for royalties and send angry letters. If they find a misprint or a single line is missing, your life is in danger. I will give him thirty dollars a week and let him sit and scribble. We could publish the magazine half in German, half in Yiddish. You two together could be the editors. Friedel would be satisfied to be the editorial—how do you call it?— superintendent."

"You told me yourself that Dr. Walden hates Yiddish."

"Today he hates it, tomorrow he will love it. For a few pennies and a compliment you can buy all these intellectuals."

"You shouldn't have told him that I am a Yiddish writer."

"There are a lot of things I shouldn't have done. In the first place I shouldn't have been born, in the second place I shouldn't have married Friedel, in the third place I never should have begun this funny comedy, in the fourth place ... Since I haven't mentioned your name, he will never find you. It's all because of my admiration for great men. I always loved writers. If a man had something printed in a

newspaper or a magazine, he was God. I read the
Neue Freie Presse as if it were the Bible. Every
month I received *Haolam,* and there Dr. Walden
published his articles. I ran to lectures like a madman. That is how I met Friedel. Here is our Dr.
Walden."

Dr. Walden seemed shaky. His face was yellow.
He had forgotten to button his fly. He stared at us
and muttered. Then he said, "Excuse me," and he
went back into the washroom.

4.

Dr. Walden had asked for my address and telephone
number, and I gave him both. I could not cheat this
learned man. The day after his arrival in New York,
Liebkind Bendel left for Mexico City. Lately he was
always flying to Mexico. I suspected he had a mistress there, and most probably business, too. In a
strange way, Liebkind Bendel combined the roles of
merchant and art connoisseur. He went to Washington to try to get a visa for a Jewish writer in
Germany, and there he became a partner in a factory that produced airplane parts. The owner was a
Jew from Poland who was in the leather business
and had not the slightest knowledge of aviation. I
had begun to realize that the world of economy,
industry, and so-called practical matters was not
much more substantial than that of literature and
philosophy.

One day when I came home after lunch, I found a
message that Dr. Walden had called. I telephoned him
and I heard a stammering and a wheezing. He spoke
to me in Germanized Yiddish. He mispronounced
my name. He said, "Please come over. I am kaput."

Liebkind Bendel had put Dr. Walden in an Orthodox Jewish hotel downtown, though the two of us
lived uptown. I suspected that he wanted to keep
him as far away as possible. I took the subway to

Lafayette Street and walked over to the hotel. The lobby was full of rabbis. They seemed to be having a conference. They strolled up and down in their long gaberdines and velvet hats. They gesticulated, clutched at their beards, and all spoke at the same time. The elevator stopped at each floor and through the open doors I saw a bride being photographed in her wedding dress, yeshiva boys packing prayer books and shawls, and waiters in skullcaps cleaning up after a banquet. I knocked on Dr. Walden's door. He appeared in a burgundy-red bathrobe down to his ankles. It was covered with spots. He wore scuffed slippers. The room reeked of tobacco, valerian drops, and the rancid smell of illness. He looked bloated, old, confused. He asked, "Are you Mr.—what is the name—the editor of *Jugend?*"

I told him my name.

"Do you write for that jargon *Tageblatt?*"

I gave him the name of my newspaper.

"Well—*Ja.*"

After Dr. Walden tried again and again to speak to me in German, he finally changed to Yiddish, with all the inflections and pronunciations of the village he came from. He said, "What kind of calamity is this? Why all of a sudden did she fly to California? For years I could not make up my mind whether to take this trip or not. Like Kant, I suffer from travel phobia. A friend of mine, Professor Mondek, a relative of the famous Mondek, gave me pills but they prevented me from urinating. I was sure my end had come. A fine thing, I thought, if the airplane arives to New York with me dead. Instead, she is gone. I just cannot grasp it. I asked someone and he had not heard of this plane crash. I called her number and an old woman answered. She must be deaf and senile—she sounded incoherent. Who was the other little man who met me at the airport?"

"Lipman Geiger."

"Geiger—a grandson of Abraham Geiger? The Geigers don't speak Yiddish. Most of them are converted."

"This Geiger comes from Poland."

"What was his connection with Miss Eleanor Seligman-Braude?"

"Friends."

"I am completely bewildered." Dr. Walden spoke half to me, half to himself. "I know English from reading Shakespeare. I have read *The Tempest* in the original a number of times. It is Shakespeare's greatest work. Each line is deeply symbolic. A masterpiece in every way. Caliban is actually Hitler. But here they speak an English that sounds like Chinese. I don't understand a single word they say. Did Miss Eleanor Seligman-Braude have any family?"

"Distant relatives. But as far as I know she kept away from them."

"What will happen to her fortune? Usually rich people leave a will. Not that I have any interest in such matters—absolutely none. And what about the body? Isn't there going to be a funeral in New York?"

"Her body is somewhere in the ocean."

"Do they fly from California to New York over the ocean?"

"It seems that instead of east the plane flew west."

"How could this be? Where was this crash reported? In what newspaper? When?"

"All I know is what Lipman Geiger told me. He was her friend, not I."

"What? A riddle, a riddle. One should not go against one's own nature. Once, Immanuel Kant was about to take a trip from Königsberg to some other town in Prussia. He had traveled only a short distance when there was rain, lightning, and thunder, and he immediately gave orders to turn back. Somewhere I knew all the time that this trip would be a fiasco. I have nothing to do here—absolutely nothing. But I cannot fly back to London in my present condition. To go by ship would be even worse. I will tell you the truth, I brought almost no money with me. My great friend and benefactor, Dan Kniaster, is now a refugee himself. I worked on an encyclopedia, but we left the plates in Berlin— even the manuscripts. The Nazis had placed a time bomb in our office and we just missed being torn to pieces. Does anybody know that I am in New York? I traveled, as they say, incognito. As things are now, perhaps it would be useful to let the newspapers know. I have many enemies here, but perhaps somewhere a friend might be found."

"I think Lipman Geiger notified the newspapers."

"There is no mention of me anywhere. I asked for the papers." Dr. Walden pointed to a pile of Yiddish newspapers on a chair.

"I will do my best."

"At my age one should not undertake such adventures. Where is that Mr. Geiger?"

"He had to fly to Mexico but he will be back soon."

"To Mexico? What is he doing in Mexico? So, this is my end. I am not afraid of death, but I have no desire to be buried in this wild city. True, London is not much quieter but at least I have a few acquaintances there."

"You will live, Dr. Walden," I said. "You will live to see the fall of Hitler."

"What for? Hitler still has something to spoil on this earth. But I have already committed all my blunders. Too many. This unlucky trip is not even a tragedy. Just a joke—well—*ja*, my life is one big joke, from the beginning to the end."

"You have given much to humanity, to the Jewish reader."

"Trifles, rubbish, junk. Did you personally know Miss Seligman-Braude?"

"Yes—no. I just heard of her."

"I didn't like that Geiger—a buffoon. What do you write in the Yiddish newspapers? What is there to write about? We are returning to the jungle. *Homo sapiens* is bankrupt. All values are gone—literature, science, religion. Well, for my part I have given up altogether."

Dr. Walden took a letter from his pocket. It was stained with coffee and ashes. He scrutinized it, closing one eye, wincing and snorting. "I begin to suspect that this Miss Seligman-Braude never existed."

5.

Late one evening when I was lying on my bed fully dressed, brooding about my laziness, neglected work, and lack of will power, I got the signal that I was wanted on the pay telephone downstairs. I ran down the three flights of steps, lifted the receiver, which dangled from a cord, and heard an unfamiliar voice saying my name. The voice said, "I am Dr. Linder. Are you a friend of Dr. Alexander Walden?"

"I have met him."

"Dr. Walden has had a heart attack and is in the Beth Aaron Hospital. He gave me your name and telephone number. Are you a relative?"

"No relative."

"Doesn't he have any family here?"

"It seems not."

"He asked me to call Professor Albert Einstein, but nobody answers. I cannot be bothered with such errands. Come tomorrow to the hospital. He is in the ward. That's all we could give him for the time being. I'm sorry."

"What's the situation?"

"Not too good. He has a whole list of complications. You can visit him between twelve and two or six and eight. Goodbye."

I searched for a nickel to call Friedel but found

only a fifty-cent piece and two dollar bills. I went out
on Broadway to get change. By the time I had it and
found a drugstore with an unoccupied telephone
booth, more than half an hour had passed. I diáled
Friedel's number and the line was busy. For another
quarter of an hour I kept on dialing the same number and it was always busy. A woman entered the
next booth and lined up her coins. She looked back
at me with a smug expression that seemed to say,
"You're waiting in vain." As she spoke, she gesticulated with her cigarette. From time to time she
twirled a lock of her bleached hair. Her scarlet,
pointed claws suggested a rapaciousness as deep as
the human tragedy.

I found a penny and weighed myself. According to
this scale, I had lost four pounds. A slip of cardboard
fell out. It read, "You are a person with gifts but you
waste them on nothing."

I will try once more, and if the telephone is still
busy I will go home immediately, I vowed to myself.
This scale told the bitter truth.

The line wasn't busy. I heard Friedel's mannish
voice. At that very moment, the lady with the
bleached hair and scarlet nails hurriedly left the
booth. She winked at me with her false eyelashes.
"Mrs. Bendel," I said, "I am sorry to disturb you. Dr.
Walden has had a heart attack. They have taken
him to Beth Aaron Hospital. He is in the ward."

"Oh, my God! I knew that nothing good would
come of that joke. I warned Liebkind. It was a
crime—absolutely a crime. That is the way Liebkind
is—a trick occurs to him and he doesn't know when
to stop. What can I do? I don't even know where he is
now. He was supposed to stop in Cuba. Where are
you?"

"In a drugstore on Broadway."

"Perhaps you could come here. This is no trifling
matter. I feel guilty myself. I should have refused to

write that first letter. Come up, it's still early. I never go to sleep before two o'clock."

"What do you do until two?"

"Oh, I read, I think, I worry."

"Well, this evening is lost already," I mumbled or thought. I had only a few blocks to walk to Liebkind Bendel's apartment on Riverside Drive. The doorman there knew me. I went up to the fourteenth floor, and the moment I touched the bell Friedel opened the door.

Friedel was short, with wide hips and heavy legs. She had a crooked nose and brown eyes under masculine brows. As a rule, she dressed in dark clothes, and I had never noticed a trace of cosmetics on her. Most of the time when I visited Liebkind Bendel, she immediately brought me half a glass of tea, spoke a few words, and returned to her books and manuscripts. Liebkind Bendel used to say jocosely, "What can you expect from a wife who is an editor? It's a miracle that she can prepare a glass of tea."

This time Friedel had on a white sleeveless dress and white shoes. She was wearing lipstick. She invited me into the living room, and on the coffee table stood a bowl of fruit, a pitcher filled with something to drink, and a plate of cookies. Friedel spoke English with a strong German accent. She indicated the sofa for me and sat down on a chair. She said, "I knew it would end badly. From the beginning, it was the Devil's own game. If Dr. Walden dies, Liebkind will be responsible for his death. Old men are romantic. They forget their years and their powers. That inbecile Frau Schuldiener wrote to him in such a way that he had every reason to give himself illusions. One can fool anybody, even a sage." (Friedel used the Yiddish word *"chochom."*)

One could even fool Liebkind Bendel, something whispered in my brain—a dibbuk or an imp. Aloud I said, "You should not have permitted things to go so far, Madame Bendel."

Friedel frowned with her thick brows. "Liebkind does as he pleases. He doesn't ask my advice. He goes away, and I really don't know where or for what purpose. He was supposed to go to Mexico. At the last minute he announced that he wanted to stop in Havana. He has no business either in Havana or in Mexico City. You probably know much more about him than I do. I'm sure he boasts to you about his conquests."

"Absolutely not. I haven't the slightest idea why he went and whom he is seeing."

"I do have an idea. But why talk about it? I know all his Galician tricks. . . ."

There was silence for a while. Friedel had never spoken to me in such a manner. The few conversations we had had dealt with German literature, Schlegel's translation of Shakespeare, and with certain Yiddish expressions still in use in some German dialects, which Friedel had discovered were derived from Old German. I was about to answer that there were decent people among the Galicians when the telephone rang. The instrument stood on a little table near the door. Friedel walked over slowly and sat down to answer it. She spoke softly, but I could tell that she was talking to Liebkind Bendel. He was calling from Havana. I expected Friedel to tell him immediately that Dr. Walden was sick and that I was visiting. But she didn't mention either fact. She spoke to him with irony: Business? Certainly. A week? Take as much time as necessary. A bargain? Buy it, why not? I do my work as always—what else is there?

As she spoke, she threw sidelong glances to me. She smiled knowingly. I imagined that she winked at me. What kind of crazy night is this, I thought. I got up and moved hesitatingly toward the door in the direction of the bathroom. Suddenly I did something that perplexed even me. I bent down and kissed Friedel's neck. Her left hand clutched mine and pressed with strength. Her face became both youthful and sneering. At the same time, she asked, "Liebkind, how long will you stay in Havana?"

And she got up and mockingly put the receiver to my ear. I heard Liebkind Bendel's nasal voice. He was telling of antiques to be got in Havana and explaining the difference in the exchange. Friedel leaned over to me so that our ears touched. Her hair tickled my cheek. Her ear almost burned mine. I was ashamed—like a boy. In one moment, my need to go to the bathroom became embarrassingly urgent.

Next morning when Friedel called the hospital, they told her that Dr. Walden was dead. He had died in the middle of the night. Friedel said, "Isn't that cruel? My conscience will torture me to my last moment."

The following day the Yiddish papers came out with the news. The same editors who Liebkind Bendel told me had refused to announce Dr. Walden's arrival in New York now wrote at length about his accomplishments in Hebrew literature. Obituaries also appeared in the English-language press. The photographs were at least thirty years old; in them Dr. Walden looked young, gay, with a full head of hair. According to the papers, the New York Hebraists, Dr. Walden's enemies, were making arrangements for the funeral. The Jewish telegraph service must have wired the event all over the world. Liebkind Bendel called Friedel from Havana to say that he was flying home.

Back in New York, he talked to me on the telephone for almost an hour. He kept repeating that Dr. Walden's death was not his fault. He would have died in London, too. What difference does it make where one ends? Liebkind Bendel was especially eager to know whether Dr. Walden had any manuscripts with him. He was planning to bring out a special number of *Das Wort* dedicated to him.

Liebkind Bendel had brought from Havana a painting by Chagall that he had bought from a refugee. He admitted to me that it must have been stolen from a gallery. Liebkind Bendel said to me, "Well, if it had been grabbed by the Nazis, would that have been better? The Maginot Line isn't worth a pinch of tobacco. Hitler will be in Paris! Remember my words."

The chapel where the funeral was to take place was only a few blocks from Liebkind Bendel's apartment, and he, Friedel, and I arranged to meet at the chapel entrance. They were all there—the Hebraists, the Yiddishists, the Anglo-Jewish writers. Taxis kept arriving. From somewhere a small woman appeared, leading a girl who looked emaciated, disturbed. She stopped every few seconds and tapped with her foot on the sidewalk; the woman urged her forward and encouraged her. It was Sarah, Liebkind Bendel's mistress. Mother and daughter tried to go into the chapel, but it was already filled.

After a while, Liebkind Bendel and Friedel arrived in a red car. He was wearing a sand-colored suit and a gaudy tie from Havana. He looked fresh and tanned. Friedel was dressed in black, with a broad-brimmed hat. I told Liebkind that the hall was full and he said, "Don't be naïve. You will see how things are done in America." He whispered something in an usher's ear and the usher led us inside and made room for us in one of the front rows. The artificial candles of the Menorah cast a subdued light. The coffin stood near the dias. A young rabbi with a small black mustache and a tiny skullcap that blended with his shiny pomaded hair spoke a eulogy in English. He seemed to know little of Dr. Walden. He confused facts and dates. He made errors in the titles of Dr. Walden's works. Then an old *rabbiner* with a white goatee, a refugee from Germany, wearing a black hat that looked like a casserole, spoke in German. He stressed his umlauts and quoted long passages in Hebrew. He called Dr. Walden

a pillar of Judaism. He claimed that Dr. Walden had
come to America so that he could continue publish-
ing the encyclopedia to which he had devoted his
best years. "The Nazis maintain that cannons are
more important than butter," the *rabbiner* declaimed
solemnly, "but we Jews, the people of the Book, still
believe in the power of the word." He appealed for
funds to bring out the last volumes of the encyclopedia for which Dr. Walden had sacrificed his life,
coming to America in spite of his illness. He took out
a handkerchief and with a corner dabbed away a
single tear from behind his misty glasses. He called
attention to the fact that among the mourners here
in the chapel was present the universally beloved
Professor Albert Einstein, a close friend of the de-
ceased. A general whispering and looking around
began among the crowd. A few even rose to get a
glimpse of the world-famous scientist.

After the German *rabbiner*'s sermon, there was a
further eulogy given by the editor of a Hebrew
magazine in New York. Then a cantor in a hexago-
nal hat, with the face of a bulldog, recited "God Full
of Mercy." He sang in loud and lugubrious tones.

Near me sat a young woman dressed in black. She
had yellow hair and red cheeks. I noticed a ring with
a huge diamond on her finger. When the young
rabbi was speaking in English, she lifted her veil
and blew her nose into a lacy handkerchief. When
the old *rabbiner* spoke in German, she clasped her
hands and wept. When the cantor cried out, "In
Paradise his rest shall be!," the woman sobbed with
as much abandon as the women in the old country.
She bent over as though about to collapse, her face
drenched with tears. Who can she be, I wondered. As
far as I knew, Dr. Walden had no relatives here. I
remembered Liebkind Bendel's words that somewhere in New York might be found a true admirer
of Dr. Walden's who would really love him. I had

realized long ago that whatever anybody can invent already exists somewhere.

After the ceremony, everyone rose and filed past the coffin. I saw ahead of me Professor Albert Einstein looking exactly as he did in his pictures, slightly stooped, his hair long. He stood for a moment, murmuring his farewell. Then I got a glimpse of Dr. Walden. The undertakers had applied cosmetics. His head rested on a silk pillow, his face stiff as wax, closely shaved, with twirled mustache, and in the corners of his eyes a hint of a smile that seemed to say, "Well, *ja,* my life was one big joke—from the beginning to the end."

Translated by the author and Dorothea Straus

The Primper

Why should a wealthy girl remain unmarried? This, my children, nobody can explain.

Suitors had been suggested. Her two sisters and three brothers married in due time, but she, Adele— her real name was Hodel—remained a spinster. We lived in their house and despite her being at least twenty years older than I, we became friends. The matchmakers were still after her, although then she was already past forty. Her father, Reb Samson Zuckerberg, was a rich man and a partner in a sugar refinery. Her mother came from a learned family.

In her youth Adele was far from ugly, though she was always too thin—small, without a bust, dark-skinned like her mother. Her eyes were black and so was her hair, though later on it became streaked with gray. In our town they called such hair cemetery grass. Still, uglier women than she got husbands. Old maids were a rarity in those times even among tailors and shoemakers. There isn't such a thing as a Jewish nunnery.

There are girls who cannot find a husband because of their bitter disposition, or because they are too choosy. Adele didn't have the time to be bitter. All her troubles were caused by her madness for clothes. She simply could not think about anything else. You don't believe it? A preacher came to our town and he said that everything can become—how do you call it—a passion, even eating sunflower seeds.

Adele's mind was all wrapped up in clothes. Even when she was introduced to a man, her first remark, when I later spoke to her, was on how he dressed.

She would comment that his shirt collar was open,
that his coat was unbuttoned, or that his boots were
not polished. She looked for things that others didn't
pay attention to. Once she told me about a man that
had tufts of hair in his nostrils, and this disgusted
her. What woman is interested in such trifles? Once
she complained that the prospective bridegroom
smelled bad. I remember her saying "All men stink."
This is a terrible thing to say. Are we women all
made of rose petals? She had a strange habit of
washing all the time. She often carried a bottle of
smelling salts with her. Whenever I treated her to
tea or applesauce, she was always finding specks of
dust or soot on the dish. In those times when a dress
or a suit was made for a person, it was worn for
years, but if Adele wore something three times, this
was already much. After her father's death she
inherited his house and the stores located there. The
old man had also set aside a dowry for her, but all
this fortune went into the things she put on her
back.

Even though she was an old maid, she was invited
to weddings, circumcisions, engagement parties. She
had many relatives in Lublin and also in Warsaw.
She kept on bringing them gifts and she made a big
deal about each item. Every trinket had to be just so
and right for the occasion.

Her one pet phrase from the time I first met her
was: "I have to go for a fitting." One day it was a
cape, then a skirt, the next time a tunic or a blouse.
She always had to keep appointments with shoemakers, milliners, furriers, and seamstresses. Everything had to match. If the dress was green she had to
have green shoes and a green hat. The hat had to
have a green feather, and the parasol had to be
green. Who in Lublin bothered with such nonsense?
Maybe ladies of the manor or the wife of the governor.

And was one fitting of a garment enough? Here

she found a wrinkle, there the peplum was crooked. She subscribed to the fashion magazines from Paris where all the new styles were described. As a rule, the fashions first came to Warsaw and then about a year later to Lublin. But since Adele received the magazines direct from the fashion makers, everything became topsy-turvy with her. They just began to wear shorter dresses, when she was already ordering longer ones. The tailors got all confused. When she walked out on Lewertow Avenue, the passersby stopped to look at her and thought she was mad.

As long as her father and mother lived, the matchmakers never lost hope. They arranged introductions with men, and each time she had an appointment to meet the man, she dressed up like a bride. Nothing ever came of it. When her parents died, the matchmakers began to ignore her. How long could they run after one like her? When a person doesn't want anybody, she is sooner or later left alone.

I married when I was seventeen. When she was in her fifties, I already had grown-up children. At thirty-six I became a grandmother. We had a dry-goods store. We sold remnants, linings, sackcloth, trimmings, and buttons. Our store was in her building and she was always looking for something: a button, a ribbon, lace, beads. She stood for hours poking and browsing. My husband, he should rest in peace, was by nature an angry man. He had no patience with her. "What is she searching for?" he would ask. "For last year's snow? For whom is she adorning herself, for the Angel of Death?" He himself didn't know how right he was. She came to ask me questions as though I was an authority. "Can one wear a green shawl over a brown cape? What does one wear to a party celebrating the birth of the first-born son?"

You young people don't know it, but at that time the fashions were different: a rotonda, a hobble skirt, a reverende, and others that I don't even remember myself. You may have the idea that in the olden times people walked around in shabby clothes. Far from it. Those who could afford it were dressed to the teeth. But this with Adele was, heaven spare us, craziness. She had maybe fifty crinolines. All her closets were packed. She also had a liking for furniture and antiques. Her parents left her plenty of baubles, but a hardly a week passed without her buying some additional knicknacks: one kind of a mirror and then another kind; a chair with straight legs and one with crooked legs.

She didn't give away her old things. Instead, she looked for customers to whom to sell them. When you buy something, the merchant expects to be well paid. When you want to sell it, the buyer tries to get it for nothing. She was cheated and robbed. As I said, she was all dried up—skin and bones. She simply didn't have time to eat. She had a kitchen and dishes that were fit for a king, but she seldom cooked anything. In former years she had had a maid. Now she let the maid go because all the money went for frippery. At that time, fat was beautiful. Even heavy women wore hip pads and bustles to appear rounder. A corset was worn only when you went abroad. Adele put her corset on every morning as surely as a pious Jew his fringed garment. Shrunken and emaciated as she was, she needed a corset like a hole in the head, but she wouldn't dare cross the threshold without one, as if people would notice the difference. Nobody cared a hoot. She could have walked out naked. Her sisters were already grandmothers and even great-grandmothers. Adele herself could have been a grandmother. Just the same, my door would open and Adele would come in, black as coal, with sunken cheeks and bags under her eyes, saying: "Leah Gittel, I am going to the spas and I have nothing to wear."

The rich people who suffered from gall-bladder or

liver ailments used to go every summer to Carlsbad, Marienbad, or at least to Nalenczow. The very fat ones went to Franzenbad to lose some of their weight. Some would travel to Piszczany to take the mud baths. Have the rich anything to worry about? Another reason for going there was to arrange marriages. They took their daughters with them and walked them around like cows in the marketplace. There was no lack of matchmakers and young men who were looking for rich girls. They flocked there as to a fair. The girls were supposed to drink the mineral waters while the mothers had a sharp eye for prospective bridegrooms.

If you have daughters, what can you do? But what did Adele want at the baths? She went just to parade around and to see what the women were wearing. They knew her there and they poked fun at her. She walked all alone or she attached herself to a crony from Lublin and followed her around. She avoided men and they certainly didn't run after her. Instead of improving at the spas, she came back even more wasted than before. She saw everything, heard everything, knew of all the intrigues. Even then, not everybody was a saint. Daughters of rich houses became acquainted with officers, charlatans, and the devil knows who else. A girl would drop a handkerchief and immediately there emerged a skirtchaser who picked it up and bowed as though she was a countess. He followed her and tried to make arrangements. The mother tagged along, almost bursting from anger, but she didn't dare to say anything. The new times had already begun. When did the new times begin? The eggs had become cleverer than the chickens. Still, a girl had to have, how do you call it, a spotless reputation, and if she behaved too badly, she fell into people's mouths. One way or another, there was always trouble. Just the same, girls became engaged. What else?

But Adele spent her money for nothing. She bought

heaps of silk, velvet, lace, whatnot. At the border she had to pay duty and all the bargains melted away.

Yes, for Rosh Hashana and Yom Kippur she bought a pew in the synagogue, but the way she dressed up for these holidays was unbelievable. She prepared herself a wardrobe as if it was her wedding. Actually, she was never pious. In the synagogue she did not pray, but gaped at the women's outfits. Her pew was occasionally near mine. The cantor would intone the liturgy, the women were bathed in tears, but Adele would keep whispering in my ear about dresses, jewelry, about what this one was wearing, how the other one decked herself out. She was already in her sixties then. The truth was that she never looked right in spite of her primping. There was a shabbiness about her which clothes could not hide. Somehow she always looked disheveled and haggard, as if she were sleeping in her garments. Yet nobody could have imagined she was capable of doing what she did later!

2.

There is an opinion that old maids don't live long. Sheer nonsense. That Adele survived her two sisters and three brothers. She lost her teeth and remained with an empty mouth. Most of her hair fell out and she had to wear a wig. In time I lost my husband, but I remained in the same building, which slowly became a ruin. I had to give up the store.

Why am I telling all this? Yes, Adele. She continued to adorn herself, to run to tailors, and to look for bargains just as in her youth. One day when I came into her apartment she began to talk to me about whom to leave her possessions to. She had written a will and provided for all her relatives—the women, not the men. This niece will get this fur coat, the other niece a different fur coat; one will inherit the

Persian rug, another the Chinese rug. No one refuses an inheritance, but who wants clothes forty years old? She had frocks from the time of King Sobieski. She had linen which she had never put on and if one just touched it, it disintegrated like a spider web. Each summer she stored her belongings in mothballs but the moths got in just the same. She had perhaps a dozen trunks and she opened them all for me. These things had cost her a king's ransom, but what was it all worth? Even her jewelry was no longer in style. In the old times they liked heavy chains, large brooches, long earrings, bracelets which weighed a pound. Now the young women like everything light. Well, I listened to her and I nodded.

Suddenly she said: "I am prepared for the next world also!" I thought she was leaving something for poor brides or orphans, but she opened a chest for me and showed me her shrouds.

My dear people, I have seen much in my life but when I saw these shrouds I didn't know whether I should laugh or cry: the most precious linen, and reams of lace; a cowl that would fit the Pope. I said to her: "Adele, the Jews are not permitted luxurious burial clothes. I'm not a scholar but I know. The Gentiles dress up their dead according to their means, but Jews have to be buried all alike. And why should a corpse look so fancy? To please the worms?" And Adele said: "Still, I like beautiful things."

I understood that she was out of her mind and I said to her: "For my part, it's right, but the burial society will not go along with it." I think she went to ask the rabbi and he told her that shrouds had to be made of plain linen. Scissors couldn't even be used, the linen had to be torn. The women didn't sew it, they basted it. Why fuss about a body after it has ceased to be?

According to the law, when someone died the first day of a holiday the funeral took place on the second day. This was permitted. But how about shrouds?

One is not allowed to sew shrouds on the holiday. There were old women who prepared their shrouds in advance, and if there was a need they gave them away to be used for others, and the family or the community replaced them. Even if they didn't, how much does a few yards of linen cost? There was a belief that giving away a shroud would bring long life, and everybody wants to live, even those who have one foot in the grave.

In that month of Elul there was a real epidemic. Rosh Hashana eve and the day after, a score of people died. The women of the burial society learned that Adele had shrouds prepared and they came to ask for them. Who would refuse a thing like this? But Adele said: "I won't give away my shrouds." She opened her chest to show them her treasure. The women took one look and spat. They left without bidding her a good holiday. I wasn't there but Adele came into my house crying. How could I help her? My heart was heavy with my own troubles. When my husband was alive, Rosh Hashana was Rosh Hashana. He used to blow the ram's horn in the synagogue. He recited the benediction not over grapes like everybody else but over a pineapple which cost five rubles. When a woman is alone and her children are married and scattered, what remains? And here she came to cry on my shoulder. She was afraid that the corpse might take revenge on her. I comforted her. If the dead, I told her, would interfere in the matters of the living, the world could not exist. When one departs from this earth, all scores are forgotten.

I don't know if it was because of the shrouds or if I had just become depressed, but I stopped visiting her. She didn't come to me either. Actually, what could we have spoken about? She had neither children nor grandchildren. Sooner or later she would begin to babble about her outfits. She became bent and wrinkled. She even seemed to me dirty. Her face developed many warts. We had separate entrances and I had almost forgotten about her.

One day a woman, a neighbor of mine, came in and said: "Leah Gittel, I want to tell you something but don't be shocked. In our age we mustn't permit ourselves to get too upset."

"What happened," I asked. "The sky has fallen down, or the thieves of Piask turned honest?"

She said: "When you hear it, you will think that I am mad, but it's true just the same."

"*Nu,*" I said. "Stop beating about the bush and come out with it." My neighbor gave me a frightened look and said: "Adele is about to convert."

"I am afraid," I said to her, "you are really out of your mind."

"I knew you would say this," she replied. "A priest visits her every day. She tore the mezuzah from her doorpost."

"The dreams I had last night and the night before should fall on the heads of our enemies," I said. "I can understand if a young person becomes an apostate because she thinks it might help her to improve her situation. Some will sell the eternal hereafter for a few good years on earth. But why should an old woman convert?"

"This is what I would like to know," my neighbor said. "I knocked at Adele's door but she did not open it. Please go there and see if you can find out what happened. The priest comes to her every day and he stays there for hours. Somebody saw her entering a nunnery."

I was completely flabbergasted. "Well," I said, "I'm going to find out."

I was sure that the whole thing was a mistake or a lie. Even the insane have some sense. Just the same, when I wanted to get up, my legs were as heavy as wood. I knew my neighbor; she was not the kind of person to invent things.

I approached Adele's door and there was no mezuzah on her doorpost. Where the mezuzah had hung, the paint was faded. I knocked at the door but no one answered. It must be a dream, I said to myself. I pinched my cheek and it hurt. I kept on knocking until I heard steps. Adele's door had a peephole covered from the inside with a flap. When one lives alone, one is always afraid of thieves, and especially with her loaded closets. She stared at me with one eye and it gave me the jitters. She opened the door just a crack and asked me angrily: "What do you want?"

"Adele, don't you recognize me?"

She grumbled as she opened the door and let me in. She looked at me suspiciously and her face was as pale as death.

I said: "Adele, we have been friends for all these years. Have I wronged you in some way? And why did you remove the mezuzah? Is there, God forbid, truth in what I heard?"

"It's true, I'm not a Jewess any more," she said. Everything became black and I had to sit down even though she didn't ask me to. I simply collapsed into the chair. I was about to faint but I held on. I asked: "Why did you do it?" And she replied: "I don't have to account to anybody but I did it because the Jews shame the dead. The Christians dress a corpse in his finest. They place him in a coffin and cover him with flowers. The Jews wrap their dead in rags and throw them into a muddy hole."

To make a long story short, she converted because she wanted to be bedecked in her grave. She told it to me plainly and openly. It all began with the lace on her shrouds. She brooded so long and worried herself sick until she went to the priest. . . .

If I wanted to tell you everything we spoke about that day, I would have to sit with you until tomorrow morning. On that day she looked and behaved like a witch. I pleaded with her to reconsider, but it was like talking to a stone. "I can't stand," she said "to be dumped like garbage." She hated shards over her eyes and a rod between her fingers. She disliked the Jewish funeral and the sobbing of the mourners and the horses draped in black. A Christian hearse is decorated with wreaths and the attendants following carry lanterns and are dressed ceremoniously like knights of old. She opened her closet and showed me her new burial attire. Woe to me, she had equipped herself with a whole trousseau. She had already bought a grave in the Catholic cemetery and ordered her monument. Crazy? Certainly she was crazy, but it all had to do with her vanity. Moving is not an easy business for an older person, but I moved out immediately and so did the other neighbors. Even the storekeepers went elsewhere. The street toughs wanted to beat her up, but their elders warned them not to dare touch her. The Poles would have killed all of us. After we moved out, I was told that she bought herself a lead coffin lined in silk and she kept it in her house until the day of her death. She lived only nine months after her conversion. Most of the time she lay sick in bed. An old nun was bringing her food and medicine. She wouldn't let anybody else in.

She left her possessions to the Church, but the thieves got to them first. Her brothers and sisters were all dead. It had rained for days before she died and her grave was full of water and mud.

Yes, a passion. A person begins to yearn for something and soon this yearning floods the brain. Only later a niece of Adele's told me that her aunt never went to a doctor when she was ill, because she had a birthmark on her breast. For the same reason she avoided marriage, because she would have had to go to the ritual bath and show her defect. She always reeked of perfume.

I often say, one cannot become too much taken with anything, not even the Torah. In Rovna there was a young scholar who studied Maimonides so much, he became an unbeliever. They nicknamed his Moshka Maimonides. He knew all of Maimonides by heart. Saturday he would sit by the window with a cigarette in his mouth and recite Maimonides. When the rabbi came to reprimand him, they engaged in a debate and Moshka tried to prove to him that according to Maimonides there is no prohibition against smoking on the Sabbath. One Sabbath he was chased out of town and he ran straight into the Vistula and drowned. In his eulogy the rabbi said: "Maimonides will intercede for him. No one knew him better than this madman."

Translated by the author and Ruth Schachner Finkel

Schloimele

One day, soon after my arrival in the United States, I sat in my furnished room, unknown as only a Yiddish writer can be, and tried, with the help of Harkavy's Dictionary, to learn English from the Bible. The door opened and a pink-cheeked young man with cherry-dark eyes came in. He smiled, dimpling, his small mouth girlishly red, and asked, "Are you the writer from Warsaw?"

"I am."

He looked around at me and my room and I looked at him. There was something familiar about him, with his adolescent face. But his body seemed middle-aged, the shoulders broad, the neck wide and plump. The hands were too large for his short body. In a red shirt, yellow trousers, a multicolored tie, carrying a thick briefcase, he had the appearance of a comedian. With his slightly hoarse, intimate voice he said, "Mr. Bernard Hutchinson recommended me."

"Hutchinson?"

"His name is really Holzman, but he became Hutchinson here. He writes Hollywood scripts. Your story was in—what's the name of that Yiddish newspaper?—and he thought it would make a good play. I'm producing an off-Broadway play; yesterday's *Village Journal* gave it a rave. Oh, I forgot to introduce myself: Sam Gilbert. In Yiddish my name is Schloimele. That's what my mother calls me. I came to this country at the age of five from a village in Poland—I forget the name. It always slips my mind when I try to recall it." He slapped his forehead as though killing a fly.

"It's somewhere near Radom. I remember mud, deep mud; the women wore high boots, like men. I'm writing a play myself, but right now I'm producing one by my friend, Sylvia Katz, a talented girl. Too much talent! But temperamental. She's the star. Take if from me, she'll go places. We'll get married soon. Hollywood wants me. All I have to do is sign a contract—five hundred dollars a week, a plush office—the works. But my heart's in the theater. I want to put on a Jewish show, in English, naturally, with the taste of home, like onions and schmaltz herring—so the goys will know we're not just a lot of money-grubbers. We have a culture."

"I don't know what story you mean. I've published several."

"Wait. I wrote down the title."

Schloimele opened his briefcase on my rickety table; papers and photographs fell out. When I bent down to pick them up, more escaped—actors, dancers, men with wild expressions, half-naked girls, white and Negro. After rummaging a long time, Schloimele was still unable to locate his piece of paper. Becoming upset, he lit a long cigar he had drawn from his front pocket. The cigar looked incongruous in his baby face, from which clouds of smoke arose.

"It's about a girl who disguises herself as a yeshiva boy," he said. "When Sylvia heard about it, she was hysterical. It's just the part for her. The one she has now isn't right, even though she wrote it. Anyhow, the reviewers are enthusiastic. But the theater's too small; audiences don't like going off-Broadway. I have some rich 'angels'—that's what they call play investors. We're looking for a theater. Besides, the one we have is condemned. If you don't grease palms all the way up, you get into trouble. A bunch of grafters all of them, from the cop on the beat to the top man. As you say in Yiddish: 'Who smears well, rides well.' You think you can dramatize your story? We'll sign a contract. I tell you what, come and have dinner with us. The play's not on tonight. I'll introduce you to Sylvia. She's American-born but *haimisch*. Every Friday night her mother lights the candles. Sylvia's gefilte fish melts in your mouth. Her blintzes are famous. Her Yiddish is good, with all the *taam*—how do you say it? A true Jewish daughter!" Schloimele smiled sweetly, his eyes blinking.

"Both of us are penniless and here we are getting married. My father's furious. Her mother wants a millionaire son-in-law, nothing less. Men are wild about Sylvia. The director who wanted to take me to Hollywood is madly in love with her. But Sylvia and I are fated for each other."

Schloimele spoke in a mixture of Yiddish and English. "This isn't the place for you," he said. "A writer needs inspiration. When you're successful they'll buy you a house in Woodstock or somewhere and you'll look out at trees, a river, hills. Love is important too. My mother has a saying: 'One is none.' New York's full of pretty girls. When they find out how talented you are, they won't leave you alone. Here's my address."

2.

After a long search I found the house where Schloimele and Sylvia lived in Greenwich Village. I entered a room in which red candles in glass candlesticks burned on a long, green-covered table. Young men and women sat everywhere, on a bench, on the floor, smoking, trying to be heard above the general din. There was a smell of roasted meat, whisky, perfume, and garlic. They fanned themselves as they drank, the girls with their pocketbooks, the men with magazines or folded newspapers. Schloimele ran to greet me; Sylvia exclaimed and hugged me. Much taller than Schloimele, blond and slim, she had blue eyelids, the lashes heavily mascaraed.

Kissing me as though we were related, she called out, "Here's the author of our next play."

I was introduced to girls—blondes, brunettes, redheads—to bushy-haired young men in open shirts of every color, in shorts, with sandaled feet. There were a few Negroes as well. The dinner had been delayed on my account; I sat at the head of the table. Sylvia insisted that I remove my jacket. She weighed it in her hand. "Goodness! What are you carrying? Your collected works?"

"Europeans don't know about tropical suits yet," Schloimele explained.

"You'll dissolve in clothes like this," Sylvia said.

She needn't have said it. My shirt was soaked. I wore a stiff collar, starched cuffs, and cuff links. A discussion started with dinner and everyone shouted at top pitch. They spoke of the modern theater; I don't know what excited them so much. I heard them mention Stanislavsky, Reinhardt, Piscator again and again. A young man with a thick furry chest called another one "Fascist." A girl with her back bared to the waist drank a tomato-juice toast to the new theater. All the girls kept saying "darling" to and kissing a huge dog that had come with one of the guests. My steak was half raw, the gravy bloody. For dessert I had a cake made entirely of sweet cream; my demitasse was ink-black and strong as liquor. Although they had fussed about me at first, I was now abandoned. I told Schloimele I had to leave.

"But the evening's just begun!" Sylvia protested as her crimson fingernails proffered my jacket. Before I left she gave me a prolonged kiss and promised she would contact me soon.

The little streets of the Village confused me and it took some time to reach the subway. The passengers were chewing gum and reading the morning papers. Kneeling among strewn newspapers and peanut shells, a Negro boy shined shoes. A beggar blew a tune on a horn and then extended a paper cup whose

nickels and pennies tinkled. A drunk made a speech.
He predicted that Hitler would save America, and
then vomited. On the seat next to me, a tabloid
someone had left described a bride killed by a jealous
suitor at the church entrance. The photograph showed
her in gown and veil, sprawled out on the steps. The
murderer, flanked by two policemen, posed for the
camera. Mussolini had called himself a genius. Hitler
had threatened to attack Poland. In Moscow, some
more old Bolsheviks had been arrested.

Obviously, the evening had been a total loss. My
story had none of the elements that those young
people wanted to bring into the theater. Unable to
eat either meat or cake, I had remained hungry. I
left the subway, walked three blocks to my rooming
house, and barely squeezed into a tiny elevator
where a huge Negro sat on a pile of dirty linen. The
fifth-floor corridor was narrow and ill-lit, the bathroom constantly occupied, my room hot as an oven.
Lying fully dressed on my bed, I waited tensely for
the bathroom door to open. I felt a sore swelling
where Sylvia had kissed my cheek. She must have
had the lips of a vampire.

3.

For a year I had not heard from Schloimele. One
day, as I sat in a Broadway cafeteria, he came up to
my table. I barely recognized him. He had grown
fatter. Smiling, greeting me, he asked permission to
sit down, and carried over his tray full of blintzes,
sour cream, onion rolls, and milk, saying, "It's a
funny thing. I intended to go to Childs, but something made me come here instead. How are you?
What's new? Everything's over between Sylvia and
me. She married a goy and she's ready to divorce
him. Promised her the sun and the moon, her own
theater, a Hollywood role. What a bluffer! It nearly
killed her mother. But this is America. Who cares

for parents? We were practically married, lived together, had one bed. Suddenly who does she fall for but a faker! I could have had a Broadway theater but now the deal's off, naturally. I'm connected with a new group and still want to produce your story. I tried phoning you. We have a wonderful new actress. Sylvia wouldn't have been right disguised as a yeshiva boy. She's too big, too noisy. The minute she steps on stage, she starts screaming. Actually, she's always like that, scares the 'angels' with her aggressiveness. Her analyst explained to me that her father's a schlemiel so she has to compensate. Bonnie's the opposite. Right now we're only living together, but we plan marriage. Her mother's dead, her father a taxi driver in Cleveland, remarried, with other children. My office is at Forty-eighth Street and Sixth Avenue. Come up some time! We're a stock company, rehearsing a play, but we plan to open in New York. Hutchinson's with us again. He didn't see eye to eye with Sylvia, but Bonnie's easygoing. The twenty-five thousand dollars we need is practically ours."

"Twenty-five thousand dollars!"

"So what? On Broadway that's peanuts. The sky's the limit when you're a success. You can make millions. What? Just write it your own way. I've doctored a number of plays. The main thing is to keep it moving. Hold the audience's interest. Tomorrow afternoon at twelve-thirty be in my office. I'll have Bonnie there too. She's dying to meet you, knows all about you. She and Sylvia were friends. Of course, they're a little cool toward each other now. But we still get together. I even offered her a part in the play. But Sylvia always has to be the star. She's *meshugga*."

Schloimele chewed as he spoke. When he finished, he got coffee and cheese cake for himself and me. "I'm getting too heavy," he said, "but in my profession you've got to eat with everyone—lunch, dinner,

sometimes between meals. I must lose at least twenty
pounds. How do you do it? What's life without food
and love? May I smoke?"

"Go right ahead."

He lit a cigar, blew smoke in my face, and said, "I
wanted to act but I'm better as a manager. I'm a
brother, a father for them, what have you. A pregnant girl needs an abortion. It's a racket, illegal, but
what can you do? Be at my office at twelve-thirty
tomorrow, on the dot."

The next day I climbed three narrow flights of
stairs in a house on a corner of Sixth Avenue. The
open doors of the rooms revealed half-dressed girls
singing drawn-out mournful songs of unfulfillment
which I learned were "the blues." Radios roared,
victrolas blared. I opened the door of a tiny room
whose walls were covered with photographs, posters,
and faded newspapers, and found a smallish girl
with a crooked nose, owlish eyes, and hair cropped
like a boy's. Schloimele, on the telephone, nodded
and winked. The girl hastily freed a chair of magazines and signaled me to sit there. Schloimele was
saying, "You can't do this to us! We're a solvent
company. We'll pay, we're not about to skip town.
After all, we're a young group, we deserve a break. If
the play's a hit. . . ."

Apparently the person on the other end had hung
up. "Hello, hello!" Schliomele called. Then, to the
girl, to me, and to no one in particular, he announced, "The guy's crazy, a madman plain and
simple."

4.

Our meetings, accidental as they were, began to
embarrass me. I had no play; Schloimele had no
theater. He and Bonnie had broken up. He had a
new girl, a head taller than he, with a long nose,
black woolly hair, and a mustache. She had a bass

voice and openly admitted membership in the Communist Party. Her ambition was to organize a leftist theater group to play Brecht, Toller, Romain Rolland's *The Wolves,* and the Soviet dramatists. "Yiddish is all right," she said, "if it serves the masses. But a play about a girl masked as a yeshiva boy isn't for us. The progressive theatergoer wants the theater to reflect his time, his struggles, his role in society." The girl, Beatrice, had her own way of doing things. She would light a cigarette, inhale twice, and extinguish it in her cup of coffee. Her nails were bitten to the roots, her fingers yellow from tobacco. Despite the fact that she lived with Schloimele and tried to open a theater with him, she ridiculed him. In the cafeteria she was always ordering him about. One minute she wanted mustard, and then horseradish. She had to have a frankfurter with sauerkraut, then a corned-beef sandwich with pickled cucumber. Her coat pockets were as deep as those of a man and stuffed with newspapers and magazines. She even had a mannish cough. When she went to the bathroom Schloimele said, "Don't take her seriously. The yeshiva boy role is just right for her. She'll be a hit."

I decided to make an end to our meetings and idle talk, but we kept running into each other. No matter how often I assured Schloimele that I had no theatrical ambitions, he kept talking about my nonexistent play. The moment I came through the turnstile of the cafeteria, he would jump up and run toward me on his short legs—silver, napkin, and plate in hand. All he wanted was to do favors for me. Would I like to go to the opera? Was I interested in music? His purse was full of tickets. A former geisha acquaintance would become my lover. Or perhaps I'd like to try marijuana? He could get anything wholesale—a coat, suit, shirts, watch, typewriter, liquor. Doctors, druggists, masseurs, editors, and owners of umbrella factories were among his intimate friends. It was painful for me always to decline, and once I even accepted two tickets for a new comedy. When I arrived at the theater with a girl, I found it shut. The reviewers had massacred the play, and it closed the second night.

As the years went by, Schloimele symbolized for me wasted time and my own failure. I could never get a publisher, or he a theater. As he grew stouter, I grew leaner. Many times we were each on the verge of marriage, but remained bachelors. Both of us planned trips to Europe, to Palestine, but the years passed and we never left New York. Even though he always boasted of his enterprises, I could not understand how he earned a living, nor did he really know what I was doing. I published an occasional article in the Yiddish press, did some translating, editing, proofreading, even some ghostwriting. Schloimele seemed to have become a small-time impresario. In ten, fifteen years, he never lost his cheerfulness. His body grew huge and he suffered from asthma, but his eyes gleamed with a youthful energy and good nature that no setbacks could diminish. As for me, my notebook was still full of plans for novels, stories, essays. Strangely enough, neither of us knew the other's address or telephone number. Sometimes weeks, months went by without our meeting. Then we'd meet every day, even twice a day. We were both strangers and intimate friends. He discussed his affairs; I, mine. There was nothing else to chatter about. Even though there wasn't much about him that I liked, I had to admit we had something in common. Neither of us could ever see his projects through. We had each been disappointed in women; or perhaps it was the other way around. They always started off idealistically but in the end married insurance agents, accountants, butchers, and waiters.

Around my bald spot the hair had turned gray. Schloimele's black shock grew thin and threaded with white. No longer did he introduce me to girls but to middle-aged women. I became involved with a widow much older than I; she already had grandchildren. We could neither stay together nor separate. She was always afraid of being found out by her son, her daughter-in-law, her daughters and sons-in-law. At night her language was passionate and she bit my shoulder; in the morning she told me she had bought herself a plot in the cemetery near her husband. Suddenly she stopped dyeing her hair and in a few weeks it became white. She gave up her apartment in Brooklyn, went to live with her daughter on Long Island. She said to me over the telephone, "There must be an end to everything."

I tried to look up my former girlfriends, but that summer no one was around. The married ones were occupied with their families, the single ones were in Europe or California. Some had moved or had unlisted telephone numbers. I tried to develop a new relationship, but had no luck. I lost all desire to write. My fingers grew sluggish. The fountain pens sabotaged me, either leaking or withholding ink. I couldn't read my own handwriting. I skipped letters, left out words, made ridiculous mistakes, wrote long, stilted sentences. Often I said the opposite of what I intended, as if a literary dibbuk had gotten into me. My notebooks, even my manuscripts vanished. My nights were sleepless. I stopped receiving mail, wasn't called to the telephone. The moment I put on a shirt it was wet with perspiration. My shoes hurt. I cut myself when I shaved. Food spotted my ties. My nose was clogged; I could barely breathe. My back itched and I developed hemorrhoids.

I had saved some vacation money but did not know where to go. In the cafeteria I found Schloimele eating noodles and cottage cheese. Round as a barrel, with a bloated face, blue shadows beneath his eyes, and a dirty collar, he still had an animated expression as he beckoned me to sit as his table. I joined him with a cup of coffee.

"What happened to you?" Schloimele asked. "I kept looking for you, but—"

"I suppose you've found a theater by now?" I said, realizing that my irony was cruel.

"Huh? There'll be one. What's a theater after all? A hall with chairs. There are millions of dollars to be made on Broadway. If you only knew how to get them."

Schloimele pushed a spoonful of noodles into his mouth, swallowed, choked, washed them down with milk. He lifted a noodle that had dropped on his lapel, and ate it.

"How do you like the weather?" he asked. "A man has to be out of his mind to stay in town in this sweltering heat. Why don't you get away? Oh, it's not that easy, I know. One has commitments. A Yemenite actress is here from Israel, very talented. Imagine, her husband is a Litvak from Vilna."

"Really?"

Schloimele glanced at me sideways, smiling. "Why don't we go away together?"

"Two men?"

"What of it? We are not fairies. We'll find women."

"Where should we go?" I asked, amazed at myself.

"A friend of mine has a hotel at Monticello. He'll charge us next to nothing. It's a nice place, the air is good, food homecooked—sour cream, cottage cheese, blueberries, blintzes, anything your heart desires. He has a casino, needs entertainers. Let's organize something. You could lecture."

"Never."

"No is no. But what harm will it do? Read them a few pages and they'll love it. After stuffing themselves all day long with derma and pancakes, they need amusement. Do you have a humorous sketch?"

That night I couldn't sleep. My furnished room felt as if it were on fire. No breezes came through the open window, only New Jersey mosquitoes that buzzed lustily and bit me. I squashed some of them, but this did not teach the others a lesson. Poisonous fumes traveled from the cleaning establishment across the building lot. The stench made my head reel. For a moment I imagined that someone was climbing down the fire escape. I grew tense. True, I had no valuable possessions that a robber might want, but New York was full of maniacs. Cats meowed; a truck, unable to start on the avenue, groaned, shuddered, and shook its metal insides. Above the roofs a red strip of sky glowed. I was thirsty, but the water from the faucet was tepid and rusty. Although I wanted to urinate, I hadn't the strength to put on a bathrobe and cross the narrow corridor to the bathroom, which was probably occupied. Naked, standing between my bed and the limping table on which my never finished novel lay, I scratched myself.

A few days later I gave up my room, packed my belongings in two suitcases, and took the the subway to the bus terminal. I was early, but Schloimele was there before me, with an old-fashioned trunk and three valises. He wore a straw hat, a pink shirt, and a bow tie. Although I had met him two days before, I barely recognized him. This was not the Schloimele I knew but an elderly man, gray-haired, bent, with a yellow complexion, a wrinkled double chin, and sad eyes under bushy brows. For a while he stared at me in bewilderment as if he, too, could not believe what he saw. Then he started, a smile lit up his face, and in a split second he became Schloimele again. He waved to me, spread his short arms, and gestured as if to embrace me. He called: "Welcome, *shalom!* I spoke to the Yemenite actress about your play. It's just the part for her. She's absolutely delirious!"

Translated by Alma Singer and Elaine Gottlieb

The Colony

It was all like one long dream: the eighteen-day
boat trip to Argentina, the encounter with my Polish
landsleit in Montevideo and Buenos Aires, my speech
in the Theater Soleil, and then the trip by car to the
old Yiddish colony in Entre Rios where I was sched-
uled to lecture. I went there in the company of a
Yiddish poetess, Sonya Lopata, who was to read her
poems. The spring Sabbath day was a warm one. We
passed by sleepy little towns bathed in sunlight,
everywhere the shutters closed. The dusty road
stretched itself between huge wheatfields and ranches
where thousands of oxen fed without being tended.
Sonya kept on talking to the chauffeur in Spanish, a
language which I do not know. At the same time she
patted, pinched, and pulled my hand; she even dug
the nail of her index finger into it. The calf of her leg
she pressed against mine. It was all both strange
and familiar: the bright sky without a single cloud,
the wide horizon, the midday heat, the smell of
orange trees which drifted God knows from where.
Sometimes it seemed to me that I had experienced
all this in a former life.

About two o'clock the car stopped before a house
which was supposed to be a hotel or an inn. The
chauffeur knocked at the door, but nobody came to
open it. After he had banged and cursed a long time,
the owner appeared, a sleepy little man. We had
awakened him from his siesta. He tried to get rid of
us with all kinds of excuses but the chauffeur refused to be cheated of his dinner. He argued with
him profusely. After much haggling and many
reproaches we were let in. We passed through a

patio paved with colored stones and decorated with cactuses planted in large tubs. We entered a darkish hall which held tables without a single guest. It reminded me of the story by Reb Nachman Bratslaver about a palace in the desert where a feast for demons was prepared.

Finally the owner came to and went to wake the cook. Again we heard talk and complaints. Then the cook woke his assistant. It was three hours before we finished the meal. Sonya said to me, "This is Argentina."

There was a long trip in a ferry over a river as wide as a lake. The car approached the Jewish colony. The wheatfields swayed in the heat like a green sea. The road became even dustier. A Spanish cowboy on horseback drove a herd of cattle to slaughter. He chased the animals with wild cries and whipped them to make them run. They were all lean, covered with scales of dirt, and one could see the fear of death in their distended pupils. We passed the carcass of an ox of which nothing was left but hide and bones. Crows still tried to get the last bit of nourishment from it. In a pasture a bull copulated with a cow. He mounted her high, his eyes bloodshot and his long horns protruding.

All day long I did not notice the Sabbath, but when the sun began to set I suddenly felt the closing of the Sabbath day and remembered my father chanting the "Sons of the Mansion" and my mother reciting "God of Abraham." I was overcome by sadness and longing. I grew tired of Sonya's caresses and moved away. We passed a synagogue by the name of Beth Israel. There was no candle to be seen and no voice to be heard. Sonya said to me, "They are all assimilated."

We came to the hostel where we were to stay. In the patio stood a billiard table and barrels filled with torn books. A Spanish-looking woman was ironing a shirt. Along the patio, on both sides, doors

led into rooms without windows. I was given a room,
Sonya one near me. I had expected someone to
receive us, but nobody came. Sonya went to change
her clothes. I came out to the patio and stopped at
one of the barrels. Great God! It was full of Yiddish
books with library markings on them. In the dusk I
read the titles of books which had enchanted my
youth: Sholom Aleichem, Peretz, L. Shapiro, and
translations from Hamsun, Strindberg, Maupassant,
Dostoevsky. I remembered the bindings, the paper,
the print. Although it is unhealthy to read in twilight, I strained my eyes and read. I recognized each
description, every phrase, even the misprints and
transposed lines. Sonya came out and explained it
all to me. The old generation of colonists had spoken
Yiddish. There had been a library here; they had
organized lectures, had invited Yiddish actors. The
new generation was raised on Spanish. However,
from time to time they still brought in a Yiddish
writer, a reciter, an actor. A special fund was set
aside for this. It was done mostly to avoid the criti-
cism of the Yiddish press in Buenos Aires. There still
remained two or three old people who might enjoy
these activities.

After a while a member of the committee showed
up. He was short, broad, with black hair which was
almost blue, and with the black shining eyes of a
Spaniard or an Italian. He spoke to us in a broken
Yiddish. He winked at the hotel owners and joked
with them. His cheeks had a mango redness. The
night fell black and thick, with a darkness that no
lamp could penetrate. The crickets seemed to make
a different sound than in Europe or in the United
States, where I now lived. The frogs croaked differently. The stars had different formations. The south-
ern sky pressed low with its unfamiliar constellations.
I imagined I heard the whining of jackals.

Two hours later I gave my speech. I spoke about
Jewish history, Yiddish literature, but the boorish

men and fat women in the audience seemed not to
understand what I said. They didn't even listen.
They ate peanuts, talked, screamed at their children. Beetles, butterflies, all kinds of insects flew
through the broken windowpanes and cast flying
shadows on the walls. The electricity went off and
then on again. A dog had entered the hall and began
to bark. After my lecture Sonya read her poems.
Then they gave us a supper of extremely fatty and
spicy foods. Later somebody took us back to the
hostel. The colony was badly lit, the ground full of
ditches and mounds of earth. The man who led the
way told us that the colonists had become rich in
recent years. They didn't farm any more but hired
Spaniards or Indians to do their work. They themselves went often to Buenos Aires. Many of them
had Gentile wives. Their main amusement was
playing cards. The colonies which Baron de Hirsch
had built to take the Jews away from their insub-
stantial businesses and turn them into useful farm-
ers were falling apart. As the man spoke, passages
from the Bible came into my mind. I thought of
Egypt, the Golden Calf, and the two calves which
Jeroboam the son of Nebat established in the cities
of Beth-el and Dan, saying, "Behold thy gods, O
Israel." There was something Biblical in that aban-
doning of one's origins, forgetting the efforts of the
fathers. To this spiteful generation there should
have come a prophet, not a writer of my kind. When
the man left us, Sonya went to her room to wash up
for the night, and I returned to the barrels of books. I
could not read them now, but I touched their covers
and pages. I breathed in their moldy smell. I dug a
book out of the pile and tried to read its title by the
light of the stars. Sonya come out in night robe and
slippers, her hair loose.

"What are you doing?" she asked. And I answered,
"I am visiting my own grave."

2.

The night was dark and long. Tepid breezes wafted through the open door. From time to time I heard what seemed to me the steps of a beast lurking in the darkness, ready to devour us for our sins. All the endearments, the whole game and procedure of love had passed, but I could not fall asleep. Sonya was smoking and she was overcome by a garrulousness which I sometimes suspect is the number-one passion with women. She spoke in a nagging tone.

"What does a girl of eighteen know? He kissed me and I fell in love with him. He immediately began to talk about practical details: getting married, children, an apartment. My father was no longer alive. My mother had gone to live with her sister, a widow, in Rosario. She was actually her maid. Men ran after me, but they were all married. I worked in a textile factory. We made sweaters, jackets, all kinds of knitted goods. We were paid pennies. The workers were all Spanish women, and what went on there I cannot describe to you. They were always pregnant and they seldom knew by whom. Some of them supported their lovers. The climate in this country makes you crazy. Here sex is not a caprice or a luxury. It attacks you like hunger or thirst. In those days the pimps still played a big part in our community. They were the bosses in the Yiddish theater. When they didn't like a play, it was immediately taken off the boards. The struggle with them had already begun. The others isolated them completely. Here the elders of the burial society are the real leaders. They refused to sell them plots in the cemetery. They were not let into the synagogue on the New Year and Yom Kippur. They had to establish their own cemetery and their own synagogue. Many of them were already old, has-been pimps, their wives former whores.

"What was I saying? Yes, then they still played a big role and tried to get hold of every woman who was alone. They had special men who did the seducing. As a matter of fact, my own boss was after me. I began to write—but who needs poetry here? Who needs literature? Newspapers, yes. Even the pimps read the Yiddish papers every day. When one of them died, whole pages of obituaries appeared. You came here in the best time of the year, spring. But all year round the climate is terrible. In summer the heat is unbearable. The rich go to Mar del Plata or to the mountains, but the poor remain in Buenos Aires. In winter it's often bitter cold, and modern heating didn't exist in those days, not even the kind of ovens they used to have in Poland. One simply froze. Now there is steam heat in the new buildings, but the old houses still have stoves which give out smoke but no heat. It seldom snows, but it sometimes rains for days and the cold gets into your bones. There is no lack of sickness here and women suffer even more than the men—bad livers, kidneys, whatnot. This is the reason the burial society is so strong.

"A writer does not write just for his files. I tried to find recognition in the newspapers and magazines, but when they see a young girl, and in addition not an ugly one, they're drawn to her like flies to honey. The big shot who himself led the war against the pimps became interested in me. He had a wife, but she had a lover. Why he consented to such conduct I will never know. He must have loved her immensely. Here there is not much religion. They go to synagogue only on the Days of Awe. The Gentiles have many churches, but only the women worship there. Almost every Spaniard here has a wife and a mistress.

"To make it short, I came to the editor, and he said to me almost openly, 'If you sleep with me, I will publish your work.' The critics disguised their meaning. However, they wanted the same thing. I wasn't so holy, but a man has to please me. To go to bed with someone cold-bloodedly, this I cannot do.

"And there was Leibele, my present husband. He also wrote poems and had published some of them. He had even brought out a little book. In those times when somebody's name was printed black on white, he appeared to me like a genius. He showed me a review by some critic in New York. He had a job with the burial society. Till today I don't know what he did there. Most probably he was somebody's assistant. We went to the rabbi and got married. We moved into the Jewish section on Corrientes. It soon appeared that his job wasn't worth a penny. He earned little and what he earned he spent. He had a whole bunch of friends, little writers, beginners, amateurs who attach themselves to Yiddish culture. I never knew that such creatures existed. He was never alone, always with them. They ate together, drank together, and if I had allowed it, he would have slept with them as well. Not that he was a homosexual. Far from it—he was not sexual altogether. He was one of those who cannot stay alone for a minute. Every night I had virtually to drive out his cronies, and every night my husband begged me to let them stay a little longer. They never left before two o'clock. In the morning I had to go to work. Wherever he took me, to the theater, to a restaurant, to a lecture, even just for a walk, his bunch of schlemiels followed. They could babble and discuss each bit of nonsense forever. Some men are jealous, but he didn't even know that jealousy existed. When one of his colleagues kissed me, he was overjoyed. He wouldn't have minded if they had gone further. This is how he was and how he still is. When he heard that I was going with you on this lecture, he was in seventh heaven. You are to him a god, and no one can be jealous of a god.

"We had no children and things might have come to an end, but a divorce makes sense only if you are

in love with somebody else. However, the years
passed and I didn't fall in love with anyone. The few
affairs I had were with married men. In the beginning I had a high opinion of my husband's writing,
but then he disappointed me in this too. I grew as a
poetess—at least the critics praised me—but my
husband stagnated. He began to be more and more
enthusiastic about my poems. Everyone wants to be
admired, but his admiration irritated me. He infected
the others too. My house became a kind of temple,
and I its idol. One thing he forgot: we had to eat and
pay rent. I still went to work and came home in the
evening dead tired. I was a second George Sand. Just
the same, I had to cook supper for him and his
parasites. I stood over the pots and they analyzed my
verses and marveled at each word. Funny, isn't it?

"Lately things are a little easier. I stopped
going to work. Once in a while I get a subsidy
from the community—we now have a few patrons of
the arts. From time to time I publish something
in a newspaper, but basically everything remains
the same. Occasionally he earns a little money,
but not enough!"

"Why don't you have children?"

"What for? I don't even know if he can father
children. I suspect that we are both barren." Sonya
laughed. "If you remained here, I would have a child
with you."

"What for?"

"Yes, what for? Women have such a need. A tree
wants to give fruit. But I need a man to look up to,
not someone I always have to apologize for. Recently
we even stopped sleeping together. It's all platonic."

"Does he consent?"

"He doesn't need it. All he wants is to discuss
poetry. Isn't that strange?"

"Everything is strange."

"I have castrated him spiritually, that is the truth."

3.

At dawn Sonya returned to her room. I covered
myself and fell asleep. I was awakened by sounds I
had never heard before. I imagined that I heard the
voices of parrots, monkeys, and birds whose beaks
are shaped like bananas. Through the open door
there drifted in the fragrance of oranges mingled
with the scent of fruits and plants which I could not
identify. The breeze which blew in was warmed by
the sun and seasoned with exotic herbs. I breathed
deeply. Then I washed at the faucet and stepped
outside. The barrel with books still stood there,
waiting for a Yiddishist redemption. I left the patio
and saw women and children dressed in Sunday
finery—the mothers with mantillas on their heads
and lace on their sleeves, prayer books in hand—
riding to church on horseback. In the distance I
could hear the ringing of church bells. All around
me stretched the wheatfields and pastures. The grass
was full of flowers: yellow, white, all colors and
shapes, and the grazing oxen blithely chewed up all
these wonders.

A sound played in the air, a mixture of birds' song
and breezes in the trees. It reminded me of the story
from the Talmud about the North Wind playing on
King David's lyre and awakening him to midnight
studies. Sonya came out in a white dress embroidered
with red and blue. She looked fresh and was in a
playful mood. It seemed to me that only now I saw
her for the first time as she really was: small and
broad, with high cheekbones and the slanted eyes of
a Tartar. She had a high bosom, rounded hips, and
muscled calves like the magician's helpers who used
to come to our courtyards to roll barrels on their
soles and swallow fire.

Who knows where she came from, I thought. Perhaps from the Khazars. What doesn't a people go

through in two thousand years of exile? But nature has a memory.

Sonya gave me a sideways glance. She smiled questioningly, knowingly, with a wink. I remembered the passage in Proverbs, "Such is the way of an adulterous woman: she eats, and wipes her mouth, and says, 'I have done no wrong.' " Yes, the Enlightenment which our poets praised in such lofty phrases and called the "Daughter of Heaven" has made us all into lechers and harlots. Nobody cared about serving us breakfast and we went to look for a coffee shop. We strolled like honeymooners. The chauffeur who had brought us here was to come for us at one o'clock. We were told that he had a mistress among the laborers in the colony. Most probably he would be hours late. After walking a few minutes, we came upon a house. On the porch sat an old man in a gray jacket and gray cap, the kind they used to wear in Warsaw. The color of his face reminded me of the Warsaw porters: reddish, bluish, with the stubble of a gray beard. His hairy throat with its pointed Adam's apple was heavily veined. Although he was without prayer shawl or phylacteries, he rocked back and forth as he recited from a prayer book. As we came nearer, he lifted up his eyes, which might once have been blue but were now yellowish, spotted, and bloodshot.

I said to him, "You are praying, aren't you?"

The old man hesitated, and answered hoarsely (I imagined that I recognized a Warsaw voice): "Do I have something better to do? You are the speaker, isn't that right? I was at your lecture last night. Did they let you talk, the scoundrels? They need a speaker like I need a boil. All they need is to stuff themselves and play cards. May their guts rot in hell! And you, young lady—what is your name?—I heard your poems, yes, I heard them. I couldn't understand them all. I am a simple fellow, but. . . ."

He closed the prayer book and rose. "You will eat with me."

We tried to decline; the old man lived alone. But he said, "When will I have a chance like this? I am eighty-one years old. When you visit again, I will be lying there." And he pointed toward a grove of trees which must have hidden the cemetery.

The old man's house was full of broken-down furniture. His dishes seemed not to have been used for a long time. On an uncovered table in the living room there lay fresh eggs, still encrusted with the dirt of chickens. He prepared an omelette for us. He cut thick slices of whole-wheat bread, full of bran and kernels. On his half-paralyzed legs he hobbled back and forth, bringing us more things to eat: gooseberry jam, stale cookies, dried cheese. As he served us, he spoke.

"Yes, I had a wife. Fifty-four years we lived together like doves. I never heard a bad word from her. Suddenly she lay down and it was all over. The children wandered off. What was there for them here? One son is a doctor in Mendoza. A daughter is married in Brazil and lives in São Paulo. One son died and left three orphans. I always thought that I would be the first to go. But what can you do? If one is destined to live, one must live. A woman is not so helpless when she is alone. As you see, I am one of the first colonists. When I came here, it was all wasteland. You couldn't even buy a piece of bread. While on the ship we all sang Zunser's hymn, 'The Lord's Blessing Is in the Plough.' We were told that peasants are healthy because they live in the lap of nature, and that kind of poppycock. But the moment we arrived an epidemic broke out. Children fell ill and died. Older people also became sick. There was talk that the water was poisoned, or who knows what. The baron sent us delegates who were supposed to be agriculturalists, but they couldn't tell wheat from rye. They gave us endless advice; noth-

ing helped. We all wanted to leave but didn't have
the fare. We had signed contracts and were debtors.
They bound us hand and foot; still they were—what
do you call it—philanthropists. A great man came to
us from Paris and spoke only French. We didn't
understand a word he said. Of Yiddish they were
ashamed, these charity lords.

"The Spanish people in the neighborhood hated
us. They always shouted, 'Go back to Palestine!' One
day a rain started and continued for eight days
without stopping. The rivers overflowed their banks.
There was a flood. In the middle of the day it became
as dark as night. There was such thundering and
lightning that we thought the world was coming to
an end. It hailed too. The hailstones were as large as
goose eggs. One chunk of ice made a hole in a roof
and destroyed the house. How does ice come from the
sky? There were among us a few elderly people and
they began to recite their confessions. They believed
the Messiah was about to come and that this was the
war between Gog and Magog. Those who could write
wrote long letters to the baron, but he never answered.
The women did one thing; they cried. There came to
us a young man, Hershelle Moskver. They called
him—how do you say?—an idealist. He had long
hair and wore a black blouse with a sash. He had
already been to the Holy Land and had left it.
'There,' he said to us, 'is a desert. Here the earth is
fat.' He brought with him a young woman. Her
name was Bella. She was beautiful, black like a
gypsy, with a mouth full of white teeth. All the men
fell in love with her. When she entered a room, it
became brighter. She comforted and helped everyone. When a woman gave birth, she was the mid-
wife. But the women began to complain that she had
come here to seduce their husbands. There was a lot
of gossip and fighting. In the middle of all this, Bella
contracted typhoid fever and could not be saved. Her
enemies had put a curse on her. Hershelle Moskver

stood at her grave and refused to recite the Kaddish.
Three days later he was found hanged. Do you want
another cup of coffee? Drink, my good friends, drink.
When will I have such an honor again? If you want,
come with me to the cemetery. It's right here. I will
show you everything. The whole colony is buried
there."

Our breakfast finished, the old man took his cane
and we walked to the cemetery. The fence was
broken. Some headstones were bent, others had top-
pled over. They were all grown over with weeds and
wild flowers, the engraved letters green with moss
and half erased. Here and there protruded a rotting
wooden tablet. The old man pointed toward a hill.
"There lies Bella, and next to her, Hershelle Moskver.
They lived together, and . . . how is it in the Bible?"

I helped him out. "Lovely and pleasant in their
lives, and in their death they were not divided."

"Yes, you remember. My memory has weakened.
What took place seventy years ago is clear to me like
yesterday. What happened yesterday seems far away.
It's all the years, the years. I could sit with you
seven days and seven nights and I wouldn't be able
to tell you a tenth of what we suffered. And does the
younger generation know it? They don't want to
hear a thing. Everything was prepared for them. All
work is now done with machines. They get in a car
and drive to Buenos Aires. Are you two husband and
wife?"

"No, we are friends."

"Why don't you get married?"

"He already has a wife." Sonya pointed to me.

"Well, I will sit down here."

The old man sat on a bench. Sonya and I walked
among the graves and read the inscriptions on the
headstones. The air smelled sweet, like honey. Bees
hummed as they flew from flower to flower. Huge
butterflies fluttered over the graves. The wings of
one butterfly had the black and white stripes of a

prayer shawl. Sonya and I came over a hill and saw a stone with two names, those of Bella and Hershelle Moskver.

Sonya took my hand and began to pinch and pull. She dug her nails into the flesh. We stood by the stone and could not move away. Every few moments another kind of bird sounded his call. A strong perfume filled the air. In Sonya's hair all sorts of insects gathered. A ladybug landed on my lapel. A caterpillar fell into the cuff of my pants. The old cemetery teemed with life, death, love, vegetation. Sonya said, "If only we could remain here like this."

After a while we returned to the bench where the old colonist waited. He had fallen asleep. His toothless mouth was open and he looked as stiff as a corpse. But his eyes under his shaggy brows seemed to smile. A butterfly had settled on the visor of his cap. It remained still, congealed in thoughts as ancient as its species. Then it shook its wings and flew off in the direction of the hill where Bella and Hershelle lay buried—the Romeo and Juliet of Baron de Hirsch's grandiose dream to turn Russian Jews into Argentine peasants.

Translated by the author and Evelyn Torton Beck

The Blasphemer

Faithlessness can also lead to insanity. In Malopol, our village, this is what happened to Chazkele. I knew him well; I even went to cheder with him one winter. His father, Bendit, was a coachman. He lived on the hill among the poor. He had a dilapidated hut, a broken-down stable, and a nag called Shyva, who was as emaciated as a skeleton and terribly old. This horse lived more than forty years. Some believed that it was over fifty. Why this animal existed so long, no one could understand, because Bendit drove it six days a week, made it carry heavy loads, and fed it a mixture of straw and a few oats. It was said that Shyva was a reincarnation of a man who went bankrupt and came back as a horse to pay his debt with hard work.

Bendit was small, broad-shouldered, with yellow hair, a yellow beard, and a face full of freckles. He addressed the horse as if it were human. He had six children and a wife, Tsloveh, who was famed for her curses. She cursed not only people but her cat, her chickens, even her washtub. Besides her living children, Tsloveh had a whole brood in the cemetery. She began to curse her infants when they were still in her belly. When the baby kicked her, Tsloveh would scream, "May you not live to see the light."

Her children, five girls and only one boy—Chazkele, who was the third-born—always squabbled among themselves. When my father had to go to Lublin, I was sent to fetch Bendit and so I was familiar with their house. The woman walked around half naked and barefoot. Since Chazkele was good in cheder, he

was provided with a gaberdine and boots. I was told
that he had been taught the alphabet and learned to
read, and even studied the book of Genesis, all in one
year. Chazkele had hair that was so yellow that it
almost blinded you. His face was like his father's—
white and densely freckled. I think his eyes were
green. Even though Tsloveh was a faithful wife and
never even looked at another man, Bendit called his
son Chazkele Bastard. The girls also had nicknames:
Tsipa the Snake, Zelda the Sloven, Alteh Dripnose,
Keila Garbage, Rickel the Scratcher. Tsloveh herself was called in town Tsloveh Bigmouth. Once,
when Bendit fell ill and Tsloveh went to the synagogue to pray at the Holy Ark, she addressed the
Almighty, "Couldn't you find anyone to strike but
Bendit? He must feed a wife and six worms. Father
in heaven, it's better you plague the rich."

She began to name all the community leaders of
Malopol. She advised God whom to give a boil on his
side, a swelling on his rear, a burning of his insides.
Fulcha the beadle had to drag her away from the
scrolls.

His father and mother both loved Chazkele. No
small thing, an only son, and a scholar in addition.
But the name Bastard remained. At the slightest
provocation, Bendit removed the belt from his pants
and whipped him. Tsloveh used to pinch him. There
was a type of pinching in Malopol that was called
"the little fiddle." It was a drawn-out, thin pinch that
makes you see stars. Chazkele's sisters were proud
of him and boasted about him to others, but at home
they needled him and called him bench warmer,
bookworm, and other such nicknames. When his
olders sister, Tsipa the Snake, gave him his meal,
she would say, "Eat until you choke," or "Drink
until you burst." Two or three girls slept together on
a pallet, but Chazkele had a bench bed for himself.
Whoever made his bed would say to him, "Go to
sleep and don't wake up."

Even in cheder, Chazkele began to ask questions
about God. If God is merciful, why do small children
die? If He loves the Jews, why do the Gentiles beat
them? If He is the Father of all creatures, why does
He allow the cat to kill the mouse? Our teacher,
Fishele, was the first one to predict that Chazkele
would grow up a nonbeliever. Later, when Chazkele
began to study in the study house, he plagued the
principal of our yeshiva, Reb Ephraim Gabriel, with
his queries. He found all kinds of contradictions in
the Bible and in the Talmud. For example, in one
place it is written than God cannot be seen and in
another that the elders ate and drank and saw Him.
Here it said that the Lord doesn't punish the children for the sins of their fathers and elsewhere that
He takes revenge on the third and fourth generations. Reb Ephraim Gabriel tried to explain these
things as well as he could, but Chazkele would not
be put off so easily. The enlightened ones in Malopol
were pleased with Chazkele's heresies, but even
they advised him not to overdo it if he didn't want to
be persecuted by the fanatics. But Chazkele would
answer, "I don't give a damn. I want the truth."

He was slapped and thrown out of the study house.
When Bendit heard these goings on, he gave Chazkele
a sound lashing. Tsloveh wailed that, instead of joy,
he only brought shame upon her. She went to cry on
her mother's grave and to pray that Chazkele might
see the right way. But Chazkele remained obstinate.
He made friends with the town musicians, with
Lippa the leech, with Lemmel the watchmaker, all
people with little faith. On the Sabbath, he no longer
prayed in the synagogue with the community but
stood in the antechamber with the rough youths. For
a short time, he even tried to learn Russian from the
druggist's daughter, Stefania. When he reached the
age of his bar mitzvah, his father brought him a pair
of phylacteries from Lublin, but Chazkele refused to

put them on. He said to his father, "What are they, nothing but the hide of a cow."

He got a heavy beating, but blows no longer bothered him. His build was small, like his father's, but he was strong and agile as an ape. On the thirty-third day of Omer, when it is the custom for boys to go to the forests, he climbed up the highest tree. When he was in the mood, he helped his father carry heavy sacks of grain or barrels of kerosene. He got into brawls with Gentile boys. Once he fought a whole bunch of them alone and got a good thrashing. When any of the townspeople scolded him, he answered with insolence. He would say to an elder, "You are God's Cossack, aren't you? Why don't you stop giving false weights and false measures in your store?"

When Bendit convinced himself that this boy would not grow up to be a rabbi, he apprenticed him to Zalman the blacksmith; but Chazkele had no patience to fan the bellows all day. I don't know why he did it, but he stole books from the study house and went to read them in the women's section of the synagogue, which was empty all week long. When something in a book didn't please him, he erased the words with a pencil or he tore out a page. Once he was caught tearing out pages from a book and from then on he wasn't permitted to enter the study house. My father didn't allow me to talk to him. Neither did the fathers of other young men permit their sons to associate with him. Chazkele was as good as excommunicated. He threw off the yoke of Jewishness completely. It was rumored that he smoked on the Sabbath. He went with Sander the barber to the tavern and drank vodka with him and ate pork. He took off his gaberdine and managed to get a short jacket somewhere and a Gentile cap. Even before he had grown a beard, he asked Sander to shave him. He searched only for sin. Bendit grew tired of beating him and no longer treated him as a son, but his mother and sisters still sided with him. Once on the Feast of Booths, Chazkele peeked into the booth of Reb Shimon the warden and made some nasty remark. Reb Shimon and his sons came out and beat him up, even though it was a holiday. He went home dripping with blood. Late at night, three of Chazkele's sisters, Keila, Rickel, and Alteh, stealthily entered Reb Shimon's booth and defecated there. In the morning, when Reb Shimon's wife, Baila Itta, went into the booth and saw the mess, she fainted. The rabbi sent for Bendit and warned him that if his son did not stop this scandalous behavior, he would forbid the townspeople to travel in his wagon and to send merchandise with him.

That feast day, even though it was forbidden, Bendit beat Chazkele with a heavy stick for such a long time that Chazkele lost consciousness. For months after, Chazkele was almost timid. I was told that he even began to study again, although I never met him in the study house. Then, a few days after Passover, Bendit's nag died. It lay with its protruding ribs in front of the stable, wet with sweat, salivating, urinating, heaving its sides. Crows hovered on the straw roof, ready to pick at the eyes of the carcass. Tsloveh and her daughters stood over the dying horse, wringing their hands and lamenting. Bendit cried as if it were Yom Kippur. I was there myself. Everybody went to look. The next day, early in the morning, when one of those who prayed in the study house opened the Ark to take out the holy scroll, he found horse dung and a dead mouse there. A pauper who slept in the study house bore witness that Chazkele had gone there late at night and poked around in the Ark. There was an uproar in Malopol. Butchers and barrelmakers went to Bendit's hut, intent on seizing Chazkele and punishing him for the sacrilege. Tsloveh met them at the door with a pail of slops. His sisters tried to scratch their eyes out. Chazkele hid under the bed. The crowd pulled him out and gave him what he deserved. He tried to defend himself, but they dragged him to the rabbi and there he confessed to everything. The rabbi asked, "What was the sense of it?"

And Chazkele said, "A God who can so torture an innocent nag is a murderer, not a God." He spat and cried. He spoke such words that the rabbi's wife had to stop her ears.

Bendit came running and the rabbi said to him, "Your Chazkele is what the Bible calls 'stubborn and rebellious.' In ancient times, such a one was taken to the gate of the town and stoned. Today, the four death punishments of the court—stoning, strangling, burning, and beheading—have been abolished. But Malopol will not stand for this rascal any more." On the spot, the elders had decided to buy Bendit another horse, on the condition that Chazkele leave town. And so it happened. The next morning, Chazkele was seen walking on the road to Lublin, carrying a wooden box like a recruit. Tsloveh ran after him, bemoaning him like a corpse.

There was a community he-goat in Malopol, a first-born which, according to the law, was not to be slaughtered. He chewed the straw from the thatch huts, peeled the bark from logs, and, when there was nothing better to eat, he nibbled at an old prayer book in the synagogue yard. He had two crooked horns and a white beard. After Chazkele had gone, the people discovered that the he-goat was wearing phylacteries. Before he left, Chazkele fastened the head phylactery between the goat's horns, and the arm phylactery he bound to one of its legs. He even formed the letter "shin"—the initial of the holy name Shodai—with the phylactery straps.

You can just imagine the outcry in Malopol. At that time, I myself had begun to veer, so to speak, from the straight path. Against my father's wishes, I started to learn bookbinding. Several of my friends and I planned to go to America or to Palestine. First,

I didn't want to serve the czar or to have to maim
myself to avoid the service. Second, we had become
enlightened and we no longer believed in boarding
at the house of the fathers-in-law and letting our
wives provide for us. I never went to America or to
Palestine, but at least I moved to Warsaw. After
Chazkele left Malopol, he became our idol for a
while.

2.

The salesmen who went to Lublin for merchandise
brought back news of Chazkele. The thieves of Piask
tried to make him a partner to their foul business,
but Chazkele declined. He would not steal other
people's property, he said. One should live honestly.
In Lublin, there were strikers who wanted to depose
the czar. One of them even threw a bomb into a
barracks. The bomb didn't explode, but the one who
threw it was torn to shreds by the Cossacks' spears.
When these rebels heard about Chazkele, they wanted
to make him one of them. But Chazkele said, "Is it
the czar's fault that he was born a czar? Are the rich
to blame for being lucky? Would you throw money
away if you had it?" This was Chazkele. He had an
answer for everything. One might think that he was
ready to go to work and earn his bread, but he had
no desire to work, either. He apprenticed himself to
a carpenter; but when his master's wife asked him to
rock the baby, Chazkele answered, "I'm not your
nanny." He was thrown out immediately. There
were missionaries in Lublin who attempted to convert him, and Chazkele asked them: "If Jesus is the
Messiah, then why is the world full of evil? And if
God can have a son, why can't he have a daughter?"
The soul catchers realized that he was a hard nut to
crack and let him go. He refused to accept alms. He
slept on the street and almost died from hunger.
After a while, he left for Warsaw.

I had moved to Warsaw, too. I got married and became a bookbinder on my own. I met Chazkele and proposed to teach him the trade, but he said, "I'm not going to bind Bibles and sacred books."

"Why not?" I asked him.

"Because they are full of lies," he said. He wandered around on the Jewish streets—Krochmalna, Gnoyna, Smocha—dressed in tatters. He would stop on the square on Krochmalna Street and engage in discussions with anyone. He blasphemed God and the Anointed. I never knew that he was so well versed in the Scriptures and in the Talmud. He poured out quotations. He would stop a few bums who didn't know the alphabet and inform them that the earth is round and that the sun is a star, or some such thing. They thought he was crazy. They punched him in the nose and he fought back. No matter how strong he was, they were stronger. A few times, he was arrested. So he sat in jail and enlightened the prisoners. He had nine measures of talk and was always ready to argue. According to him, nobody knew the truth—everyone deceived himself. I once asked him what, then, should be done, and he replied, "There's nothing to do. Wise are those who make an end to everything."

"If that's so," I asked, "why do you wander around in this chaotic world?"

And he said, "What's the hurry? The grave won't run away."

It seemed that there was no place in the world for Chazkele, but he finally did find something. Across the square, there was a brothel. The whores used to stand at the gate of the building each evening and sometimes even in daylight. The other tenants did everything they could to get rid of them, but the pimps bribed the authorities. It was just across from the window of my apartment and I saw it all. The moment evening fell, men began to appear there in shabby clothes; also soldiers and even schoolboys.

The fee was, if I'm not mistaken, ten kopecks. Once I saw an old man with a long gaberdine capote and a white beard enter there. I knew him quite well, a widower. He most probably thought that no one saw him. What can an old man do if he has no wife?

I met Chazkele on the street. For the first time, he was decently dressed and he carried a bundle. I asked what he carried there and he said stockings. "Have you become a peddler?" I asked, and he said, "Women do need stockings." After a while, I saw him enter the brothel. He even stopped to talk to one of the prostitutes. To make it short, Chazkele sold stockings—but only in the brothels. This had become his livelihood. I was told that the loose females loved his talk and this is why they bought from him. He went to them during the day, when they had no guests. I often saw him walk by, and each time the bundle grew larger. Who could be better company for Chazkele? The streetwalkers were delighted with his banter. They fed him and accepted him as their own. How strange; the thieves in Warsaw had their leader, Berelle Spiegelglas, and now these dames had their Chazkele. Berelle Spiegelglas behaved sedately. Thieves have wives and children. They don't spit on everything. Loose women besmirch everybody. Chazkele stood with these creatures and told them about the sins of King David, King Solomon, Bathsheba, Abigail. They became high and mighty. If such saints could sin, why can't they? Everyone needs some justification.

Once a tart appeared who was different from the rest. Most of these girls came from poor little villages; many of them were sick. All they wanted was to make a few groschen. This one was brazen, healthy, with red cheeks and the eyes of a vulture. I still remember her name, Basha. In the middle of the summer, she wore boots. As a rule, the pimp stood a few steps away or across the street and kept an eye on his property, so they shouldn't hide some money in their stockings or waste time with the urchins who came just to babble. Once in a while, these flesh dealers used to beat up one of their ladies and the screaming could be heard along the whole street. The policeman had been bought off and he played dead. But this Basha did what she wanted. She uttered such filth, and carried on so, that the neighbors had to close their windows in order not to hear her obscenities. She mimicked everyone, she teased the passersby. There was always a circle of ruffians around her and she held forth for them. You know their way of thinking: all women are rotten; everyone can be bought; the whole world is one whorehouse. My Miriam came home one day and said, "Chaim, it's an ordeal to go out in the street. It's a danger to bring up children here." The moment I saved up a few rubles, I moved out to Panska Street.

Still, I visited Krochmalna Street from time to time. I got work there from the cheders and study houses. Everybody knew that Chazkele was from my town and they told me about him. He became the teacher of the wanton females. He wrote letters for them. He dealt not only in stockings but in kerchiefs and underwear. He had met Basha, and they had fallen in love. Somebody told me that she came from a decent house and that she took to this profession not because of poverty but because she liked to wallow in dirt. When the pimps learned that she loved Chazkele, they became jealous and wanted to break his neck. The girls took his part. To make it short, Basha left the brothel and went to live with Chazkele. One might think that someone like Basha wouldn't care about being respectable, but she wanted to take Chazkele to the rabbi and get married according to the law of Moses and Israel. Females all dream about marriage. However, Chazkele refused. "What is a rabbi? An idler in a fur hat. And what is a canopy? A few yards of velvet. And what is a ketuba? A piece of paper." Basha insisted. For their kind to

get married is a real achievement. But Chazkele
was stubborn. The hoodlums sided with Basha now
and wanted to knife him. The couple had to move to
Praga, on the other side of the Vistula. There, no
one knew them. Chazkele could no longer sell stockings in the brothels, because the underworld accused
him of shaming one of their own. He came out with a
pushcart at the Praga bazaar, but he was not the
only one. Besides, he spoiled his own business. A
matron would come over to him to buy a pair of
garters or a spool of thread and he would say to her,
"Why do you wear a wig? It's not written anywhere
in the Torah that one has to cut off one's own hair
and wear someone else's. It was all invented by the
rabbis." On the Sabbath, the market was deserted—
but Chazkele brought out his wares. The strong men
of the Sabbath Observers Society learned about him
and they went out and threw all his merchandise
into the gutters. Chazkele got a beating. Even as
they were tearing him to pieces, he argued: "To sell
a handkerchief is a sin, and to break a man's nose is
a holy deed?" He quoted the Bible to these ignoramuses. He was suspected of being a missionary and
he was banished from the market.

Meanwhile, Basha gave birth to a boy. When a
male child is born, one has to circumcise him, but
Chazkele said, "I won't take part in this ancient
ritual. The Jews learned it from the Bedouins. If God
hates the foreskin, why are children born with it?"
Basha begged him to give in. Praga is not Moscow.
It's full of pious Jews. Who has ever heard of a father
who refuses to let his son be circumcised? His windowpanes were smashed. On the eighth day, a quorum of porters and butchers stormed in, together
with a mohel, and they circumcised the baby. Two
men seized and held Chazkele. A father has to recite
the benedictions. Nothing could force Chazkele to
say the holy words. Basha lay in bed behind the
screen and poured out deadly curses on him. In the

beginning, she had liked his foul language; but
when a woman goes to live with a man and she
becomes a mother, she wants to be like anyone else.
From then on, their life became one bitter quarrel.
She used to beat him up and drive him out of the
house. Her cronies had to make a collection for her.
After a while, she took the infant and went back to
the brothel. Did she have a choice? The madam took
care of the child. I knew that madam and her husband, Joel Bontz, as well. He used to pray in the
little synagogue at number 12. In 1905, when the
revolutionaries fought with the pimps, a bunch of
the Red ones forced their way into the brothel and
beat up the girls. It was in the morning. The madam
ran into the little synagogue and screamed, "You
stay here and pray, and there our merchandise is
being ruined."

After Basha left him, Chazkele fell to pieces. He
again walked around in rags. He couldn't peddle
anything any more and became a beggar. But even
as a panhandler, he was a failure. He would stand in
front of the synagogue, stretch out his hand, and
dissuade the worshippers from praying. "To whom
are you praying?" he would say. "God is deaf. Besides, He hates the Jews. Did He rescue His people
when Chmielnizki buried children alive, and did He
save them in Kishinev?" Nobody wanted to give a
groschen to a heretic like this. Not a day passed
without his being slapped. He would pick up a cigarette stub on the Sabbath and go smoke it on Hasidic
Twarda Street. He got a kopeck or two somewhere
and ate pork sausages on Yom Kippur in front of
Aaron Sardiner's synagogue. There was a group of
freethinkers in Warsaw and they offered to help
him. He antagonized them also. I was told that he
used to go to the madam's home to try to see his son
and she wouldn't let him in. He went to Basha's
brothel and she, too, chased him away. In the summer, he slept in a courtyard. In the winter, he went

to the "circus." This is what they called the poor-house. I met him several times in the street. He looked old and unkempt. He wore one boot and one slipper. He couldn't even afford to shave his beard. I said to him, "Chazkele, what will be the end of you?"

"It's all God's fault," he said.

"If you don't believe in God," I asked, "with whom do you wage war?"

"With those who speak in His name," he answered.

"And who created the world?" I asked.

"And who created God?" Chazkele asked in return.

He became sick and they took him to the hospital on Chysta Avenue. There he indulged in such antics and created such bedlam that they wanted to throw him out. A sick man was chanting the psalms and Chazkele told him that King David, the author of Psalms, was a murderer and a lecher. He told such wild jokes that the other patients held their stomachs from laughter. One man had a boil that had to be opened. He laughed so much at Chazkele's jokes that the boil burst open. To this day, I don't know what was wrong with Chazkele. Before his death, he asked that he be cut to pieces and thrown to the dogs.

Who listens to a madman? He was taken to the cleansing room and candles were placed at his head. He was dressed in shrouds and a prayer shawl, and the community gave him a plot in the suburban cemetery. Basha, his former mistress, and her company rode after the hearse in droshkies. His son was five or six years old and he recited Kaddish at the grave. If there is a God and Chazkele must account to Him for his deeds, it will be quite gay in heaven.

Translated by the author and Rosanna Gerber

The Wager

The Friday evening meal was over, but the candles were still burning in the silver candlesticks. A cricket chirped behind the stove, and the wick in the lamp made a slight sucking sound as it drew up the kerosene. On the covered table stood a crystal decanter with wine and a silver benediction cup, an engraving of the Wailing Wall upon it; near them lay a bread knife with a mother-of-pearl handle and a challah napkin, embroidered in golden thread.

The master of the house, still young, had blue eyes and a small yellow beard. His Sabbath caftan was not made of satin, as was the custom with the Hasidim, but of silk. He also wore a crisp collar around his neck and a ribbon that served as a tie. The mistress wore a dress with a design of arabesques and a blond wig adorned with combs. She had the face of a young girl: round, without a wrinkle, with a small nose and light-colored eyes.

Outside, the snow lay in great drifts, gleaming under the full moon. The frost was forever trying to paint a tree, a flower, a palm leaf, or a bush upon the windowpanes, but in the warmth of the room the patterns quickly melted away.

On a chair sat the family cat, content after a meal of tidbits thrown to it from the table, its belly full of kittens. Its eyes, green as gooseberries, stared at the guest. He was a straight-backed man, dressed in a weekday caftan girdled with a cord, and with a beard that seemed to have been made of dirty tufts of cotton. His nose was red, for he had already downed at least half a bottle of vodka. From under his thick brows a pair of needle-sharp eyes looked out. The hand, which he rested on the white table-cloth, had horny nails, a network of veins, and was covered with tufts of hair.

He said: "It's a long story. Not for today. You will probably want to go to sleep now."

"Sleep?" the mistress of the house cried. "It's only fifteen after six. Look!" And she pointed to the clock with a long pendulum and the hours indicated by Jewish letters.

Her husband said: "What's the hurry? You cannot sleep through the long winter night anyway. We shall still have tea and pastry later on."

"Oh, when I was young, I could snore through twelve hours at a stretch. But when you're older, you cannot sleep. I doze off and I wake up right away. I lie on the hard bench and think all sorts of idle thoughts."

"Tonight you'll sleep on a soft bed."

"What's the good? After that, the bench will seem still harder. . . . As you see me now, you must think that my family was some low scum, that I was born in a poorhouse. Nonsense! My father was a merchant. On my mother's side, I come of ritual slaughterers and lumber merchants. I'm from Hrubieshov. My grandfather was a leader of the community there. My father owned a store—pots and hardware. We were not wealthy, but we got along quite well. My mother had borne eight children, but only two sons remained alive—myself and my brother Bendit. My name is Avrom Wolf.

"When people have only two children left, they tremble over them and hope to gain some pride and pleasure from them. But neither of us liked to study. We were sent to the best cheders, but our minds remained far from the Torah. My brother Bendit—he was my elder by two years—was fond of pigeons. He build a pigeon-cote on our roof, and the pigeons came flying to him from near and far. He fed them hempseed, peas, millet, and anything else he could get hold of. He was also fond of a glass of vodka. In that he's like me, he-he. . . . But he had golden hands.

"Our father wanted him to become a teacher, but all he was good for was carpentry. Whenever a table, a chair, or a bench was broken, Bendit repaired it in a wink. Once a cornice split off a wardrobe. It needed a carver to fit in the broken piece, but Bendit carved it out, replaced it, and polished it so that you could not tell the difference. He wanted to apprentice himself to Faivel the carpenter, but our mother would not hear of it. She cried that she would rather die than see her Bendit become a workman. In the end, both of us hung around without anything to do.

"There were enough idlers in Hrubieshov, and we became part of the company. We spent our days in taverns. On Saturdays, we went out to the Yanev Road, where the seamstresses went strolling, and had our fun with them. We never had to worry where the next meal would come from, and when the stomach is full the Devil's never far away. We cheated on prayers and we broke the rules of the Sabbath.

"In those days there lived an atheist in Shebreshin—a certain Yekl Reifman. Zamosc was full of—what do you call them now? Maskilim, men who preached 'enlightenment.' They said that God had not created the world, and other things of this kind. All week Leibush's tavern was empty, because the peasants came to drink only on market days—on Thursdays. Our gang would sit there, guzzling vodka and palavering of this and that. We were forever making wagers: how many hard-boiled eggs a man could eat, how many mugs of beer one could drink down.

"A few years earlier one of these wagers had ended badly. A cart driver, Yoineh Khlop, had made a bet that he could eat an omelette of thirty eggs. He put it all away and washed it down with a full pitcher of beer. Then his guts burst, and he was done for. You'd think that after such an incident the fellows would quiet down, but not they! They continued to prattle and to brag. We held contests to see who'd force the other's hand down, and in this I was the champion. I had great strength. If I weren't so strong, I'd be rotting in the earth by now.

"Anyway, one winter a wild young fellow had come to our town from Zamosc, Yosele Baran by name. I don't remember exactly why or to whom he had come. Perhaps for no special reason, or perhaps to buy wheat. His father was a grain broker, and Yosele helped him out a bit. On the following day we all went to the tavern and had ourselves a time. Yosele took a piece of pork from his pocket and began to eat it. We had ordered some kosher sausage from Leibush, but Yosele wanted to show he was a big shot. A discussion began, and Yosele declared that there was no God. A dead man, he said, was no more than a dead fish. Moses had not ascended to heaven. And so on, and so forth.

"There was among us a certain Tovele Kashtan, a redhead and a rascal, and he said: 'All the same, if you were told to spend a night with a corpse in the morgue, you'd get your pants full.' Yosele immediately flew into a temper. 'I am not afraid,' he said, 'either of the living or of the dead. If you're a coward, don't turn it on anybody else.' Both of them were hotheads, Yosele and Tovele.

"One word led to another, and they made a wager. Yosele Baran bet twenty-five rubles that he would spend a night with a corpse in the hut where the dead were cleansed. Tovele Kashtan also put up twenty-five rubles. In those years it was a fortune, especially to us, but both were in a rage over the challenge. Yosele had to go somewhere, and we all agreed to meet later.

"It was only after Yosele had gone that we realized there were no corpses in town. First of all, nobody had died in Hrubieshov. Second, no dead man was left overnight in the hut, unless it was a stranger or a pauper from the poorhouse. We talked it over, until someone thought of a trick: one of us would impersonate a corpse. He would lie down on the table, with candles at his head, and Yosele would think it was a dead man. We'd play a joke on Yosele that he would long remember.

"All this was almost fifty years ago, but as I talk, it seems to me that it was only yesterday. As it chanced, our parents had gone to Izhbitza to a wedding. My brother Bendit tried to persuade me to play the corpse. The others helped him out. They promised me half the purse.

"To tell the truth, I was unhappy over the whole business, but they plied me with drink after drink. They said that if I played some tricks under the sheet to frighten Yosele, he would surely run away, and we'd be left with the kitty. I allowed myself to be talked into it. Life was too good to us; we had to ask for trouble.

"My brother Bendit and I went home. I put on a pair of my father's long underwear and his shirt, to look as though I was wrapped in a shroud. Our father was a giant of a man, a head taller than I. The path to the cemetery was covered with snow, like today. We took a roundabout way to avoid being seen. There was a gravedigger in town, Reb Zalmon Ber, but he lived far from the cemetery. He was also a water carrier. Since there was no corpse in the hut, he had nothing to do at the graveyard.

"We prepared two candles and waited. As soon as Tovele, Yosele, and the rest came into sight, I was to play dead. In the meantime we cracked sunflower seeds, putting the shells into our pockets. The whole business looked like a joke. Who could have thought it would lead to such a misfortune?

"After a while we saw them coming. Night had fallen, but the sky was still red with the sunset. We saw them plodding through the snow. I took off my boots and jacket and stretched out on the bench. My brother covered me with a sheet. He hid my clothes under the bench, lit the two candles, and went out.

"Why deny it? I felt uneasy, but I knew that the gang would soon burst in and the game would start. Twelve and a half rubles weren't to be found under every bush.

"It did not take long for the company to arrive. I heard my brother's voice among theirs. They spoke in undertones as is proper in the presence of the dead. Yosele Baran asked who the dead man was, and he was told that it was a tailor's apprentice, a lonely orphan who had died in the poorhouse.

"Suddenly Yosele went over and uncovered my face. I thought the game was up, but I must have been white as a corpse, for he drew up the sheet at once. I remained there benumbed. I held my breath and tried to make no movement. We had to win the bet. Soon the others left. There was no lock on the door, but I heard them piling up snow outside and tramping it down with their feet so that Yosele could not open the door if he lost his nerve. Across the road from the cemetery hut there was a ruined building, and the band of jokers was to spend the night there playing cards. It was agreed that, if Yosele should become frightened, he was to shout and they would come for him. But Yosele Baran was no coward. Through the sheet I saw him lighting a cigarette. He sat down bravely on an overturned pail and laid out a pack of cards.

"It may be only a joke, but when you're lying in the cemetery hut on the bench where the corpses are washed, with two candles burning at your head, it gives you a queer feeling. My heart was hammering so hard that I was afraid Yosele would hear it."

"My dear man, don't tell any more," the mistress begged. "It's a terrible story. . . . I'll be afraid to sleep tonight. . . ."

"Silly, it wasn't a real corpse," her husband reassured her.

"Still, I'm frightened."

"If you're frightened, say a prayer to ward off the Evil Ones. . . ."

"It's not a story for the Sabbath."

"If you don't want me to, I won't tell any more," said the guest. "You're young people. . . . You are only beginning to live. . . ."

"Really, Reizele, you shame me before our guest," the husband said. "You shouldn't be such a coward. After all, everybody dies. We shall also be dead some day."

"Oh, stop it!"

"Forgive me, I'll go to sleep," said the guest.

"No, no, dear man. I'm the master of the house, not she. If she doesn't want to hear, she can leave the table. . . ."

"Really, I do not wish to cause trouble between man and wife," the guest said. "You will make up, and the anger will be turned against me. . . ."

"No, go on with the story. If my husband wishes it, then I will hear it too."

"You will have bad dreams."

"Go on, go on. I am curious myself."

"Where was I? Oh, yes, I lay there and looked at Yosele Baran through the cloth. He was laying out his deck of cards, but every now and then he'd throw a glance in my direction. I knew very well that he was nervous, and I was anxious for the jest to be over. When you're lying without moving, you suddenly get an itch on the shoulder, the head, the back. Saliva collects in your mouth, and you must spit it out. How long can a man lie like a stone?

"I stirred a little, and the room was so quiet that the bench creaked. Yosele turned his head and the cards dropped from his lap. He stared at me, and I saw that his teeth were beginning to chatter. I wanted to sneeze, but I did my best to hold it back. I was already thinking of sitting up and saying, 'Yosele, they're putting something over on you,' but I did not

want him to get into a rage. To make it short, I
sneezed.

"What happened after that can't even be described.
He jumped and let out a gurgling sound like a
slaughtered ox. I sat up and wanted to tell him it
was all a trick, but I got tangled in the cloth and
accidentally put out the candles. I heard something
fall, and it became quiet. I thought that Yosele had
fainted and wanted to revive him, but I could see
nothing in the dark. I had not even had sense enough
to bring matches with me. I began to scream like a
madman. Then I fell and struck Yosele. The moment
I touched him, I knew he was dead. You know such
things."

"God in heaven, the misfortunes that can happen
in this world!" the woman cried.

"I remember running to the door and trying to
force it open. But the snow piled up by the fellows
must have turned to ice. Now I was alone with a
corpse, and in pitch darkness. My dear friends, I
fainted with the shock. I don't know to this day how I
lived through it.

"And now the real mixup begins. The fellows in
the ruined building became so excited over the card
game that they forgot all about the wager. Suddenly
someone remembered, and they went to the cemetery
hut to take a look. I learned all this forty years later.
They came to the hut and saw it was dark inside.
There were cracks in the walls, but no windows.
They began to call: 'Yosele! Avrom Wolf!' But nobody answered. They quickly cleared away the pile
of snow, forced the door, and saw two corpses in the
light of the stars. They had not brought a lantern,
and the moon was out.

"There were three of them: my brother Bendit,
Tovele Kashtan, and a certain Berish Kirzhner, a
big shot. But boys will be boys. Everybody is afraid
of death, even the greatest braggarts. They ran like
mad. Berish fell and broke a leg. Tovele Kashtan

ran to knock at the rabbi's window. The rabbi was up late, studying the Torah. Tovele rushed in, half frozen, and began to stutter and shake.

"Before the rabbi called the beadle, and before the beadle roused the householders, and before they all got dressed and lit their lanterns, it was almost dawn. They went to the cemetery, and on the way they found Berish Kirshner, already stiff. He could not get up and he had frozen to death."

"God in heaven! . . ."

"I had come to in the meantime and managed somehow to trudge my way home. I expected to find Bendit there, but the house was empty. Bendit thought that I had died of fright and he ran away from the city. He did not dare to face our father and mother. I know all this now. But then I knew only one thing: Bendit was not there.

"The town was in an uproar. The rabbi sent the beadle to call me, but when I saw him at the door, I hid in the attic. Berish Kirzhner's family—they were all butchers—had given Tovele Kashtan a thrashing. They'd beaten his lungs to a pulp. I hid out for two days, still hoping that Bendit would return. But on the third day, when our parents were due back from Izhbitza, I packed a bag and left town. I couldn't look my parents in the eyes and listen to their wailing and shouting. It was already known all over town that I had pretended to be dead, and I got all the blame. Yosele Baran had a large family, with plenty of strong-arm boys; they would have battered me to hash.

"I went to Lublin and apprenticed myself to a baker.

"But kneading those huge buckets of dough gave me a rupture, may God preserve you from such things. Besides, the other apprentices resented me because I was a stranger, and wouldn't play their games. Matchmakers came to me with offers, but I did not like the girls. Also, everybody wanted to know all about me: where I had come from, who my father was. I played the fool, and people thought I was a bastard.

"All this time I was hoping to find some traces of my brother. I looked for him everywhere: in synagogues, in taverns, in hostels. There was a blind musician in Lublin, Dudie by name. Dudie played at all the weddings. When Dudie struck up the wedding march or the welcome dance, the girls wept and laughed. The other musicians became jealous and did all they could to spite him. He had no wife, and so he went out on the road. I met him over a glass of beer and became his guide. At first we traveled only to nearby towns. Later we wandered throughout the breadth and length of Poland.

"Everywhere I sought my brother. I asked everybody I met whether he had seen such and such a man, and described him as best I could. But no one had met him. As long as Dudie lasted, everything was fine. Weddings are jolly occasions. Relatives and guests come from all over. When people dance and sing and play, you forget your troubles. I had heard so many wedding jesters that I began to babble in rhymes myself. Whenever we came to a small town without a jester, I took charge of the entertainment. But Dudie was sinking from day to day. His hands began to tremble. At one of the weddings he dropped, and there was no more Dudie.

"If I were to tell you all I had gone through, I'd have to stay here for a year. They had married me off too, but it didn't work. They palmed off an old maid on me, and she took to me like a starved person to a roast. I am ashamed to talk about it. She was consumptive, and people with consumption don't know when to stop.

"I became a rope winder. Her uncle had taught me the trade. It took no great skill, but it could be done only outside, when it was warm. I'd stand there, drawing out the rope, and every five minutes she'd come out. 'Avrom Wolf, come in.' Now it was one excuse, now another. They get fever from their sick lungs, and the fever drives them crazy. People stood around and laughed in their fists. The children mocked her: 'Avrom Wolf, come in. . . .' When I reproached her, she would get into a coughing fit and spit blood. I wanted to divorce her, but she wouldn't hear of it. The town was not near any river, and I'd have had to go somewhere else for a divorce.

"I suffered for five years. During her last year she spent more time in bed than on her feet. But as soon as her sickness would ease up a bit, she'd start her old song. How can you tell about such things? On the last day she suddenly felt better. She sat up like a healthy woman and talked of going to another town to see a doctor. I brought her a glass of milk and she drank it. Her face was flushed, and she looked prettier and younger than on our wedding day. I went outside to my rope. When I came in, she seemed asleep. I looked more closely and could not hear her breathing. She was gone.

"After her death I was offered match after match, but I wouldn't hear of marriage any more. I could not stay in that town any longer. I sold the house for a song, with everything in it, with the rope wheel and the bit of hemp, and went off wandering over the land. When your heart is heavy, it is difficult to stay in one place. Your feet carry you as they will. How much does a man need when he is alone? A piece of bread and a place to sleep at night. People don't forget you. In every town there is a poorhouse. Good folks like you take one in as a guest. I still kept looking for my brother, but I had lost all hope of finding him.

"It says in some book that the Messiah will come when the people give up hope. And so it was with me. I came to a small town, Zychlin. My boots were falling apart. Since I had a few groschen, I asked for a cobbler who was good and cheap. I was directed up a street on a hill. I walk along this street, and the cobbler sits outside on a bench and scrapes a worn-down sole. I walk over and he lifts his head. I look—it's my brother Bendit.

"I cannot help it. Every time I talk about this meeting, I must cry; it was like Joseph and his brothers. I knew him, but he did not recognize me. I was about to tell him I was Avrom Wolf, but I wanted to be sure it was he. I asked him: 'Where are you from?' And he answered sharply, 'What did you come here for, to babble or to have your boots repaired?' The moment he spoke, I knew it was Bendit. I said to him: 'Are you from the Lublin region?' And he said, 'Yes, I am.' 'From Hrubieshov?' He looked a bit stunned, and then he asked, 'Who are you?' I said, 'I have regards to you from your brother.' The shoe dropped from his hands, 'What brother?' he asked, and I said, 'Your brother Avrom Wolf.' 'Avrom Wolf is alive?' he asked, and I said, 'I am Avrom Wolf.'

"He jumped up and wailed as if it were Yom Kippur. His wife came out, barefoot and ragged. She carried a pail of slops, and she spilled it over her feet. I asked, 'What has become of our mother and father?' And he began to cry. 'They've long gone to the better world. Father died the same year. Mother suffered a while longer.' My brother learned about it years later."

"Is your brother still alive?" the master of the house asked.

"I don't know. He may be. I stayed there for a week. After that I picked up my bundle again. He didn't have enough bread for himself."

"Why didn't you try to let your father and mother know you were alive?"

"I was afraid. I was ashamed. I don't know why myself. They lost two sons at once."

"But why didn't you write them?"

"Who knows? I didn't write."

"Where's the sense of it?" the master asked.

The guest did not reply.

The mistress took out a handkerchief and put it to her eyes. "Why are people so crazy?"

"Reizele, let us have some tea."

The guest raised his head. "Maybe you'd give me another glass of vodka instead?"

"Drink it all down, whatever's left."

"I'm not a drunkard, but when your heart grows bitter you want to forget the sorrow."

The guest turned up the glass. He grimaced and shook himself. Then he pushed away the bottle and said: "I'll never tell my story to anyone again. . . ."

Translated by Mirra Ginsburg

The Son

The ship from Israel was due to arrive at twelve o'clock, but it was late. It was evening before it docked in New York, and then I had to wait quite a while before any passengers were let off. Outside it was hot and rainy. A mob of people had come to wait for the ship's arrival. It seemed to me that all the Jews were there: assimilated ones, and rabbis with long beards and sidelocks; girls with numbers on their arms from Hitler's camps; officers of Zionistic organizations with bulging portfolios; yeshiva boys in velvet hats, with wildly growing beards; and worldly ladies with rouged faces and red toenails. I realized I was present at a new epoch in Jewish history. When did the Jews have ships?—and if they did, their ships went to Tyre and Sidon, and not to New York. Even if Nietzsche's crazy theory about the eternal return were true, quadrillions and quintillions of epochs would have to pass before the smallest part of anything happening in the present would have happened before. But this waiting was tedious. I measured everybody with my eyes, and each time I asked myself the same question: What makes him my brother? What makes her my sister? The New York women fanned themselves, spoke all at once with hoarse voices, refreshed themselves with chocolate and Coca-Cola. A non-Jewish toughness stared out of their eyes. It was hard to believe that only a few years ago their brothers and sisters in Europe went like sheep to the slaughter. Modern Orthodox young men with tiny skullcaps hidden like plasters in their dense hair spoke loudly in English and cracked jokes with the girls, whose behavior and

clothes showed no sign of religion. Even the rabbis
here were different, not like my father and grandfather. To me, all these people appeared worldly and
clever. Almost all, except myself, had secured per-
mits to board the boat. And they got acquainted
unusually fast, shared information, shook their heads
knowingly. The ship's officers began to descend, but
they seemed stiff in their uniforms, which had epau-
lettes and gilded buttons. They spoke Hebrew, but
they had accents like Gentiles.

I stood and waited for a son whom I hadn't seen in
twenty years. He was five years old when I parted
with his mother. I went to America, she to Soviet
Russia. But apparently one revolution was not enough
for her. She wanted the "permanent revolution."
And they would have liquidated her in Moscow if
she hadn't had someone who could reach the ear
of a high official. Her old Bolshevik aunts who
had sat in Polish prisons for Communist activity
had interceded for her, and she was deported together with the child to Turkey. From there, she
had managed to reach Palestine, where she had
brought up our son in a kibbutz. Now he had come
to visit me.

He had sent me one photograph taken when he
had served in the army and fought the Arabs. But
the picture was blurred, and in addition he was
wearing a uniform. Only now, as the first passengers began to come down, did it occur to me that I did
not have a clear image of what my son looked like.
Was he tall? Was he short? Had his blond hair
turned dark with the years? This son's arrival in
America pushed me back to an epoch which I had
thought of as already belonging to eternity. He was
emerging out of the past like a phantom. He did not
belong in my present home, nor would he fit into any
of my relationships outside. I had no room for him,
no bed, no money, no time. Like that ship flying the
white-and-blue flag with the Star of David, he con-

stituted a strange combination of the past and the
present. He had written me that of all the languages
he had spoken in his childhood—Yiddish, Polish,
Russian, Turkish—he now spoke only Hebrew. So I
knew in advance that, with what little Hebrew I
possessed from the Pentateuch and the Talmud, I
would not be able to converse with him. Instead of
talking to my son, I would stammer and have to look
up words in dictionaries.

The pushing and noise increased. The dock was in
tumult. Everyone screamed and shoved themselves
forward with the exaggerated joy of people who have
lost the standard to measure achievement in this
world. Women cried hysterically; men wept hoarsely.
Photographers took pictures, and reporters rushed
from person to person, conducting hurried interviews.
Then there occurred the same thing that always
occurs when I am part of a crowd. Everyone became
one family, while I remained an outsider. Nobody
spoke to me, and I didn't speak to anybody. The
secret power which had joined them kept me apart.
Eyes measured me absent-mindedly, as if to ask:
What is *he* doing here? After some hesitation, I tried
to ask someone a question, but the other didn't hear
me, or at least he moved away in the middle of my
sentence. I might just as well have been a ghost.
After a while I decided what I always do decide in
such cases, to make peace with fate. I stood out of the
way in a corner and watched the people as they came
off the boat, sorting them out in my mind. My son
could not be among the old and middle-aged. He
could not have pitch-black hair, broad shoulders, and
fiery eyes—one like that could not have stemmed
from my loins. But suddenly a young man emerged
strangely similar to that soldier in the snapshot—
tall, lean, a little bent, with a longish nose and a
narrow chin. This is he, something screamed in me. I
tore myself from my corner to run to him. He was

searching for someone. A fatherly love awoke in me.
His cheeks were sunken and a sickly pallor lay on
his face. He is sick, he has consumption, I thought
anxiously. I had already opened my mouth to call
out, "Gigi" (as his mother and I had called him as a
small boy), when suddenly a thick woman waddled
over to him and locked him in her arms. Her cry
turned into a kind of barking; soon a whole bunch of
other relatives came up. They had snatched a son
from me who was not mine! There was a kind of
spiritual kidnapping in the whole thing. My fatherly
feelings became ashamed and stepped back in a
hurry into that hiding place where emotions can
stay for years without a sound. I felt that I had
turned red with humiliation, as if I had been struck
in the face. I decided to wait patiently from now on
and not allow my feelings to come out prematurely.
Then for a while no more passengers emerged. I
thought: What is a son after all? What makes my
semen more to me than somebody else's? What value
is there in a flesh-and-blood connection? We are all
foam from the same caldron. Go back a number of
generations and all this crowd of strangers probably
had a common grandfather. And two or three generations hence, the descendants of those who are relatives now will be strangers. It's all temporary and
passing—we're bubbles on the same ocean, moss
from the same swamp. If one cannot love everybody,
one should not love anybody.

More passengers came out. Three young men
appeared together, and I examined them. None was
Gigi and even if one were, no one would snatch him
from me anyhow. It was a relief when each of the
three went away with someone else. None of them
had pleased me. They belonged to the rabble. The
last one had even turned round and thrown a belli-
cose look at me, as if he had in some mysterious way
caught my deprecating thoughts about him and
those like him.

If he is my son he will come out last, it suddenly occurred to me, and even though this was an assumption, somehow I knew that it would happen that way. I had armed myself with patience and with that resignation which is always there in me ready to immunize my failures and curb any desire I might have to free myself from my limitations. I observed each passenger carefully, guessing his character and personality from the way he looked and was dressed. Perhaps I only imagined it, but each face gave me its secrets and I seemed to know exactly how each of their brains was working. The passengers all had something in common: the fatigue of a long ocean trip, the fretfulness and unsureness of people arriving in a new country. Each one's eyes asked with disappointment: Is this America? The girl with the number on her arm angrily shook her head. The whole world was one Auschwitz. A Lithuanian rabbi with a round gray beard and bulging eyes carried a heavy tome. A bunch of yeshiva boys were waiting for him, and the moment he met them he began to preach with the angry zeal of one who has learned the truth and is trying to spread it quickly. I heard him say, Torah . . . Torah . . . I wanted to ask him why the Torah hadn't defended those millions of Jews and kept them from Hitler's crematoria. But why ask him when I knew the answer already?—"My thoughts are not your thoughts." To be martyred in God's name is the highest privilege. One passanger spoke a kind of dialect which was neither German nor Yiddish but a gibberish out of old-fashioned novels. And how strange that those who waited for him should chatter in the same tongue.

I reasoned that in the whole chaos there are precise laws. The dead stay dead. Those who live have their memories, calculations, and plans. Somewhere in the ditches of Poland are the ashes of those who were burned. In Germany, the former Nazis lie in their beds, each one with his list of murders, tortures, violent or half-violent rapes. Somewhere there must be a Knower who knows every thought of each human being, who knows the aches of each fly, who knows each comet and meteor, each molecule in the most distant galaxy. I spoke to him. Well, Almighty Knower, for you everything is just. You know the whole and have all the information ... and that's why you're so clever. But what shall I do with my crumbs of facts? ... Yes, I have to wait for my son. Again, no passengers were coming out and it seemed to me that everyone had disembarked. I grew tense. Hadn't my son come on that ship? Had I overlooked him? Had he jumped into the ocean? Almost everybody had left the pier, and I felt the attendants were ready to put out the lights. What should I do now? I had had a premonition that something would go wrong with that son who for twenty years had been for me a word, a name, a guilt in my conscience.

Suddenly I saw him. He came out slowly, hesitantly, and with an expression that said he didn't expect anybody to be waiting for him. He looked like the snapshot, but older. There were youthful wrinkles in his face and his clothes were mussy. He showed the shabbiness and neglect of a homeless young man who had been years in strange places, who had gone through a lot and become old before his time. His hair was tangled and matted, and it seemed to me there were wisps of straw and hay in it—like the hair of those who sleep in haylofts. His light eyes, squinting behind whitish eyebrows, had the half-blind smile of an albino. He carried a wooden satchel like an army recruit, and a package wrapped in brown paper. Instead of running to him immediately, I stood and gaped. His back was already bent a little, but not like a yeshiva boy's, rather like that of someone who is used to carrying heavy loads. He took after me, but I recognized traits of his mother—

the other half that could never blend with mine. Even in him, the product, our contrary traits had no harmony. The mother's lips did not pair with the father's chin. The protruding cheekbones did not suit the high forehead. He looked carefully on both sides, and his face said good-naturedly: Of course, he didn't come to meet me.

I approached him and asked unsurely, *"Atah* Gigi?" He laughed. "Yes, I'm Gigi."

We kissed and his stubble rubbed my cheeks like a potato grater. He was strange to me, yet I knew at the same time I was as devoted to him as any other father to his son. We stood still with that feeling of belonging together that needs no words. In one second I knew how to treat him. He had spent three years in the army, had gone through a bitter war. He must have had God knew how many girls, but he had remained as bashful as only a man can be. I spoke to him in Hebrew, rather amazed at my own knowledge. I immediately acquired the authority of a father and all my inhibitions evaporated. I tried to take his wooden box, but he wouldn't let me. We stood outside looking for a taxi, but all the taxis had already gone. The rain had stopped. The avenue along the docks stretched out—wet, dark, badly paved, the asphalt full of ditches and with puddles of water reflecting pieces of the glowing sky, which was low and red like a metal cover. The air was choking. There was lightning but no thunder. Single drops of water fell from above but it was hard to know whether these were spray from the former rain or a new gust beginning. It hurt my dignity that New York should show itself to my son so gloomy and dingy. I had a vain ambition to have him see immediately the nicer quarters of the city. But we waited for fifteen minutes and no taxi appeared. Already I had heard the first sounds of thunder. There was nothing else to do but walk. We both spoke in the same style—short and sharp. Like old friends who know one another's thoughts, we did not need long explanations. He said to me almost without words: I understand that you could not stay with my mother. I have no complaints. I myself am made of the same stuff. . . .

I asked him, "What kind of a girl is she—the one you wrote me about?"

"A fine girl. I was her counselor in the kibbutz. Later we went into the army together."

"What does she do in the kibbutz?"

"She works in the barns."

"Has she at least studied?"

"We went to high school together."

"When are you going to marry?"

"When I go back. Her parents demand an official wedding."

He said this in a way that meant—naturally, we two don't need such ceremonies, but parents of daughters have a different logic.

I signaled a taxi and he half protested. "Why a taxi? We could have walked. I can walk for miles." I told the man to drive us across Forty-second Street, up the lighted part of Broadway, and later to turn into Fifth Avenue. Gigi sat and looked out through the window. I was never so proud of the skyscrapers and of the lights on Broadway as that evening. He looked and was silent. I somehow grasped that he was thinking now about the war with the Arabs, and all the dangers which he had survived on the battlefield. But the powers which determine the world had destined that he should come to New York and see his father. It was as if I heard his thoughts behind his skull. I was sure he too, like myself, was pondering the eternal questions.

As if to try out my telepathic powers, I said to him, "There are no accidents. If you are meant to live, you have to remain alive. It is destined so."

Surprised, he turned his head to me. "Hey, you are a mind reader!"

And he smiled, amazed, curious, and skeptical, as if I had played a fatherly trick on him.

Translated by the author and Elizabeth Pollet

Fate

I used to visit a relative who lived on Park Avenue. He was a lawyer, an investment specialist. There were quite a few rich widows and spinsters among his clients. Every now and then he'd give a party and invite them.

It was at one of these parties that I met Bessie Gold. She was in her fifties, small, slim, with sunken, darkly rouged cheeks. Her yellow eyes were made up with blue eye shadow and inky mascara, as if for the stage. She used an orange-color lipstick and her nails were lacquered to match. On her hairy, veined wrists she wore heavy bracelets from which dangled an assortment of charms. Their clinking and clanging made me think of a prisoner's chains. She was as emaciated as a consumptive and her legs in their mesh stockings were thin as sticks. We sat next to each other, each of us holding a glass of champagne.

Bessie alternated between a sip of champagne and a puff on her cigarette. I noticed that her neck was thin and blue like that of a plucked chicken. Her chest was flat and freckled. A pair of men's ears adorned with diamond earrings protruded from her newly blonded hair. She turned to me and said: "Are you really a writer?"

"I try to be one."

"Why don't you describe my life? Don't think I've always been a champagne-drinking lady. I wasn't born in this country. I was born in Europe. My parents spoke Yiddish. I used to speak Yiddish myself, but I've forgotten most of it. We lived on the East Side and my mother kept boarders—and everything else that goes with it. I don't have to tell you how immigrants lived in those days. We had three dark rooms, and a toilet in the hall. My father worked fifteen hours a day in a sweatshop. In season he used to sleep in the factory, because before he could get home it was already daybreak and time to start working again. There were some union shops at the time, but he was a timid greenhorn and was exploited right and left. He worked such long hours that he began to spit blood.

"I had one brother and two sisters and they all left home early—egotists who refused to help carry the burden. I always had a sense of responsibility. It was the cause of my misfortunes. I slaved with my mother. I cooked, baked, went to Orchard Street for bargains, washed the boarders' clothes, and managed to sneak time to read a book. I never finished high school, but I learned English well enough to give lessons to foreigners. What didn't I do? My father died after long suffering and my mother was left physically and spiritually broken. She barely understood what was said to her. She kept going to the cemetery to cry her bitter heart out on Papa's grave. There was no longer any point in keeping boarders, and so I went to work in a shop as a draper. You know what that is? They put a dress on a mannequin and you fit it. One usually studies to be able to do this, but I had a knack for such things. I could come into any shop and within three days know everything there was to know. Naturally I made enemies.

"From childhood, I always acted older than my years. My mother used to call me 'the old child.' She came from Poland, but Papa was a Litvak. I was a worrier, always searching for security. I became like a husband to my mother. Every Friday I brought her my 'payday' as they call it. Not a penny was missing. Other girls, my sisters included, ran around with boys; enjoyed their youth. But I had one goal: to marry a decent young man, have a home and a family. I had a mother's instincts. I already loved my unborn children. Why don't you drink? A little champagne won't hurt you.

"If I were to tell you everything I've lived through, it would take three thick volumes. I'll make it short. I met a young man. We fell in love and got married. He was tall, good looking, gay. He seemed to have all the virtues. My family could barely believe that I had got myself such a man. He came from Rumania. However, I soon found the fly in the ointment. He didn't like to work. One day he had a job, the next day he didn't. I had saved a few hundred dollars and we rented an apartment uptown. I paid for the furniture, for everything, even the bills for our honeymoon in Ellenville. Such was my fate from the beginning.

"I soon realized, however, that he was keeping things from me. Our neighbor kept calling him to the telephone. We didn't have one. He began getting letters in pink envelopes. He would stuff them into his pocket and never open them in my presence. I suspected that he was having an affair with another woman, but my nature is such that I didn't mind too much. Just so long as he came home to me at night. I was born humble. What did I have to offer him? Before I married, when I quarreled with my mother, she called me a board. Such words stick in your mind and poison your blood. When my husband kissed me, the tears came to my eyes as if he were doing me the greatest favor. One day he disappeared with all our savings. He even took my few jewels away with him. I never saw his face again."

"And you've never heard from him since?"

"No, never. I was told about the Missing Persons' Bureau, but I thought to myself, if he doesn't want me, why look for him? You can't force a person to love. And I didn't want him put behind bars. He was the father of the child I was carrying.

"I promised I wouldn't tell you a long story, but these are the bare facts. I gave birth to a girl. Words cannot describe the joy I felt when I became a mother. True, I had been deserted, but I had tasted a few months of happiness. All my life I had been surrounded by old maids and schlemiels, and by comparison I seemed fortunate. I vowed that my child would never know want. She would have everything that I had missed—a comfortable home, education, nice clothes, all that her heart desired. How did I manage it?

"I found a good-hearted woman, a divorcée, who shared my apartment and took care of the child. My mother had died and I had gone to work in a department store, selling dresses. I did so well that I was soon made an assistant buyer. An assistant buyer rarely gets to be the buyer, but somehow I, the green girl from the East Side, became a buyer for one of the big stores. Don't laugh. It was quite an achievement.

"The other buyers went out and had a good time. Some of them weren't above taking a bribe from a manufacturer. I, fool that I was, slaved for the store. Still, I earned enough to send my Nancy to a private school. She always got the best. One thing I couldn't give her and that was a father. I could have married again. I was legally divorced. But those who wanted me, I didn't want. A man had to please me. If he proved to be a fool or a bore, he disgusted me. There were some that were interested in my few dollars— half gigolos, parasites. I felt that every penny of mine belonged to Nancy. She grew tall and beautiful. She took after her father. The house seemed to light up when she came into it. She was blond and blue-eyed, like a *shiksa*. Some day I'll show you her picture. I have three albums filled with her pictures. That's all I have."

"Did something happen to her?"

"No, God forbid. Not what you think. She's alive

and healthy. May she, as they say in Yiddish, outlive my bones. She did the same thing as her father had done. She walked out on me. As long as she needed me, I was Mummy, and Mum, and Darling Mother. Just as soon as she graduated from Smith and found a rich boy, a Harvard graduate, she began to find fault with me. I foresaw everything, knew exactly how it would end, just as surely as I know now that we will eat supper, have coffee, and go home. How I knew isn't quite clear to me. Some say that I'm psychic. I think about someone I haven't seen in ten years, and suddenly the door opens and there he is. In short, I had served my term and was no longer needed.

"I might mention that over the years I became very successful. My buying trips were reported in the fashion columns. I traveled to Paris, London, Rome, and whatever I bought, the women grabbed up. If I had gone into business for myself I could have become rich, but I made enough to have a beautiful apartment and to spoil my daughter.

"Yet she turned out to be a girl without a heart. There was one thing she knew: I, I, I. She treated me as if I were her slave. Her rich fiancé called me a vulger *Yenteh* from the East Side, and that was enough to make my own child despise me. She didn't even try to hide how she felt. I said to her: 'I don't know which one of us is the more vulgar.' When she heard these words, she flew into such a rage that she spat at me—she literally spat in my face and screamed: 'My daddy was right to get rid of you. I love him even though I never knew him, and you're a fishwife from Orchard Street.' She even tried to hit me.

"I saw my role was finished and said: 'That's enough.' She immediately packed her bags. She, too, took my jewelry, just as her daddy had done. She slammed the door and was gone. Nevertheless, I hoped that her anger would pass. After all, what had

I done? But a voice inside me said, 'You will never see her again.' When she left, my heart became like a stone, and my blood froze in my veins. I was sure that my end had come and I prayed to God that I would die quickly.

"There are moments when life is worthless. Why else do people commit suicide? I fell into my bed and didn't leave it for a week. It was the Christmas season, and there I lay, my nerves in tatters, unable to hold down even a spoonful of water. I had already discovered that there was no limit to how much suffering I can bear. Somebody once called me a masochist. I didn't even know then what the word meant. Yet such people let themselves be tortured for pleasure. It was no pleasure to me. I lay there like a beaten dog and licked my own wounds until my sense of responsibility got the best of me.

"Now I'll tell you something that you'll hardly believe. If you have a few minutes more, listen to this."

"Yes, of course, I'll listen."

"They say there are no miracles, but what happened to me was a miracle. One day a man came into my office. He was neither young nor old, about fifty, tall, handsome, with graying temples. He was a manufacturer and came on business. We made the usual small talk about prices, styles, and the foibles of the customers. 'Who knows what a woman will like?' he said. 'And are men more predictable?' I asked. It happened to be at the time when Rockefeller married that daughter of a Lithuanian peasant, and the newspapers were full of the story. 'Yes,' my visitor replied. 'A man does know exactly what he likes.' 'What does he like?' 'I, for example, like you.' In our business, one is accustomed to such banter, but why deny it, I'm not a woman who attracts men. Once in a while some man would make a pass at me, but it never went further than that. I got used to being alone. It became second nature to me.

" 'Thank you for the compliment,' I said.

" 'It's not a compliment. You're the kind of woman that appeals to me.'

" 'How do you know that I'm not married?'

" 'You're not wearing a wedding ring.'

"Why make a long story of it? He was completely serious. He forgot about his business. Right then and there he proposed to me. I thought he was kidding. Such a good-looking man, and rich to boot. He was a widower without children. What did he see in me? In those days I was always dead tired. I dressed well, but what did clothes mean to a man like that? We had dinner together that night. We were sitting in a restaurant and he told me that God himself had sent me to him. Now listen. He took out his checkbook and said: 'Here is a check for $25,000. Does that prove how serious I am?' I suddenly became frightened. 'You don't even know me,' I said, and I began to tell him my whole story. He also told me about himself. He had been married to a rich girl with a thousand caprices, who ran around with other men. It was closing time and we were the last guests in the restaurant. The waiters eyed us and gradually began turning out the lights. Dawn was breaking when we left.

"Yes, it was love at first sight. I don't understand what he saw in me. It will always remain a riddle. He explained it in this way: he'd had a certain type of woman in mind, and he'd been looking for her. I was his ideal. I have to laugh, excuse me."

The woman began to laugh. Tears streamed from her eyes and she blew her nose. The bracelets on her wrist jangled hollowly. When she took her lace handkerchief away, her face had changed. She had the look of a pious woman who had been interrupted in her prayers. The bags under her eyes had puffed up. I said: "You were married and he died."

"Yes. Are you psychic too? Your cousin must have told you.

"The few years that we spent together were the happiest ones I can possibly imagine. It was too good to last. He was fit and healthy, a giant of a man. We had had dinner and were about to go to the theater. 'Wear your mink jacket, because it's cool outside,' he said. It was in November. If I were to mention everything he bought me, the trips we took and the wonderful hotels we stayed at, it would take too long. It seems that heaven had decided Bessie should have four happy years. He went to the closet, took out my jacket, and fell down like a log. He didn't even sigh. I began to scream with all my might. The neighbors ran in. He was dead.

"Do I have to tell you how I loved him? A good word, or even a smile, and I overflow. It's enough if someone doesn't actually insult me. If God had been good to me, he would have taken me at the same time. My only wish was to die. However, the courage to take a rope and hang one's self, or jump out of a window, I do not have. Only those who are not accustomed to pain can do that. I've been suffering since childhood, and even during my few lucky years I had a premonition that things would end badly. In a way, in those years I suffered more than ever.

"Now let me tell you what happened with our dog. It was too late for us to have children. My husband had a wonderful dog, a Great Dane. He was as large as a calf and clever, at least I thought so. When I walked him, everybody stopped to look. My husband was mad about him. I used to tease him about loving his dog more than his wife.

"After my husband died, the dog was all I had left. I'm not speaking about money. My husband left me a fortune. I knew that it was his sacred wish that I be good to the dog, and whom else did I have to be good to? What can you do for a dog? What there was to do I did. He lived in luxury. Steak every day. Twice a day I took him for a walk and sometimes it seemed to me that he was leading me on the leash and not I him. He dragged me wherever he pleased. Passerby laughed. I knew that I was overdoing it, but I also knew that there would never be anything else to fill the emptiness of my life.

"The dog had the eyes of a human being. I talked to him. He sat there and seemed to listen and to understand each word. Perhaps he really understood. Recently I read an article about animals. It said that they can guess our thoughts and are clairvoyant. I believed that the dog was just as attached to me. He ate from my hands. I washed and combed him. I ordered a mink coat for him to wear in cold weather. He slept on my bed at night. I tried many times to drive him away because he was so huge, so heavy. It seemed as if a lion were lying at my feet. But he wasn't the kind of animal that can be pushed away.

"My husband had had many friends and relatives, yet after his death they all left me strictly alone. Don't ask me why. That's my fate. They hadn't been really friendly toward me even when he was alive. How had I wronged them? But then, how had I wronged my own daughter?

"You won't believe this, but suddenly I noticed that the dog was becoming hostile toward me. He grew grouchy and sometimes even malicious. He stopped putting his paws up on my lap and licking my face. Every now and then he would growl like a wolf. Do you mean to tell me that you too have something against me, I thought. I comforted myself by saying that it was only my imagination, my inferiority complex. Soon I could no longer ignore his ill temper and his snarling look. Luckily, a dog cannot pack his bag and leave. I really couldn't understand it. If one is kind to an animal, it is usually faithful. There was no one I could talk to about it, and I would have been ashamed to. At first he just misbehaved and acted spoiled. Then he began to bark the moment he saw me and to bare his teeth. He seemed possessed. I was afraid to let him sleep on my bed any longer, and locked him in the kitchen at night. I wanted to give him away, but when I thought of my husband and how he had loved him, I just couldn't bring myself to do it. Who knows what goes on in the mind of an animal? They also have their moods and I hoped that the dog would begin to act normally again.

"One evening I had returned from a restaurant where I had eaten supper—alone, of course. I put the dog's leash on to take him out. Suddenly he stood up on his hind legs and began to lick me affectionately as he used to do. 'So, you want to make peace? *Mazel tov.*' I bent down to kiss him and then, my dear friend, a terrible thing happened. The dog snapped at my nose and almost bit it off. That is why I use so much makeup—to cover the scar.

"That night I thought that I had been disfigured for life, or that I would bleed to death. I was alone in the house and I dragged myself to the telephone and called for help. The blood was gushing from me and the dog ran after me and tore off my skirt. They shot him later. What can you do with such a monster? The moment I got the operator on the phone, I fainted. I woke up in the hospital. They had to operate on me because I could not breathe. When I recovered, I had a plastic job done.

"I told you that I never saw my daughter again. That is not exactly true. She came to visit me in the hospital. It was right after the operation and I was still under the influence of the anesthetic. I saw her as if through a fog. She spoke to me, but I don't know to this day what she said. She looked changed. Her face had become hard. It was not my child. She was all dressed up. I might have thought that it was a hallucination, excepting that the nurse later told me that my daughter had been to visit me. It was the last time that I saw her.

"I spent three weeks in the hospital and then two weeks more in the private clinic of the plastic surgeon. It cost a fortune but, considering everything, the operation was a success. My case was written up in the medical journals. But the mental hurt the accident caused me no doctor, no analyst can cure. When your husband leaves you, your only daughter runs away from you, and the dog whom you've been feeding and treating with kindness tries to destroy you, there must be something the matter. What is it? Am I so evil, so ugly, such a nuisance? I don't expect an answer. I no longer expect anything from man or beast, that's the truth.

"Since this misfortune, I live completely alone. An acquaintance offered to give me a parrot or a canary, but I said, 'The dog I loved bit me. The bird will probably peck out my eyes.' People such as I are lepers."

For a while neither of us said anything. Then she asked, "What does it all mean?"

"You called it fate."

"What is fate?"

"One's own trap."

"I've trapped others, too. Well, let's finish our champagne. Cheers, *lechayim*."

We clicked glasses. She took a sip, half grimaced, and licked her lips. She looked at me questioningly, and with a sad smile. The scars and creases around her nose showed through her makeup.

"I'm not fooling myself," she said. "I realize that it was all my fault. Even what happened with the dog."

"What makes you say that?"

The woman did not reply. Something oily and spiteful appeared in her gaze. It is hard to define exactly what it was: self-pity, pride, the hidden satisfaction of those who know they are dangerous to themselves and to others. Suddenly I knew that although she sounded so sincere, there was much more to her story than she cared to reveal. I became aware of the uncanny power in this frail woman with her glib talk and cat-like movements. I was gripped by the desire to get away from her, lest I too become involved in her weird complexities. She seemed to guess that she had frightened me. Her yellow eyes measured me with sly reproach.

"Go, better join the other guests," she said. "Fate such as mine is contagious."

Translated by the author and Elizabeth Shub

Powers

As a rule, those who come for advice to the newspaper where I work do not ask for anyone in particular. We have a reporter who turns out a regular column of advice to readers, and anyone dropping around is usually referred to him. But this man asked especially for me. He was shown my room: a tall man—he had to bend his head to come through the door—without a hat, with a shock of black hair mixed with gray. His black eyes, under shaggy brows, had a wild look that rather frightened me. He had on a light raincoat, although it was snowing outside. His square face was red from the cold. He wore no tie, and his shirt was open, showing a chest covered with hair as thick as fur. He had a broad nose and thick lips. When he talked, he revealed large, separated teeth that appeared unusually strong.

He said, "Are you the writer?"

"I am."

He seemed surprised. "This little man who sits at this table?" he said. "I imagined you somewhat different. Well, things don't have to be exactly as we imagine them. I read every word you write—Yiddish and English both. When I hear that you've published something in a magazine, I run right out to buy it."

"Thank you very much. Please sit down."

"I'd rather stand—but—well—I will sit down. May I smoke?"

"Certainly."

"I should tell you I am not an American. I came here after the Second World War. I've been through Hitler's hell, Stalin's hell, and a couple of other hells

273

besides. But that's not why I came to you. Do you
have time to listen to me?"

"Yes, I have."

"Well, everybody in America is busy. How do you
have time to write all those things and to see people
too?"

"There is time for everything."

"Perhaps. Here in America time disappears—a
week is nothing and a month is nothing, and a year
passes by between yes and no. In those hells on the
other side, a day seemed longer than a year does
here. I've been in this country since 1950, and the
years have gone like a dream. Now it's summer, now
it's winter, the years just roll away. How old do you
think I am?"

"In the forties—maybe fifty."

"Add thirteen years more. In April I will be sixty-
three."

"You look young—knock on wood."

"That's what everybody says. In our family we
don't turn gray. My grandfather died at ninety-three
and he had hardly any gray hair. He was a blacksmith. On my mother's side, they were scholars. I
studied at a yeshiva—I was a student at the yeshiva
of Gur, and for a while in Lithuania. Only until I
was seventeen, it's true, but I have a good memory.
When I learn something, it stays stuck in my brain.
I forget nothing, in a sense, and this is my tragedy.
Once I was convinced that poring over the Talmud
would be useless, I took to studying worldly books.
The Russians had left by that time and the Germans
had taken over. Then Poland became independent
and I was drafted into the army. I helped to drive the
Bolsheviks to Kiev. Then they drove us back to the
Vistula. The Poles are not too fond of Jews, but I
advanced. They made me a top sergeant—*chorázy*—
the highest rank you can reach without military
school, and after the war they offered to send me to a
military academy. I might have become a colonel or

something, but the barracks was not my ambition. I read a lot, painted, and tried to become a sculptor. I began to carve all sorts of figures out of wood. I ended up making furniture. Cabinet work—I specialized in repairing furniture, mostly antiques. You know how it is—inlays fall out, bits break off. It takes skill to make the patch invisible. I still don't know why I threw myself into it with such enthusiasm. To find the right grain of wood, the right color, and to fit it in so that the owner himself couldn't spot the place—for this, one needs iron patience, and instinct too.

"Now I'll tell you why I came to you. It's because you write about the mysterious powers: telepathy, spirits, hypnotism, fatalism, and so on—I read it all. I read it because I possess the powers you describe. I didn't come to boast, and don't get the idea I want to become a newspaperman. Here in America I work at my trade and I earn enough. I'm single—no wife, no children. They killed off my family. I take a drink of whisky, but I'm not a drunkard. I have an apartment here in New York, and a cottage in Woodstock. I don't need help from anybody.

"But to get back to the powers. You're right when you say a person is born with them. We're born with everything. I was a child of six when I first began to carve. Later I neglected it, but the gift stayed with me. And that's how it is with the powers. I had them but I didn't know what they were. I got up one morning and it came into my mind that someone in our building was going to fall out the window that day. We lived in Warsaw on Twarda Street. I didn't like the thought—it frightened me. I left for cheder, and when I came home the courtyard was black with people. The ambulance was just arriving. A glazier had been replacing a pane in a window on the second floor, and had fallen out. If such things had happened once, twice—even five times—I might have called it coincidence, but they happened so frequently there could be no question of coincidence. Strange, I began to understand that I should conceal this—as if it were an ugly birthmark. And I was right, because powers like this are a misfortune. It's better to be born deaf or lame than to possess them.

"But, no matter how careful you are, you can't hide everything. Once, I was sitting in the kitchen. My mother—peace be with her—was knitting a stocking. My father earned good money, even though he was a laborer. Our apartment was comfortable, and as clean as a rich man's house. We had a lot of copper dishes, which my mother used to scour each week until they shone. I was sitting on a low bench. I wasn't more than seven years old at the time. All of a sudden, I said 'Mama, there's money under the floor! There is money!' My mother stopped knitting and looked at me in amazement. 'What sort of money? What are you babbling about?' 'Money,' I said. 'Gold pieces.' My mother said, 'Are you crazy? How do you know what's under the floor?' 'I know,' I said. Already I realized that I shouldn't have said it, but it was too late.

"When my father came home for dinner, my mother told him what I had said. I wasn't there, but my father was so astonished he confessed that he had hidden a number of golden coins under the floor. I had an older sister and my father was saving a dowry for her—putting money into a bank was not the custom for simple people. When I returned from cheder, my father began to question me. 'Are you spying on me?' Actually, my father had hidden the money when I was in cheder and my mother was out marketing. My sister had gone to visit a friend. He had locked and bolted the door, and we lived on the third floor. He had even been careful enough to stuff the keyhole with cotton. I got a beating, but no matter how I tried I could not explain to him how I knew about those coins. 'This boy is a devil!' my father said, and he gave me an extra box on the ear.

It was a good lesson to me to keep my mouth shut.

"I could tell you a hundred things like that about my childhood, but I'll add just one. Across the street from our home there was a store that sold dairy products. In those years, you went to the store to buy boiled milk. They boiled it on a gas range. One morning my mother gave me a pan and told me, 'Go to Zelda across the street and buy a quart of boiled milk.' I went over to the store and there was only one customer—a girl who was buying a few ounces of butter. In Warsaw they used to slice the butter from a big chunk with a bow, like the ones children carried at the Feast of Omer when they went picnicking in the Praga forest. I looked up and saw a strange thing: a light was burning over Zelda's head, as if there were a Hanukkah lamp in her wig. I stood and gaped—how was it possible? Nearby, at the counter, the girl spoke to Zelda as though there was nothing out of the way. After Zelda weighed the butter on the scale and the girl left, Zelda said, 'Come in, come in. Why are you standing there on the threshold?' I wanted to ask her, 'Why does a light burn over your head?' But I already had a hunch that I was the only one who saw it.

"The next day, when I came home from cheder, my mother said to me, 'Did you hear what happened? Zelda from the dairy store dropped dead.' You can imagine my fright. I was only about eight. Since then I've seen the same kind of light many times over the heads of those who were about to die. Thank God, I haven't seen it for the last twenty years. At my age, and among those I spend my days with, I could see those lights all the time."

2.

"A while ago, you wrote that in every great love there is an element of telepathy. I was struck by this and decided that I had to see you. In my own life this

happened not once, not ten times, but over and over
again. In my young years I was romantic. I would
see a woman and fall in love with her at first sight.
In those days you couldn't just approach a woman
and tell her you were in love with her. Girls were
delicate creatures. A mere word was considered an
insult. Also, in my own way, I was shy. Proud, too.
It's not in my nature to run after women. To make it
short, instead of talking to a girl, I would think
about her—day and night, I fancied all kinds of
impossible encounters and adventures. Then I began
to notice that my thoughts took effect. The girl I had
been thinking about so hard would actually come to
me. Once, I deliberately waited for a woman on a
crowded street in Warsaw until she appeared. I'm no
mathematician, but I know the odds that this woman
might cross that street at that very time were about
one in twenty million. But she came, as though
attracted by an invisible magnet.

"I'm not too credulous; even today I have my
doubts. We want to believe that everything happens
in a rational way and according to order. We're
afraid of mysteries—if there are good powers, it's
likely there are also evil ones, and who knows what
they might do! But so many irrational things
happened to me I would have to be an idiot to ignore
them.

"Perhaps because I had this kind of magnetism, I
never married. Anyway, I'm not the kind of man
who is satisfied with one woman. I had other powers,
too, but those I'm not going to boast about. I lived, as
they say, in a Turkish paradise—often with as many
as five or six lovers at the same time. In the drawing
rooms where I used to fix furniture, I often made the
acquaintance of beautiful women—mostly Gentiles.
And I always heard the same song from them—I was
different from other Jews, and all that kind of chatter. I had a room with a separate entrance, and
that's all a bachelor needs. I kept brandy and liquors

and a good supply of delicacies in my cupboard. If I were to tell you what took place in this room on my sofa, you could make a book out of it—but who cares? The older I grew, the clearer it became to me that for modern man marriage is sheer insanity. Without religion, the whole institution is absurd. Naturally, your mother and my mother were faithful women. For them there was one God and one husband.

"Now I come to the main point. In spite of all the women I had in those years, there was one I stayed with for almost thirty years—actually, until the day the Nazis bombed Warsaw. That day thousands of men crossed the bridge to Praga. I wanted to take Manya with me—Manya was her name—but she had the grippe, and I couldn't wait for her. I had plenty of connections in Poland, but in such a catastrophe they are not worth a sniff of tobacco. Later I was told that the house where I lived was hit by a bomb and reduced to a pile of lime and bricks. I never heard from Manya again.

"This Manya might have been considered an ordinary girl. She came from some little village in Greater Poland. When we met, we were both virgins. But no power and no treachery on my part could destroy the love between us. Somehow she knew of all my abominations and kept warning me that she would leave me, get married, and whatnot. But she came to me regularly every week—often more. The other women never spent the night in my room, but when Manya came she stayed. She was not particularly beautiful—dark, not tall, with black eyes. She had curly hair. In her village they called her Manya the Gypsy. She had all the antics of a gypsy. She told fortunes from cards and read palms. She believed in all kinds of witchcraft and superstitions. She even dressed like a gypsy in flowered skirts and shawls, wore large hoop earrings, and red beads around her neck. There was always a cigarette between her lips. She made a

living as a salesgirl in a lingerie shop. The owners
were an elderly couple without children, and Manya
became almost a daughter to them. She was an
excellent saleswoman. She could sew, embroider,
and even learned how to make corsets. She managed
the whole business. If she had been willing to steal,
she could have had a fortune, but she was one
hundred per cent honest. Anyhow, the old people
were going to leave her the store in their will. In
later years, the old man had a liver ailment, so they
traveled to Carlsbad, Marienbad, and to Piszczany.
And they left everything with Manya. Why did she
need to get married? What she needed was a man,
and I was that man. This girl, who could barely read
and write, was, in her way, very refined—especially
in sex. In my life I had God knows how many
women, but there was never one like Manya. She
had her own caprices and peculiarities, and when I
think about them I don't know whether to laugh or
cry. Sadism is sadism and masochism is masochism—
are there names for all this nonsense? Each time we
quarreled we were both terribly unhappy, and making peace was a great ceremony. She could cook fit
for a king. When her bosses went to the spas, she
cooked meals for me in their apartment. I used to
say that her food had sex appeal, and there was some
truth in it. This was her good side. The bad side was
that Manya could never make peace with the idea
that I had other women. She did everything she
could to spoil my pleasure. By nature I am not a liar,
but because of her I became one. Automatically. I
didn't have to invent lies—my tongue did it by itself,
and I was often astonished at how clever and far-
sighted a tongue can be. It foresaw events and
situations—a matter I realized only later. However,
you cannot fool anybody for thirty years. Manya
knew my habits and she never stopped spying on
me; my telephone used to ring in the middle of the
night. At the same time, my business with other

women gave her a perverse enjoyment. Now and again I confessed to her and she would ask for details, call me the worst names, cry, laugh, and become wild. I often felt like an animal trainer—like one who puts his head in the mouth of a lion. I always knew that my successes with other women made sense only as long as Manya was in the background. If I had Manya, the Countess Potocka was a bargain. Without Manya, no conquest was worth a groschen.

"It sometimes happened that I returned from one of my adventures, perhaps at an inn or at a nobleman's estate, and I would be with Manya that same night. She refreshed me and I would begin all over again as if nothing had happened. But as I grew older I began to worry that too much love might do me some damage. I am something of a hypochondriac. I read medical books and articles in the newspapers. I worried that I might be ruining my health. Once, when I returned completely exhausted and was to meet Manya, the thought ran through my mind: how good it would be if Manya would get her period and I would not have to spend the night with her. I called her and she said, 'A funny thing happened, I got my holiday'—this is what she called it—'in the middle of the month.' 'So you've turned into a miracle worker,' I said to myself. But I remained skeptical about its really having anything to do with my wish. Only after such things repeated themselves many times did I realize that I had the power to give orders to Manya's body. Every word I'm telling you is pure truth. A few times I willed her to become sick—of course, just for a while, because I loved her very much—and she immediately got a high fever. It became clear that I ruled over her body completely. If I had wanted her to die, she would have died. I had read books and pamphlets about mesmerism, animal magnetism, and such topics, but it never occurred to me that I possessed this power myself, and in such measure.

"Besides being able to do anything I wanted with her, I also knew her thoughts. I could literally read her mind. Once, after a bitter fight, Manya left, slamming the door so hard that the windowpanes trembled. The moment she left, it occurred to me that she was going to the Vistula to drown herself. I grabbed my overcoat and started after her silently. She went from one street to another and I trailed her like a detective. She never looked back. Finally she reached the Vistula and began to move straight toward the water. I ran after her and grabbed her shoulder. She screamed and struggled. I had saved her from death. After that, I ordered her in my mind never to think of suicide again. Later she told me, 'How strange, I often used to think of making an end to myself. Lately these thoughts have stopped completely. Can you explain this?'

"I could have explained everything. Once when she came to me, I told her, 'You have lost money today.' She became pale. It was the truth. She had returned from a savings bank and had lost six hundred zlotys."

3.

"I will tell you the story about the dog and one story more and that will be enough. One summer—it must have been 1928 or 1929—I was overcome by a terrible fatigue. Hypochondria, too. I was entangled in so many affairs and complications that I almost fell apart. My telephone rang constantly. There were bitter quarrels between Manya and me that began to take on an uncanny character. At the place where she worked, the old man's wife had died, and Manya kept threatening to marry him. She had a cousin in South Africa who wrote her love letters and offered to send her an affidavit. Her great love suddenly turned to terrible hatred. She talked about poisoning herself and me. She proposed a double suicide. A fire kindled in her black eyes, which made her look like a Tartar. We are all the descendants of God knows what murderers. Did you or someone else write in your newspaper that every man is potentially a Nazi? At night I usually slept like the dead, but now I suffered from insomnia. When I finally fell asleep, I had nightmares. One morning I felt that my end had come. My legs were shaky, everything whirled before my eyes, there was a ringing in my ears. I saw that if I did not make some change, I would be finished. I decided to leave everything and go away. I packed a bag. As I packed, the telephone rang madly, but I did not answer it. I went down the street and took a droshky to the Vienna depot. A train was about to leave for Krakow, and I bought a ticket. I sat down on the secondclass bench and I was so tired that I slept through the whole trip. The conductor woke me at Krakow. In Krakow I again took a droshky and told the driver to take me to a hotel. The moment I entered the hotel room, I fell down on the bed in my clothes and dozed until dawn. I say dozed, because my sleep was fitful—I slept and I did not sleep. I went to the toilet and voices screamed in my ears and bells rang. I literally heard Manya crying and calling me back. I was on the verge of a breakdown. But with my last strength I curbed myself. I had fasted for a day and a night, and when I woke at about eleven o'clock in the morning I was more dead than alive. There are no baths in the Krakow hotel rooms—if you wanted a bath, you had to order it from the maid. There was a washstand and a pitcher of water in the room. Somehow I managed to shave, eat breakfast, and get myself to a railroad station. I rode a few stops, and there the rails ended. Of course I wanted to go to the mountains, but it was not the line to Zakopane but a spur. I arrived at a village near Babia Góra. This is a mountain apart from the other mountains—a mountain individualist—and few tourists go there. There was no hotel or rooming house and I got a room with an old peasant couple—*gazdas*. I guess you know the region and I don't have to tell you how beautiful it is. But this particular village was especially beautiful and wild, perhaps because it was so isolated. The old pair had a dog—a huge specimen—I don't know what breed. They warned me that he would bite and one should be careful. I patted him on the head, I tickled his neck, and he immediately became my pal. That's an understatement—the dog fell madly in love with me—and it happened almost at once. He did not leave me for a minute. The old couple rented the room every summer, but the dog had never become attached to any lodger. To make it short, I ran away from human love and fell into canine love. Burek had all the ways of a woman, even though he was a male. He made scenes of jealousy that were worse than Manya's. I took long walks and he ran after me everywhere. There were whole packs of dogs in the village and if I only looked at another dog Burek became wild. He bit them, and me too. At night he insisted upon sleeping on my bed. In those places, dogs have fleas. I tried not to let him into my room, but he howled and wailed so, he woke half the village. I had to let him in and he immediately jumped on the bed. He cried with a human voice. They began to say in the village that I was a sorcerer. I didn't stay long, because you could die there from boredom. I had taken a few books with me, but I soon read them all. I had rested and was ready for new entanglements. But parting from Burek was not an easy business. He had sensed, with God knows what instinct, that I was about to leave. I had telephoned Manya from the post office and had received telegrams and registered letters in that Godforsaken village. The dog kept on barking and howling. The last day, he went into some kind of spasm; he foamed at the mouth. The peasants were afraid he was mad. Until then, he hadn't even been tied up, but his owner got a chain and tied him to a stake. His clamor and his tearing at the chain shattered my nerves.

"I returned to Warsaw, sunburned but not really rested. What the dog did to me in that village, Manya and a few other females did in Warsaw. They all clung to me and bit me. I had orders to mend furniture, and the owners kept phoning me. A few days passed—or perhaps a few weeks; I don't remember exactly. After a difficult day, I went to bed early. I put out the lamp. I was so exhausted that I fell asleep immediately. Suddenly I woke up. Waking up in the middle of the night was not unusual for me, but this time I woke with the feeling that someone was in my room. I used to waken with a heaviness in my chest, but this time I felt an actual weight on my feet. I looked up and there was a dog lying on my blanket. The lamp was out, but it wasn't completely dark because a street lamp shone in. I recognized Burek.

"At first I had the idea that the dog had run after the train to Warsaw. But this was sheer nonsense. In the first place, he was tied up; then, no dog could run for so long after an express train. Even if the dog could have found his way to Warsaw by himself—and found my house—he could not have climbed up three flights of stairs. Besides, my door was always locked. I grasped that this was not a real dog, flesh and blood—it was a phantom. I saw his eyes, I felt the heaviness on my feet, but I didn't dare to touch him. I sat there terrified, and he looked me in the eyes with an expression utterly sad—and something else for which I have no name. I wanted to push him off and free my feet, but felt restrained. This was not a dog but a ghost. I lay down again and tried to fall asleep. After a while I succeeded. A nightmare? Call it a nightmare. But it was Burek just the same. I recognized his eyes, ears, his expression, his fur. The next day I wanted to write to the peasant to ask about the dog. But I knew that he couldn't read, and then I was too busy to write letters. I wouldn't have got an answer anyhow. I am absolutely convinced that the dog had died—what had visited me was not of this world.

"That wasn't the only time he came—over a number of years he kept returning, so that I had ample time to observe him even though he never appeared in the light. The dog was old when I left the village, and the way he looked that last day, I knew that he couldn't have lasted long. Astral body, spirit, soul— call it what you like—it is a fact so far as I'm concerned that a ghost of a dog came to me and lay on my legs, not once but dozens of times. Almost every night at first, then rarely. A dream? No, I wasn't dreaming—unless the whole of life is one dream."

4.

"I will tell you one last incident. I have already told you that a number of the women with whom I had affairs I met in the drawing rooms where I went to repair furniture. This plain man who sits here has made love to Polish countesses. What is a countess? We are all made of the same stuff. But once I met a young woman who really made me jump out of my skin. I was hired to go to a noblewoman's house in Vilanov, to mend an old pianoforte decorated with gilded garlands. While I was working, a young woman glided through the drawing room. She stopped for no more than a second, saw what I was doing, and our eyes met. How can I describe to you how she looked? Both Polish aristocrat and strangely Jewish—as if, by some magic, a gentle yeshiva student had turned into a Polish *panienka*. She had a narrow face and black eyes, such deep ones that I became confused.

They actually burned me. Everything about this woman was full of spirituality. Never before have I seen such beauty. She disappeared in an instant, and I remained shattered. Later I asked the owner who that beauty was, and she said it was a niece who was visiting. She mentioned the name of some estate or town from which she came. But in my confusion I wasn't able to pay attention. I could easily have learned her name and address if I hadn't been so dazed. I finished my work; she did not show up again. But her image always stood before my eyes. I began to think about her day and night without stopping. My thoughts wore me out, and I decided to make an end of them, no matter what the cost. I was so mixed up that, even though I knew Warsaw like my ten fingers, I got lost in the streets and made silly mistakes. It went on like this for months. Slowly my obsession weakened—or perhaps it just sank deeper inside me; I could think about someone else and at the same time brood about her. So the summer passed and it was winter, then it was spring again. One late afternoon—almost dusk—I don't remember if it was April or May—my telephone rang. I said hello, and no one answered. However, somebody was holding the receiver at the end of the line. I called again, 'Hello, hello, hello!' and I heard a crackle and a stammering voice. I said, 'Whoever you are, be so good as to speak up.'

"After a while I heard a voice that was a woman's voice but also the voice of a boy. She said to me, 'You once worked in Vilanov, in such and such a house. Do you happen to remember someone passing through the drawing room?' My throat became tight, and I almost lost the ability to move my tongue. 'Yes, I remember you,' I said. 'Could anyone forget your face?' She was so quiet I thought she had hung up. But she began to speak again—murmur is more like it. She said, 'I have to talk to you. Where can we meet?' 'Wherever you wish,' I said. 'Would you want

to come to me?' 'No, out of the question,' she said.
'Perhaps in a café—' 'No, not in a café,' I said, 'Tell
me where you could meet me and I will be there.'
She became silent; then she mentioned a little street
near the city library, way uptown, near Mokotow.
'When do you want it to be?' I asked. And she said,
'As soon as possible.' 'Perhaps now?' 'Yes, if you can
make it.' I knew that there was no café, no restaurant, not even a bench to sit on in that little street,
but I told her that I was leaving at once. There had
been a time when I thought that if this miracle
should happen I would jump for joy. But somehow
everything was silent in me. I was neither happy nor
unhappy—only amazed.

"When I arrived at our meeting place, it was
already night. The street had trees on both sides and
few lamps. I could see her in the half darkness. She
seemed leaner, and her hair was combed up in a bun.
She stood near a tree, wrapped in shadow. Except for
her, the street was deserted. She started when I
approached her. The trees were blooming and the
gutter was full of blossoms. I said to her, 'Here I am.
Where can we go?' 'What I want to tell you can be
said right here,' she replied. 'What do you want to
tell me?' I asked. She hesitated. 'I want to ask you to
leave me in peace.'

"I was startled, and said, 'I don't know what you
mean.' 'You know very well,' she said. 'You don't
leave me in peace. I have a husband and I am happy
with him. I want to be a faithful wife.' It wasn't
talking but stammering. She paused after each word.
She said, 'It wasn't easy to learn who you were and
your telephone number. I had to invent a story about
a broken chest to get the information from my aunt.
I am not a liar; my aunt did not believe me. Still, she
gave me your name and address.' Then she became
silent.

"I asked, 'Why can't we go somewhere to talk it
over?' 'I can't go anywhere. I could have told you this

on the telephone—it is all so strange, absolutely insane—but now you know the truth.' 'I really don't know what's on your mind,' I said, just to prolong the conversation. She said, 'I beseech you, by whatever is holy to you, to stop tormenting me. What you want I cannot do—I'd rather die.' And her face became as pale as chalk.

"I still played the fool and said, 'I want nothing from you. It is true that when I saw you in your aunt's drawing room you made a strong impression on me—but I haven't done anything that should upset you.' 'Yes, you have. If we weren't living in the twentieth century, I would think you were a sorcerer. Believe me,' she went on, 'I didn't come easily to the decision to call you. I was even afraid that you might not know who I was—but you knew immediately.'

" 'We cannot stand here on the street and talk,' I said. 'We have to go somewhere.' 'Where? If someone who knows me should see me, I am lost.' I said, 'Come with me.' She hesitated for a while, and then she followed me. She seemed to have difficulty walking on her high heels and she took my arm. I noticed, even though she was wearing gloves, that she had most beautiful hands. Her hand fluttered on my arm, and each time a shudder ran through my body. After a while the young woman became more relaxed with me, and she said, 'What kind of powers do you possess? I have heard your voice several times. I have seen you, too. I woke up in the middle of the night and you were standing at the foot of my bed. Instead of eyes, two green beams shone from your sockets. I woke my husband, but in a second you vanished.'

" 'It's a hallucination,' I said. 'No, you wander in the night.' 'If I do, it's without knowing it.'

"We approached the shore of the Vistula and sat down on a log. It's quiet there. It's not completely safe because it's full of drunks and bums. But she sat with me. She said, 'My aunt will not know what has become of me. I told her that I was going for a walk. She even offered to accompany me. Give me a holy promise that you will let me go. Perhaps you have a wife and you wouldn't want anybody to molest her.'

" 'I have no wife,' I said, 'but I promise you that, as far as it depends on me, I will not molest you. That's all I can promise.'

" 'I will be grateful to you until my last breath.'

"That is the story. I never saw the woman again. I don't even know her name. I don't know why, but of all the strange things that have happened to me this made the strongest impression. Well, that's all. I won't disturb you any more."

"You don't disturb me," I said. "It's good to meet a person with such powers. It strengthens my own faith. But how did it happen that Manya had the grippe when you left Warsaw? Why didn't you order her to get well?"

"What? I ask myself this question constantly. It seems that my power is only negative. To heal the sick, one must be a saint and, as you see, I am far from being a saint. Or it may be—who knows—that to have a woman along in those days was dangerous."

The stranger hung his head. He began to drum on the table with his fingers and to hum to himself. Then he got up. It seemed to me that his face had changed; it had become gray and wrinkled. Suddenly he looked his age. He even appeared less tall than before. I noticed that his raincoat was full of spots. He gave me his hand to say goodbye, and I accompanied him to the elevator.

"Do you still think about women?" I asked.

He thought it over as though he hadn't grasped my words. He looked at me sadly, with suspicion. "Only about dead women."

Translated by the author and Dorothea Straus

Something Is There

As a rule, Rabbi Nechemia from Bechev knew the cunning of the Evil One and how to subdue him, but the last few months he had been plagued by something new and terrifying: wrath against the Creator. A part of the rabbi's brain quarreled with the Lord of the Universe, rebelliously arguing: Yes, you are great, eternal, all mighty, wise, even full of mercy. But with whom do you play hide-and-seek—with flies? What help is your greatness to the fly when it falls into the net of the spider that sucks out its life? Of what avail are all your attributes to the mouse when the cat clamps it in its claws? Rewards in Paradise? The beasts have no use for them. You, Father in heaven, have the time to wait for the End of Days, but they can't wait. When you cause a fire in Feitl the water carrier's hut and he has to sleep with his family in the poorhouse on a cold winter's night, that is an injustice beyond repair. The dimming of your light, free choice, redemption, may serve to explain you, but Feitl the water carrier needs to rest after a day's toil, not to toss about on a bed of rotten straw.

The rabbi knew well that Satan was talking to him. He tried every means to silence him. He submerged himself in the icy water of the ritual bath, fasted, and studied the Torah until his eyes closed from weariness. But the Devil refused to be thwarted. His insolence grew. He screamed from morning till night. Lately, he had begun to defile the rabbi's dreams. The rabbi dreamed of Jews being burned at the stake, of yeshiva boys led to the gallows, of violated virgins, tortured infants. He was shown the cruelties of Chmielnitzki's and Gonta's soldiers and those of the savages who consume the limbs of animals before the beasts expire. Cossacks impaled children with their spears and buried them still alive. A Haydamak with a long mustache and murderous eyes ripped open a woman's belly and sewed a cat inside. In his dream, the rabbi waved his fists toward heaven and shouted, "Is all this for your glory, Heavenly Killer?"

The whole court at Bechev was on the verge of collapse. The old rabbi, Reb Eliezer Tzvi, Rabbi Nechemia's father, had died three years before. He had suffered from cancer of the stomach. Rabbi Nechemia's mother had developed the same disease in her breast. Besides the rabbi, one daughter and a son remained. The rabbi's younger brother, Simcha David, became an "enlightened one" while his parents were alive. He left the court and his wife, the daughter of the Zhilkovka rabbi, and went to Warsaw to study painting. The rabbi's sister, Hinde Shevach, had married the son of the Neustater rabbi, Chaim Mattos, who immediately after the marriage sank into melancholia and returned to his parents. Hinde Shevach became an abandoned wife. Since he was considered insane, Chaim Mattos was not permitted to go through divorce proceedings. Rabbi Nechemia's own wife, a descendant of the rabbi of Kotzk, had died together with her infant at childbirth. The matchmakers proposed various mates for the rabbi, but he gave them all the same answer: "I will think it over."

Actually, no appropriate match was offered. Most of the Bechev Hasidim had deserted Reb Nechemia. In the rabbinical courts, the same laws prevailed as among the fish in the sea: the big ones devoured the little ones. The first to leave were the rich. What could keep them in Bechev? The study house was half ruined. The roof of the ritual bath had caved in. Weeds grew everywhere. Reb Nechemia was left with a single beadle—Reb Sander. The rabbi's house had many rooms, which were seldom cleaned, and a layer of dust covered everything. The wallpaper was peeling. Windowpanes were broken and not replaced. The entire building had settled in such a way that the floors all slanted. Beila Elke, the maid, suffered from rheumatism; her joints became knotted. Reb Nechemia's sister, Hinde Shevach, had no patience for housework. She sat on the couch all day long reading books. When the rabbi lost a button from his coat, there was no one to sew it on.

The rabbi was barely twenty-seven years old, but he appeared older. His tall figure was stooped. He had a yellow beard, yellow eyebrows, yellow sidelocks. He was nearly bald. He had a high forehead, blue eyes, a narrow nose, a long neck with a protruding Adam's apple. He had a consumptive pallor. In his study, Reb Nechemia, wearing a faded housecoat, a wrinkled skullcap, and shoddy slippers, paced back and forth. On the table lay a long pipe and a bag of tobacco. The rabbi would light it, take one puff, and put it down. He would pick up a book, open it, and close it without reading. He even ate impatiently. He bit off a piece of bread and chewed it while walking. He took a sip of his coffee and continued to pace. It was summer, between Pentecost and the Days of Awe, when no Hasidim go forth on pilgrimages, and during the long summer days the rabbi had time enough to brood. All problems blended into one—why the suffering? There was no answer to be found to this question, neither in the Pentateuch, in the books of the Prophets, in the Talmud, in the Zohar, nor in the *Tree of Life*. If the Lord is omnipotent, He could reveal Himself without the aid of the Evil Host. If He is not omnipotent, then He is not really God. The only solution to the riddle was that of the heretics: There is neither a judge nor a judgment. All creation is a blind accident—an inkwell fell on a sheet of paper and the ink wrote a letter by itself, each word a lie, the sentences in chaos. In that case, why does he, Rabbi Nechemia, make a fool of himself? What kind of rabbi is he? To whom does he pray? To whom does he complain? On the other hand, how can spilled ink compose even a single line? And from where does the ink and the sheet of paper come? *Nu*, and from where does God come?

Rabbi Nechemia stood at the open window. Outside, there was a pale blue sky; around a golden-yellow sun, little clouds curled like the flax that is used to protect the ethrog in its case. On the naked branch of a desiccated tree stood a bird. A swallow? A sparrow? Its mother was also a bird, and so, too, its grandmother—generation after generation, thousands of years. If Aristotle was right that the universe always existed, then the chain of generations had no beginning. But how could that be?

The rabbi grimaced as if in pain. He formed a fist. "You want to conceal your face?" He spoke to God. "So be it. You conceal your face and I will conceal mine. Enough is enough." He decided to put into action what he had contemplated for a long time.

2.

That Friday night the rabbi slept little. He napped and awoke intermittently. Each time he fell asleep, horrors seized him anew. Blood flowed. Corpses lay strewn in the gutters. Women ran through flames, with singed hair and charred breasts. Bells clanged. A stampede of beasts with ram's horns, pig's snouts, with skins of hedgehogs and pussy udders emerged from burning forests. A cry rose from the earth—a lament of men, women, serpents, demons. In the confusion of his dream, the rabbi imagined that Simchas Torah and Purim had fallen on the same day. Had the calendar been altered, the rabbi wondered, or had the Evil One taken dominion? At dawn an old man with a crooked beard, wearing a torn robe, ranted at him and shook his fists. The rabbi tried to blow the ram's horn to excommunicate him, but instead of a blast the sound was a wheeze that might have come from a deflated lung.

The rabbi trembled and his bed shook. His pillow was wet and twisted, as if it had just been wrung out from the washtub. The rabbi's eyes were half glued together. "Abominations," the rabbi muttered. "Scum of the brain." For the first time since he could remember, the rabbi did not perform the ablutions. "The power of Evil? Let's see what Evil can do! The sacred can only stay mute." He walked over to the window. The rising sun rolled among the clouds like a severed head. At a pile of garbage, the community he-goat was trying to chew last year's palm leaves. "You are still alive?" the rabbi addressed him. And he remembered the ram whose horns were caught in the thicket which Abraham had sacrificed instead of Isaac. He always had a need of burnt offerings, the rabbi thought of God. His creatures' blood was a sweet savor to Him.

"I will do it, I will do it," the rabbi said aloud.

In Bechev they prayed late. On the summer Sabbaths there was barely a quorum, even counting the few old men who were supported by the court. The night before, the rabbi had resolved not to put on his fringed garment, but he did so anyway out of habit. He had planned to go bareheaded, but reluctantly he placed the skullcap on his head. One sin at a time is enough, he decided. He sat down on his chair and dozed. After a while, he started and got up. Until yesterday the Good Spirit had attempted to reprimand the rabbi and to threaten him with Gehenna or a demeaning transmigration of the soul. But now the voice from Mount Horeb was stifled. All fears had vanished. Only anger remained. "If He does not need the Jews, the Jews don't need Him." The rabbi spoke no longer directly to the Almighty but to some other deity—perhaps to one of those

mentioned in the Eighty-second Psalm: "God standeth
in the Congregation of the mighty, He judgeth among
the Gods." Now the rabbi agreed with every kind of
heresy—with those who deny Him entirely and with
those who believe in two dominions; with the idolators
who serve the stars and the constellations and those
who uphold the Trinity; with the Karaaites, who
renounced the Talmud; with the Samaritans, who
forsook Mount Sinai for Mount Gerizim. Yes, I have
known the Lord and I intend to spite Him, the rabbi
said. Many matters suddenly became clear: the primeval snake, Cain, the Generation of the Flood, the
Sodomites, Ishmael, Esau, Korach, and Jeroboam,
the son of Nebat. To a silent torturer one does not
speak, and to a persecutor one does not pray.

The rabbi hoped that somehow at the last moment
a miracle would occur—God would reveal Himself or
some power would restrain him. But nothing happened. He opened the drawer and took out his pipe,
an object forbidden to the touch on the Sabbath. He
filled it with tobacco. Before striking the match, the
rabbi hesitated. He admonished himself, "Nechemia,
son of Eliezer Tzvi, this is one of the thirty-nine
tasks prohibited on the Sabbath! For this, one is
stoned." He looked around. No wings fluttered; no
voice called. He withdrew a match and lit the pipe.
His brain rattled in his skull like a kernel in the
nutshell. He was plummeting into the abyss.

Usually the rabbi enjoyed smoking, but now the
smoke tasted acrid. It scratched his throat. Someone
might knock at the door! He poured a few drops of
ablution water into the pipe—another major viola-
tion, to extinguish a fire. He had a desire for further
transgression, but what? He wanted to spit on the
mezuzah but refrained. For a while, the rabbi listened
to the turmoil within him. Then he went out into the
corridor and passed along to Hinde Shevach's room.
He pulled at the latch and tried to open the door.

"Who is there?" Hinde Shevach called out.

"It is I."

The rabbi heard her rustling, murmuring. Then she opened the door. She must just have awakened. She wore a house robe with arabesques, slippers, and on her shaven head a silk kerchief. Nechemia was tall, but Hinde Shevach was small. Though she was barely twenty-five years old, she looked older, with dark circles under her eyes and the grieved expression of an abandoned wife. The rabbi rarely came to her room, never so early and on the Sabbath.

She asked, "Has something happened?"

The rabbi's eyes filled with laughter. "The Messiah has come. The moon fell down."

"What kind of talk is that?"

"Hinde Shevach, everything is finished," the rabbi said, astounded by his own words.

"What do you mean?"

"I'm not a rabbi any more. There is no more court unless you want to take over and become the second Virgin of Ludmir."

Hinde Shevach's yellowish eyes measured him crookedly. "What happened?"

"I've had my fill."

"What will become of the court, of me?"

"Sell everything, divorce your schlemiel, or leave for America."

Hinde Shevach stood still. "Sit down, you frighten me."

"I'm tired of all these lies," the rabbi said. "The whole nonsense. I'm not a rabbi and they're not Hasidim. I'm leaving for Warsaw."

"What will you do in Warsaw? Do you want to follow in Simcha David's path?"

"Yes, his path."

Hinde Shevach's pale lips trembled. She looked for a handkerchief among her clothes on a chair. She held it to her mouth. "What about me?" she asked.

"You are still young. You're not a cripple," the

rabbi said, baffled by his own words. "The whole
world is open to you."

"Open? Chaim Mattos is not allowed to divorce
me."

"He's allowed, allowed."

The rabbi wanted to say, "You can do without
divorce," but he was afraid that Hinde Shevach
might faint. He felt a surge of defiance, the courage
and the relief of one who had rid himself of all yokes.
For the first time he grasped what it meant to be a
nonbeliever. He said, "The Hasidic institution is
sheer mendicancy. Nobody needs us. The whole
business is a swindle and a falsehood."

3.

It all passed smoothly. Hinde Shevach locked herself
in her room, apparently crying. Sander the beadle
got drunk after Havdalah, the ushering out of the
Sabbath, and went to sleep. The old men sat in the
study house. One recited the Valedictory Prayers,
another read the *Beginning of Wisdom*, a third
cleaned his pipe with a wire, a fourth patched a
sacred book. A few candles flickered. The rabbi gave
a final look at the study house. "A ruin," he
murmured. He had packed his satchel himself. Since
his wife's death, he had grown accustomed to fetching
his own linen from the chest where the maid placed
it. He took out several shirts, some underwear, and
long white stockings. He didn't even pack his prayer
shawl and phylacteries. What for?

The rabbi stole away from the village. How
convenient that the moon was not shining. He did
not take the highway but walked along the back
roads, with which he had been familiar as a boy. He
did not wear his velvet hat. He had found a cap and a
gaberdine from the days when he was a bachelor.

Actually, the rabbi was no longer the same man.
He felt that he was possessed by a demon who

thought and chattered in its own peculiar manner.
Now he passed through fields and a forest. Even
though it was Saturday night when the Evil Ones
run rampant, the rabbi felt bolder and stronger. He
no longer feared dogs or robbers. He arrived at the
station only to learn that he would have to wait for a
train until dawn. He saw down on a bench, near a
peasant who lay snoring. The rabbi had recited
neither the Evening Prayer nor the Shema. I will
shave off my beard, too, he decided. He was aware
that his escape could not remain a secret and that
his Hasidim might seek him out and find him.
Briefly, he considered leaving Poland.

He fell asleep and was awakened by the ringing of
a bell. The train had arrived. Earlier, he had bought
a fourth-class ticket because in those carriages there
is never any illumination; the passengers sit or
stand in the dark. He was apprehensive of encountering citizens of Bechev, but the car was full of
Gentiles. One of them struck a match, and the rabbi
saw peasants wearing four-cornered hats, brown
caftans, linen trousers—most of them barefoot or
with rags on their feet. There was no window in the
car, only a round opening. When the sun rose, it cast
a purple light on the bedraggled lot of men, who
were smoking cheap tobacco, eating coarse bread
with lard, and washing it down with vodka. Their
wives reclined on the baggage and dozed.

The rabbi had heard about the pogroms in Russia.
Bumpkins such as these killed men, raped women,
plundered, and tortured children. The rabbi huddled
in a corner. He tried to cover his nose from the
stench. "God, is this your world?" he asked. "Did you
attempt to give them the Torah on Mount Seir and
Mount Paran? Is it among them that you have
dispersed your chosen people?" The wheels clammered
along the rails. Smoke from the locomotive seeped
through the round hole. It reeked of coal, oil, and
some indiscernible smoldering substance. "Can I

become one of these?" the rabbi asked himself. "If God doesn't exist, neither did Jesus."

The rabbi felt a strong urge to urinate but there were no facilities. These passengers seemed to be flea- and lice-ridden. He felt an itch beneath his shirt. He began to regret having left Bechev. "Who prevented me from being an infidel there?" he asked himself. "At least I had my own bed. And what will I do in Warsaw? I have been impetuous. I forgot that a heretic too needs food and a pillow under his head. My few rubles will not last long. Simcha David is a pauper himself." The rabbi had been informed that Simcha David was starving, wore tattered clothes, and in addition was stubborn and impractical. "Well, and what did he expect? There is no lack of charlatans in Warsaw."

The rabbi's legs ached and he lowered himself to the floor. He shoved the visor of his cap lower on his forehead. Jews boarded the train at various stations; someone might recognize him. Suddenly he heard familiar words. "Oh, my God, the soul which Thou gavest me is pure; Thou didst create it, Thou didst form it, Thou didst breathe it into me; Thou preservest it within me; and Thou wilt take it from me but wilt restore it unto me hereafter. . . ." "A lie, a brazen lie," something in the rabbi exclaimed. "All have the same spirit—a man, an animal. Ecclesiastes himself admitted this; therefore, the sages wanted to censor him. Well, but what is a spirit? Who formed the spirit? What do the worldly books say about that?"

The rabbi slept and dreamed that it was Yom Kippur. He stood in the synagogue yard along with a group of Jews who wore white robes and prayer shawls. Someone had locked the synagogue, but why? The rabbi lifted his eyes to the sky and instead of one moon he saw two, three, five. What was that? The moons seemed to rush toward one another. They became larger and more radiant. Lightning struck, thunder rolled, and the sky blazed in flames. The

Jews emitted a howling lament: "Woe, Evil is prevailing!"

Shaken, the rabbi awoke. The train had arrived in Warsaw. He had not been in Warsaw since his father—blessed be his memory—fell ill and went there to see Doctor Frankel a few months before his demise. Father and son had then traveled in a special carriage. Sextons and court members had accompanied them. A crowd of Hasidim had waited at the station. His father was led to the house of a rich follower on Twarda Street. In his living room Father interpreted the Torah. Now Nechemia walked along the platform carrying his own valise. Some of the passengers ran, others dragged their luggage. Porters shouted. A gendarme appeared with a sword on one side, a revolver on the other, his chest covered with medals, his square face red and fat. His tallowy eyes measured the rabbi with suspicion, hatred, and with something that reminded the rabbi of a predatory beast.

The rabbi entered the city. Trolley cars clanged their bells, droshkies converged, the coachmen flicked their whips, the horses galloped over the cobblestones. There was a stench of pitch, refuse, and smoke. "This is the world?" the rabbi asked himself. "Here the Messiah is supposed to come?" He searched in his breast pocket for the scrap of paper bearing Simcha David's address, but it had vanished. "Are the demons playing with me already?" The rabbi returned his hand to the pocket and withdrew the paper he had been searching for. Yes, a demon was mocking him. But if there is no God, how can there be an Evil Host? He stopped a passerby and asked for directions to Simcha David's street.

The man gave them. "What a distance!" he said.

4.

Each time the rabbi asked how to reach Smotcha Street, where Simcha David lived, he was advised to take a trolley car or a droshky, but the trolley seemed too formidable and a droshky was too expensive. Besides, the driver might be a Gentile. The rabbi spoke no Polish. He stopped to rest every few minutes. He hadn't eaten breakfast; still, he didn't know whether or not he was hungry. His mouth watered and he felt a dryness in his throat. The smell of freshly baked rolls, bagels, boiled milk, and smoked herring drifted from the courtyards. He passed by stores that sold leather, hardware, dry-goods, and ready-made clothes. The salesmen vied for customers, tore at their sleeves, winking and interspersing their Yiddish with Polish. Saleswomen called out in a singsong, "Apples, pears, plums, potato kugel, hot peas and beans." A wagon laden with kindling tried to pass through a narrow gate. A cart piled high with sacks of flour forced its way through another gate. A madman—barefoot, wearing a caftan with one sleeve missing and a torn cap—was being chased by a bevy of boys. They called taunts and threw pebbles at him.

"Mother cooked a kitten," a young boy sang out in a high-pitched voice. Blond sidelocks hung down from his octagonal cap.

The rabbi proceeded to cross the street and was nearly run down by an express wagon drawn by two Belgian horses. Women wrung their hands and scolded him. A man with a dirty gray beard who carried a sack on his shoulders said, "You'll have to recite a Thanksgiving benediction this Saturday."

"So, Thanksgiving." The rabbi spoke to himself. "And what does he carry in the sack—his portion in Paradise?"

He finally reached Smotcha Street. Someone pointed out the gate number to him. At the gate a girl was selling onion rolls. He entered a courtyard where children were playing tag around a huge, freshly tarred garbage receptacle. Nearby, a dyer dipped a red skirt in a kettle filled with black dye. In an open window a girl was airing a feather bed, beating it with a stick. The first people he asked knew nothing of Simcha David. Then one woman said, "He must live in the attic."

The rabbi was unaccustomed to so many steps. He had to stop to catch his breath. Refuse littered the stairway. Apartment doors stood ajar. A tailor was sewing on a machine. One flat contained a line of weaving looms where girls with bits of cotton in their hair deftly knotted threads. On the higher stories, holes gaped in the plastered walls and the smell became stifling. Suddenly the rabbi saw Simcha David. He had emerged from a dark corridor, capless, in a short jacket spattered with paint and clay. He had yellow hair and yellow eyebrows. He carried a bundle. The rabbi was amazed that he recognized his brother; he looked so much like a Gentile. "Simcha David!" he called.

Simcha David stared. "A familiar face, but—"

"Take a good look."

Simcha David shrugged. "Who are you?"

"Your brother, Nechemia."

Simcha David didn't even blink. His pale blue eyes looked dull, sad, ready for all the bizarre things time might bring. Two deep wrinkles had formed at the corners of his mouth. He was no longer the prodigy of Bechev but a shabby laborer. After a while he said, "Yes, it's you. What's wrong?"

"I've chosen to follow you."

"Well, I can't stop now. I have to meet someone. They're waiting for me. I'm late already. I'll let you into my room so you can rest. We'll talk later."

"So be it."

" 'I had not thought to see thy face,' " Simcha David quoted from Genesis.

"*Nu,* I thought you had already forgotten everything," the rabbi said. He was more embarrassed by his brother's quoting the Bible than by his coolness.

Simcha David opened the door of a room so tiny it

reminded the rabbi of a cage. The ceiling hung
crookedly. Along the walls leaned canvases, frames,
rolls of paper. It smelled of paint and turpentine.
There was no bed, only a dilapidated couch.

Simcha David asked, "What do you want to do in
Warsaw? These are hard times." He left without
waiting for a reply.

Why is he in such a rush, the rabbi wondered. He
sat on the couch and looked around. Nearly all the
paintings were of females—some nude, some half
nude. On a little table lay brushes and a palette.
This must be the way he makes a living, the rabbi
thought. It was clear to him now that he had acted in
folly. He shouldn't have come here. One can suffer
pain anywhere.

The rabbi waited for an hour, two, but Simcha
David didn't return. Hunger gnawed at him. "Today
is a day of fast for me—a heretic's fast," he told
himself. A voice inside him teased, "You deserve
what you're getting." "I don't repent," the rabbi
retorted. He was ready to wrangle with the Angel of
God as he once struggled with the Lord of Evil.

The rabbi picked up a book from the floor. It was
in Yiddish. He read a story about a saint who,
instead of going to the Evening Prayer, gathered
kindling for a widow. What is this—morality or
mockery? The rabbi had expected to read a denial of
God and the Messiah. He picked up a pamphlet
whose pages were falling out, and read about colonists
in Palestine. Young Jews plowed, sowed, dried
swamps, planted eucalyptus trees, fought the Bedouins. One of these pioneers had perished and the
writer called him a martyr. The rabbi sat bewildered.
If there's no Creator, why go to the Holy Land? And
what do they mean by a martyr?

The rabbi grew tired and lay down. "Such Jewishness is not for me," he said. "I'd rather convert!" But
where did one convert? Besides, to convert, one had
to pretend belief in the Nazarene. It seemed that the

world was full of faith. If you didn't believe in one
God, you must believe in another. The Cossacks
sacrificed themselves for the Czar. Those who wanted
to dethrone the Czar sacrificed themselves for the
revolution. But where were the real heretics, those
who believed in nothing? He had not come to Warsaw
to barter one faith for another.

5.

The rabbi waited for three hours, but Simcha David
didn't come back. This is how the modern ones are,
he brooded. Their promise is not a promise; they
have no sense of kinship or friendship. Actually,
what they worship is the ego. These thoughts
perturbed him—wasn't he one of them now? But
how does one curb the brain from thinking? He
gazed about the room. What could thieves find of
value here? The naked females? He went out the
door, closed it, and walked down the stairs. He took
his valise with him. He was dizzy and walked
unsteadily. On the street, he passed a restaurant but
was ashamed to enter. He didn't even know how to
order a meal. Did all the patrons sit at the same
table? Did men eat together with women? People
might ridicule his appearance. He returned to the
gate of the house where Simcha David lived and
bought two rolls. But where could he eat them? He
remembered the proverb "One who eats in the street
resembles a dog." He stood in the gateway and bit
into the roll.

He had already committed sins that were punish-
able by death, but eating without washing his hands
and without reciting a benediction disturbed him.
He found it difficult to swallow. Well, it's a matter of
habit, the rabbi comforted himself. One must get
accustomed even to being a transgressor. He ate one
roll and put the other into his pocket. He walked
aimlessly. On one street, three funeral processions

drove past him. The first hearse was followed by
several men. A few droshkies rode after the second.
No one accompanied the third. "Well, it doesn't
make any difference to them," the rabbi said to
himself. " 'For the dead know not anything, neither
have they any more a reward,' " he quoted Ecclesiastes.

He turned right and went by long, narrow dry-
goods stores lit up inside by gas lamps although it
was midday. From wagons nearly as large as houses,
men were unloading rolls of woolens, alpaca, cottons,
and prints. A porter walked along with a basket on
his shoulders, his back bent under the load. High-
school boys in uniforms with gilded buttons and
insignias on their caps toted books strapped to their
shoulders. The rabbi stopped. If you didn't believe in
God, why raise children, why support wives? According to logic, a nonbeliever should care only for his
own body and for no one else.

He walked on. In the next block a bookstore
displayed books in Hebrew and Yiddish: *The Generations and Their Interpreters, The Mysteries of Paris,
The Little Man, Masturbation, How to Prevent
Consumption.* One book was titled *How the Universe
Came into Being.* I'm going to buy it, the rabbi
decided. There were a few customers inside. The
bookseller, a man with gold-rimmed glasses attached
to a ribbon, was talking to a man who had long hair
and wore a hat with a wide brim and a cape on his
shoulders. The rabbi stopped at the shelves and
browsed among the books.

A salesgirl approached him and asked, "What do
you want—a prayer book, a benedictor?"

The rabbi blushed. "I noticed a book in the window
but I've already forgotten its name."

"Come out, show it to me," the girl said, winking
at the man with the gold-rimmed glasses. She smiled
and dimples formed in her cheeks.

The rabbi had an impulse to run away. He pointed to the book.

"Masturbation?" the girl asked.

"No."

"Vichna Dvosha Goes to America?"

"No, the one in the middle."

"How the Universe Came into Being? Let's go back inside." The girl whispered to the store owner, who now stood behind the counter. He scratched his forehead. "It's the last copy."

"Shall I take it from the window?" the girl asked.

"But why do you need that book in particular?" the store owner said. "It's out of date. The universe didn't come into being the way the author describes. Nobody was there to tell."

The girl burst out laughing. The man in the cape asked, "Where do you come from, the provinces?"

"Yes."

"For what did you come to Warsaw? To buy merchandise for your store?"

"Yes, merchandise."

"What kind of merchandise?"

The rabbi wanted to answer that it was no business of his, but it wasn't in his nature to be insolent. He said, "I want to know what the heretics are saying."

The girl laughed again. The merchant took off his glasses. The man in the cape stared at him with his big black eyes. "That's all you need?"

"I want to know."

"Well, he wants to know. Will they allow you to read it? If they catch you with such a book, they'll throw you out of the study house."

"No one will know," the rabbi replied. He realized that he was speaking like a child, not like an adult.

"Well, I guess the Enlightenment is still alive, the same as fifty years ago," the man in the cape said to the owner. "This is the way they used to come to Vilna and ask, 'How was the world created? Why does the sun shine? Which came first, the chicken or the egg?' " He turned to the rabbi. "We don't know, my dear man, we don't know. We have to live without faith and without knowledge."

"So why are you Jews?" the rabbi asked.

"We have to be Jews. An entire people cannot become assimilated. Besides, the Gentiles don't want us. There are several hundred converts in Warsaw and the Polish press attacks them constantly. And what would conversion accomplish? We have to remain a people."

"Where can I get the book?" the rabbi asked.

"Who knows. It's out of print. Anyway, it only states that the universe evolved. As to how it evolved, how life was created, and all the rest, nobody has an inkling."

"So why are you unbelievers?"

"My dear man, we have no time to engage in discussions with you. I have one copy and I don't want to stir the dust," the owner said. "Come back in a few weeks when we redo the window. The universe won't turn sour in that short a time."

"Please forgive me."

"My dear fellow, there are no unbelievers any more," said the man in the cape. "In my time there were a few, but the old ones have died and the new generation is practical. They want to improve the world but don't know how to go about it. Do you at least earn a living from your store?"

"So-so," the rabbi muttered.

"Do you have a wife and children?"

The rabbi didn't answer.

"What is the name of your village?"

The rabbi remained silent. He felt as timid as a cheder boy. He said, "Thank you," and left.

6.

The rabbi continued to walk the streets. Dusk was falling, and he remembered that it was time for the

Evening Prayer, but he was in no mood to flatter the Almighty, to call Him a bestower of knowledge, a reviver of the dead, a healer of the sick, a freer of the imprisoned, or to implore Him to return His holy presence to Zion and to rebuild Jerusalem.

The rabbi passed a jail. A black gate was opened and a man bound in chains was led in. A cripple without legs moved about on a board with wheels. A blind man sang a song about a sunken ship. On a narrow street, the rabbi heard an uproar. Someone had been stabbed—a tall young man with blood gushing from his throat. A woman moaned, "He refused to be robbed, so they attacked with their knives. May hell's fire consume them. God waits long but punishes well."

Why does He wait so long, the rabbi wanted to ask. And whom does He punish? The stricken, not the strikers. Police arrived, and the siren of an ambulance wailed. Young men in torn pants, the visors of their caps covering their eyes, rushed out from the gates, and girls with their hair disheveled, worn-out slippers on their bare feet. The rabbi was afraid of the mob and its noise. He entered a courtyard. A girl with a shawl over her shoulders, her cheeks as red as though painted with beets, said to the rabbi, "Come in, it's twenty groschen."

"Where shall I go?" the rabbi asked uncomprehendingly.

"Come right downstairs."

"I'm looking for a place where I can lodge."

"I will recommend you." The girl took his arm.

The rabbi started. For the first time since he had grown up, a strange woman was touching him. The girl led him down dark steps. They walked through a corridor so narrow that only one person could pass at a time. The girl walked ahead, dragging the rabbi by his sleeve. A subterranean dampness hit his nostrils. What was this—a living grave, the gate to Gehenna? Someone was playing on a harmonica. A woman was ranting. A cat or a rat jumped over his feet. A door opened and the rabbi saw a room without a window, lit by a small kerosene lamp, its chimney black with soot. Near a bare bed that had only a straw mattress stood a washbasin of pink water. The rabbi's feet stuck to the threshold like those of an ox being led into the slaughterhouse. "What's this? Where are you taking me?"

"Don't play dumb. Let's have fun."

"I'm looking for an inn."

"Hand over the twenty groschen."

Could this be a house of ill repute? The rabbi trembled and withdrew a handful of change from his pocket. "Take it yourself."

The girl picked up a ten-groschen coin, a six-groschen coin, and a four-groschen coin. After some hesitation she added a kopeck. She pointed to the bed. The rabbi dropped the remaining coins and ran back through the corridor. The floor was uneven and full of holes. He nearly fell. He bumped into the brick wall. "God in heaven, save me!" His shirt was drenched. When he reached the courtyard, it was already night. The place stank of garbage, gutter, and rot. Now the rabbi deplored that he had invoked the name of God. His mouth filled with bile. A tremor ran through his spine. These are the pleasures of the world? Is this what Satan has to sell? He took out his handkerchief and wiped his face. Where do I go now? "Whereto shall I flee Thy countenance?" He raised his eyes, and above the walls hovered the sky with a new moon and a few stars. He gazed bewildered, as if viewing it for the first time. Not even twenty-four hours had passed since he had left Bechev, but it seemed to him that he had been wandering for weeks, months, years.

The girl from the cellar stepped out again. "Why did you run away, you silly yokel?"

"Please forgive me," the rabbi said, and he walked out into the street. The crowd was gone. Smoke rose

from chimneys. Storekeepers were locking their stores
with iron bars and locks. What had happened to the
young man who was stabbed, the rabbi wondered.
Had the earth swallowed him? Suddenly he realized
that he was still carrying his valise. How was this
possible? It seemed as if his hand clutched it with a
power of its own. Perhaps this was the same power
that created the world? Maybe this power was God?
The rabbi wanted to laugh and to cry. I'm not even
good at sinning—a bungler in every way. Well, it's
my end, my end. In that case there's only one way
out, to give back the six hundred and thirty limbs
and sinews. But how? Hanging? Drowning? Was the
Vistula nearby? The rabbi stopped a passerby.
"Excuse me, how do you get to the Vistula?"

The man had a sooty face, like a chimney sweeper.
From under his bushy, coal-black eyebrows, he stared
at the rabbi. "For what do you need the Vistula? Do
you want to fish?" His voice barked like a dog's.

"Fish, no."

"What else, swim to Danzig?"

A jester, the rabbi thought. "I was told there is an
inn in the neighborhood."

"An inn near the Vistula? Where do you come
from, the provinces? What are you doing here, looking
for a teaching job?"

"Teaching? Yes. No."

"Mister, to walk the Warsaw cobblestones, you
need strength. Do you have any money?"

"A few rubles."

"For one gulden a night, you can sleep in my
place. I live right here in number 14. I have no wife
I will give you her bed."

"Well, so be it. I thank you."

"Have you eaten?"

"Yes, in the morning."

"In the morning, huh? Come with me to the tav
ern. We'll have a glass of beer. A snack, too. I'm the
coal dealer from across the street." The man pointed

with a black finger to a store whose doors were barred. He said, "Be careful, they may steal your money. A man from the provinces has just been taken to the hospital in an ambulance. They stabbed him with a knife."

7.

The coal dealer walked up the few steps to the tavern. The rabbi stumbled along after him. The dealer opened a glass door and the rabbi was struck by the odor of beer, vodka, garlic, by the sounds of men's and women's loud voices and of dance music. His eyes blurred. "Why do you stop?" the coal handler asked. "Let's go." He took the rabbi's arm and dragged him.

Through vapor as dense as in the bathhouse of Bechev, the rabbi saw distorted faces, racks of bottles on the wall, a beer barrel with a brass pump, a counter on which sat platters of roasted geese, plates of appetizers. Fiddles screeched, a drum pounded; everyone seemed to be yelling. "Has something happened?" the rabbi asked.

The coal dealer led him to a table and screamed into his ear, "This is not your little village. This is Warsaw. Here you have to know your way around."

"I'm not used to such noise."

"You'll get used to it. What kind of teacher do you want to be? There are more teachers here than pupils. Every schlemiel becomes a teacher. What's the good of all the studying? They forget anyhow. I went to cheder myself. They taught me Rashi and all that. I still remember a few words: 'And the Lord said unto Moses—' "

"A few words of the Torah are also Torah," the rabbi said, aware that he had no right to speak after having violated so many commandments.

"What? None of it's worth a cock's crow. These boys sit in the study house, shaking and making crazy faces. When they're about to be drafted, they rupture themselves. They marry and can't support their wives. They breed dozens of children, who crawl about barefoot and naked . . ."

Perhaps he is the real unbeliever, the rabbi thought. He asked, "Do you believe in God?"

The coal dealer placed a fist on the table. "How do I know? I was never in heaven. Something is there. Who made the world? On the Sabbath I go to pray with a group called 'The Love of Friends.' It costs a few rubles, but how does the saying go—let it be a mitzvah. We pray with a rabbi who barely has a piece of bread. His wife comes to me to buy ten pounds of coal. What are ten pounds of coal in the winter? I add a piece just for good measure. If there is a God, then why does He allow the Poles to beat up the Jews?"

"I don't know. I wish I did."

"What does the Torah say? You seem to know the fine points."

"The Torah says that the wicked are punished and the righteous rewarded."

"When? Where?"

"In the next world."

"In the grave?"

"In Paradise."

"Where is Paradise?"

A waiter approached. "For me, light beer and chicken livers," the coal dealer ordered. "What do you want?"

The rabbi was at a loss for an answer. He asked, "Can one wash one's hands here?"

The coal dealer snorted. "Here you eat without washing, but it's kosher. They won't serve you pork."

"Perhaps I will have a cookie," the rabbi muttered.

"A cookie? What else? Here you have to wash everything down. What kind of beer do you want? Light? Dark?"

"Let it be light."

"Well, give him a mug of oat beer and an egg cookie." After the waiter left, the coal dealer began to drum the table with his sooty nails. "If you haven't eaten since morning, that isn't enough. Here, if you don't eat you'll drop like a fly. In Warsaw you have to be a glutton. If you want to wash your hands for the benediction, go into the toilet. There's a faucet there, but you'll have to wipe your hands on your coat."

"Why am I so unhappy?" the rabbi asked himself. "I am sunk in iniquity just like the rest of them— even worse. If I don't want to be Jacob, I have to be Esau." To the coal dealer, he said, "I don't want to be a teacher."

"What do you want to be, a count?"

"I would like to learn some trade."

"What trade? If you want to be a tailor or a shoemaker or a furrier, you have to begin young. They take you as an apprentice and the master's wife tells you to pour out the slops and to rock the baby in the cradle. I know. I learned to be a carpenter and my master never let me touch the saw or the plane. I suffered with him for four years and when I left I had learned nothing. Before I knew it, I had to go serve the Czar. For three years I ate the soldier's black bread. In the barracks you have to eat pig, otherwise you have no strength to carry the gun. Did I have a choice? When I was discharged, I went to work for a coal dealer and this has been my trade since. Everybody steals. They bring you a wagon of coals that should weigh one hundred pood but it weighs only ninety. Ten pood are stolen along the way. If you ask too many questions, they knife you. So what can I do? I pour water on the coal and that makes it heavier. If I didn't do it, I would go hungry. Do you understand me?"

"Yes, I understand."

"So why chatter about a trade? You most probably

warmed the bench in the study house all these
years, didn't you?"

"Yes, I studied."

"So you're good for nothing except to be a teacher.
But you have to be fit for that also. There's a Talmud
Torah on the block where they had a softy of a
teacher. The boys who study there are all hoodlums.
They played so many tricks on him he ran away. As
for the rich, they want a modern teacher who wears
a tie and knows how to write Russian. Do you have a
wife?"

"No."

"Divorced?"

"A widower."

"Shake hands. I had a good wife. She was a little
deaf but did her job. She prepared my meals, we had
five children, but three died when they were babies.
I have a son in Yekaterinslav. My daughter works in
a hardware store. She boards with her employers.
She doesn't want to cook for her papa. Her boss is a
rich man. Anyhow, I'm alone. How long have you
been a widower?"

"A few years."

"What do you do when you need a female?"

The rabbi blushed and then became pale. "What
can one do?"

"For money, everything can be had in Warsaw.
Not here on this street. Here they're all infected.
You go to a girl and she has a little worm in her
blood. You get sick and you begin to rot. There's a
man in the neighborhood whose whole nose has
rotted off. On the better streets the whores have to
be inspected every month at the doctor's. It costs you
a ruble to be with one of them, but at least they're
clean. The matchmakers are after me but I can't
make up my mind. All the women want is your
rubles. I was sitting with one right here in the
tavern and she asked me, 'How much money do you
have?' She was an old hag and ugly as sin. I said to

her that how much money I had saved up was none
of her business. If for one ruble I can get a girl who is
young and pretty, why do I need such an old bag? Do
you follow me? Here's our beer. What's the matter?
You're as pale as death."

8.

Three weeks had passed, but the rabbi still wandered
about in Warsaw. He slept at the coal dealer's. The
coal dealer had taken him to the Yiddish theater
after the Sabbath meal. He had also taken the rabbi
with him to the races at Vilanov.

Every day except Saturday, the rabbi visited
Bresler's library. He stood at the bookshelves and
browsed. Then there was a table where one could sit
and read. The rabbi came in the morning and stayed
until closing time. In the afternoon he went out and
bought a roll, a bagel, or a piece of potato kugel from
a market woman. He ate without a benediction. He
read books in Hebrew, in Yiddish. He even tried to
read German. In the library he found the book that
he had first seen in the shop window, *How the
Universe Came into Being.* "Yes, how was it created
without a creator?" the rabbi asked himself. He had
developed the habit of talking to himself. He tugged
at his beard, winced, and shook as he used to in the
study house. He muttered, "Yes, a fog, but who made
the fog? How did it arise? When did it begin?"

The earth was torn away from the sun, he read—but
who formed the sun? Man descended from an ape—but
where did the ape come from? And since the author
wasn't present when all this happened, how could he
be so sure? Their science explained everything away
in distance of time and space. The first cell appeared
hundreds of millions of years ago, in the slime at the
edge of the ocean. The sun will be extinguished
billions of years hence. Millions of stars, planets,
comets, move in a space with no beginning and no

end, without a plan or purpose. In the future all
people will be alike, there will be a Kingdom of
Freedom without competition, crises, wars, jealousy,
or hatred. As the Talmud says, anyone who wants to
lie will tell of things that happen far away. In an old
copy of the Hebrew magazine, *Haasif,* the rabbi read
about Spinoza, Kant, Leibnitz, Schopenhauer. They
called God substance, monad, hypothesis, blind will,
nature.

The rabbi clutched at one of his sidelocks. Who is
this nature? Where did it get so much skill and
power? It took care of the most distant star, of a rock
in the bottom of the ocean, of the slightest speck of
dust, of the food in a fly's stomach. In him, Rabbi
Nechemia of Bechev, nature did everything at once.
It gave him abdominal cramps, it stuffed his nose, it
made his skull tingle, it gnawed at his brain like the
gnat that plagued Titus. The rabbi blasphemed God
and apologized to Him. One moment he wished
death upon himself and the next he feared sickness.
He needed to urinate, went to the toilet but couldn't
function. As he read, he saw green and golden spots
before his eyes and the lines merged, diverged, bent,
and passed over one another. "Am I going blind? Is it
the end? Have the demons already got hold of me?
No, Father of the Universe, I will not recite my
confession. I'm ready for all your Gehennas. If you
can be silent for an eternity, I at least will remain
dumb until I give up my soul. You are not the only
man of war," the rabbi spoke to the Almighty. "If I
am your son, I too can put up a fight."

The rabbi stopped reading in an orderly fashion.
He would take out a book, open it at the middle, run
through a few lines, and replace it on the shelf. No
matter where he opened, he encountered a lie. All
books had one thing in common: they avoided the
essential, spoke vaguely, and gave different names
to the same object. They knew neither how grass
grew nor what light was, how heredity worked, the

stomach digested, the brain thought, how weak na-
tions grew strong, nor how the strong perished.
Even though these scholars wrote thick books about
the distant galaxies, they hadn't yet discovered what
went on a mile beneath the crust of the earth.

The rabbi turned pages and gaped. He would lay
his forehead on the edge of the table and nap for an
instant. "Woe to me, I have no more strength."
Every night, the coal dealer tried to persuade the
rabbi to return to his own village. He would say,
"You will collapse and they won't even know what to
write on your headstone."

9.

Late one night when Hinde Shevach slept, she was
awakened by steps in the corridor. Who creeps around
in the middle of the night, Hinde Shevach wondered.
Since her brother had left, it was as silent in the
house as in a ruin. Hinde Shevach got up, put on a
house coat and slippers. She opened a crack in the
door and noticed a light in her brother's room. She
walked over and saw the rabbi. His gaberdine was
torn, his shirt was unbuttoned, his skullcap was
crumpled. The expression on his face was entirely
altered. He was bent like an old man. In the middle
of the room stood a satchel.

Hinde Shevach wrung her hands. "Are my eyes
deceiving me?"

"No."

"Father in heaven, they're searching for you all
over. May the thoughts that I had be scattered over
the wastelands. They're already writing about you
in the newspapers."

"So, well."

"Where were you? Why did you leave? Why did
you hide?"

The rabbi didn't reply.

"Why didn't you say you were leaving?" Hinde Shevach asked despondently.

The rabbi dropped his head and didn't answer.

"We thought you were dead, God forbid. I telegraphed Simcha David but no answer came. I wanted to sit the seven days of mourning for you. Heaven save me! The whole town is in an uproar. They invented the most gruesome things. They even informed the police. A policeman came to ask me for your description and all the rest of it."

"Too bad."

"Did you see Simcha David?" Hinde Shevach asked after a hesitation.

"Yes. No."

"How is he making out?"

"Eh."

Hinde Shevach gulped. "You're as white as chalk, all in tatters. They dreamed up such stories that I was ashamed to show my face. Letters and telegrams came."

"Well . . ."

"You can't just get rid of me like this." Hinde Shevach changed her tone. "Speak clearly. Why did you do it? You're not just a street urchin, you're the rabbi of Bechev."

"No more rabbi."

"God have mercy. There will be bedlam. Wait, I'll bring you a glass of milk."

Hinde Shevach withdrew. The rabbi heard her go down the steps. He seized his beard and swayed. A huge shadow wavered along the wall and ceiling. After a while Hinde Shevach returned. "There is no milk."

"Nu."

"I won't go until you tell me why you left," Hinde Shevach said.

"I wanted to know what the heretics say."

"What do they say?"

"There are no heretics."

"Is that so?"

"The whole world worships idols," the rabbi muttered. "They invent gods and they serve them."

"The Jews also?"

"Everybody."

"Well, you've lost your mind." Hinde Shevach remained standing for a while and stared, then she walked back to her bedroom.

The rabbi lay down on his bed fully clothed. He felt his strength leaving him—not ebbing away but all at once, rapidly. A light he never knew was there flickered in his brain. His hands and feet grew numb. His head lay heavy on the pillow. After a time, the rabbi lifted an eyelid. The candle had burned out. A pre-dawn moon, jagged and dimmed by fog, shone through the window. In the east, the sky reddened. "Something is there," the rabbi murmured.

The war between the rabbi of Bechev and God had come to an end.

Translated by the author and Rosanna Gerber

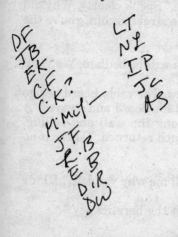